Martin Penalver is English-born with Spanish history throughout his family. Born in 1968 in Colchester he lived by the sea in Clacton for the first eleven years of his life before circumstances took him to London where he began his graduation in life. Noted at an early age for his reading skills and imaginative writing, Martin left school not to write but to find his own destiny in the world.

Over a period of years he succeeded in management within the retail sector before moving into the plastics sector in his mid twenties. During this time he would occasionally write pieces of poetry, songs and quotes more for fun or the moment then for any gain. One such piece of poetry 'River Of Dreams' was entered locally by a friend It went on to win. Following that it won a national placing and was published, he also won critical acclaim for his poems 'The Shadow Dancer' and 'Ticking Of The Clock'. In addition Martin edited and wrote for 'Gazetta Di Castel Di Frinton' for three years before writing this, his first novel 'In Search Of An Angel'.

Visit his website: www.martinpenalver.com

ISBN: 1-905988-15-X   978-1-905988-15-0

Cover by Sue Cordon

Published by Libros International

www.librosinternational.com

Acknowledgements

To my dear parents who gave me life and taught me well. I love you now and always.

To my brothers and sisters and extended family that share in my adventures and judge me not, thank you.

To Ken Douglas, thanks for your unwavering support and optimism, a friend always and to your family who make me feel part of them whenever I am in their company.

To Jimmy, thank you for all the research and knowledge you willingly shared over a beer and to Ian Hughes who gave me so much encouragement throughout. Thank you.

To Iveta Vesala, thank you so much for all your invaluable help with research and translations. I wish you happiness always.

To Debbie who supported me throughout and to Werner, Brenda & George, lifelong friends.

To Jill Morrison who has been my teacher along the way. Your touch and knowledge shaved the rough edges away and crafted my work. I cannot thank you enough.

To Sue Cordon for the finishing touches. A true artist.

To Carol Cole, thank you for your help in bringing the book to life.

To all my friends who I can count myself lucky to have, humbly I say there are many and I cannot list them all but you know who you are and I class you all as family, I can only hope I can repay your friendship with my own. May life treat you all as well as you have treated me.

To Kaciey & Demah for knowing me as I am and for being who you are. You are two special people.

Finally to you, the reader, may your Angel guide you towards your dreams.

In Search of an Angel

Martin Penalver

Libros International

In memory of Thomas Dean, 1948-2007
Dedicated to those I love and to those who know how to love.
There is an Angel.

'Each of us lives our lives like an artist.
So take care in the pictures that you paint.
For in old age you will be left to view an exhibition of a lifetimes work.'

Martin Penalver, 2006

PROLOGUE

I wasn't sure if she had heard me. She looked at me, wax-like, her lips portraying a wizened smile.

'See you later then, Roz,' I bellowed on account of her more than poor hearing. She smiled, but didn't answer. Our conversation was over for today.

I leant away from the crooked wooden fence that divided us as she gave that familiar little wave and turned away. I noticed she was not hunched in the way many eighty-three year-olds can be, especially considering the amount of gardening she had done over the years.

Roz had now wandered around the side of her small white bungalow and I stood alone. The sun felt lovely on my face as the delicate sea breeze flowed around me. I walked back towards my own front door. I did not know *how*, but I knew I was close to knowing, to finding, at last…

My name is Steve Bidante. Not Steven but Steve and don't ask me why. You get given names and when you have children then you do the giving. Right? This is my story. My quest if you like. I am not a religious man but I have spent the last few years of my life searching for something we all look for in some way or another. Call it a guiding light, call it a god, call it a faith. Call it anything that fits your conviction. All I know is I wanted to find it this side of life's curtain.

I wanted to find an angel.

CHAPTER ONE

The town of Clacton-on-Sea has been my home for the last thirty odd years. The other three years of it were spent gaining an education in life in the big city of London. From the age of eleven through to fourteen I lived there - through chance not choice.

As a child you have little choice in the things you do. Your parents tell you what is right and what is wrong, what to say and what not to say. On reflection it's a tough call to be a parent. I mean, if they get it wrong then they can mould you into a shape that gets disfigured. To be fair, neither of my parents got it wrong. In fact, they were as good as it got in my eyes. I comfort myself with that thought often.

I live in a quaint two-bedroom bungalow on Gorse Hill in a suburb of Clacton-On-Sea known as Great Clacton. My home is in a lovely location perched on the top of the hill and so gazes upon the green countryside that surrounds the area. History states that it was the beginning of the Clacton story back in the days when it was pretty much all farming land.

The second house belongs to my neighbour Roz and has done for God knows how long. She's a lovely old lady who has a major hearing problem, especially when it suits her.

The hill is at the top of an old valley that stretches down below. The road leading down splits grassy fields which in turn cover the entrances to two cemeteries. It is a wide valley that slopes for a quarter of a mile taking you to the very outskirts of Clacton town itself.

You may think living so near to two cemeteries is strange, but it's not like that at all. The cemetery on the left houses a sweet little chapel. Behind the chapel or church as you might call it - (I told you, I am not a religious man but to me, chapel suits this building better) - lies the older of the two gardens where there are many old headstones. It's a peaceful place and very pretty.

Across the road lies the newer cemetery. Again it's nothing you would associate with a horror movie. Simply picturesque and tranquil. To the left of this cemetery there's a children's play area while twenty metres away a small brook sends gurgles of water along as it passes this little spot in the universe.

The area is complemented by four ancient willow trees spread across the front of the landscape almost as if they have been painted onto the scene. I never tire of this quiet, almost holy part of my world.

Not many people live in Great Clacton. On the whole it is populated by elderly and middle-aged people, mainly due, I think to the bungalows which suit them. I got some strange looks when I first moved in, as if I didn't belong. Maybe they thought that I had some secret of a youth cream that they had missed out on. After a while, when they realised I was no trouble - simply younger than they were - the street became even nicer to live in. I suppose you could say we all look out for each other.

To sum up Clacton-On-Sea itself. Think of London, the big city of England. Think of escaping the smog and grime for a day out on the beach. Over the years you will find or know of someone who has been to Clacton. In its heyday in the early 1920s, people flocked to the place. They went to visit the pier with its fun and rides and to wander about the beach in their full-length bathing costumes. To sit on the deck chairs and perhaps dream of one day living here. I think a place with a beach is always going to have that special feeling for some people. A beach is a wonderful asset and for many years Clacton *did* enjoy the fruits of its own tree, so to speak. But gradually all that has changed.

Many older people in the town say it was when Butlin's shut down that things began to go downhill. Butlin's for those who don't know was - and still is in other seaside towns such as Skegness - a holiday camp in the best British tradition. A place to take the whole family for a break in the days before cheap flights and internet deals. A place where the kids were just British kids being entertained by the famous Red Coats while their parents relaxed in the evenings and enjoyed some kind of cabaret act. Even though we lived in Clacton it was always our holiday destination too.

I remember those days well when I was a young child until eventually the owners decided to close the place down. It needed major renovation and the first real foreign trips, to places such as Spain, were beginning to win hearts. It was maybe the death knell of this seaside town The holidaymakers left, the jobs went and the council sold the land to another investor named, as I recall, Atlas Park. It was supposed to take entertainment onto the next level but about six months later, the only level was *ground* level, as it was razed after going bust.

So we were left with a cocktail of people. The slow paced, easy-going pensioners and the fast moving and fast talking London folk. Not always the best combination.

Add to that the crime that has drifted into the town like an unwanted cancer with many elderly being mugged by the young. Add the drug culture that is beginning to enslave many towns across the country and you can see that I probably think Clacton-On-Sea has seen better days. It has, but I am not complaining, not at all because I love it here. I have friends, I have work, and I have a holiday to take tomorrow.

See, that's another great thing about living here by the sea. I have fresh air and long beaches to empty the mind of dust and set the cobwebs free, whilst just an hour away lies Stansted airport, a launch pad to the world. Tomorrow I'll be at that launch pad getting ready to fly to Spain to spend a week with my pal Ray Skee.

Ray, for the record, is one of my best friends. Everyone has friends in different kinds of categories. For men, there are those who you may have an odd drink with. There are friends who you may have a meal with as a couple, if you have a girlfriend (which I don't right now). Then there are real good friends like Ray Skee. Someone who you can talk to about *anything*. Who never judges and always supports and, best of all, a mate who, if you don't see him from one day to the next, is *exactly* the same as the last time you saw him.

Ray and I haven't seen each other for about nine months so when he called me about three weeks ago to invite me out to his place in Los Alcazares, Spain, I jumped at the chance. 'Just grab a flight, mate,' he said. So I did and got a nice deal too.

So now you know a bit about Clacton and my mate Ray.

The strange thing about all of this is that I live here in this town again. You see, I'd been a part of it from the age of zero until I was eleven. Then, after a three-year absence, destiny brought me back here.

Here I am then, living in my nice bungalow at the top of the hill by the cemetery. I have a nice job and I have some nice friends. So what is so strange about that, I hear you say?

I haven't mentioned my family, have I? Well, they aren't far away. My dear family. With the exception of my granny, they are all inside that cemetery on the right.

CHAPTER 2

I've suffered with dreams and nightmares from an early age. One in particular.

I open my eyes. The clock on my left automatically flicks three black pieces of plastic over to show the white numbers: 8.00. Simultaneously sound emits from the built-in radio.

'It's eight o'clock. John Lennon shot dead in Manhattan.'

December the 8th 1980. Yesterday John Lennon was alive. Yesterday so were my parents.

A shadow appears at the door. It's Granny. As the radio announcer describes the scene she walks slowly in with a cup of tea, which she puts down on the side next to the alarm clock.

'Former Beatle John Lennon was shot dead by an unknown gunman who opened fire outside the musician's New York apartment last night. The forty year-old was shot several times as he entered the Dakota, his luxury apartment building opposite Central Park, on Manhattan's Upper West Side, at eleven o'clock local time.'

My grandmother strokes my forehead. 'Steve. Morning,' she whispers gently.

I don't answer. 'Good morning, Steve,' she says again. I try to smile but nothing happens. My lips curl the wrong way. I try again but this time they curl even more the wrong way and my eyes start to water. I sit up and grab her in one movement. She hugs me and I feel tears rain down from my eyes. Confused - hopeless - real tears. Shedding pain and loneliness and so much more. I don't even know the names of how to describe them.

Granny holds me tighter as she whispers in my ear 'It's alright, it's alright.'

But it's not alright. I shake inside as the tears take a hold on me. I can't stop them and I can't stop shaking. I only know I need to hold my granny longer. She's all I have left and I don't want to let her go. I can't let go - even if I want to - and I don't. The moments go by. Maybe one. Maybe ten.

Her shoulder is wet now and I am shivering a little. She senses the tears are subsiding and sits down gently next to me, easing me back. My body goes limp. She eases me back onto the mattress and tucks a pillow behind me and I slump onto it. Her eyes are glazed and she looks very sad. I don't want her to be sad.

'Sorry, Granny, sorry. Don't be sad.' The words quiver from my mouth as my lips just won't do what they are supposed to do. Soft wet tears run down my face and I wipe them away with my pyjama sleeve.

'You silly boy,' she says as a small smile appears. Not a real smile but a sad smile as if she has no control either.

'Don't be sorry, Boy,' she says. Her name for me when she is being kind is "Boy".

'Why Granny? Why?' The words tumble desperately from my mouth. My voice sounds small and quiet.

It was late when the policeman came last night. I know it was late because I was in bed and I didn't go to bed till it was just past ten. I loved staying with her. When Mummy and Daddy and I arrived in East Ham yesterday, we had a yummy lunch. Granny and Mummy cooked it while Daddy and I played in the garden. Granny has a long garden and her house is lovely. I like it because it's near a park and it's off Lonsdale Avenue where there's a nice sweet shop. If I'm good when I come here I'm allowed to go to the shop and buy sweets.

I must have been good because normally I leave when Mummy and Daddy do, but yesterday Granny asked if I could stay. I jumped about while Mummy and Daddy discussed arrangements. Granny smiled at me when they said I could stay, and I smiled back. I was very happy especially when they said I could stay until Wednesday. It's the eleventh and Daddy said he would pick me up when he delivered his blinds in London. I could help him and then go home.

I love helping my dad. He makes blinds and they call him Bob. His van has *Bob the Blind Man* written on it and he goes around delivering his blinds to all the big warehouses in London.

When they left, Mummy kissed me and we waved "goodbye" from the door, watching them as they got into the car and waving more as they drove off. After they'd gone Granny made some sandwiches for tea. I had three types yesterday. She knows I like different kinds of sandwiches so she made me peanut butter, Marmite and strawberry jam ones, all cut into triangles like only Granny can do.

She bustled around doing Granny things and then we sat in the front room and she got out the chess set and we played three games. I won two and she won one. When it got late she told me to get ready for bed so I went upstairs and brushed my teeth and put on my pyjamas that she keeps safe for when I stay. They are light blue with claret stripes, like West Ham, the local team. I'm going to see them one day soon. Daddy told me he would take me, just like my granddad took him before granddad went to heaven.

Granny tucked me in and wished me sweet dreams. I told her the same and then I went to sleep. Sometime later I was woken up by a knocking sound. I heard Granny at the door and some voices. I got up quickly to see what was happening and went to the top of the stairs. The light was on and it was so bright that it hurt my eyes so that I had to rub them.

I saw a policeman *and* a police lady at the bottom of the stairs. They were talking to Granny but then they stopped and looked at me. I looked back at them because I hadn't done anything wrong.

Everything changed then. Everything was in slow motion like the football replays on the telly. My granny was crying and the policeman and the police lady looked very sad.

There were lots of words but I only heard the important ones.

My mummy and daddy are dead. They died in our car on the way home.

'But why, Granny? Why?' I say again

'They are safe in heaven now, Boy,' she replies.

I don't like that answer. 'But I don't understand, Granny. *I* need them. Why have they left me?'

She thinks and then looks at me sadly and says, 'Steve, sometimes sad things happen and we don't understand them but we have to try to understand them.'

I look at her because I still don't understand.

She hesitates. 'They're safe now. *They're* in heaven but *you're* here and you're safe too.'

I want to be in heaven now as well if that's where Mummy and Daddy are. 'Why didn't I die?' I ask Granny, 'Why didn't I go with them and then I'd be dead too? Wouldn't I Granny? Wouldn't I?' The tears start to stream down my face again.

Granny's getting upset now too. She wipes her eyes and says, 'Steve, do you know what an angel is?'

I nod. I *do* know because I've seen one on our Christmas tree but I don't know if they're real because Daddy never told me. I know Father Christmas isn't real because he did tell me that last Christmas when I was ten.

'Well, angels....' she said and then stopped for a moment. 'Angels, they protect us and they look after us and things like that.'

I sniffle a bit while I think. 'So Granny, where *are* these angels? Why didn't they look after Mummy and Daddy?'

Now I watch as she sniffles too while she thinks. 'Steve...' she says really slowly. 'Your mummy and daddy are in heaven and it's in heaven that there are angels, okay?'

I nod a little, trying to understand.

'And you,' she says, 'you are my little angel and you and I will look after each other now, okay?' Granny looks very sad now. She's shaking a bit, holding my hand and I feel that trembling too. I don't like seeing her upset.

'Okay, Granny,' I say. 'I'll look after you.'

'Good boy,' she says doing that smile thing which is not really a real smile.

We look at each other for a moment.

'Granny?' I say, questioningly.

'Yes, Steve,' she answers patiently.

'The angels live in heaven, don't they? But do they ever come down to earth?'

She stops the way she does when she is *really* thinking.

'Yes, yes, I'm sure they do. I'm certain, Boy, because we all have a guardian angel *somewhere* you see...' she replies, and then she smiles the lovely smile that means she likes what she just said... I think.

'Well, Granny,' I say with a deep breath, 'then I am going to try and find an angel, and one day when I do I am going to ask them why my mummy and daddy went to heaven.'

CHAPTER THREE

Now twenty years later I still have that recurring dream as well as many others. That is when it must have begun. That is when my search began.

But today I have no such thoughts. Today, I am on holiday.

I've never been good at getting up early and this flight to Spain meant exactly that. Thankfully my mate Harry gave me a morning call on his way to pick me up and chauffeur me to the bright lights of Stansted airport. You can always rely on Harry. He is one of life's natural comedians and what he may not have in Adonis good looks he more than makes up for in personality. I am not saying he is ugly by any means. He stands about five eleven with cropped blonde hair and no unusual characteristics. That is with the exception of a larger than normal nose and a set of gnashers that have earned him the affectionate nickname, Doctor Teeth.

He works in the city with historical pieces and antiques so for him getting up early is no big deal. I don't know how he does it and sometimes wonder why he does, but Harry likes the big house and the good life with his wife and two kids and he has all that. All in all he is a top guy.

After live entertainment courtesy of Doctor Teeth himself, I arrived at Stansted in good spirits. The airport was alive with people all going somewhere. All shapes and sizes, cultures and nationalities bustling around below the shining lights. It almost seemed like some kind of spaceport. I went through the usual rigmarole of security which seemed to take longer and longer each time I travelled. I found myself wondering if all the security actually made anyone feel more secure, because I noticed people eyeing each other suspiciously.

Once all the checks were over I took a quick stop at the

newsagent's to grab a paper and then a couple of minutes wandering around the perfume store where there was just about every fragrance I had ever heard of. I sampled a Gautier one and after spraying a little on each wrist, I cupped my hand and sprayed four large doses into it before putting the sampler back on the glass shelf. As I walked the hundred metres to the Wetherspoon's bar, I splashed it on my face and behind my ears and felt instantly refreshed.

I have to admit I am a nervous flyer, so to soothe those nerves I ordered a beer and a red wine from the bar and sat myself down at a nearby table. Although it was still early in the morning, I had an hour to kill and it helped dampen the edginess I felt in my stomach before a flight.

I once heard that there is more chance of being killed by the hind legs of a donkey than in an air crash, but that theory never works for me when I get close to flying. I smoked three cigarettes quickly whilst necking down the drinks and then of course I needed the toilet before boarding. Wandering into the lavatory I felt a combination of happiness and tiredness combined with a hint of euphoria from the alcohol. Washing my hands, I splashed water onto my hair and looked into the mirror. I looked okay considering the time of day. I pushed my dark brown hair back with my fingers. My face looked slightly tanned but could do with improvement. I was sure Spain would assist with that! I grinned at myself in the mirror. Holiday time, Steve!

A glance at the clock outside the toilet told me to speed up my step. Reaching the transit lounge for my journey to gate twelve, I breathed deeply and attempted to gather myself for the flight ahead. I looked to see if any other passengers were displaying the slight tension I felt but most seemed oblivious to anything but getting there first.

When we were all on the plane there the safety procedure that I always listened to. Perhaps out of superstition - as if someone up in heaven might notice if I didn't. And then moments later I saw the early morning light and the landscape blurring from the window next to me. I leant back as the plane lifted up with an overwhelming surge of g force. We were off.

The steep climb sent a momentary rush through me. I waited for the ascent to finish and for the plane to steady. While this was happening I faced my usual battle with the anxiety that challenged me each time I flew. Thoughts seemed to jump around my head like grains of rice on a drum, until at last, the plane settled in the sky as it found its level. The welcoming bing bong sound meant we could relax; well it did to me. As soon I heard it I felt better. Soon after, the trolley trundled up the aisle offering the only chance of eating or drinking that I would get for the next two hours or so. I ordered my favourite combination of red wine and black coffee before settling down for the journey ahead.

The sky looked wonderful outside. I sipped my wine in tandem with the coffee and watched the clouds puff gracefully around the craft. As a small child I remembered sitting next to my father and watching the clouds thinking they could be jumped and skipped on. One cloud to the next all the way to the big castle in the sky. Sadly, when I grew up I lost that dreamy vision. As the plane glided across the sky I thought about the trip ahead.

I remembered when I had first met Ray Skee, just after I'd returned from London. I was walking home from school across the local playing field, when I saw this bloke on a bike racing towards us across the bumpy green grass. He just kept on heading towards our group, until he was almost upon us. Thankfully I wasn't his target. One of the kids walking with me was suddenly hurled up in the air like a rag doll before landing on his arse. I was stunned as I watched this idiot laughing crazily as he circled around us on his bike.

It seemed he knew some of the group I was with but not me of course because I was new in town. After celebrating his demolition of this poor kid he suddenly noticed me and said, 'Who are you then?'

He didn't scare me though with his mass of wavy hair – big,

but stupid. 'Who are *you*?' I retorted aggressively. I'd learnt from my time in London that the minute you back down from a bully - and this guy looked like one - was the time you got trampled. That would probably last for the rest of your school life and I had two years of mine left. I didn't fancy playing the victim with this lump treading on my head or whatever the hell he got up to when he had you by the balls.

He seemed somehow pleased with my hostile answer.

'I'm Ray Skee,' he replied. 'Pleased to meet you.'

And that was how we met.

Despite the unusual circumstances, for the rest of my school life, Ray became a great friend. He was, and still is, a strange character but I love the fellow. He liked fish finger sandwiches for lunch which I found strange, yet no one would dare take the mick out of him for it.

School kids can be cruel and the smallest thing can be your downfall, but even though Ray had many weird things about him, nobody pushed him. A couple of bigger kids tried and landed flat on their backs. My favourite thing about Ray Skee is that the bloke has absolutely no fear. Unless you know someone who is like that, it is nearly impossible to describe. When you have no fear it makes a difference. The other guy usually does.

He wasn't a bully at school, just a bit soft in the head at times. Coldly intelligent at others. There were occasions when I was just the foil for his next plan but he never tried to dominate me. We treated each other equally, even back then and I liked him for that. He was a big strong bloke, stronger than me for sure, yet he had a dignity that meant he would sometime cock his ear like a dog when I said something he considered to be important.

We stayed close friends even after our schooldays. I got into computers for a living while Ray went into the Fire Service. A perfect job for a big built five foot eleven lump like him. The job gave him freedom of movement which he utilised by buying a place in Spain three years ago. Now he just travels back and forwards to work and stays in brigade digs when on duty in London. This has dual benefits for him and also me. It means that I can hop on a plane like this and catch up with my pal.

Ray Skee, top-drawer fireman, who has saved lives and seen death that I can only imagine in dreams *or* nightmares.

CHAPTER FOUR

The last twenty years have not always been easy. Any child who loses his immediate family suffers dramatically. Our family was small enough anyway, after that night it was just the two of us. Looking back on it now I feel more for my grandmother who had to hold the last pieces together and to take on the challenge of bringing up a child in her sixties.

For me as a young boy, the world seemed a lonely confusing place after that. As I was growing up, I began to understand what it was all about but looking back it was a harsh place, about to get much harsher.

I felt the gentle rocking of the plane, another hour to go till we landed, time for a doze. I closed my eyes and my mind drifted in semi consciousness.

****

It's grey outside as I walk to the car. All around me is dreary and meaningless. My hand holds hers. It feels warm and yet has coldness about it. I hold it as it leads me to the door. We get in the black car.

Silence surrounds me. She looks at me from time to time and she gives me a reassuring smile which means I have to try and smile but I can't.

I stare out the window as the car eats up the miles from my new home in London on our way to Clacton, my old home. I have seen these views many times before. I remember that building, I remember that house. But it was different then. Now it's silent and I'm afraid. I look up to the front of the car where I see the man driving us. He just drives.

I close my eyes and then open them and look again. Nothing

is different. But I imagine Mummy turning to me 'Are you alright, Steve?' I only see her in my mind because she is not here now. Now there is only the driver and me and Granny in the back.

I feel sick.

I feel so afraid and lonely. Granny is holding my hand but she doesn't feel like my granny at the moment. She's taking me somewhere I don't want to go.

Eventually the car stops. The man opens the door and I get out. Granny looks at me and pulls at my suit to straighten it. Then she pulls my tie straight. I don't say anything.

'There you are, Steve, that's better,' she says, looking satisfied.

I look at her and still say nothing. I have never worn a suit before. It feels funny - awkward. I want to take it off and run away. Run to that field across the road and hide. She takes my hand again.

'Come along,' she says. I do as she asks.

I walk with Granny to where there are a small crowd of people. They are all wearing suits and things. All black - like the sky. We stand by a building which looks like a church but different. I've been to church before with Mummy and Daddy but not a church like this. My granny is talking quietly to a man in a white robe that looks like a man I saw before in a church I went to with Mummy and Daddy. I can't hear what they're saying but he's looking at me.

'Hello, Steve.'

'Hello, sir,' I reply, because Mummy told me to call the man in church "sir" and this man looks like him.

He smiles at me but I think it's a sort of sad smile.

I don't like it here. The people around me are quiet too. Perhaps they don't want to be here either.

No one talks to me now. I just look around and keep close to Granny and we wait for a while. The rain falls and it's wet and horrid.

Two shiny black cars pull up by the church. I watch Granny

walk with the man in white and they are talking to the people in the car. I don't know them. I look around a bit but not too much because I feel very shy and scared. I don't know which I feel the most.

I see Mrs. Edwards standing by some flowers. She's my next-door neighbour and friends of Mummy and Daddy. She looked after me lots of times when they went out together. She won't be looking after me again because I don't live there any longer. I live with Granny now.

Granny comes towards me. 'Steve,' she beckons and takes my hand again. And then we're walking inside the big doors of this place They're so big! Like one really big door cut in half. We're inside now and it's cold and it smells. I don't know what this is but I hate the place. Granny and I walk to the wooden seats. I have to slide along to sit down. We sit at the front as the other people come in. I don't count them like I might sometimes do with people. Nobody sits with us.

'Granny,' I whisper. It sounds loud like a shout in this place.

Granny looks at me and leans close towards me bending down to reach. I can smell her granny perfume now.

'What, Steve?' she whispers, but she is quieter than me at whispering.

'Why are we sitting alone?' I whisper again, but in my best whispering voice.

I look at her. She looks very nice really. She's wearing a black bonnet which I haven't seen before. It looks old. Not old like rubbish, but old like from a long time ago. She sits straight for a moment, looking at me and I know what she is thinking.

She bends towards me again and whispers a reply, 'These seats are for family, Steve.'

She sits up straight again and I watch her hand go to her shiny black bag. Nothing else is shiny but everything is black today. She pulls out a handkerchief.

I watch Granny pat her eyes but she doesn't notice me

because she is looking straight ahead. I think about what she just said.

I hold her hand because I love her and she's upset. I can tell. She smiles a little but her eyes look sad and I can't see her very well because my eyes aren't working properly now. I think I'm going to cry. The man in the white robe comes in the door and music plays. It's organ music and I've heard it before in the other church I went to but not this song. Everyone stands up so I do the same. So does Granny.

Everybody looks towards the big doors. Now I know why the doors are so big. Some people come in carrying a box. More people are behind them carrying another box. I know what's inside those boxes but I don't know which one is which. I start to cry.

I cry a lot. Not like a baby but like a grown-up and I don't wipe my tears because I don't care. 'Mummy,' I whisper but I'm not whispering because I can feel everyone looking at me and they're sad too.

I shout, '*Mummy*! *Daddy*!' And then Granny is holding me and all the people are looking at me now. All at once.

'Shhh, Shhh,' she says as we sit down. She wipes my face with her handkerchief.

The music stops. The man in the white robe is standing by the boxes and he is talking now. I can't make much sense of his words.

'Mumble... mumble... Michael and Patricia... mumble... mumble... taken from us... mumble... mumble ... tragedy.'

Granny holds my hand. I feel cold and I'm shaking. I don't like the man in the robe. He's not like the other man I met before. He's talking about my mummy and daddy but I've never seen him before. What does he know about them?

He mumbles a lot more. It's like he doesn't know what to say. I want to shout again but I can't because I know I mustn't.

We stand up. I hear a noise. People are holding books and we're singing just like we did in church when I went with Mummy and Daddy. I don't sing though. I just look at the boxes and I cry more, but quietly now. Crying in a whisper.

The song finishes and the man talks some more. He talks about God and he talks about life and he talks about lots of things, but I don't hear very much. I look at the wooden boxes and I think of my parents. I think of lots of times with them and I miss them more than ever right now. I miss things like my mummy saying 'Good night darling.' I miss my daddy saying 'You're a good boy.' As I think of these things I cry and cry and cry and I can't stop.

The time goes by. We sing a sad song. The man in the white robe talks some more. Then he stops and he says we must go somewhere now. My granny is talking to me, 'Steve, Steve,' she says. I look at her and she's crying too. 'Come on, Boy.' Her face is kind now. She leads me outside where it feels very light but it's still raining.

Granny bends down towards me 'Are you alright, Boy?' She gives me a little cuddle.

'Granny,' I say in my questioning voice that she always understands.

'Yes, Steve?' she replies, the way she does.

'Do you think that God is crying too?' I point to the sky.

Granny laughs and cries at the same time. She shakes and her throat goes funny, like when I hiccup. 'Yes, Steve,' she says. 'God is crying.'

'Well, Granny,' I say. 'If God is crying, then why did he do it?' I feel angry now.

'Oh, Steve,' Granny says.

I look at her, waiting for an answer.

'Because, darling,' she says, 'even God makes mistakes sometimes.'

We walk across the road past some big willow trees. I know they're willows because I read a book called *The Wind in the Willows* once. I liked it a lot and I like willows a lot too. When I read the book Mummy pointed the trees out to me. I like to think willow trees can talk.

The cars arrive and we're standing by some holes in the

ground. The men lift the boxes out of them and the man in white says things about ashes and things. Granny holds my hand really tight. I say nothing. Just watch.

The people put my mummy and daddy in the ground and I know I will never see them again. Never, ever, ever.

I cry more than I have ever cried in my whole life and I fall on the ground.

When I stop crying people are around me but not saying anything. They look awkward. I'm wet and my trousers are muddy. Mrs. Edwards is next to me and so is Granny. Mrs. Edwards says, 'Hello, Steve. Are you alright?'

I'm not *feeling* alright but I nod anyway and look at Mrs. Edwards.

'Dear Steve… poor boy… I'm so sorry,' she says.

'What for? You're not God,' I whisper, but so quietly only I hear it.

The people start to leave. They talk to Granny and some of them say "sorry" to me. I just look at them. I walk to the flowers where the boxes are and I look. The flowers are pretty and bright and *beautiful*. They look wrong here. Here it is grey and God is crying and I am crying.

'Steve?'

I look around.

'Hello, Steve.'

I see a lady in black. She's quite tall but I don't know her. I've never seen her before like some of the other people here. She's pretty and I like her immediately but I don't know her.

'I don't know you,' I say.

She kneels down next to me. 'I knew your mummy and daddy, Steve.'

I look at her eyes. She has beautiful blue eyes. Like the sky in summer. 'Well, *I've* never seen you before,' I say, but not nastily.

She looks at me kindly and smiles. 'That's true, Steve, but I *do* know them and I have a message for you from them.'

'You do?' I say, 'But…'

'They love you very much, Steve.'

I say nothing. I like her voice – it's soft like a blanket and it reminds me of Mummy.

'Will you remember something for me?' she asks me, smiling tenderly.

'Yes,' I say.

'No one is gone until you forget them, so you'll never lose hope if you keep remembering.'

I nod as I think about what she is saying.

'It's important that you remember today, Steve.'

'I will,' I say.

'If you do, then one day you'll find what you are searching for and you'll know love.'

'I understand.'

'Will you remember that for me?'

'Yes.'

'Good boy,' she says standing up. 'Goodbye, Steve.' She smiles sweetly at me.

'Goodbye, lady,' I reply.

I watch her walk a few steps away as Granny comes up to me.

'Come on, Boy,' she says.

I walk with her towards the car that brought us here. I feel better now.

'Are *you* alright, Granny?' I ask.

She looks at me. 'Yes, are you?'

'Yes,' I say. 'Yes.'

She turns her head slightly towards me. 'Who was that lady you were talking to?'

'She…,' I say, then stop. 'Granny…,' I whisper.

'Yes, Steve.'

'I think she was an angel.'

Granny looks around but the lady has gone.

I dreamt about her again several weeks later. I was very ill and couldn't start my new school. One night, when I was at my worst, she came in my dream and spoke to me again. It was almost the same as before.

She said, 'Always have hope. If you do, then one day you will find what you are searching for and you'll know love.'

I got better quickly after that.

CHAPTER 5

'Sir! Sir! Excuse me, sir.'

I felt my left arm being shaken. My eyes snapped open immediately, unsure of my surroundings.

'Wake up, sir,' I looked up to see the flight attendant smiling at me.

'We'll soon be beginning our ascent into Alicante, sir. Please can you put away your tray and fasten your seat belt.'

'Sorry,' I mumbled as my mind stumbled to adjust. I must have dropped off. Damned sleep, damned flashbacks, come on, get with it, Steve.

Slowly things started to come back into focus as I became aware of my surroundings. I tried to put thoughts of yesterday away until I got home. Then, if needed, I would give Pat a call. He was the only one I trusted or could talk to about any of this. The only one who understood.

I looked out of the window and saw the dry landscape of Spain coming closer. As the plane eased downwards I gazed at the crystal blue water of the Mediterranean, shimmering like a sparkling jewel in a crown.

A couple of bumps and a decent landing later, we disembarked into a fine looking day.

¡Viva España! The land of big easy and warmth and that's not just the sun but the people too. *¡Tranquilo!* as the locals say. A word I never tire of repeating back home in Blighty.

I loved Spain for all sorts of reasons: the fact that families and friends ate out so often; that older people were respected by the younger generation - almost in a Mafia Godfather kind of way. I even loved silly things, like you can smoke when and where you want - although that may change in the future,

I felt good about everything but that's what a holiday does to a man. I smiled to myself as I made my way from the plane. The flight attendant thought the smile was meant for her and smiled back at me.

The steps down from the plane led to a wonderful Alicante morning. I felt the surge of heat slap me in the face as I breathed in the distinct Spanish air.

Inside the terminal building I lit up a cigarette as I walked towards baggage reclaim. Nobody looked at me strangely like they would have done in England and I strolled straight through passport control.

After collecting my bag I wandered down the slope towards the exit. The décor was fresh and light. At the bottom I headed for the sliding doors which led out into the arrivals hall. As they opened and shut for the people in front of me, I saw a mass of faces. Everyone waiting for someone. Some holding cards up for people they had never seen in their lives before while others probably waited for people they had not seen for a lifetime.

I looked around; no Ray.

Walking through the throng of people I saw something that caught my eye near the back of the crowd.

A white card held aloft with bold letters: **BIDANTE HOMELESS CHARITY**

I smiled as Ray's face appeared from behind the card and as I approached he smirked and laughed that crazy laugh that my ears had really missed.

'You dickhead!' I grinned as we hugged like long-lost brothers, his bear-like arms squeezing the air from me.

'Hello, Steve, welcome to Spain!' he bellowed.

'Good to see you, buddy,' I said as we released each other.

'You too, mate. You too,' Ray replied. 'Did you have a good flight?'

I didn't divulge my sleeping thoughts, which were still in my mind but simply replied, 'As good as it gets, Ray, as good as it gets.'

'Well, it's great to have you here,' he enthused as we walked towards the outer doors. Outside we headed for the car park where the sunshine hit me again. 'Lovely, eh, Ray? All this weather?' I commented looking up at the sun.

He grinned. 'You get used to it, but me - I even think I'm losing the English habit of talking about the weather. You see, it doesn't really change too much round here!'

'You got the best of both worlds, Ray,' I laughed.

Ray looked at me. Now that he was older the wavy hair had been replaced by a shaven patch - a reminder of the way his hair used to be. He looked in good shape – the picture of health in fact.

'I told you I was going to do it, Steve. Once all the logistical headaches were out the way the rest was easy. Now I live here, work back home and earn English money which I spend in heaven.' He gave me a look of satisfaction as he accentuated the word heaven.

I remembered when he first talked about it. We were on a boys' trip to Benidorm and someone mentioned "property". He went out later that same day and looked at some because that night he spoke about it. Within six months he had bought.

Ray Skee. Whatever he does, he doesn't mess about!

'Here we are.' Ray stopped and pointed to a battered white convertible Jeep. I didn't mind what he drove but, just in case I did, he seemed ready to cover his tracks as if he had been in this position before with someone who gave a damn about cars.

'It isn't much, Steve,' he said sheepishly, 'but it gets me about and it doesn't matter if it gets covered in Sahara sand *and* you can bump into parking spaces. Plus it hasn't got a roof which is great when it rains because it gets a wash!'

'Just drive safe, brother. That's all I ask.'

'Never any different, buddy!' he laughed.

He revved it up and swerved out of the parking space much too fast for my liking. If I had to declare one thing I hated about Ray, just one thing, it would be easy. Two things would be very hard but one, easy: his bloody obsession with speed.

He drives everything and anything to the max. Even that pushbike all those years ago on the day I met him.

We stopped with the radiator of the Jeep practically kissing the barrier of the car park exit. Ray leant over and popped some coins into the slot. As soon as the arm creaked upwards he was off, foot flat down on the floor bombing around the corner much too fast. I watched nervously as he cut across the junction narrowly avoiding another car. The angry driver waved his fist and beeped his horn but Ray just laughed like a madman.

After eating up a dozen or so miles he actually slowed down but that was only due to traffic lights. Pulling out a cigarette, he lit it before offering me the packet.

He drove more slowly while we smoked, which meant we could actually talk without the engine roaring in our ears.

'So, how's home, Steve? Tell me the latest.'

'Nothing major, Ray,' I replied. 'I was out last week with Sharon for a drink – she's good. Laurence turned up - looking smooth as usual. We had a nice night and before you say it - yes, Sharon still thinks he's the business.'

He soaked up my words and nodded as if everything was okay. I'd always suspected that he had a soft spot for Sharon and not such a soft one for Laurence. He'd never said much about it but at times he looked at her in a certain way. To me, Sharon was simply my friend and the closest thing to a sister I could ever have.

'How's the job, Ray? You saved any lives recently?' I asked, noticing that he was picking up speed again. Much to my relief, he slowed again so I could hear what he was saying.

'It's good, buddy, I finished my last shift a few day ago. A house fire in Stratford - saved a few Paddies,' he added nonchalantly.

'What happened?' I was always fascinated with Ray's tales about his work. I guess it was pretty sadistic but in truth I didn't want to hear the horror stories - just the hero stuff.

'Nothing out of the ordinary really,' he replied. 'An Irish

couple who hadn't got around to fitting a smoke alarm. They were lucky a neighbour spotted the flames, I can tell you.'

'You saved them?'

'Yeah, course we saved them!' Ray grinned.

I had to admire the fellow. It all came so easy to him. I relaxed even as he put his foot back on the floor. It was great to be in Spain again with my pal.

The journey to Los Alcazares flew by. We arrived at Ray's flat with a bump as he swerved the car up the steep kerb and into the parking area below the modern building he now called home. I followed him as he pulled out a key card and slid it over an impressive looking grid by the large front door of the building. A click and it opened into an imposing hallway graced with decorative mini palm trees.

'I like it, Ray,' I said, knowing he would never have chosen to live in a dump.

'You haven't seen anything yet, buddy.' A few seconds later and the steel door in front of us opened to reveal a clean-smelling marble lift.

'To the penthouse!' he said hitting a button.

At the top I followed him to his own door where he swiped his card again. Swinging it open he revealed what would be my home for the next few days.

When we went into the flat a clean fresh light almost made me want to shield my eyes. I followed Ray along a long, narrow hallway past a bathroom, into a wide open-plan lounge where white marble floors complemented cream walls. Bright light shone through a large set of patio doors ahead. He strode across and opened them, immediately inviting noisy hustle and bustle from outside into the flat. I strolled around getting to know my angles and discovered a spacious kitchen-cum-diner which, together with two roomy bedrooms, led off the end of the lounge.

'Very smart. Very smart.' I smiled as I wandered out onto the balcony where Ray stood sparking up another cigarette.

'This is perfect, Ray.' I couldn't help but be impressed.

'Will be when the cranes leave,' he answered, as we gazed around. Stubbing out his cigarette, he grabbed my arm, 'Come! Check this out!' He walked back through the lounge towards the front door motioning me to hurry after him.

'Come on! Come on!'

I followed as he nearly ran back down the hall leading out to the lift. To the left of the lifts there was a smaller door that I had not noticed on the way in. Ray opened it with his card and I followed him as he bounded up a dark, narrow flight of stairs. At the top he swung another door open and immediately a warm cascade of light invaded the area. I stepped outside and saw him wandering along the roof. But this was not *just* a rooftop. It was a massive garden-cum-terrace that covered the whole of the building. From here I could see the golden sands of the beach stretching across the landscape layered with the blue of the shimmering sea below.

'The business or what?' Ray yelled across from the other side of his vast concrete sun lounge.

'Is all this yours?' I called back to him feeling an inner joy. Not just for the splendour of the place and not just because I could imagine relaxing out here in the evenings with my thoughts and the stars. It was more on account of the smile Ray was displaying. I had never seen him look so happy.

'It is bloody superb, Skee,' I shouted. 'I'm even happier about calling you my friend now I know where to come for a free holiday.'

The rest of the day was like a dream. The warm sun beat down on us as we wandered along the promenade taking in beers from the many bars we stopped at. We heard sweet music being played from a variety of different bands during the long, dreamy afternoon. Peruvian pipes whisked along on the gentle sea breeze made the beer taste even better. After a couple of hours my head and body felt more relaxed than it had been for many a day. As we walked slowly along the paved promenade, Ray stopped and pointed to a bar and I simply followed. It was his town; he knew it.

After a meal of delicious paella I felt livelier, albeit pretty drunk. Afterwards Ray suggested we relaxed in a typical Irish bar just off the square. It felt lovely and cool after the heat of the day. I sat on a beer barrel and looked around at the décor while he ordered two pints of Guinness from the waitress who also provided us with some salty crisps and nuts to get the drinking buds going. Easy music blended with the soft atmosphere of the half full bar.

We chinked glasses. 'To us, *salud!*' he grinned.

'*Salud!*' I replied and sipped the cold Guinness.

'So tell me, mate,' Ray's speech was slightly slurred. 'Laurence and Sharon. Still not got it on then?'

I took another gulp of beer and pulled out a cigarette from the packet on the table.

'No,' I replied, remembering the feeling I had that he liked her. 'He just wants to be pals I think, Ray. She'd love something else but it isn't going to happen. I guess she needs to find someone to really love her, you know.'

He nodded agreement but didn't give anything away regarding his feelings.

'What about Harry boy? How's he doing?'

'Same as ever,' I replied. 'Richer, but still not allowed a ticket to go away on holiday! Still a top bloke though, Ray - and she's okay too. They just can't work that trust stuff out together, I guess.'

'Bloody mad, the lot of them. Give him my best,' he replied with a wink as he took another swig of the black stuff. He knew that Harry and Sofia were happy enough. It was just that Sofia thought that every woman on the planet wanted to tear Harry's clothes off. I was never sure what she was seeing to get that idea, but it wasn't what we were.

'So, any love on the horizon out here, Ray?'

He almost choked on his Guinness. 'Not really, mate. I don't have the time, not with the brigade and all the coming and going. The only love I can find out here with my schedule costs me about thirty euros and we don't talk,' he said with a faint smile. 'Seriously, Steve. That's the hardest part, getting time to meet a really nice girl. And you, my old mate?' He looked at me questioningly.

'No, buddy,' I said truthfully, because I knew what Ray meant. 'I work too much, talk too much and think too much. Nothing happening for me at the moment but you never can tell. Always got to hope, I guess.'

The truth of the matter was, I *did* want to meet someone but I was scared stiff. I'd met a couple of nice girls in the last year but there was no spark in the ignition if you get my meaning. I blamed it on my childhood, on the fact I'd become aware of something more around me. Some strange things had happened to me which had left me with a feeling that my life was somehow already mapped out for me. I thought I would know when the right girl came along. Either that or my theory would go up in smoke leaving me with a lonely, female-free existence.

We stayed in the bar for at least three more hours. It was hard to tell but it got late and everything was blurred. In the end, after drinking flaming *samboukas* - and plenty of them - the call of drunken sleep beckoned us home.

It took us a while to get back because my legs frequently let me down, much to Ray's amusement. His bulk of a body seemed to absorb the drink much better than mine. Back at the flat he grabbed two glasses and poured tequila into them. I drew on my last scrap of willpower to focus on the glass he handed me.

'Steve, my son. This holiday will live long in our minds. I just know it. *Salud* my friend!'

'*Salud!*' I replied gulping the filthy liquid down in one. The break would be great and his words rang true. Trying to look sober I realised I could see at least three of him. One Ray Skee was more than enough. I had to go to bed.

At that moment I could never even have guessed how much drunken words sometimes shine true.

CHAPTER SIX

The morning light stretched into my room, its brightness prising my eyelids slowly open. The whiteness made me feel as if I was still dreaming in some pure and heavenly place. As my eyes and mind gradually adjusted to my surroundings, I tried to recall the events of the night before.

I sat up on the edge of the cream futon that I would call bed for the next week feeling a little sick. It had been a heavy day. Ruffling my hair with my fingers, I slipped on some clothes and wandered out the room to take a peek at Ray. He was sound asleep - snoring like a pig.

I made a pot of coffee and then grabbed the keys from the table and went up onto the rooftop. It took a moment for my eyes to adjust. It was another fresh sunny day. I pulled out a cigarette and lit up, breathing in a load of trashy smoke which made me cough. Jesus, I'd got to give this crap up.

As my brain started to fully awaken, I leant against the railings and admired the wonderful view.

'This is the life,' I said out loud. As I sipped my coffee I reflected that it had not always been like this.

The dreams didn't come as often now but they sometimes threw up an event that left me thinking. The trouble was that I needed to speak to a shrink about things. Mention it to most people and they would probably refer me to one anyway. But there was always Pat. He was the only one I could speak to openly and easily and that's another strange thing. Why him?

When I looked back over my life, meeting Pat was one of the strangest experiences. Not because of the actual meeting but because of what he became to me. I could never have imagined it.

It was a long time ago when all that happened but still as clear as if it was yesterday. Travelling back to London with Granny after the funeral she explained this was going to be my new home. I should have felt glad I guess; I liked it at her house and I loved *her,* but it was never going to be the same again though, was it? Carrying on minus two loving parents in a house that was not home, in a place that you hardly knew apart from a park and a sweet shop. Who wouldn't struggle with that?

Soon after I arrived, within days of the funeral, I remember being very ill. Granny was really worried and the doctor visited a lot. I can't remember how long I was ill for though. That part is hazy because I was in and out of sleep. Fever. Vomiting. Eventually I got better and she fussed around me more than ever. I couldn't go to school of course and then after I was better I found out they couldn't fit me in anywhere straight away mid term. That led to even emptier days.

I hung off Granny at first but like any kid I wanted someone my own age to play with, to talk to. I spent the first months staying in and listening to music, writing, trying to entertain myself. Being in a new town at eleven was tough. I'd left all my friends and it was hard to meet new ones, I wasn't even sure if I *wanted* new ones. I just wanted things the way they were and I struggled to accept that back then.

I wasn't nasty or bad to Granny. I did all she told me and she was good with me but I was growing up and fast. Soon I was wandering round the streets on my own or sitting in the park by Lonsdale Avenue, but it wasn't my *real* home. At home I had a beach and the sea and friends *and* my parents. Here I had a sewer bank to look at and people on benches in the park sniffing glue or drinking methylated spirits. Other children were not so friendly either. They just looked at me like some forbidden stranger they had never seen. Which, in many ways is what I was - a stranger. Even to myself.

I waited to see that woman again, the one who told me to

have hope - either in my dreams or in real life. She seemed real to me although I'd only seen her in dreams; she was more real than the world around me.

When I found out I had a place at a school for the next term I remember having mixed feelings. I would start my second year at senior school in a new place, meet new friends. It was all going to be new. On the first day Granny checked me over to make sure I was neat and tidy and before I left she gave me one last tip which I will never forget.

'It may be best not to mention about your mummy and daddy, Boy.'

Those were her words and when I asked her why, she said that it was something that just came to her. Something she needed to tell me. Granny said that in her day you didn't talk about things and she didn't think that it had changed. She talked all the time while she pulled and prodded me, adjusting my blazer and tie. I didn't really understand what she meant until she began to talk about my granddad and I realised then that she must be very sad sometimes too. She had lost a husband in the war and now a son and daughter-in-law.

I listened to what she said and nodded before setting off up the road to my new school. On the way I didn't think about the day ahead or myself. I thought about my grandmother and what she had said and of how hard it must be for her.

'Oh, my Cyril was a hero,' she would tell anyone who visited the house and had time to listen. She'd lost him in the war when they were just kids really and he had left her with the task of bringing up a son while grieving a husband.

She'd told me a lot about Granddad because of course I had no memory of him. Only through faded black and white pictures and stories did I get an idea of who he was. I realised on that walk to school that day that even though he was dead long ago, it didn't matter. For her, Cyril was very much alive and still a hero.

Surprisingly the first days at school were good. It was all

new and some of the children were interested in me just *because* I was new. They would ask where I came from and listen with interest when I described this lovely place with its beach and the sea. It was almost as if they never knew such places existed. I suppose if you knew no different then you would assume everywhere was just like East Ham.

I did my best to keep my secret to myself, just like Granny told me to. But even so, after a week or two, the problems started. The children who had asked the questions about me had told other children and some of the bigger or nastier ones wanted to know why I lived in East Ham. Why would I want to live here and not by the sea? Was I a liar?

I was only telling the truth but it got worse. Some of the teachers even called me Clacton with a sneer as if it was a made-up name from a made-up place. Then one day I was asked the question I had dreaded and that was the day I first met Pat.

I was standing by the tuck shop alone eating crisps and just looking around. I liked to watch in case I saw another child who I sort of knew. I didn't have any proper friends yet, only ones who asked questions and then went off.

A group of boys from a different year from mine came up. I'd seen one of them and I didn't like him much. I think his name was John Patrick but I know they called him Jettee for short. He came right up to my face and spoke.

'So Clacton, what we all want to know is why your parents left that lovely place to come here?'

When I didn't answer straight away, he glanced back at his friends before looking at me again and then swinging a punch that landed in my stomach knocking the wind out of me.

'I'm talking to you!' he shouted, as I dropped to my knees. I'd never felt so much pain and it was hard to breath.

'You think you're too good to live around here?' he yelled while the others stood around smirking and mumbling in agreement.

I got unsteadily to my feet.

'No,' I answered weakly, feeling sick.

Jettee came close and grabbed my by the throat twisting my shirt as he did so.

'So your *parents* think they're too good to be here then, do they?' His face was contorted with anger.

I was so scared that I said it. '*My parents are dead.*'

I had not wanted to say those words, not just because of what Granny had said but because to me they were not.

Jettee paused for a moment. He seemed slightly thrown by my words but he soon grabbed his composure. Instead of showing sympathy, he said, 'Well, that makes you a bastard, right? You're a bastard from Clacton!'

I didn't know then what a bastard was so I couldn't say if I was or I wasn't. He seemed to take that as an insult because after nodding to his friends that I was indeed, a bastard, he decided I was now a *rude* bastard.

'Answer me, Clacton. Tell the lads you're a bastard, right?' He had me up against the wall again pushing my face back against the rough bricks.

It was then I met Pat, or should I say he met me.

'Leave him be!' I heard someone say in a strange accent.

Jettee released his grip and I turned to see a short, well built boy standing there. He had a blazer on with his collar turned up. I hadn't seen him before but Jettee obviously had.

'Come on, Pat,' he said. 'This kid from Clacton, he's a bastard. A cocky bastard at that.'

I noticed a change in his voice, a touch of fear when Pat approached him and the other boys moved aside. I watched as Jettee wilted like a dying flower in front of me.

'I said leave him be,' Pat repeated. 'You touch him again and your parents will have no son going home. Ya got that?' he snarled.

Jettee got it. He gave me a last glance but there was no anger in his look in case Pat saw it, I suppose. Then they were gone and it was just me and him.

He looked me up and down. 'Ya alright?' he said in that strange accent.

'Yes thanks' I said, brushing myself down and feeling a little stupid.

'What did you do wrong?' he asked.

'Nothing. They just don't like me.'

Pat looked at me with a touch of humour in his eye. 'They just don't like you?'

He didn't understand.

I repeated the words but I hated saying them. 'My parents are dead. That's why I'm at this school. I used to live somewhere else but now I live here, and… they didn't like it. They said I'm a bastard.'

I waited for Pat to say something. Not for sympathy but just to hear him speak. He blew a sigh out from his cheeks and looked down at the ground for a moment before speaking again.

'You're not a bastard - a bastard is a lad without a father.'

'Right,' I said.

'Sorry to hear about your parents. That's sad, that is. What's your name?'

'Steve. Steve Bidante,' I replied.

Pat came close to me but I didn't feel scared this time.

'Well, Steve Bidante. You've got yourself a friend in Pat Reilly.' He offered me his hand.

'Are your parents dead too then?' I said, shaking it.

'No be'Jesus!' he replied and went to walk off.

'Pat,' I called after him, 'what does "be'Jesus" mean and… what's that accent?'

He turned his head and he was grinning. 'It's Irish, Steve. *I'm* Irish.'

And that's how I met Pat Reilly. It turned out he was the toughest kid in school aside from his four brothers.

The strangest thing about a boy like Pat Reilly helping out a boy like me was not just the fact of why would he? That was strange because he had no reason except that he was destined to be there that day.

Looking back now I realise that chance meeting was to change both our lives.

CHAPTER SEVEN

'Good morning!' Ray said, as he ambled out onto the terrace.

'Fancy some breakfast, Stevey boy?'

'Sounds good!' I replied, snapping out of my reverie. The mention of breakfast made me feel hungry. 'I'll just grab a shower and be with you.'

The coldness of the shower massaged my body and mind and left me feeling revitalised and with a renewed sense of purpose. Twenty minutes later I was ready to go.

We wandered from the flat down towards the seafront and along the pretty promenade where we came to a terracotta-coloured Andalucian style café-bar. I was amused when Ray called out for two English breakfasts. With the way my stomach felt I had to approve of his choice.

One well cooked meal later and I started to feel better still. I lit up a cigarette while Ray went to order some more coffee, listening as he chattered away, noticing how much his Spanish had improved.

'You really have got this language thing going, Ray,' I commented when he returned.

'¡Si, amigo! Hablo español!' he laughed. 'But seriously,' he continued, leaning towards me, 'I live here - so I try. The problem with Spain isn't the *Spanish*. They're great and if you make the effort then you're in clover. Thing is, most expatriates – especially the English and Germans - want to live their own way in someone else's country. Great for the Spanish income but it's a pain, man, a pain.'

'I hadn't really thought of it like that,' I said.

He gave me a frustrated look before continuing to make his point.

'Okay, listen up. The typical bloody tourists from England

come out here, determined to let their hair down in the two weeks' holiday they've worked all year for. Usually fourteen days of getting so pissed up, they fall over. Then you have your typical ex-pats. They move out here, hate the weather 'cos it's too hot - as if they didn't bloody know that after coming here on holiday for the last ten years! So they arrive, build their little communities and instead of integration we end up with fucking little Britain!'

He leant back in his seat. I could see the anger in his eyes and hear it in his voice so I decided to try reason.

'The Spanish seem a tolerant people, Ray,' I said. 'I suppose it's the British mentality that makes them behave that way when they go to another country on holiday. You know, forget the rules, enjoy themselves. You can't change that, nor can the other people who want to live by the rules - the Spanish way.'

It worked, I sensed his anger dissipating.

'Yeah, you're right. And we just ate a full English breakfast!' He smiled, holding up his hand for me to slap, as he breathed the anger out.

'Do you fancy relaxing down on the beach for a bit?'

It sounded good to me. 'It won't take us long to walk back to the flat to get our bits,' I said, nodding.

Ray shook his head. 'I've a better idea. How about heading for Guardamar in the Jeep?'

'Where?' The name meant nothing to me.

'*Guar...da...mar,*' he said slowly, 'a twenty-minute ride tops - and it's kind of out the way. You know - where the Spanish people go.'

I sensed he was trying to prove a point about his integration into the Spanish way of life.

'Why not,' I replied. 'You're the boss.' I gave him a friendly whack on the arm.

'It's got a decent beach bar too, mate,' he said with a grin.

We walked back to the flat and picked up some towels and beach clothes for the afternoon. I also grabbed a book and my shades and a fresh pack of cigarettes courtesy of Ray.

When we were in the Jeep and on our way Ray explained that Guardamar was only about forty kilometres up the road from Los Alcazares. As we raced out onto the open road, he told me about the town. He said that it was not as busy as Los Alcazares, that there was no nightlife and that he preferred the beaches and quieter way of life. It was a predominantly Spanish town which, thankfully, the English seemed to have bypassed.

The traffic was light and he made the most of it, hitting speeds that turned my stomach a little. But even this was diluted by the blend of warm sunshine and the feeling of freedom Before long we left the main road and turned right where Ray had to slow down to negotiate the narrow streets. This allowed me to observe the historical architecture of the town centre where people ambled about between the pretty shops and cafés.

The approach to the beach was different from what you would expect. We turned into a narrow lane that was lined with palm trees that shaded the road and made it look like a kind of nature park. Trundling gently over the speed bumps, aloe vera peeked out from the edges, almost touching the Jeep.

We continued along the avenue for around a mile until it opened out into a wide, open parking space. There were only five or six cars there and Ray parked the Jeep in one of the shaded bays where it would be shielded from the blistering heat. Grabbing our things from the back of the Jeep, we walked the short distance across the park to the sea. The sandy beach stretched out for miles in front of us. Walking across the decking that led onto the beach, we passed a large wooden straw-roofed hut with chairs stacked around it. 'Beach bar,' Ray said unnecessarily. 'Open later, I guess.'

The beach was deserted. Glancing at my watch, I was surprised to see that it was already after two. Siesta time for most of the Spanish. Gazing at the golden sands all around me, I saw that there were neat stacks of it piled up at the back of the beach. It gave me the impression that I had walked into a desert with sand dunes, but the water was no mirage. It was real and in front of me.

'Beautiful!' I said out loud.

We settled down about two hundred metres to the right of the bar and stripped down to our shorts. I strolled by the sea while Ray splashed into it. The cold water cooled my feet where they stung from walking on the hot sand. Looking around me, all I could see for miles was raw beauty. This was one hell of a spot.

After a bit I walked back to where we had left our things and laid out the towels. I pulled out my book and settled down to do a bit of reading in this lovely setting. As I fingered through to find my place, I glanced around for Ray. He was at least three hundred metres away now, swimming along the coastline. I forgot about him as I became engrossed in the book.

After about an hour of reading, smoking and sipping water while the sun massaged my body, I looked around for Ray again. Eventually I saw him kneeling down, maybe thirty metres away, deep in conversation with two girls. I squinted to get a better look at them. What a boy, I thought to myself before going back to the book.

About ten minutes later, Ray hurled himself down next to me, spraying my sticky, sun soaked body, with a wall of sand. Brushing it from my hair and spitting out a few grains from my mouth, I folded down the corner of the page and put the book down. End of reading time it seemed.

'Hi, mate!' Ray blurted the words out like a kid.

I helped him along. 'Looks like you were having a good chat, buddy,' I said with a smile.

'Oh yes,' he replied. 'Lovely day, Steve, and I just met two gorgeous girls!' He was obviously waiting for a response but I replied with silence.

'Well,' he continued after a few moments, 'I was wandering back and saw this amazing body lying on the beach. Naturally I had to investigate and it happens that they're two German girls who're staying here in Guardamar!'

'You speak German now as well?' I enquired, laughing. 'Is there no end to your talents?'

'I remembered enough, my son' he grinned. 'I did some roofing in Hamburg, remember? Anyway the tall and short of it is that the girls are coming back here tonight. I said I would have a word with you and we would meet up with them. What do you say?'

I wasn't so sure. Knowing Ray as long as I had, I knew that any meeting he'd arranged with girls did not necessarily mean any meeting at all. I had to admire his tenacity. He worked on a "no fear" theory - even with woman. I'd seen him knocked back on more than a dozen occasions in the past. Sometimes be given non-existent mobile numbers even. To his credit, if you can call it that, he would keep going and maybe ten females later he would find someone who fitted the bill, or at least didn't knock him back.

He waited impatiently for my answer.

'So which one have you got your eye on then?' I asked.

'Christina,' he announced proudly, as if I could know which one that was and then added, 'the one in the beige bikini.' He leant closer before adding enthusiastically, 'The one with the body to die for!'

I couldn't help but laugh. This was a Ray Skee moment. As far as he was concerned he had hit the jackpot and God help the girl now.

When I looked over at the girls, they waved acknowledgment and I found myself waving back. From where I was, Christina did indeed look to have a shapely body. Her long dark hair and tanned body made her stand out on the beach like a pretty shell in the sand. The girl beside her was wearing a blue all-in-one swimsuit as if she was trying to hide her defiantly paler skin. She had very short, tightly curled, black hair and looked almost white compared with her friend. She was not jumping out at me.

'So what's her friend's name?' I asked cautiously.

'Danni, short for Danielle, I suppose,' he said, as he drew deep on a cigarette while at the same time looking damned pleased with himself. I looked back at the beach and thought about it.

'It'll be a right laugh, Steve, come on.' He poked his face in front of mine, giving me his best puppy-eyed look. I felt almost sick but I had to admit that it was funny.

'I'll think about it! Now get lost!' I laughed.

'Great,' he said. 'I'm going for another dip and then we'd best be getting back, especially if we have to get ready for later.' With a "you know what I mean" wink, he was off, leaping into the sea. I lay there thinking about the position he had put me in. A definite no-win scenario. You see, I knew what was coming. He was going to badger me like hell to come back here later and I would probably want to come back even less than I did right now. Not because I was being awkward or boring, it was because I knew if - and when - we came back, I would cease to exist while he gave every gram of his attention to the girl in a quest for... well, you can guess.

I was packing my stuff away when Ray raced back from his swim.

'Right, he said, 'let's head back and get something to eat.'

On our way back to the Jeep, Ray prattled on about Christina's beauty, her silky voice and her endless legs while I offered little in the way of enthusiasm. As we drew level with the Jeep he stopped and put his arm around me. 'It'll be great, Steve - you and me, mate, come on.'

'We'll see,' I replied. I needed more time before making the decision to return. I wasn't sure why but I knew this was going to be a near impossible situation to get out of. I just wanted time to think and maybe hope this sudden passion for a German lady might wear off.

Ray nodded approvingly, as he skidded across the sandy car park and headed home.

'What time would we be meeting them?' I shouted above the drone of the engine.

'Midnight' he yelled, smiling.
Bloody midnight.
Typical Ray Skee.

CHAPTER EIGHT

As I showered I knew that I had already made my mind up that I would go with Ray. I hadn't told him yet because I wanted to watch him testing his powers of persuasion. As the powerful spray cleansed the sand from me I felt lucky to be here. I saw myself as a fatalist so it was just another piece of luck - only this time good.

Like everyone I have my runs of bad luck but I guess the timing of some events in my life has made me believe in fate. One instance was meeting Pat Reilly. The tough Irishman has a soul that's as deep as an abyss. It was he who first made me realise that some things are meant to be and that I must follow my dreams. When I told him I had dreams – more like visions really - he didn't even bat an eyelid. He just listened and believed and it was then I knew that I was not alone.

But there were lots more examples - both good and bad. Losing my parents was, of course the worst piece of bad luck that can happen to any child - if you can call it that. If I'd been religious, that event alone would have shaken my belief, but fate - fate's different. It led me to believe that all events are somehow linked. One example of this that stays in my mind took place in my second term at school in London.

I was in the changing rooms getting ready for a badminton class, sitting on the tiled concrete floor with my towel as a cushion, when I got the urge to go for a wee. It wasn't desperate - it came on suddenly because seconds earlier I hadn't felt it. I was undecided about whether to go or not, wondering if I should try anyway but it was not a wee I needed; it was one *I felt* I needed. When I did decide to go, I strained at the urinal with little success. Just as I was about to give up and put myself away, I heard an almighty crash from the changing rooms followed by lots of noise. Running back in to see what the commotion was I saw a huge iron support girder with its tip embedded in the concrete floor. Walking past the silent boys I stood by the metal tip looking at where my towel lay beneath it. It could have, and should have, been me.

Perhaps I did need that wee after all.

****

Nine o'clock in Spain is early enough to be eating and, unlike home, it's a real event for everyone including people like Ray and me. We sat outside a restaurant on the promenade at Los Alcazares. It was a beautiful evening, perfect weather for the T-shirts and slacks we were wearing. We ordered a selection of *tapas* and it was as I picked out delicious pieces and put them onto my plate that Ray tried to work his magic.

'You fancy it later then, Steve, you know… Guardamar?'

Between mouthfuls of food I shot him uncertain glances made in acting school. 'Maybe, Ray, maybe,' I said with a hesitant nod.

I thought he'd changed the subject until he said, 'Did I ever tell you about the time in Turkey?'

He hadn't. I didn't even know that he'd been there. I shook my head and as I did so grabbed a blackened slice of roasted pepper and washed it down with red wine.

'Well, when I was there on holiday a while back, I was on one of those boat tours to some caves just off the coast. These were, apparently, notorious for filling up with water at certain times. The guide told us only the locals knew how to navigate them and this is where my story begins….'

His voice changed and I was intrigued - Ray lived on the edge and had some great stories to tell.

'As the boat floated up to this great rock of a cave, we watched as a local man swam off underneath and into its mouth. While this was happening, the guide told us about the mystery of the cave. You know, smuggling and all that kind of thing.' Ray glanced at me to make sure I was listening.

'Well, about ten minutes later when our boat had travelled around the cave, lo and behold, the man popped out from the other end! We all clapped because it seemed pretty amazing. But I had my doubts, Steve.'

Now that I was enjoying a succulent piece of calamari, I was more than happy for Ray to continue, but again he waited for me to show interest.

'Okay, Ray,' I said, 'doubts about what?'

Bingo! Ray continued talking so I could continue eating!

'I had doubts that the cave was full of water and it was then that I got the urge to follow his lead and go under. I have no idea why but I just felt a need to do it.'

'So what happened?' I was surprised.

Ray looked serious. 'I dived down and swam hard and discovered that the cave *did* have water in it but I wasn't going to turn back. Before I knew it everywhere was pitch black. I didn't know where the hell I was going so I had to go on. I was swimming as fast as I could but it was pretty tight under there. I figured I was somewhere in the middle, but it was impossible to be sure and then, suddenly, I felt it.' He paused for effect.

'What?' By now I was hooked.

'Fear,' Ray said, as if the word itself was foreign to him. He even *looked* scared now, sitting there telling me.

'So here was I in the middle of this cave, feeling my coordination vanishing as the fear gripped me. My lungs were getting tight and I was starting to panic. Mate, I felt real bloody panic.'

'So what did you do?'

'Well, I just panicked more,' he said, raising his eyebrows at the memory. 'I was running out of juice in my lungs and I wasn't sure where to swim to. The cave was bigger now but still no air - just water and I really thought that was it. All I could do was just swim as fast as I could and then...'

Completely hooked I just stared at him.

'Then... my luck changed,' he said. 'Suddenly I felt a gap above my head. Not sure how but there it was, a rise in the cave that gave me my life - a bloody air pocket! I couldn't believe my luck. For a few minutes I just gasped air in.'

'Then what happened?' I asked, gulping wine in the way that he must have gulped air. 'Did you know how to get out?'

'Well,' he replied, looking as if he was thoroughly enjoying himself now, 'I figured the guide must've used the air pocket, so I had to be near the other side. If I got lost all I had to do was to go back for more air until I found a way out. And that's exactly what I did do!' He folded his arms in triumph.

I stared in disbelief.

'It was an unbelievable feeling when I came out,' he said. 'And thing is, no one was clapping me. They were just staring and the guide was looking pretty angry - or amazed - hard to tell. I got back in the boat and I tell you, mate, I was shaken up while all the time they were telling me off and staring at me like I'd done something special. Pretty much said I was lucky to be there.' He paused. 'And you know what?'

'What?'

'I had to agree and that's the moral of the story.' He stopped and looked at me with those big blue eyes.

I took a breath. 'Good story, what *is* the moral again?'

'The moral of the story is...' He grinned. 'Shall we meet those girls tonight 'cos I'm lucky to be able to.'

'You idiot,' I laughed. Whether the story was true or not was one thing. Ray's powers of persuasion were another. I didn't mention that I had already decided to go. Let him have his moment of glory.

****

Darkness surrounded us as we drove down the long road that led us back to the Guardamar beach. There was no lighting which made it not only inky black, but eerie black too. I wondered if it could really happen that two girls would come to this beach in blackness to meet two men they had only met briefly. The idea seemed laughably improbable.

As the Jeep reached the car park the headlamps picked out a bright light by the beach hut we'd been at earlier that day and we saw that the bar was open. Ray pulled over and parked and clambered out hurriedly but soon slowed down apparently in an attempt to look cool.

Nearing the hut, we saw that the night was lit by a large bonfire and further along the beach we saw that there were smaller fires scattered about. It was much livelier than I had expected. Spanish couples sat chatting and laughing with their friends in the firelight. It was a magical setting. There were about twenty or thirty people sitting around the bar area. The tables and chairs that, earlier in the day, had been neatly stacked were now arranged in a circle near the big fire. It was as we approached the bar that Ray spotted what he had been looking for. A group of people were sitting at a long table talking and I saw Christina illuminated in the flickering light. Danni sat opposite her and to their right there were two shadowy figures.

Ray kissed Christina on the cheek and then sat down next to her, immediately beginning to chat animatedly. I followed slowly behind, mumbling 'hello' to everyone and then equally falteringly asking them if anyone would like a drink. They all said they were okay except Ray that is, who raised his head and said, 'Cheers mate, a beer, ta,' before returning his eyes to Christina's. Or her breasts; it was hard to tell.

'*Hola, dos cervezas, por favor,*' I said and was rewarded with two beers. I walked back across the sand with them to where the others were sitting to find that Ray now had his arm around Christina and seemed to be pushing his lips towards hers. I broke up the moment by waving a beer in front of him and saying cheerily, 'One for you!'

As Ray took the beer he glared at me as if I'd walked in on him having sex. He wasn't going to be saying much tonight!

As I looked along at the others, the girl with the short dark hair that I had seen that afternoon, looked up at me.

'Please sit, please sit,' she said, in a strongly accented voice.

I did as I was told and, as I clicked back the ring pull on my beer, Danni introduced herself.

'Hello, I am Danni and this is Christina.' She said the words slowly, as if learning them as she spoke and at the same time pointing at the girl I already knew was Christina, who gave me a small wave before turning back to Ray.

'Hi Danni,' I smiled unconvincingly as she continued to introduce the others further along the table

'That is Susie and Krilla.' I followed her eyes and looked across at a couple sitting a little away from us. It was difficult to see them clearly because the firelight flickered and shifted away from them but they waved and I responded. This could be a long evening, I thought, as my earlier hopes for the evening drained away.

Danni was very friendly and chatted away nineteen to the dozen while the others just gazed at each other. She told me that she and Christina were old friends and that they were staying at her parents' place. She also said that they had only arrived that day but would be going home tomorrow. I won't bother to get to know you then, I thought to myself, with a wry grin. We talked for a while, exchanging small talk. She said that she was East German but now lived in Cologne in the west where she had a good job. I told her I lived in England by the sea and that I fixed computers. Danni said that she liked England and had been to London where she loved the grand architecture of the buildings, statues and monuments. Try living in the East End, I thought.

It was an hour or so before I heard Ray's dulcet tones again.

'Shall we go for a walk?' I looked up and saw him holding Christina's hand. Susie and Krilla stopped chatting immediately. 'Sure,' they said and Danni looked at me. We all got up and headed along the beach. There was some pier or jetty or something stretching out about a mile away in the distance. I hadn't noticed it earlier in the day but now it was illuminated with small coloured lights all around it.

As we wandered slowly along the beach we passed small fires with groups of people laughing and chatting, shadows dancing in the firelight across their happy faces. It was a lovely still night and the moon loomed large in the sky. As Danni walked by my side, I felt that the setting was perfect. The girl was not.

I was getting sick of watching Ray and Christina exchange tongues and when Danni looked at me and said, 'Shall we walk back?', I agreed immediately.

When we got back to our seats, Susie and Krilla went to order more drinks and for the first time I saw them clearly under the lights. He was tall with a shaven head and a rugged look about him as if he played a lot of sport or something. She was small and pretty with dark brown hair pulled back, showing wide brown eyes and dark unblemished skin. She was quite beautiful.

As we sipped drinks I watched Krilla fondle Susie and wished suddenly that it was me. She didn't appear to be in the mood for him. 'I am tired, we must go soon,' she said in English which I guessed was for my benefit.

I could see that Ray was getting desperate. He really wanted that girl.

'Shall we all meet tomorrow?' he said in a loud voice.

The girls discussed what he had suggested and then explained that they wanted to spend the day at the beach and do some shopping. Basically, we were not invited and Krilla looked quite happy about it. He seemed to want the girls to himself, especially Susie.

'How about tomorrow night?' said Susie, in perfect English. I looked at her, her voice was enchanting. As her eyes met mine, I swear I saw a flicker of a smile fly straight towards me in the night air. Something in my stomach did a somersault but I remained silent just looking back, trying to return the smile while all the time the others continued to discuss things around me.

Finally it was agreed we would meet again and Ray said that we could come back to Guardamar. I wasn't happy about following him around again.

'What about Los Alcazares?' I found myself saying. 'It's lovely there and we can show you around the place. You'd all love it.' I knew I sounded like a tour guide.

Silence followed for the briefest of moments, but it seemed like an eternity. At least if they went for the Los Alcazares angle I could go home if things got messy and I knew the place a bit by now. I could almost feel myself squirming as I waited for someone to say something. I looked at Ray. He was not going to help me out. He was going wherever Christina went.

'Steve, I think that's a great idea.' It was Susie.

She had come to my rescue yet she would be going home tomorrow.

'Don't you?' she said looking at Krilla and then at me again. She was so beautiful and seemed more so now after saving me. I sensed she must have felt my awkwardness and quickly saved me.

'Yes,' Krilla said gruffly, in his strongly accented English before speaking quickly to Susie in German. A few seconds passed and then Susie spoke again, her eyes softening after the heatedness of the discussion.

'We'll come to Los Alcazares,' she smiled. 'It will be very nice, I am sure.'

Her words sank into me as if they were said just for me. We said our goodbyes and, as I hugged Susie, I felt her small body close to mine. The embrace lasted for seconds but it seemed so much longer than everyone else's. Maybe it was just me. I felt as if I was falling into a dream. My stomach turned and my heart leapt. The hug ended leaving emptiness.

'See you tomorrow, then,' I said.

'I look forward to it,' she replied softly.

On the way back we stopped at the garage where we had arranged to meet the girls the next day. Ray put in some petrol while I went into the shop and on impulse bought an ice cream. When I came out Ray had pulled the Jeep over next to some coaches, which were parked to the side of the garage in a kind of lay-by.

As I wandered up to him I saw that he was speaking to a woman and he turned when he heard my footsteps.

'Won't be a minute,' he said sharply before following her behind the coach. I stood there for a moment before realising what he was doing. He was getting his fill from a goddam prostitute!

As I sat on the wall nearby and ate my ice cream, I thought of him with Christina. I thought about Susie and how much I liked her. God, I couldn't remember the last time I felt like that - if ever. It was a strange sensation. As for Ray, well he had seemed to be involved with the German girl, but now he appeared to not care at all. Ten minutes later and he returned, smiling. I didn't ask about his visit to the lady of the night and he didn't mention it. As we drove back to the flat in silence I realised something about my pal.

Mine and Ray's idea of love was completely different.

CHAPTER NINE

Only having a few hours sleep didn't stop me from dreaming and any new dream was something to be taken into consideration - and this was a new dream. I'd had many that recurred, especially when the lady in black - as I now called her - came with her message about love and hope.

This particular dream was so vivid it was more like the ones I called visions. At least I called them that when I talked to Pat about them. It was simple enough really. I felt as if I was awake within the dream, as if it was real. It was dark and I was in a confined space. I tried to feel my way around but stumbled over, falling onto a hard floor, hurting myself. I felt panic as I walked forward, suffocated by a fear of falling. As the fear took over and I began to fall, I woke. I was sweating and as I sat on the edge of the bed I noticed something very bizarre. Both my knees hurt.

****

I buttoned up my shirt slowly, a nice white number with beige jeans and desert boots. It looked okay. Pretty summery yet not overdressed. Stop it Steve, I said to myself, don't worry, just enjoy. For some reason I felt apprehensive about the night ahead. Was stage fright this bad?

We were waiting at the garage just before nine o'clock and dusk was beginning to fall before I saw the car approaching. It pulled over to where we were standing beside the Jeep. Danni immediately wound down her window and smiled, 'Hi Guys!' while the others waved from inside the car.

'Hi!' we said in unison before Ray slipped around to the other side to talk with Christina leaving me standing and smiling like some dumb kid. Soon we were driving into Los Alcazares town with them following behind. It was a perfect summer night and the lights twinkled ahead of us revealing busy shops and lots of people ambling about. It took us a while to find two parking places close to each other but eventually we managed to park just two streets off the seafront.

The six of us strolled towards the front under Ray's direction. He was our tour leader and I was happy with that. But again, it was Danni and me who were *together* - at least when it came to walking down the street. As you would expect, Ray was all over Christina and I could hear Krilla and Susie giggling just behind me. *Krilla, the bloody Gorilla,* I thought to myself.

We settled outside a Cuban-style bar that had a sexy Latin American feel perfect for the company we were in. As the loud music wafted from within I felt both relaxed and alive. Everything seemed to be turning out better than I had anticipated and I started chatting to everyone once I realised that Ray was not going to be involved with the rest of the group. He'd already isolated himself from us, sidling close to Christina so I decided to make a real go of it and get to know the others.

Krilla turned out to be a real nice guy. He was into computers like me and worked on graphic design - unlike me, but we had enough in common to hit it off whilst not enough to turn the night into a computer seminar.

Susie's English was the best by far and after a couple of drinks she really came out of her shell. She and Krilla were flying back in the early hours of the morning but I had no idea exactly when they were leaving. I was really enjoying spending time with them, especially Susie, and I found myself getting more and more attracted to her.

'You're a lucky man, Krilla,' I said, as we leant at the bar waiting to be served.

'Of course I am with looks like mine,' he joked.

'I mean with Susie. She's something else,' I said, ordering the drinks.

'*Ja*,' he smiled. 'I think I am getting somewhere with her!'

I said nothing for a moment, trying to control my exploding mind. They weren't together then? Of course not! I thought back to the night before. Her body language had been saying that she didn't want him all over her, not that she was being moody. He had no bloody chance. *Yes!* No chance!

'Cheers,' Krilla held his glass up to mine, interrupting my thoughts.

'Cheers, Krilla!' I smiled.

Back outside I felt light as a feather. I looked at Susie. She was wearing a silky summer dress - light cream printed with soft rose petals - and she looked stunning. She was small but beautifully formed with deep brown eyes that were capable of seducing the strongest man on the planet. As she gazed out into the night, I was overwhelmed by the strength of my feelings and had to summon every ounce of my willpower to look happy but not obsessed.

The time was clocking on and I noticed Danni keeping tabs on it because she was taking Susie and Krilla to the airport. I knew that I had to act fast.

'Shall we take a wander for a last couple of drinks?' I suggested just before midnight.

Danni looked uninterested and I got the impression that she had picked up that I wasn't interested in her. I sipped my drink during the ensuing discussion and was relieved when it ended in agreement. Good, still time to ask.... On the way I collared Ray for his mobile which he grudgingly lent me while telling me I should get with the times and buy my own. I didn't see the point, especially when he had one I could borrow.

I dialled the number and waited for him to pick up.

'Speak now or forever hold your peace.'

I loved the way he said that.

'Hi Pat - Steve here. How're you?'

'Steve, I can't...'

But I didn't have time to listen. 'Look Pat,' I interrupted, 'I want to run something by you, so listen up. I'm with a really lovely German girl, I mean *really* lovely. I haven't got much time so I was going to ask for her email address or something. What do you think?'

'Steve, I haven't got the time right now,' he said shortly.

I felt stupid. Why was I asking him anyway? 'Okay, sorry to trouble you, Pat. I'll call you when I get back and we can meet up, alright?'

'Fine, that's fine, and Steve... do what you thinks right, okay?' He was obviously in a hurry.

I started to speak again but all I heard from the mobile was a musical sound informing me that the call was over.

****

At a glance, the streets in Los Alcazares all look pretty much the same – they all concertina back and so a few streets are, in reality, only about three hundred metres. At one am, the six of us went into Monroe's bar that was, as you would expect, themed with Marilyn Monroe memorabilia everywhere.

We bought some drinks and pushed our way through to the back where the owners had carved out darkened, softly lit alcoves which were much more suited to romance than the busy bar. The place bounced around with live music beating out of the speakers that were perched all over the place. It was nearly impossible to talk without getting close but that suited me. It gave me the excuse I needed to move closer to Susie. She smelt delicious and I felt as close as if we were lying next to each other.

I managed, during the snatched conversation, to say what I had planned.

'Susie, would you like to have my email address?' I said boldly. 'It's been really special meeting you and it would be even more special to keep in touch.' I felt more sincere about her than I had done about anyone in my life.

I waited for the answer. Almost as if my life depended on it. 'That would be really great,' she replied, nodding.

Even as her words echoed around my mind I got to work. With a pen and paper that I had borrowed from the bar, I listened as she told me her email address and I wrote down mine. Tearing the piece of paper carefully down the middle, I gave her one half and slipped my half into my pocket, where I constantly checked its safety throughout the remainder of the night.

Time is the fire in which we burn and its gradual flames engulfed us. Danni was getting edgy about the time and wanted to leave for the airport and eventually it had to happen. I felt the sadness mounting. I never wanted this night to end.

It was a sad walk back to the cars, with me trailing on my own at the back, all the time watching Susie who was walking in front of me. She seemed to be trying to be cheerful, maybe not even trying. I watched each step that she took. She looked stunning – seeming almost to glide along and her silhouette took my breath away. A cacophony of feeling raged inside me but there were no words, only a silent submission to the moment.

We said our goodbyes at the garage and Krilla shook my hand and Christina gave me a polite kiss on each cheek. Danni hugged me with a warmth that I did not share and then …Susie.

To describe a violin playing is to sometimes explain the impossible, the sea crashing against the shore, the sound of the birds on the first day of spring. You have to just *feel* it. We hugged. It felt incredible. A massive surge of emotion ran riot within me as we clung to each other in every sense of the word, and then….

Absolute emptiness surrounded me there on that sandy path in that lonely place at that moment. Not since I stood as a child on that rainy day had I felt so alone.

One last smile lifted us but the reality was all too real. The yellow car turned and they all waved their last goodbyes from inside until their faces blurred in the darkness. It was just me and Ray. I looked at him and felt nothing, my great friend Ray. I would swap a thousand Rays at that moment for one more hour with her. Wrong but true.

'You liked her, didn't you?' We had been driving silently along the empty streets.

'Yeah, I did.' My voice sounded empty and crackly.

I was in no mood for idle chat so, as soon as we arrived home, I sneaked off. It had nothing to do with Ray. Sometimes you just need space to stop feeling so lonely. Double-edged stuff, you know.

I laid on the bed and put my hands behind my head and sighed out loud.

She was on her way back to Germany and I was here. Each second took her further away from me. Would I ever see her again?

I closed my eyes and waited for sleep to come.

For once, I waited and prayed that my subconscious would not betray me.

'Please dream, please dream,' I whispered as the blanket of sleep took the pain away.

CHAPTER TEN

I was back on Guardamar beach. She was leaving for Germany. I turned away only to hear her voice whisper my name. I spun around and saw her coming closer... closer. I reached out my arms and she fell into them. We clung to each other and again the feeling of wholeness washed over me like a fresh wave. We explored each other's bodies My skin touched her soft skin. Our eyes were ablaze... it was perfect.

****

My first waking thought was of the night before and the girl. I gathered myself together and tried to wake Ray up, easier said than done. No movement at all; he was sleeping like a corpse with the only evident sign of life being loud irregular snoring. I made some coffee, borrowed his mobile again and called my grandmother to check on her.

'Hello?' her voice was comforting to my ear.

'Hi, Granny, it's Steve,' I said out of habit.

'Who is this please?' Her voice sounded unsure and I realised that the number displayed on her handset would be unknown. If she didn't recognise the number, she would want to know who it was, rather then actually listening to who I just said I was. It was an age thing. God bless her. She was getting old. I used the next few minutes of Ray's credit up explaining that it was me. Eventually we agreed we knew each other and had a brief chat about mundane things.

****

I could have thought of lots of different ways of spending my last day with Ray but one I hadn't even considered was climbing a Spanish mountain. It was Ray's way of relaxing on a simmering hot day. As soon as he woke up he told me that he had decided that he was going to take me up the mountain that I just happened to mention looked beautiful from the terrace. I had mentioned nothing about climbing the damned thing…. But that's what we did because once he had an idea in his head that was it. Maybe I should have been more assertive and said 'no' but I went along with it and wished I hadn't.

The mountain seemed to grow alarmingly with each kilometre closer we got to it.

'Higher than Ben Nevis!' Ray announced as we breakfasted on coffee and croissants in a nearby café and gazed at its rocky mass. I tried again to persuade him to do something more suitable to the weather – like water-skiing but in the end I succumbed.

'A stroll,' he said, reassuringly.

Screw Ray Skee.

We didn't have the right gear to help us with the climb and my welfare depended on him. He was my guide and I knew that he had done things like this before. I also knew he could be a little crazy. It was a small gamble but he did look as if he was taking the whole thing seriously.

I saw that his eyes were alert as we followed a narrow trail up the left side of the beast. Seeing a track of sorts gave me a feeling of security making me feel that it would be easy. Think again. Ray navigated the winding unpredictable ascent with ease; at least it appeared that way while I struggled, finding the ascent hellish. I clawed at the craggy roots that protruded like handgrips from the massive rock, toiling behind my mountain goat friend. The distance between us widened as his assurance and natural ability added to his confidence, while mine seemed to diminish with each minor slip I made.

Before long determination replaced despair and I got used to the stones sliding away from beneath me and grabbed onto branches and roots to support me before taking the next step. I was determined to achieve this thing. It became my mission in life. By the time we reached the summit three hours later, I was feeling faint and terribly sick from the climb and the fierce heat of the sun. I watched as Ray peered precariously over the edge, shouting like he'd just climbed Everest. But I'd done it! Scrambling, holding, slipping, cursing – I'd followed goatman up the "hill". Having got to the top I concentrated more on not being sick than I did on vertigo. At least the journey down would be easier. Fools think like that, don't they?

The view was, without doubt, stunning. The sea glittered all around making the land below look insignificant by comparison. The fishing traps stood out in the glistening Mediterranean like tadpoles in a pond. Sadly I could not bring myself to walk to the edge of the great rock. Screw fear, it stops you doing stuff.

Much to my surprise the journey down was just as tough but in a different way. This time it was more a question of not slipping and falling down to certain death.

'You won't die, Steve. Not likely, serious injury maybe. Die, nah,' he called casually back to me as I grabbed onto a branch to save myself, yelling with panic. Screw Ray Skee.

The descent was steep with only unreliable branches to cling to. I prayed that the mountain would once again show me mercy. Ray on the other hand seemed to have it all sussed and I followed his lead by half sitting and shuffling down the most dangerous parts. The hardest thing about the descent was going slowly. We walked along the top of the rock and followed a different path on the opposite side and Ray explained that the angle showed that it had been cut out by the Moors in the late thirteenth century. I can only surmise they too, were cloven-hoofed like our four-legged friends of the mountain or my two-footed friend leading the way.

More scares and more perspiration followed but at least I could see the ground getting nearer. My nerves were on edge until we eventually slid nearly to the bottom. Thank you, oh kind mountain! I felt high with adrenalin. My shorts and T-shirt were drenched and my hair felt as if I had dipped it in water. Ray took it all in his stride.

'A cold beer to celebrate, Steve?' he said with a grin.

'You bet,' I answered, wiping my lips in anticipation.

When the beer arrived, I looked at it for a long time but Ray swigged like a thirsty elephant that had just arrived at the swamp after a long trek.

'What you waiting for?'

'It's just….,' I said, looking at the liquid, 'you drink… and then… you drink. I mean look at this - an iced glass holding freezing liquid which I think I'm going to enjoy more than any other drink I've ever had.'

'Good for you,' he replied, signalling for another.

'What was the actual point of that, Ray?' I had to ask now that the adrenalin rush was beginning to subside.

He looked at me in between gulps, his top lip now sporting a foamy moustache.

'You like that Susie girl? Right, Steve?'

I nodded. 'Sure I do.'

'Well, that's the point. She lives miles away, a world away really. You know nothing about her yet you think you like her, so what you going to do about it? Something or nothing?' He nodded in agreement with himself before swigging down the remainder of his beer.

'I still don't get it, Ray. Sorry for my idiocy,' I stared blankly at him.

He looked pleased - like a man who was guiding another man. 'The point is…. if you want to climb to the top you've got to work hard. In my esteemed opinion, mate, you've got a mountain to climb to see that girl again.'

****

The evening was the warmest I was going to enjoy for some

time because tomorrow I was going home. My mind had already started to raise issues that needed attention when I arrived back in dear old Clacton. I had to find work and I had some catching up to do. I felt slightly envious of Ray sitting alongside me. The meal had been heavenly; I'd never tasted better veal in my life. Now, watching the world going slowly by, I knew that he would be able to do it all again tomorrow.

As we were sitting there, a small hunched figure approached our table. I took in the woman's features as she shuffled towards us, her sun withered face was full of wisdom. Her matted hair was draped around her cheeks like the dark shawl around her shoulders.

'A gypsy,' Ray said. 'No thanks, love,' he held his hand up as a barrier. Ignoring him, she stopped in front of me so that our eyes met.

I heard Ray speak but her voice overrode his as she pointed her finger at me.

'You,' she said, and I watched as she groped inside her pocket and pulled out a handful of sprigs of different flowers. I had seen these women plenty of times before but for some reason I said nothing, instead choosing to watch before judging.

'*¿Numero favorito?*' She asked in a croaky voice. I looked at her blankly.

'She's asking you for your favourite number, dummy,' Ray intervened. 'Tell her to get lost – they're a pain these people. The "looky, looky" guys are okay, they just want to sell you watches and all that but these people take bloody liberties.'

'Three, I mean *tres*,' I replied, ignoring Ray's advice.

The gypsy nodded and undid the piece of string around the flowers, carefully picking out three different sprigs and offering them to me.

'*Si, tres opciones.*'

I took them from her - they were pretty if a little squashed. One was a warm pink colour, the second had an almost cannabis like leaf while the third - well it looked like a cutting from a palm tree. The stem of each one was wrapped in tinfoil like the stuff my grandmother used to wrap the Christmas turkey in.

'*Gracias*,' I said taking the flowers. '*¿Nombres y cuenta cuesta*?' I had no idea what she had given me and how much she was going to charge. Ray laughed as I tried out my weak Spanish on her.

She shook her head. No names, great. So how much was she going to charge me?

Leaning closer to me she spoke slowly, 'Names - oleander, osmunda, palm.' She arched her back and stood up again. I took out a note and handed it to her but she shook her head and pointing at the cutting on the left said, '*¡Cuidado!*' before muttering, '*¿Tres, si?*'

She shuffled off leaving us staring at each other in amusement while I held a handful of crushed and useless flowers in my hand.

'You want to be careful of that one, mate,' Ray's voice cut into my thoughts. 'The pink one – it's oleander – deadly poisonous. No wonder she said "beware"!'

I nodded but despite that I knew that I would not be able to throw them away.

****

There was darkness all around me. I stood still and listened while trying to focus. Not a sound, the blackness seemed impenetrable. Putting my arms out in front of me I tried to identify where I was but all I could feel was nothingness. It was that dark place again.

The air felt tight as I tried to control the fear that rose with my awareness. I moved my arms around to my right and walked maybe a couple of steps before bumping into a wall. It felt smooth. Turning the other way I took a few more steps before my outstretched hands again came into contact with the wall. It felt like some kind of alleyway. Behind me the same flat surface. There was only one way to go.

Pausing for a moment I felt a trickle of sweat running down the base of my back. It felt as if the fear was eating into me. Should I go on or wait? Wait though for what?

Walking slowly, arms outstretched like a child waiting for some demon to jump out in front of me, I felt more apprehensive with each step. After I had taken about twenty paces I saw a razor thin slither of light ahead of me that became brighter with each step. Apprehension was pushed to the back of my mind as curiosity got the better of me.

The light was coming from behind an almost closed door. I ran my fingers against the panel and it felt as smooth as the walls – it apparently had no handle. I pushed it open cautiously with the tips of my fingers and saw that the illumination came from some kind of room. Somewhere in the middle there was a soft white circular glow. I felt compelled to follow it.

As I went in I tried to gauge how big it was and guessed it was roughly twenty by twenty-five but I couldn't be certain. All I could be sure of was that there was little or nothing in the room except for this eerie whiteness softened by a shadow.

As I moved further into the room I saw a chair which had obviously been there all along. As I drew level with it I swayed unsteadily and reached out to it for support not realising until that moment that I could feel a numbing pain. Apprehension engulfed me so that I didn't know what I was feeling. Was I awake or asleep?

I felt as if I was in a trance and the only option left open to me was to sit on the chair. Each second that passed the room seemed to get darker and darker until I was overcome by fear and I slumped in the chair holding on to its bulky arms. The fabric was alive to my touch and as they supported my own arms it felt as if there was an abyss below.

I was so scared that I closed my eyes for a few moments until the fear began to subside. Slowly opening my eyes again I saw a square in front of me, its frame edged by greyish white tones. There were dull sepia-coloured movements inside the frame and I felt as if I was looking at an old cinema film or cine camera clip.

At first the colour was the only thing that stood out but as I strained my eyes to see, I began to make out images within the square. The thumping in my head became louder and I began to feel sick. I saw that there was a body but the details were indistinct. Then gradually, as I stared, I saw people standing around it and was then able to identify the setting. It was a funeral.

I tried to pick out details, faces, but it was too difficult. The more I strained my eyes the more the shapes appeared to melt. The images dissolved into each other and then I saw a white room, empty except for a bed and two people. One person lay in the bed and a second leant over the bed as if talking although I couldn't hear anything. And then this image blurred and vanished. It was replaced by another unrecognisable room. It felt familiar but yet I didn't recognise it.

I saw two shapes a small distance apart and as I watched they moved closer together. They embraced and locked in a kiss, moving together in some kind of dance. It was as the shapes circled slowly around, joined together by their lips, that I saw her face. It was Susie. It had to be her, the figure, the height. I was convinced it was her but then the image started to fade taking with it the light and screen that I had been watching.

'No!' I shouted. 'Come back, don't stop, I want to see more!'

My voice echoed around me and as I sat in the inky silence, I felt a presence surrounding me and, as I sat rigidly upright in the chair, I felt something move behind me. Looking at my hands I saw that they were now visible, that it was no longer completely dark. There was a light and it was behind me moving slowly towards me and I waited, motionless, not daring to turn and look. Gradually the shape moved in front of me and I saw a figure, blurry but complete. I was transfixed, waiting for it to focus and although I heard a voice I couldn't make it out.

As the shape became clear I saw that a small girl, perhaps nine or ten years old, was standing in front of me. Her skin was as pale as the light and her almost white blonde hair, traced the sides of her face. She was beautiful in the most innocent way. Her eyes were closed and she held her hands in front of her as if praying. She was wearing shimmering white clothes that looked as if they were made from finest silk and a pendant on a chain around her neck that radiated almost as much light as her pure young beauty. I strained to see more detail but the whiteness of her skin dazzled me and I had to turn my eyes away.

I watched as she stood statue-like with her small hands clasped and her eyes shut. She was whispering softly but I couldn't make out what she was saying. I wanted to speak but dared not interrupt because her sweet voice was the only sound I wanted to hear. It captured my heart and mind like a piece of music I had waited all my life to hear. I was totally under her spell.

Then she stopped.

I waited, hardly daring to breathe, for her to do something, frozen in the moment.

'Hello,' I whispered.

Silence answered me.

'Who are you?'

She opened her eyes slowly and looked at me.

I saw a flash of the bluest colour penetrate deep into me as our eyes met.

She spoke.

'Daddy.'

CHAPTER ELEVEN

Ray drove me to the airport the next morning in his usual manner: fast – with him practising Spanish obscenities and me repeatedly asking him to slow down. As you might have guessed we arrived at the airport early.

'Cheers, Ray,' I said, as we pulled up outside the terminal doors.

'No problem, Steve.' He just grinned and again I felt envious of my friend's lifestyle. While I was boarding the plane heading back to the reality of my humdrum life, Ray would be off on another exciting day only to return to England and saving lives, whenever his firefighting duties called.

'Well…' I said, swinging my luggage from the back of the Jeep.

'I know, mate,' he interrupted, reading my thoughts. 'You can't have happy "hellos" without sad "goodbyes".' He gave me a hug and then a hearty slap on the back that made me cough.

'See you soon, buddy.'

'Okay,' I said. 'And thanks.'

He was already walking back to the Jeep.

'No problem, *amigo*,' he shouted after me as I turned and walked towards the terminal door, one friend lighter.

****

As we flew away from Spain heading towards the Pyrenees and home, I reflected on the dream I had had the night before. But I was unable to make head or tail of it so I drifted into an uncomfortable, but uneventful, sleep that lasted the journey.

Good old England welcomed me back with rain. Walking alongside tanned bodies dressed in unsuitable summer clothes the mood was one of acceptance, back to normality. The Spanish hats and toy donkeys looking completely out of place in the grim grey atmosphere of the arrival lounge. Even the officials sitting behind the passport control desk wore blank, unwelcoming expressions as we entered our homeland. Once the usual rigmarole of customs and baggage collection had been accomplished, I wandered through into the spaceship otherwise known as Stansted airport. I guessed where Harry would be and, sure enough, moments later I saw him sipping a pint of Guinness in the airport bar while flicking through the current edition of *Formula One* magazine.

'Hello, Harry!' I greeted him with enthusiasm.

He lifted his head from the magazine. 'Hi, Steve. How was the trip?'

'Good mate, real good,' I smiled.

'Ray behaving himself out there?'

'Of course – he sends his best,' I paused, grinning from ear to ear. 'He's got a lovely place out there you know, Harry.'

'Anything else happen that I should know about, Steve?' He matched my grin as if to indicate he had already heard the news.

I didn't need a second opportunity to tell him the story. 'I met a girl... a really lovely girl.'

'And...?'

That simple word stumped me. There wasn't much else *to* say. I'd no plans and I hadn't really spent any time alone with her. All I'd done was give her my email address. I tried to find the words to explain how it had felt.

'It was good for my soul, Harry,' I shrugged.

'Well, you know I don't believe in all that soul stuff,' he grinned. 'Logic and facts, that's me. So nothing happened?'

'No, not really.' I paused; it already seemed a long time ago. 'I hope to meet up again though,' I added lamely.

'Well, that all sounds great, Steve, if that's good for your soul then you just go ahead and keep it.' He finished his drink and stood up to leave. 'I'll stick with logic and facts, where things actually happen.'

Harry's world, straight down the line, black and white. There was no room for discussion. He made out that he didn't have a soul but I didn't believe that for one minute, because he had so much enthusiasm for life, but now was not the time for a debate.

As we reached his car I changed the subject to him. 'How's your luck been, Harry?' I asked. 'Kids good… Sofia okay?'

He flashed a big wide grin, exposing his big teeth. 'Yeah, the boys are great,' he said. 'And she… well, she's just Sofia.'

I didn't comment. I knew Harry loved his two boys and was a great dad and there was also no doubting that Sofia was a great mum. The problem was that somewhere down the line it had all gone wrong between them. The trust had been eroded by Sofia's insecurity and obsessive possessiveness and it caused heated arguments. It appeared that they now had a marriage of convenience except it wasn't convenient for either of them. From the outside they seemed happy enough, unless you asked, of course. The outside was where I wanted to remain, no sides taken. 'It's dangerous interfering in other people's relationships.' When Granny was younger she had told me this on more than one occasion. Remembering her words jogged my conscience. Poor Granny, I would have to go and see her soon.

We stopped for a bite to eat on the way home and as we drew up outside my house I thanked Harry and we arranged to meet up for a few drinks. It was dark and as I opened the front door I fumbled for the light switch in the narrow hallway. A pile of mail lay scattered under my feet to welcome me home. I threw my gear on the floor and walked around the bungalow turning lights on as I went while checking that everything was as I had left it. No burglars, good. Once my ridiculous routine was complete I headed into the kitchen to flick on the espresso coffee maker. Glancing at the answering machine I saw that there were four messages. I hit the play button.

Beep...'Hi, bro, it's your sis here. Hope you've had a good time. Give me a call when you're home and we'll meet up. Love ya!'

Nice one, I thought. It was always lovely to hear from Sharon. She was like a sister to me in so many ways. Maybe it was because we had both suffered similar tragedies in our lives. My parents were dead and gone whereas hers were gone but not dead. They just hadn't called her for years. We called each other "bro" and "sis" because we were so close. Our relationship had always been lovely - never sexual. She's a top girl.

Beep... 'Hello this is a message for PC Doctor – I'd like to book an appointment as soon as possible. It's Tuesday evening so can you give me a call as soon as you get this message. My name's Matthew Bowler- telephone oh-one-two-five-eight-two- double three...' I reached for a pen to jot down the number. 'Many thanks.'

Beep... 'Hello, Boy, you not back yet? Oh, I thought it was today. Never mind, give me a call when you're free, love, or pop in. Bye for now... Oh, by the way it's Granny.'

I loved the way she always told me it was her right at the end of the call when I already damned well knew it was her. Typical too - she always got the days mixed up! Even more so these days, it seemed.

Beep... 'Hey, Stevey boy, Laurence here. Let's catch up over the weekend - I heard there's a bash at The Zone. If you fancy it, bell me, kid... over and out.'

As I was debating who to call first when the phone rang making the choice for me. I picked up. 'Hello?'

'Mr. Bidante?' The caller sounded annoyed.

'Speaking,' I replied, not recognising the voice.

'It's Matthew Bowler - I called you three days ago about my computer and I haven't heard anything from you. You do fix computers, don't you?' His sarcasm made me focus.

'Oh, hello, Mr. Bowler, my apologies, sir.' I put on an

artificially apologetic voice. 'I've just this minute flown in from doing a job in the States. What can I do for you?'

'My computer.'

I began to feel that I was in some kind of comedy sketch.

'Of course, sir... I've got an appointment tonight but... just a moment....' I made a sound like flicking paper as if I was opening my diary. 'Ah, sir, I have a slot tomorrow early afternoon... say about two o'clock. Would that be okay?'

'It'll have to be, I suppose,' he said impatiently. 'But tell me, do you not have a mobile phone, Mr. Bidante?'

'I do, sir,' I lied. 'In the repair shop as we speak.' I had no desire to have a mobile and this man was one extra reason why I didn't.

'Well, fine then.' He seemed satisfied with my explanation. 'I live at number thirty-two Pallister Street. See you at two pm tomorrow, Mr. Bidante.'

'That's great, thank you, sir.' I put the phone down and scribbled a note to remind me that I had to fit the job in tomorrow afternoon. I was back in the system again. Back to the daily grind.

****

After a boring couple of hours under the watchful eye of Mr. Bowler, I finally finished the job and got paid without opening my mouth to suggest that he would benefit from a personality transplant. Rather pleased with my level of patience, I decided to go and see my grandmother who lived only about two miles away from the job.

Granny still lived in the house that she had bought when we moved back to Clacton when I'd thanked her countless times in my mind for ending my London hell. Apart from having Pat as a pal the rest had been forgettable. Odd fights and plenty of trouble, some involving Pat who tended to be a little wayward on occasions while being the deepest person I'd ever known. I remembered with a smile the day Granny told me that we were leaving East Ham, when ironically, with a little help from Pat, I hammered the last nail into my London coffin.

During a comparatively insignificant stone fight on wasteland near the sewer bank, Pat had thrown a large chunk of brick at one of the enemy. He'd missed his target and it had flown high and wide of the mark and been followed by a loud crash from behind the fence of a nearby house. He'd run like the wind with me trailing behind. The missile had, apparently, gone through the bathroom window narrowly missing a young kid in the bath. No one would have dared grass Pat Reilly up, so two hours later, when the police landed on my grandmother's doorstep, it had been me who had taken the blame and got the ticking off.

Granny had decided there and then that enough was enough. She couldn't cope with her wayward grandson. Instead of blaming me for all the unpleasant incidents that had brought people knocking on her door, she decided to move back to Clacton in the hopes that it would straighten me out.

Later she told me it was meant to be and I never argued. God bless her, she was right. I lived there with her, under her wise and watchful eye, for three years until, at the age of seventeen, I spread my wings and flew out into the big wide world. By that time I was earning enough to rent a place with my mates, which meant I could actually take a girl home. My grandmother would never have allowed such a thing under her roof! Not before I was married anyway!

I saw Granny's shape through the frosted glass door. She was walking slowly but she was in her eighties so maybe it was to be expected. Even so she was still in fine health and would probably outlive us all.

'Hello, Boy,' she greeted me with a wide smile.

'Hello, Granny,' I gave her a gentle hug for fear of crushing her fragile frame. I loved her so much. She'd been my best friend and guardian as well as my conscience and guide in those dark days. She might be small and frail now but she had the inner strength of a giant.

I followed her through to the sitting room. Nothing had changed since the days when it was my home. A pot of tea stood waiting for me - or whoever else might visit. Either she could make tea like magic or else she was addicted to the stuff. To Granny, tea solved everything. You split with your girlfriend and she'd say "have a cup of tea" - you put your head in the oven and it was "have a cup of tea" and if nothing had happened, like now, it was "like a cup of tea, Boy?". She didn't need to ask really - I never said "no" because I knew how much she liked pouring tea. It seemed to prepare her for the chat ahead.

'Well, Steve, how was Spain?' Granny asked as I watched the tea flow from the spout. 'And how's Ray? Still a little monkey?' She passed me my tea in a bone china cup and saucer that was her pride and joy.

'He's fine - doing well out there and loves the sunshine and... he's being a good boy.' I tried to look as if I was telling the truth.

'That's good then.' She smiled as if she knew that I was joking.

'So how've you been then, Granny?' I knew she would call me if anything happened of course but I always felt better if I asked, especially as she'd been a bit absent-minded lately.

'I'm fine, Boy.' She sat down in her favourite chair and I sat opposite in my usual seat. Everything was as it should be in Granny's house.

Suddenly, briefly, she looked vacant as if trying to remember what she was going to say. I was about to speak – ask her whether or not she was enjoying having her meals delivered when she suddenly recovered and beat me to it.

'Ooh, Steve, did I tell you I have these things called "meals on wheels" three times a week now? They bring you a cooked meal to your door, how about that?' She sat back looking smug.

'That's great, Granny. Is the food good?' I asked, despite the fact that she had told me three weeks before that it was.

'It's very good,' she exclaimed. 'They even make you a dessert! The other day I had apple crumble for one! Now if I do a crumble and you don't come round it goes to waste, and you know what I think of waste, don't you, Boy?'

'There are people starving...,' I replied automatically.

'That's right,' Granny sipped her tea. 'Now, did you get up to any adventures? Meet anybody special? You're getting old, you know, Steve! A nice girl is what you need.'

Dear Granny. How the world has changed, I thought as I looked at her. All it takes to bring her joy is a meal delivered to her door and yet she's so strait-laced. She can't accept that the days of no sex without marriage are long gone and that life can be lived without a partner. It's all alien to her - her world is her world and that's it and I guess it's a lovely way to be.

'Well actually, Granny, I did meet a girl.' Thinking about Susie made me feel excited and she picked up on it.

'You seem pleased with yourself, Boy! Is she nice then? Tell me all about her.'

'Well, there's not much to tell really. Her name's Susie and I met her on the beach.' I tried to thread together the thin chain of events – get them into perspective.

'We chatted a bit and I liked her and I saw her again the next night and we talked more and then she had to go home, so that's it. But we're going to keep in touch....' I said the last sentence with purpose, as if I truly believed it. Talking about it like that made the whole thing seem a bit insignificant. I didn't mention about giving her my email address because Granny wouldn't have a clue what I was talking about.

It also meant that I didn't have to tell her that the email I'd sent that morning had been returned "unknown recipient". Either I'd written the address down wrong or she'd purposely given me a wrong one. I had my doubts.

'That's nice, Boy. So when are you going to bring her round to meet me?'

'Um...,' I was stumped. 'Well, Granny, she lives abroad, that's the thing.'

'Abroad? You said she had to go home so I thought you meant she lived locally!' She chuckled softly. 'So where *does* she live then?'

'Germany,' I said.

Granny didn't respond, just sipped her tea and looked away from me.

I sensed that there was something wrong. 'Granny... you alright?'

'From Germany you said. She's German?'

'Yes, she is... what's wrong with that?'

'Would that be the same Germany that we went to war with? The same Germany where so many people died? The same Germany that saw my Cyril killed?'

I watched as tears gathered in her eyes.

God, I hadn't even thought about that and why should I have? Damn.

'Granny, it's not like that now.' I leant over to hold her hand but she pushed it away.

'Granny, please. She's a nice girl and things have changed in the world. The war is long over and lessons have been learned. I'm different, she's different. You'd like her.' I pleaded.

My grandmother looked at me with a cold hard stare, angry tears running down her cheeks.

'Changed, have they, Boy?' Her hand trembled, making her cup shake. 'Maybe they have for you but they haven't for me, not all the time I can summon up a breath.' She turned away to look out the window, the silence broken only by the sound of her slurping tea angrily.

I felt terrible. I wish I hadn't said anything. Of course for me and millions of today's children it was different, but I should have realised that for my grandmother and lots like her, the war had left deep scars.

'Sorry, Granny.'

It had no effect. She didn't even attempt to look at me as she replied, 'I don't want to talk about it, Steve. You'd best be off. I'm busy.' My grandmother was *never* busy. I *had* upset her and she wanted me to go and after more silence I decided to do as she asked.

I contemplated arguing the point. It seemed Granny was simply being unreasonable yet I had a gut feeling any further discussion would only make things worse. I opted for retreat.

'Okay, I'm sorry I upset you. Call me when you feel better,' I said as I stood up. No answer. I glanced at her again as I left, her head was hanging down as if she was deep in thought. I suppose I'd stirred up a dormant pain and I left her to her memories.

'Whew,' I sighed as I got into my car. I hadn't figured on that happening. When I thought about it I realised that there could be a lot more people with the same bigoted point of view. I'd never met a German before and for my generation there were no historical stereotypes embedded in our minds.

Three hours later, sitting in front of my computer, inhaling deeply on a cigarette I saw it. There in my inbox lay the heart stopper. One simple email that shone out amongst the others, the title subject leapt out the screen at me: *Holiday Man.*

From the moment I saw it I felt a mixture of confusion and fear. I thought about my grandmother, about the repercussions and from nowhere an overwhelming sense of apprehension surfaced. I actually felt that if I opened the email, my life would change dramatically.

I waited a little longer.

Then I opened it.

CHAPTER TWELVE

Hi holiday man,

Well, back in good old Berlin now after a nice little break. It was so nice to meet you and I think Danni really liked you! She has not stopped talking about you on the phone since we got back. I wanted to say I hope we can keep in touch and maybe one day see each other again. Something tells me we will. J
Hope to hear from you soon.

Love Susie xxxx

I recited the letter as I sat with Sharon and Laurence in The Moon bar that evening.

'So what did you write back, sunshine?' Laurence's voice rang in my ears and Sharon added her view too. 'Why a bloody German, bruv?'

'Hold on! Hold on! One at a time!' I said. 'Firstly, sis, yeah she is German and don't you start! I had all that from my grandmother!' I laughed, hoping that Sharon was being nothing like Granny; rather more like someone who had stereotypical views of other nationalities. In short, she needed to be educated.

'Sharon,' I said, 'you have to remember that the French don't wear garlic round their necks and ride around on bikes. The English don't all wear bowler hats and suits and the Germans certainly don't sit around in *lederhosen* banging their beer mugs on the table!' I gave her what I hoped was a stern look.

'I don't think it matters where they're from as long as they're fit. Is she fit, mate?' Laurence intervened.

I felt my irritation dissipate. Laurence had pretty straight views on woman; if they were pretty then it didn't matter. He had little trouble attracting the girls with his dark – almost sardonic - bad boy features and muscular frame. His nearly black, deep-set eyes seemed to hide secrets that made the girls melt with intrigue.

'Yeah, she's fit, Laurence.

We moved on with the night. It was the usual stuff, ending with me and Sharon dancing in the Zone like pieces of elastic let loose while Laurence got to know his new girlfriend via his tongue. Well, she was new that night anyway. By the time the club shut we were all a bit the worse for wear so I decided to go home.

'Don't you fancy a late drink at Sharon's? A bit of coke?' Laurence said, as if he was trying to tempt me.

'Do me a favour, you know I hate that cocaine crap, mate, ' I replied. 'You go ahead, junky. I'll see you later.' I turned towards home. 'And you, sis - keep off all that shit,' I added.

Sharon glanced at me sheepishly. 'Course I will, bruv, love ya.'

I watched as the three of them – Sharon, Laurence and the girl he had met up with in the club – linked arms and headed in the direction of Sharon's flat.

I could have got a cab for the two and a bit miles home but I fancied the walk and as I strolled the damp air revived me. I didn't pass many people on the way, just the odd lone figure, until eventually I saw the hill – my hill. As I walked up the steep incline, a cold breeze made the willows ahead sway gently under the light of the evenly spaced streetlamps. I stopped halfway up the hill to light a cigarette inhaling smoke and exhaling a combination of it and the early autumn. I let my eyes move across the landscape. Inky darkness surrounded the field and graveyards; a fine mist lay above the ground moving, ghostlike with each push from the breeze. A sense of eeriness stabbed at my skin bringing with it a new sensation as if an emotion that ran through me, was part of me, yet didn't belong there… as if a part of my heart didn't belong to me any more.

****

Dear Susie,

How lovely to read your mail when I returned home! I enjoyed the rest of the holiday of course but kept thinking about this pretty girl I was lucky enough to meet. Poor Danni, she was nice but it was not her.
I have to tell you, at first I thought you were with Krilla and when it turned out you weren't, I felt very happy. I know so little about you, and you me, but I hope we can keep in touch and one day see each other again. It would mean the world to me.
I could write much more but not sure whether to so I will just send you a hug and please know I am so happy to have met you..

Love Steve xx

I took a deep breath and pressed the send button. Grabbing a coat I decided that as it was Sunday, I would go and see my grandmother. I didn't want there to be any bad feeling between us and surely today, a "holy day", Granny would be more willing to let bygones be bygones.

Shutting the front door, I saw my neighbour kneeling beside a flower bed in her garden.

'Good morning, Roz!' I called.

Lifting her head she looked towards me. She was holding a black bin bag in one hand and a small fork in the other, tidying her garden. She was always out digging and weeding whatever the weather, her pottering seemed endless and I'd jokingly told her once that she might as well have her bed out there.

She smiled acknowledgment and waved as she stood up and walked around the centre of where she had been working. At this time of year most plants seemed to be going to sleep, at least in my garden they did, but Roz obviously knew more than me about gardening because hers still had plenty of life. Bright colours still dotted the flower beds in harmony with the leaves that fluttered from the trees.

She came slowly towards the fence that divided my bare desolate patch from her colourful, well-cultivated garden.

'*Hello, Steve!*' she bellowed.

'You okay, Roz?'

'Eh?'

Patience, Steve, I said under my breath, she *will* turn up the hearing aid in a minute. 'You okay? I've been away, haven't I? 'I turned up the volume so she could hear me, our conversations could never be private in the street.

Roz chuckled, almost like she was playing games with me to see how loud I shouted. A twist of her left ear and she carried on. 'That's better,' she said, 'I can hear you now.' Her voice decreased by several decibels.

Good.

'Nice holiday?' she said.

'Yes thanks, Roz, very nice.' At last we are getting somewhere.

'You can't beat a good holiday to clear the mind and soul. What are you doing today? Do you fancy helping in the garden?' Her expression told me she was kidding but just to make sure I used my best excuse. 'Sorry, no time today, I'm off to see Granny.'

'Is your grandmother well?'

'Yes thanks, well, not really…. I'm going to cheer her up, I hope…' I purposely dropped my voice after saying thanks so as not to divulge too much. Roz didn't know my grandmother and it wasn't her problem.

'Not happy, you say?'

I sensed that she had heard my words and found myself wondering how is it that people hear what you don't want them to but not the things you shout at them. By now I was getting impatient.

'Granny's fine, it's really nothing. I met a German girl on holiday and she's not happy about it.' I gave her a reassuring look.

'She's what? German?'

Oh please. I looked at Roz and realised that as she was old too, she might well share the same bigoted feelings about the war. Was I going to get a lecture from my neighbour as well? Please *no!*

'She's German,' I shouted just so that there would be no uncertainty that I had strong feelings for a German lady. Yes, German, and you know what? I don't give a shit. To me she is a delicate, fragile human being.

'She wouldn't like that you know.' Roz still smiled but a thinner more knowledgeable smile.

'*Who* wouldn't like *what*?' I shouted with frustration.

'No need to shout, Steve, I can hear you now, you know,' Roz said calmly. 'Your granny wouldn't like that, the fact that the girl is German.'

Tell me something I don't already know, I thought looking at Roz with a mixture of annoyance and slight bewilderment. 'I know that already, thanks. I know my grandmother pretty well and no disrespect, but you don't.'

She looked at me in surprise, which in turn made me feel a little guilty at my outburst. 'Sorry, Roz, it's just... I can't help the way I feel, you know.'

Roz gave me a searching look before she spoke again. 'You should ask your Granny *why* she doesn't like Germans.'

As she looked away something made me shudder.

'Okay, Roz, I will, promise.'

That was enough. I loved my batty old neighbour but this

was going nowhere. I knew my grandmother had lost her husband in the war but I didn't want to bring all that up again so soon.

****

'How did you lose Granddad?' I couldn't believe the words were coming from my lips.

Until that moment things had been a little tense, now Granny relaxed as if an injection had taken its effect. Usually she would seem a little absent-minded as we talked but as soon as I mentioned the subject, a fire seemed to ignite within her. It was the opposite reaction to what I had imagined. The air almost lifted with a sigh of relief.

'Sit down, Boy, and I'll tell you all about it.'

I sat.

My grandmother positioned herself, holding her usual cup of tea. Her hand was steady and she seemed to be surrounded by tranquillity.

'I'm sorry, Steve,' she said, with a wry grin.

'What for, Granny?'

'For being that way with you the other day. I got upset - overreacted a little'

'That's alright and I'm sorry too - I didn't think.'

'I know it's not your fault. You don't understand, of course.'

I nodded and waited for her to explain exactly what it was I didn't understand.

'You see, Boy, lots of people died in the war,' she began. 'Of course they did... lots of people like me got the news that their loved ones were... *gone.*' She whispered the last word and paused as if reflecting on its impact.

'I got on with it, you had to,' she continued with more spirit. 'I got what belongings he had sent home to me and we had the funeral a little later, when they brought him back to me. ' Granny's words were clear and crisp - *focused.*

'It was nineteen forty-four. Your father was just one year old.'

'That must have been tough,' I said with feeling – I'd never known that.

'It *was* tough…'she sighed. 'We'd been through the Depression together – survived the hardest times together and then… he was just twenty-one years old, Boy.'

I heard the agony in her voice and saw tears in her eyes and felt it in my own soul. The loss of my father and my mother. A deadened, blunted knife once more sharpened on my heart.

'They said - the war people…the death tellers - that my Cyril died a hero, you know. I said to them, "Isn't every soldier a hero?"'

'What did they say to that, Granny?' I felt a mixture of sadness and curiosity.

'"Well, Mrs. Bidante," they said, "he was dropped behind enemy lines into Sudetenland on a top secret mission to infiltrate German intelligence. He aided his country with information that may result in saving many lives. I'm afraid we can't tell you more then that at this time."' She looked through me. '"At this time…" - they never told me more at *any* time.' Her voice had an icy tinge, as if frozen in the history of her words, her eyes flashed with anger.

The room seemed suddenly colder.

'Granny,' I said soothingly. 'You don't have to talk about it if you don't want to.'

She breathed in slowly 'It's alright, it's alright.' I watched as she sipped tea and regained her composure.

'You see the information back then was not like it is today. I wanted to find out more but it was difficult, no one was forthcoming, doors were shut in my face. I suppose I should have consoled myself with the explanation I was given. Accepted it and moved on but it was hard. I decided to keep searching and keep waiting. You have to remember I had time on my side.' Her eyes softened.

I imagined the difficulty she must have had but that was all

I could do, imagine. In a world of media coverage and internet access, receiving information was the one thing that was not difficult to do. This was another time though, another world.

'So what happened then, Granny?'

'Something quite strange, Boy,' she said looking right into my eyes. 'Just over a year later I received a letter but it was written in a foreign language so I couldn't make head or tail of it. I took it to a friend who translated it for me.'

'What did it say?'

'It was written in Polish or something – not German anyway. From a woman who sent her condolences and her blessings – and to thank me...'

'Thank you? Thank you for what?'

'She thanked me because I was Cyril's wife,' she replied gazing ahead as if seeing a picture in her mind. 'As if it was the only way she could thank him for saving her life and the life of her daughter.'

'So you're saying...' I suddenly felt unsure of what to say. 'I mean - how was it that she found out where you lived?'

I wanted to ask if that was how my grandfather had died but couldn't find the courage to ask outright. Granny looked surprised by my question.

'Do you know, I have no idea,' she said. 'There was no address to reply to so that was that - at least I thought it was.'

'What do you mean "thought it was"?'

'A week later I received another surprise. A newspaper. Here, wait a moment.'

She lifted herself up from the chair and shuffled out into the hallway. I heard the cupboard under the stairs open and a moment later she returned with a small brown box under her arm. I watched as she lifted the lid and dipped her hand inside.

'This is where I kept all the bits they sent back to me... now let me see...' She lifted a bunch of papers and documents out. 'Ah, here we are.'

In her hand I saw a faded newspaper. She turned to the page as if she had done it many times before and then passed the paper over to me and stared out the window.

I took it and read: *Tragic End for Wife.*

The story told of the wife of a Captain Doug Gardiner who, on hearing that her husband had been killed, had taken her own life. I scanned the piece, looking for some relevance. Eventually, Granny intervened.

'At first glance I went through the paper looking for... I don't know what... but then I saw the picture of the Captain. I recognised him straight away, oh yes, I did. I knew the picture because I'd met Doug Gardiner just before your grandfather left for this mission.' I watched her head sink a little as if the newspaper was right in front of her and we were reading it together now.

I trailed my finger down the column, reading about the valiant Captain until a sentence caught my eye. I read: *"her husband died during a secret mission behind enemy lines along with Private Cyril Bidante".*

I felt my heart leap. 'So you found a link? Did you trace any of the family to find out what they knew?'

'I tried to find their family to no avail, no children, no link,' she said gravely. 'The only option I had was to wait. So I waited.'

'You waited. For what?'

'For Cyril to tell me, of course!' she said indignantly.

'Granny - Granddad is...'

She stopped me in my tracks. 'So, Steve, I waited for my Cyril to visit me in any way he could. Little messages, we all have messages you know. It just depends on whether you listen or believe.'

She eased herself up in the chair and moved closer towards me so that I could smell the familiar musky scent of her perfume. She gave me a sombre look, suddenly seeming utterly certain of herself.

'My husband - your grandfather - saved a woman and her child from German soldiers. The woman helped them and he gave his life for her. So do you understand why I find it hard when my grandson, who is all I have left, suddenly tells me he has met a German? Do you?' Her face was twisted with pain.

'Yes I do, Granny ... But you said you found no more information?' I spoke gently, scared of my own words.

'Do you dream, Boy?' she asked angrily.

'Yes, of course, we all do.'

'And in your dreams, do you see things you've never seen before? Or things you've forgotten? Or things that have no meaning at that moment but *feel* real?'

I felt as if my grandmother had just walked into my dreams and knew them inside out. I had only one answer and she seemed to know it.

'Yes, yes I do,' I whispered.

'Well then.' She relaxed and moved back a little. 'Then you know what I'm saying is true, Boy. I found peace thanks to your Granddad, he still sends me messages, you know.'

I tried to find the right words but what could I say to this frail lady that would sound right? Here I was at the beginning, maybe the end, possibly even nothing with a girl from another land. What was I supposed to say that would sound anything near right?

I needn't have worried; before I got the chance to speak she cut into the silence herself. 'But you mustn't worry,' she said with a smile. 'Just do what's right for you, Boy.'

I felt confused. 'Really?'

'Yes. If it's meant to be it will. Cyril told me that after our chat,' she added calmly.

I was completely taken by surprise. 'Um... okay,' was the only thing I could think of saying. What was she saying? That my deceased grandfather, who had died at the hands of a German, was giving me the go-ahead? Everything seemed totally bizarre.

My grandmother stood up slowly from the chair indicating that our chat was over. I was relieved and needed no further persuasion to end the conversation. I followed her through the kitchen putting her prized china cup and saucer on the chipped old kitchen unit as I went.

'Thanks, Granny.' I gave her a gentle hug at the door and kissed her lightly on the cheek.

'You sometimes look back and see things differently to how you saw them before.' She spoke quietly.

I was too puzzled to say anything.

She held the door open. 'My Cyril talks to me, Boy.'

'That's good, Granny,' I said trying to sound convincing as I stepped onto the doorstep.

'Remember when you stayed with me when you were a little boy? That terrible night when we lost your parents?'

I froze as the memories of that night spewed into my stomach, turning back only to see the door closing slowly. Her quietly spoken words squeezed through the gap between door and architrave.

'It wasn't me that asked you to stay.'

She closed the door tightly behind me.

CHAPTER THIRTEEN

I fumbled for the phone as its shrill ring woke me from my sleep. 'Hello?' I mumbled while at the same time trying to focus on the time. Ten minutes to midnight.

'Hello, *schatz!*' The voice brought me to my senses instantly.

'Susie!' I exclaimed.

'Steve, how are you?' Her voice swam into my ear, honey-coated.

'Brilliant, I mean, it's brilliant to hear your voice. Wow! Brilliant! How are you?' I blurted out the words as my heart raced. Bloody hell! It was Susie!

'I'm good!' she replied. 'I am just with friends and we are drinking *Sekt* together and I wanted to say "hello"!' Her voice danced musically down the line.

My excited reaction made my voice sound unfamiliar to my own ears. A mass of gibberish spouted from my mouth in no particular order.

'That's lovely, Susie! How's Berlin? Please say "hi" to your friends for me!'

'Of course I will and Berlin is good. Life is good... just one thing, *schatz*...'

'Eh, what does "*schatz*" mean?' I interrupted because I had no idea at all.

I heard a giggle trickle down the line into my ear, a drop of laughter that I drank thirstily as I heard it grow into a laugh.

'It means "darling"!' I could hear her friends laughing now as they cottoned on to what I'd asked. My face flushed with embarrassment.

'Ah - gotcha there, didn't I?' I tried to sound like I was joking.

'But ... *schatz*, there *is* just one thing...'

'What's that, Susie?'

'I miss you.'

I would have paid a million pounds to buy that sentence yet her words brought a mixture of elation and sadness. Life, since I'd returned from Spain, had continued the way it had before except that I now had feelings for a girl who lived a long way away. We'd exchanged emails often in the weeks since and thanks to the gift of cyberspace had shared pictures and learnt a lot about each other's lives but none of this had made up for not being able to touch, hear and see one another.

'I miss you too, Susie. I really do.' All the barriers crumbled effortlessly away.

There was a brief silence before she spoke again.

'Well, I have some news, Steve.' Her voice quivered and I could almost feel the vibration in it, a vocal arrow being readied to strike.

'What?' My short question was anything *but* short. Usually we use the word "what" to ask someone for more information, or to tell us what they mean or sometimes just because we don't understand what they're trying to say. But this time it was the bridge, the gap dividing our words. The most important "what" I'd ever "what-ed" – that's if there *was* such a word.

'I am going to come to England!' She shouted the words excitedly.

Her words skipped across the stage of my mind, leaping and bounding into all the corners, before finally dancing into my brain cells. As that last word "England" sank in, rapturous applause rang out in my head-shaped theatre and the words took a bow on its imaginary platform.

'That is fantastic! When? Where?' I stammered.

'The beginning of November - maybe the sixth till the eighth. We just have to get flights but it is decided!' Susie sounded as elated as I felt.

'Susie, that is fantastic - I'm *so* happy!' was all I could say.

And the timing too. Right after my birthday on the fourth. Perfect! If happiness could be gauged then my happy pods were overflowing. Even my pores seemed to be spitting out happiness at that moment.

'I think we are going to stay in London,' Susie explained. 'There will be four of us. Danni will come and two other friends who want to see London. So will you be able to meet me, *schatz*?'

Her last sentence seemed designed to tease me, to let me taste the thought, but I took no notice; just shouted back, '*You bet*!'

'Then, my dear Steve, I will see you soon.' Her joy was transparent and it made me feel like a giant.

'You bet, pretty lady, you bet.'

'I go now to drink, to celebrate. I will mail you tomorrow.'

'Okay, darling.' We seemed closer with every syllable we uttered..

'Mmmwah,' a virtual kiss rang into my ear. 'Bye, *schatz*.'

'Bye, darling.' I waited and listened for the sounds of disconnection before finally lowering the phone, staring at the receiver and laying it carefully back into its cradle, thanking it for giving me her voice.

****

I parked the car adjacent to Central Park and cut through to Barking Road figuring that it saved hunting for a space nearer to the pub where I had arranged to meet Pat. Whatever the time of day, the traffic was always crazy around East Ham and as rush hour approached I knew it would be folly not to walk.

Stepping onto the crisp grass I looked around the softly lit park, a sense of awareness enveloped me, stimulated by the place and the memories. No one walked through parks these days without being wary. Maybe it was a sign of the times, maybe it was simply the shadows that moved in the imagination. I walked briskly, shutting them out in the deserted park.

East Ham didn't appear to have changed much. As usual, I had driven past my old home and had a nostalgic walk along the sewer banks, breathing in the acrid stench that sometimes rose from them. I never enjoyed doing it - I just did - as if to remind myself that things were different now.

While I waited for Pat to arrive, I sipped a Guinness, reading then re-reading the menu. The one inconvenience of not having a mobile was that I had no idea where the hell he was. I just knew he was late, but then again Pat Reilly was always late. The pub began to fill up with people on their way home from work – some for a quiet drink after a hard day while others were after a cheap bite to eat.

I smiled as I spotted Pat enter the bar, his green eyes met mine and he waved before signalling to the barman for a drink. He walked over to me with a pint of Guinness in each hand.

'Good to see you, Steve,' he said, putting the glasses on the table and offering his hand.

'You too, Pat.' I took his hand. 'You look sharp.'

He slipped off his long overcoat and revealed an immaculate double-breasted suit. Things had certainly changed for Pat Reilly.

'I know, I know,' he grinned, as he rubbed his sparse hair back from his forehead. 'All part of the job.' He sat down before adding, 'You know I hate suits.'

I grinned. Pat and suits didn't go, not in my head anyway. He was just the kid who had a heart of a lion and fists to match. Strange how the world turns.

'How have you been, mate? You seemed a bit short on the phone when I called.'

Before he replied he drank a huge gulp of his Guinness as if he had waited a lifetime for the taste. Wiping the cream from his lip he said, 'Ah, sorry for that. Ma and Pa weren't so good and I was on my way to see them. As for the rest – well, I've told you before, no one tires of being surprised at an Irish brain surgeon.' He grinned at the irony.

I guess I found it amusing but it had hardly been that. Pat had always been a deep person, a thinker. While I moved back to Clacton and set about learning my trade in computers, he left with most of the teachers probably predicting a bleak future for him. But he had talent. While I was fumbling around he - two years my senior – was using his brains. Literally. He'd spent four years studying, then another four at medical school before working his arse off on a neuro-surgical training programme. He had the qualifications to earn what I could only dream about, as well as a level of job satisfaction far beyond that. Whenever I saw him I was still amazed by what he had chosen to do.

'So how was it in Spain and who was the girl?' Pat broke into my thoughts.

'It was good, Pat,' I replied, flashing a TV commercial smile. 'We've stayed in touch and I'm going to meet up just after my birthday, maybe in London.'

'Of course, it's your birthday! Jesus, Mary and Joseph!' he exclaimed. 'I doubt I'll get down for it but if she comes to London then perhaps you'll introduce her to your good old pal, Pat. You know, show her a real man!' he said with a mischievous glint in his eye. 'Just joking, Steve. I hope she's what you're looking for. Talking of which – are you still having your dreams?'

'Sometimes. I still don't know why and I still don't know what they mean.' I thought for a moment. 'All I know is that you're the only person who I feel alright to talk to about them.'

It was true. Ever since those early days Pat had been a listener, someone who understood me, or at least seemed to. It wasn't just sympathy for some screwed-up kid. He genuinely seemed to care.

'Follow your dreams, I always said it,' he smiled. 'Everything is for a reason. Everything.'

'So you still feel like that even now, Pat? Even with what you know about the human brain? What you know about the world?'

Pat glanced around as if checking for outside interference as he lit a cigarette and leant across the circular table.

'Even more so, Steve,' he said softly. 'Look, we all have beliefs. You had things happen that made you believe in angels. I was taught to be a Catholic, right?' He puffed a few times on his cigarette before continuing.

'See this, Steve?' he said, holding up the cigarette. 'This is an evil compound, the world is an evil place, and even all the religions have their faults. As a Catholic, can I condone a rapist making an innocent girl pregnant so that, as a Catholic, she would rather have the child than an abortion? No, I can't. You get it? We all have faults but we all have to believe in something. You show me a faith without fault and I will personally show you your angel. You have to have faith and you have to find it for yourself. Simple as that.'

He leant back and watched me and I nodded agreement as always marvelling at his insight.

'I guess I'm a fatalist then, Pat.'

'And so you should be,' he said raising his voice. 'I'm going to be a fully trained surgeon - a consultant - soon enough but if I'd known then what I know now, I'd have been a fucking dental surgeon. Less hours - more pay. That's the point. You make your choices and sometimes they're made for you.'

We ordered some pub grub – Pat's favourite steak and ale pie which was bathed in a dark gravy made from Guinness and of course topped with a puffy pastry lid and served with chunky chips. After we'd eaten it Pat looked at his watch.

'I've got to be heading off to see my folks, then work. You know how it is.'

'I understand, no probs, mate,' I said, then added, 'Your folks - are they alright - you didn't mention what happened.'

He raised his head and sighed. 'It was just a few days before you went to Spain; the silly dopes nearly set themselves on fire. Pa's fine but Ma got some bad burns to her arms trying to put the thing out.' He shot me a wry smile before becoming serious again. 'You can imagine, Steve. Luckily the Fire Brigade got there and saved their ruddy bacon.'

We both left soon after, stepping out together into the cold street.

'You left your car by the park?' Pat asked and I nodded. Old habits die hard.

'Drive safe and keep in touch,' he said. 'If I don't see you when Susie's here maybe you could come up for New Year? We can catch a football match while we're recovering from the hangover.'

'Sure, that'd be great. Good to see you, mate.'

We clasped hands before going our separate ways: me towards Upton Park and him in the opposite direction. Always good to see Pat, I thought, reflecting on our chat.

The traffic out of London was, as usual, heavy. My car crawled onto the A12 where I found myself in the midst of a long, impatient queue. The voice on the radio explained that there was a tailback ahead due to an earlier serious accident. After a couple of miles of snail-like progress, the flashing lights of the emergency vehicles came into view. I hated this road because somewhere along it was the place where my parents had gasped their last breath.

It was a pretty bad accident. The usual scene. Curious faces gazing from waiting cars instinctively trying to get a glimpse of the macabre scene. The crash had involved three cars and an overturned lorry. I suppose most people were looking at the cars but I found my eyes drawn to the fire engine and its crew, wondering if Ray was there, cutting the victims free.

Then a thought leapt bang into the frontal lobe of my brain, fuelled by the scene and Pat's words, 'Everything is for a reason. Everything....'

Pat's Irish parents lived in Stratford.

CHAPTER FOURTEEN

I read somewhere that the Church of England began because some king wanted to divorce his wife and it was forbidden. I made a mental note to ask Pat about it the next time I saw him, but I didn't have much time for thinking at the moment.

We enjoyed an Indian summer during the last weeks of October - at least in my mind. I had a birthday coming up but the real reason was simple. Susie was coming soon. Palm trees seemed to sprout from the ground and a carpet of flowers paved the streets. The air around me purified into sweet oxygen that tasted heavenly, making the Clacton seafront smell incredible. Pure blue waves kissed the golden sands while the residents held hands, kissed, and laughed in celebration of the paradise they had found themselves living in. Utopia had arrived, at least for me, for this is what I saw. My world became heaven on earth.

In the real world, or should I say the world I had left behind, my grandmother was in surprisingly good spirits. Perhaps the magical crystal dust of my aura rubbed off on her but she seemed to be happier than usual, although when I asked her why, she didn't seem to know most of the time. She seemed to be becoming more and more forgetful. Can't have it all, I thought to myself.

Work flowed like fine wine, job after job, happy customer following happy customer. For a change the money was coming in faster then I could spend it. Harry had put me onto two cracking jobs for a couple of companies based just sixteen miles away in Colchester. They had more than one hundred and forty machines between them and at seventy-five pounds a service, my eyes reflected pound signs.

****

'Let's go mate, cab's here.' Harry shouted as I took one last look in the mirror.

Harry chatted to the taxi driver and I sat back and enjoyed the ride. It was he who had suggested that the two of us went out for a celebratory beer. Dressed in a new shirt, courtesy of Sharon, and a pair of jeans that I'd picked up during the day, I felt on top of the world. Even Granny had played her part by remembering what my favourite brand of aftershave was and buying me some. All's fine in the world of Steve Bidante, I thought, as we sat in the back of the taxi.

It was still early when we pulled up outside the pub. The Moon has two entrances - one on the main street and the other on the seafront. I bounded up the steps of the main street entrance with Harry following closely behind. It was still relatively quiet when we ordered in the first drink of the night and Harry held it up and said, 'To my great mate. Many airport flights and many happy years!'

'Thanks, buddy.' I chinked his pint with mine then took a sip of the golden nectar. Feeling alive and vibrant, I looked at my pal, secure in the knowledge of our friendship. He knew what to say and when to say it. Whatever this night would bring it didn't matter as long as he was with me. Good old Harry.

'Hi, bruv!'

I recognised the voice instantly and turned.

'Hello, Sharon!' I grinned at her.

'Happy birthday, Steve,' she said, giving me a hug.

I noticed that there were four girls standing behind her.

'Steve, you know Kerry, Sandra and Jo and this is Nicole, all out specially for you!'

I greeted the girls. I'd seen Kerry and Jo often and I knew Sandra pretty well but I'd never met Nicole before. She seemed nice enough.

'Well, sis, thanks, what a lovely present!' I laughed, glancing at Nicole.

'I hear you only like girls made in Germany.' There was warmth in her smile.

'What you been saying, Sharon?' I laughed.

She grinned. 'Just letting the world know you're taken, Steve. Don't want these girls causing a scene, do we?'

Suddenly my drink was knocked out of my hand as two huge bodies shoved themselves between us.

'*Happy bloody birthday, Steve*!' they shouted in unison as we all fell onto the floor, a tangle of arms and legs. When we'd picked ourselves up, I saw Laurence, smartly dressed but looking as if he was plastered or drugged up - it was hard to tell. At least he was there. And Ray, good old Ray, looking pretty battered but in good enough shape. English culture at its finest!

Much to Sharon's apparent delight, Laurence began to prowl around her and her friends but Ray just gazed at her silently. I signalled to Ray and Harry to follow me to a quieter table, free from the deafening noise. Escaping the madness for a moment, I smiled at Ray and said, 'You do like her, don't you?'

'Who do I like?' he said, faking surprise. 'Oh, you mean Sharon? Yeah, she's okay, bit much for me though, more Laurence's type. Anyway,' he added, looking a bit sheepish, 'I got you something useful for your birthday, Steve.'

'You shouldn't have!' I said jokingly. I glanced at Harry as I took the box Ray held out.

'Funny,' Harry said with a smirk.

'Have I missed something?' Ray asked.

'I don't do presents, Skee,' he explained. 'I do all my giving throughout the year,' and then, seeing me smile, he added. 'Logic down the line with me, Ray, no soul, you see.'

I opened the gift and burst out laughing before embracing my pal. 'A bloody mobile, thanks, Ray! That *is* brilliant!'

'No excuse to use mine anymore,' he laughed. '*And* you can

keep in touch with that date I got you, you know, the German,' he said, winking at Harry.

****

After a great evening, by two o'clock, there were just three of us left sitting at the bar in Bailey's Club just east of the seafront. The girls had gone back to Sharon's for a late party, accompanied by Ray and I had stayed on for a last drink or two before joining them.

'Well, Laurence, not sure how you're still here but glad you are. I've just got to ask what all that was on the dance floor with Sharon, kissing and all sorts. Something you want to tell me?' I knocked back another whisky and signalled for the next round.

'Do I?' He leered at me, swaying towards the bar, his chair rocking in time with his movement. 'Good turn out tonight, though,' he slurred. 'Must've been about forty or more altogether.'

I looked at Harry. 'Yeah thanks, Harry. You're a top man, and Ray coming too. All your work?'

'No,' Harry replied, as the drinks arrived. 'He called me and I just filled him in with the details, told him about you seeing Susie soon. He reckoned he would have to come and take the credit for all the work he put in!'

Laughing, I slid Laurence's drink in front of him. 'Wakey, wakey!'

'I'll be alright once we get back to Sharon's; she'll wake me up,' he mumbled, but his head remained on the bar.

'Do me a favour, Laurence,' I said protectively. 'She doesn't need you messing her head up, you *know* she's got the hots for you, but you're not interested, are you? That's right isn't it, Harry?'

'Yeah, do the right thing, Laurence,' Harry nodded. 'You can get any woman you want and you don't need her and *she* definitely doesn't need you.'

Laurence slowly raised his head but I didn't know whether it was to reply or to drink more liquor. 'Hey, Steve, don't worry about me, mate. I'm fine. It's her you should be watching. Did you know she's now dealing gear as well as taking it?' He gazed at me through reddened eyes

'What are you saying?' He ignored me and I was so shocked that I shook him by the arm. 'What are you saying, Laurence?'

He leant forward, leering at me. 'I'm saying, my dear friend, get rid of the rose-tinted glasses and take a look at the real world. Your good little sister isn't so good.'

His words cut deep as my suspicions were confirmed. I was wrapped up in my world and had taken little, or no notice, of Sharon's ever more erratic behaviour following her nights out. I'd put her behaviour down to her wild side and pushed aside the fact that she was using again. Now, as I listened to Laurence I realised he was much more aware than I was. But a dealer? No, surely not. I couldn't see it, and I certainly didn't want to hear it tonight.

Eventually, Laurence's drunkenness rendered him more or less unconscious. I knew that by tomorrow he wouldn't even remember the chat - but I would. Rage flared up inside me as he slumped on the hard surface of the bar. What was the point though? He just took cocaine, now he reckoned she was dealing the stuff. He wasn't my problem. She was.

I signalled to Harry and we left Laurence to do what the hell he wanted.

'What a mess, Harry,' I muttered as we left.

'I know, mate,' he said. 'I don't see Sharon like you do, but it's bad news if it's true.'

'I should have seen it earlier. I guessed she was still taking the stuff, I *should* have known,' I said, angry with myself for being so blinkered.

'It's not your fault,' he reassured me. 'Look, how about giving Sharon's a miss? Come back to my place and we can have a few more birthday drinks, good idea?'

I needed another drink. My body cried out for the stuff,

especially after hearing Laurence confirm the worst. I nodded 'sure' as I climbed down from the bar stool.

'What a load of crap though, Harry.'

'Forget it, son. You've better things to think about. Like Susie.'

Her name cleansed my heart and by the time we had hailed a taxi to take us back to Harry's place, I was feeling better. Back at his luxurious, five-bedroomed Tudor-style house we sat on the decking in the garden sipping drinks oblivious to the cold air. By now, darkness was giving way to light, the chink of milk bottles sounded in between the whir of milk floats. It had been a long night.

'You know just what to say, mate.' I broke the silence induced by tiredness and drunkenness.

Harry smiled. 'Think about it, Steve. The thing is, although you can help Sharon, she's the only one who can kick the habit. And only if she wants too.'

I was about to ask him what he meant when he changed the subject.

'You haven't got any real worries. I mean no wife...yet, no kids...yet, no problems...yet,' he reasoned with a grin.

'You do alright all those things considered, Harry,' I said slowly. 'You're always happy or at least you seem that way.'

'It's all bollocks,' he replied. 'I should have been an actor, that's all.'

I decided then that it was time to sleep.

****

With countdown ticking away Cape Canaveral style, I kept myself busy to avoid feeling that I was going to burst like a balloon.

The emails kept sailing across to each other in the build-up. I read somewhere that they travel through cyberspace at something like three thousand miles a second. How I wished I could move like that!

The thought of seeing - or should I say confronting - Sharon occupied a small part of my brain but I wasn't ready yet. Ignoring her calls was hard, more so as they were on my new mobile phone and I was dying to use the thing. My thumb was busier then my ear. As my text life rocketed, my sex life lay dormant making the days pass even more slowly. Just one day to go. Each new dawn brought the excitement of the trip closer but I still craved the vital information giving me the exact details of where and when.

Then early one evening I was sitting in front of the computer watching in anticipation as the mail tumbled into my inbox, as usual scanning for Susie's. I swooped on her email with my mouse and started to read with my usual enthusiasm. I finally had the information in front of me:

WHERE- NOWHERE
WHEN- NEVER
Dearest Schatz,

I write the hardest letter I have ever had to. You have been so sweet and have not asked too much about the trip only saying lovely things to me. Steve, I have to tell you something now, it can't wait any longer. I won't be coming to London. I truly wanted to. Please believe me but some things have changed and I am confused and hurt. I will try to explain but please bear with me.

I have a friend who lives in a flat above, his name is Raimund. I have seen him from time to time and we became close. When I met you I could not get you out of my head and I think I fell in love with you. But you are not here. I have been seeing more and more of Raimund and have feelings for him. They are different to the feelings I have for you but I need to be real about all this. I have told him of you and, of course, that makes it very hard for me to come now as things have moved on with him.

I am sorry, schatz, I really am. If you were here or I there then I am sure we would be together but we are not and the truth is we are just two people who met for a moment. How could this work? I am full of doubt because my heart says YOU while my head says a man here, at home. You live there and our worlds are different. I do not even think we should keep in touch as this will not help either of us.

I feel horrible writing this, I really do. I believed for a moment when I was with you that I had found something special. I am just not strong enough to carry on. To miss you all the time hurts, there is more pain than pleasure and it is too much.

I hope you understand, schatz; I am not sure what else to say.

Sorry.

Susie x

The only sound that broke the silence was the sound of my tears hitting the keyboard.

CHAPTER FIFTEEN

Dear Susie,

Thanks for being so honest. I appreciate your words and the fact they must have been very hard to write as are mine now.

Meeting you felt so wonderful but you may be right in what you say, it could never work and I had not even considered that.. Seeing you again was all that mattered to me.

I will keep in touch if you want to. It won't be like before and all I ask is to see how we go. As for love, what is that, Susie? I only know when I think of you I feel something precious and rare.

You will always be special to me and I am proud to say I loved you in whatever form that was. I hope he appreciates you as much as I know I would.

Steve x

****

'You are a stupid bloody bitch!' I yelled, pushing my face close to hers.

'Bruv, please, you're scaring me.'

'How dare you call me your *brother*.' I trembled with anger. 'I'm no brother of yours, you drug-taking idiot! If you want to mess your own life up then fine, but quit the "bruv" shit. I asked you - no - I *begged* you not to get involved with all that and now I find out you're not only *taking* it, but bloody *dealing* the stuff.'

'Please don't, Steve.' I watched the tears sliding down her face and, taking her by the shoulders, held her at arm's length. She couldn't look me in the eyes.

'Turn off the waterworks, Sharon,' I shouted. 'Take a good look at how pathetic you look. Think about how many lives you're fucking up!'

'Please, Steve, I'm sorry,' she whispered.

I backed off while she slumped in the corner where I had pushed her during my aggressive outburst. As she sat, holding her head in her hands, sobbing, the red mist inside me cleared a little. I looked at the pathetic shape in front of me and hated myself for letting my anger take control of me - but she deserved my anger.

'Come here.' I knelt beside her, feeling a tiny pang of compassion surface.

'Oh, bruv, please don't be like that. I'm so sorry.' She reached out for me and I held her while she sobbed into my coat.

Things had to change but, as I held her, I had no idea how much they would, for us both.

****

As the season of goodwill grew on the horizon and with Christmas just around the corner, I felt that if I bumped into Santa Claus right now, I'd want to punch his lights out.

My anniversary trip to the graveyard on the eighth of December had brought me no comfort, no salvation. Just tears, as I wished for the millionth time I could hold my parents close.

The emails to Susie had ceased but the dreams continued. I wasn't looking forward to the season of goodwill. I had little goodwill to give.

Standing in one of the brightly lit shops in Clacton's West End, I flicked through packs of Christmas cards and couldn't help looking at the festive scenes with a degree of envy. Snowy landscapes with sleek horses carrying ladies and gentleman through beautifully decorated streets. Glancing out the window I saw that, back here in Clacton, a steady English drizzle rendered the streets colourless. No horses, but plenty of people walking quickly, their faces etched with the stress of fulfilling their shopping lists in the rush. I returned my gaze to the cards and found myself wondering the exact location of where those scenes were taken, because I wanted to be *there* - not here.

Deep in thought, I put them back on the rack and stared vacantly into space.

'Excuse me.' A voice close by shook me from my daydream.

'Sorry.' As I'd turned to wander from the shop I'd almost knocked a lady over. I gathered myself together and headed for the bustling streets and then for the seafront where the rain made the promenade shimmer with a clear wet reflection reminding me how much I loved Clacton - its concrete parade that gave way to steep paths cut into the hill that led down to the promenade. I stood there motionless, taking it all in, getting soaked in the process.

Noticing a woman hunched up on a bench a few metres to my right, I watched her discreetly, trying to gauge her age and guessing that she was probably in her seventies. I liked to do that, to watch people. I tried to imagine why she was there and what she was thinking. Her head was lowered as if deep in thought. Was she just lonely? That would be too easy a conclusion though just because she was on her own. And then I wondered whether she had children or a family or if she was looking forward to Christmas. If it had been Christmas Day, I could have said "Merry Christmas" to her. She might have replied but then again she might have said "Bah! Humbug!" or "What's merry about it?". I could then have engaged her in the reasons *for* liking or *not* liking the most important and meaningful day of the year for some people. In my imagination I created a sad scenario for the poor woman. She would be just another silhouette in the window of a house, lit only by the flicker of a television.

After finishing my somewhat damp cigarette, I decided to head for home and, as I turned to go, I heard a voice call out my name. I looked around to locate its source.

'When you've finished looking, perhaps you might give me a hand.' Her head emerged from inside the coat.

'Roz! What the hell are you doing here? I thought you were someone…'

'I was watching you, watching me,' she interrupted, rising slowly to her feet. 'Have you finished looking now?'

I nodded, still surprised by it being her.

'Good, then perhaps you'd like to help.'

'Help… help how…. help who?' I said, feeling rather stupid and realising that I must have been staring at her for ages.

She walked steadily towards me until we were face to face. I could feel her warm breath on me as she spoke.

'Help *yourself*, Steve.'

****

'How do you normally carry all this lot then, Roz?' I said, looking in the boot of my small car. It was filled with tins and tins of cakes, biscuits and prettily wrapped gifts.

'Usually the Salvation Army drop me off or I ride and collect a basketful at a time before I deliver it,' she replied cheerfully, twisting her earpiece.

It felt good being useful – being handed my instructions on a scrap of paper that listed the addresses of the less fortunate, who would have small gifts bestowed on them whether they liked it or not. Nothing fancy: just a sponge cake, some macaroons or maybe some chocolate biscuits.

To start with, Roz had to go everywhere with me. This, she

said, was on account of my age because I was apparently too young to just go knocking on doors. I found this beautifully strange to believe. In the ageist society we lived in, it seemed bizarre that if you are too *young* they won't open the door because they're scared of you. Of course that was tragic but it made a change from condemning old people just for being old. This time I was the victim; good on me.

Eventually I built up trust and, during the few weeks leading up to Christmas, visited lots of people more than once and got quite chatty with some of them. Most of them were elderly but there were a couple of young mums who couldn't get about so we helped out with them too. And then, of course, there were the "hidden people". Those who don't get to appear on Christmas cards - the poor and the homeless.

My estimation of Roz rocketed during that period. I marvelled not only at her incredible energy and youthfulness - despite her age - but also her pure kindness. I knew in my heart that the task she had given me made me feel useful but I didn't know why she had done it.

'Roz, what will you do for Christmas?' I'd said the words without thinking.

'I'm busy, sorry.' She answered as if it was a personal invitation from me.

'That's good,' I grinned. 'So where are you going?'

'To have dinner with the church.'

'That's nice of them to invite you,' I said, thinking how much she deserved it.

'No, you misunderstand. I'm helping to *cook* dinner for the church, for the old folk. I'm the chef,' she said, smiling vaguely.

****

Christmas morning arrived and I headed off early to my grandmother's with the couple of gifts I'd chosen for her. There was a gentle chill in the air but wintry sunshine poked through the clouds. No white Christmas but at least no bloody rain.

'Good morning, Granny, Merry Xmas!' I smiled as she opened the door warily.

'Merry Christmas, Boy.' She smiled at me with her own special brand of warmth. My only family member gave me an extra sloppy kiss on the cheek as we hugged on the doorstep. I went in and, as usual, followed her like a puppy into the kitchen.

'I've just brewed a special pot of tea,' she said gleefully, but of course it wasn't any different from her usual tea except that it was in a different pot. Perhaps that's what she meant. I nodded anyway.

'Poor Mr. Smythe passed away on the twenty-first, Steve. It's such a shame and especially this time of year.' Granny filled me in with her news as she bustled around the kitchen.

Mr. Smythe lived opposite and I'd liked him and he and my grandmother used to chat regularly. I couldn't think of a good time of year to die but I supposed Christmas made it sadder. At least for the people left behind. It also meant one less person to keep her company.

'That's a shame, Granny,' I said as she led me through to the front room. 'He was such a nice man.'

'Yes, it is, Boy and he *was* a good man.' She put the cups down and sat in her usual place as the head of her kingdom. I, her most loyal servant, sat down beside her.

'Let's open presents, shall we?' I said, handing her the two gifts and waiting expectantly for her wonderfully predictable reply.

'You shouldn't have, Boy.'

Good old Granny! It's the person who makes the habits and then the habits that make the person.

I watched as she began to unwrap the first gift, her fingers methodically easing the paper apart. Each year, for some reason, she carefully tried not to damage the paper. I always wanted to ask her if she was going to use it again but dared not, feeling sure that someone else would open a present wrapped in my previous year's paper.

'Oohh...!' she exclaimed. 'Lovely!' She held the V-shaped pillow in her hands and I could see that she was trying to figure out what it was. I showed her how to use it and a few minutes later it was being tested.

'Lovely, Boy, thank you.' She gave me an appreciative smile.

'Open the other one, Granny,' I urged. I'd always enjoyed watching other people opening their presents.

The second gift was in an envelope and peeling back the flap, she pulled out a wad of vouchers.

'Oh, Boy, that's lovely too,' she said, flicking through them. I'd bought her fifty pounds worth that she could spend at Marks and Spencer's and fifty pounds for WH Smith because she loved both shops but considered them expensive treats. Well, now she could have a field day with clothes, books and food if she wanted.

'You're a darling, Steve.' She leant away from her new pillow and kissed me. I felt a surge of pleasure. It felt like a good day already.

Then Granny gave me her present. She'd made me a parcel every year since I was a child - or should I say since I became *her* child after my parents died. This year it was packed with little bits and pieces that included ground coffee and fresh tea, together with Christmas pudding and brandy sauce. The thought that she put into making these Christmas parcels made everything taste better than if I'd bought them myself. What a wonderful lady.

The day drifted by. We ate a delicious Christmas dinner that Granny prepared for the two of us. Succulent, perfectly cooked roast turkey, with all the trimmings: crispy potatoes, fluffy Yorkshires, the works. It's more than true when they say you can't cook like Granny used to. I didn't mention the lack of vegetables, she'd simply forgotten. God bless her.

We watched the Queen's speech because my grandmother

never missed it and then an evening's television entertainment while she sucked her way through a whole packet of imperial mints. Eventually, when she drifted off to sleep, I knew that it was time for me to go home. I shook her gently and motioned that I was leaving.

She followed me to the door and, as I kissed her, I said, 'Thank you for a lovely Christmas Day, Granny.'

'Merry Christmas, Michael.'

'It's Steve, Granny.' I grinned.

'Sorry, Steve, silly me - I saw Michael yesterday,' she said, looking confused.

I shrugged. 'I'll see you soon, Granny. I love you.'

CHAPTER SIXTEEN

After a wild New Year's Eve in the company of Pat and his clan of Irish, we took in a match at Upton Park on New Year's Day. West Ham brought us back down to earth as they suffered from a hangover of their own, losing three nil. Pat was in excellent spirits though, and told us that his mother had made a good recovery. It triggered off my belief of Ray's involvement so I told him and commented on what a small world it was. He reacted very emotionally, making me call Ray there and then to verify this. I listened as he spoke to Ray, watching him wiping away tears and promising Ray that he had a good drink and a blessing or two coming his way.

Once back home in Clacton things returned to normal as everyone went back to work and their usual routine. Ray was back in Spain via a shift or two in London, while Sharon carried on taking and dealing cocaine. Laurence carried on being a gigolo and Harry carried on covering up the cracks in his marriage.

A visit from Roz brought me two jobs. One was to keep an eye out on her place while she was away for two weeks. The other was a computer job for a friend in the town. As I listened and jotted down the address, I found myself wondering whether any friend of hers would actually know how to turn a computer on.

As the month ate away, the work started to dry up, which was a pain because I, like everyone, needed the money. As always, December was the month when I'd overspent and January was the first opportunity to try to recover. By the time the job Roz had set up for me arrived, I was in no mood to wonder about anything.

I needed the money.

****

A short journey through the pale grey streets of Clacton found me at the address she had given me. Pulling up outside a medium-sized semi, in a leafy avenue on the fringe of the town, I checked that it was the right place. Roz had briefed me in a way only she could.

'The gentleman's name is Tim. He's a really nice man.' But then everyone she knows is nice. 'He just needs his computer fixing because the printer's packed up, I think.... ' That could mean anything.

Complete with my tool kit and my briefcase full of tricks, I gave the door knocker a hefty bang and stood on the doorstep feeling the cold morning dampness creeping inside my collar. I waited for what seemed like minutes, but was probably only one at the most, and still no one answered. This left me with two choices. Either I bashed the door again or just left a card and went.

Because of my loyalty to Roz, I elected the bash on the door option and gave the knocker a hefty smash. If nobody heard that then I figured they must be even more deaf than she was. Another minute and still no answer, so I made up my mind. Tim would have to get somebody else to fix his machine. While I was fumbling in my inside pocket for one of my cards, I heard a sound followed by a voice.

'Yes?'

Looking up, I saw a girl in the doorway and guessed that she was in her early twenties. She looked flustered, as if I'd interrupted her in the middle of doing something important.

'Hi there, I'm Steve Bidante, computer surgeon,' I said, by way of introduction.

'Andréa Sekhova,' she replied curtly.

We looked each other up and down. She looked pretty - and

pretty. Pretty in the face and the face looked pretty angry. Terrific.

Let's get to the point, Steve, I thought to myself.

'Hello, Andréa, is Tim in?'

'No.'

I wasn't getting anywhere. 'Could you tell him Steve came to look at the computer, please?'

I saw enlightenment dawn on her face.

'Ah, you're the *computer* man! Please come in. You must be, eh, Steve.'

As she repeated my name I realised that her broken English was indeed…broken. She was obviously foreign but where she was from was anybody's guess. The good news was that, at last, she was smiling.

'Thank you, Andréa,' I said slowly, so as not to confuse her any further.

She invited me in with a welcoming wave of her hand and I followed her into the house, trying to analyse her on the way. She was younger then I – on closer inspection maybe mid-twenties. Her skin was pale, perhaps accentuated by her dark black hair and might have made her look angrier than she actually was. She went up the stairs and signalled for me to follow. Now her body language seemed more relaxed and as I saw her turn at the top of the staircase I could see that she was indeed quite pretty in a foreign, perhaps Baltic way.

At the top of the stairs we turned left past a couple of doors. The house was a decent size and I noticed that this Tim chap must have children, either with this girl or someone else, because there were toys dotted about the floor. Andréa pointed at a door which, when I went in, turned out to be a bedroom.

'This computer is rubbish,' she said in her halting English.

'Oh you know a bit about computers, then?' I said, cheerfully, wondering why, if that was the case, she didn't fix it herself.

'Pardon…sorry? Can you speak slower please?' She turned to face me and I saw that there was confusion in her blue eyes.

'Yes - sorry,' I said, speaking really slowly. 'I – said – do – you – fix - computers?' I purposely left a gap between each word so that she would understand me.

She nodded to indicate that she had understood. 'No, but I know this computer is rubbish. See for yourself!' She pointed at a cream-coloured box nestling on a dilapidated table at the foot of the bed.

I looked at it and scratched my head. If we ever opened a computer museum in Clacton, then I would remember that machine and recommend it be displayed in a prominent position. It was *ancient* - unlike anything I'd seen for years. It had a pre-floppy five and a quarter inch drive poking out from the front of the case and this alone told me that the baby was archaic. Andréa went about her business while I waited for the ancient operating system to rumble into life. Would Windows boot up? No chance, not even a chink of light on the goddam DOS beast.

Staring at the dull screen, I wondered what to do next. The thing was, I hadn't worked on anything like that for so long that the whole thing felt alien to me. With no Windows operating system, it was like looking at another language. I'd played with DOS in the past but to be honest, that thing was as foreign to me as the girl I'd just met.

I fumbled around, typing in commands that were rejected each time with "bad command errors". After six or seven attempts, I decided that I was going to have to tell a white lie to get out of the situation. I didn't want any money, so it wasn't a lie to deceive, rather a lie to escape the hellish machine. All I had to do was to play the waiting game and I waited until I heard the sound of Andréa's footsteps coming up the stairs before making myself look as if I was busy.

'How are you getting on?' she asked.

'Well, Andréa, I am having a little difficulty getting into the program to look at the printer.' I drew the words out slowly in the hopes that she might understand.

She walked over and looked at the screen, then at me.

'You no find the program?'

'Eh, not the right one,' I bluffed.

Some key tapping and the printer screen appeared in front of me. Meaningless information relating to the dot matrix printer that hulked alongside the cream box of ageing silicon. I looked at the screen long enough to convince Andréa I knew what I was doing.

With some wire wiggling and pushing and prodding at the back of the beast I looked back at the screen as if expecting a reaction, finally I turned to Andréa and, with my most genuine look, said, 'Andréa, this computer - it is rubbish.'

'I told you,' she laughed out loud. 'It is *rubbish!*'

I was baffled by the pleasure she seemed to derive from the word "rubbish" but, hey, I was going with it. We were in agreement because for now she was on my side.

'Can you tell Tim my advice?' I said.

'Yes?'

'Get a new computer.' I smiled at her.

'I will tell him.' She laughed again.

I made my way back downstairs, chatting to her on the way. 'So you live here, Andréa? With Tim?'

'No. You must be crazy.' She turned back looking shocked.

I'd never met Tim, so didn't have any idea of the set-up, but Andréa's answer indicated that they weren't in any type of relationship. I wondered how Roz knew this Tim.

'Tim. He is my, how you say it.... boss. I look after his two children for him and his wife.'

'Oh that's, eh, nice,' I replied because I couldn't think of anything else to say. So she must be a nanny or whatever it is they call them in other countries. I'd heard about them working in London but never met one in Clacton before.

'It's okay. I teach myself English,' she said, for some reason sounding more foreign each time she spoke.

'Do you like Clacton, you been here long?' I felt like I was talking to someone from another world.

She seemed to give my question some thought and then said,

'I like it... I think. I come from country called Czech Republic.'

She must have seen my vague look because she grinned and added, 'You may remember Czechoslovakia.'

I nodded agreement.

'I come because my mother wished it so. I do not go out too much but I like what I know. Mainly I stay in and watch the television and learn the English.'

I tried to consider what it must be like for her, a girl from another country coming to England. I couldn't comprehend it so just said, 'I guess the English is useful for when you return home. Your mother will be proud of you.'

'My mother died,' she answered softly. 'She simply wished it so.' I saw tears in her eyes as she spoke. 'I do it for her, you understand?'

I suddenly felt close to the strange girl, understanding more than she could have realised. I knew loss and how it felt.

'I'm very sorry to hear that, Andréa.' I replied, trying to convey my own feelings.

For a moment we stood staring at each other until I began to feel a little awkward.

'Well, perhaps I'll see you sometime again, Andréa.' I said.

'That would be nice,' she said as we stood by the door, smiling at each other.

'Goodbye, Andréa.'

'Goodbye, Steve.'

CHAPTER SEVENTEEN

'Aye, aye!' a voice bellowed, indicating that Laurence had arrived. We were in our usual Saturday night haunt, The Moon, getting geared up for the evening ahead, when he came strutting over looking very pleased with himself.

'Bloody freezing out there, kids, but I'm in the mood for tonight.' He paused, looking around. 'Where are the others then?'

'My gang will be here about nine,' Sharon said, stressing the words *my gang*.

Laurence looked pleased with the reply. 'Good! Are we up for a boogie, Stevey boy?'

'Yeah, buddy, looking forward to it,' I said with a grin.

Now I admit I'm not the best dancer in the world, but the last couple of weeks Laurence and I had been frequenting The Zone. Instead of me standing around the bar all night watching him trying to pull girls, we'd taken to dancing. That might sound strange for two guys to go out with swaying in mind, but I can tell you one of Laurence's strengths is his dancing. He can move all right.

Whether it was because of our heated chat on my birthday about Sharon and drugs or because he was going through a phase, I couldn't be sure, but recently he'd been extra friendly. Not that he wasn't a good pal anyway. The plus side of it all was that he had been helping me to dance or "throw out shapes", as he put it. I'd actually really started to enjoy "throwing out shapes" across the dance floor. Before, I would avoid it at all costs but the lessons boosted my confidence no end and now I felt on a par with John bloody Travolta.

We'd had a couple of drinks by the time Sharon's "gang" turned up. This consisted of Kelly, Nicole and Tracy who I hadn't met before. The girls chatted between themselves about the latest goings-on in the metropolis of Clacton.

'Shall we go check out somewhere else before the club, Laurence?' I asked.

'Yeah, why not, leave the nags to it, son,' he replied with a bored look as their droning was topped by a high-pitched crescendo of laughter.

We said goodbye to them and headed off to East One, a little bar more or less opposite The Zone. The place had a good atmosphere as well as cutting down on the need to walk much further that night - and that was important. We would have been better dressed in parkas, rather than the thin jumpers we both wore, because the sea breeze made the air icy cold.

By the time we hit The Zone I was feeling pretty lively and ready to burn up the dance floor. Laurence seemed to be buzzing too, no doubt the result of a pill or two. I'd already asked him about his drug-taking but hadn't received a real answer.

Our chat had gone something like, 'Why do you need to take pills to have a laugh, Laurence?' to which he'd replied curtly, 'Why do you need to breathe to live? Fuck off and leave me alone.'

End of discussion.

Inside the club, the sounds were already thumping and so we grabbed a quick aperitif at the bar before talking each other up for the dancing ahead. We were enticed by the strobe lights and heavy dance tunes belting out of the many speakers that were dotted about everywhere. Walking confidently down to the dance floor, my feet hit the inside borders and my body seemed to turn into elastic as the beats took control of my movements.

Great tune after great tune echoed in my ears. My only contact now with Laurence was visual although we were dancing close to each other, advertising our dancing skills like birds of paradise on display. I felt tempted to copy his movements. If I could watch and admire him and think "wow", then I can only imagine what the effect of "funk master" was on the females who were watching.

After about half a dozen songs the sweat was pouring from me. The floor was packed but suddenly, through the crowd, I saw Sharon and the other girls with a couple more of their friends tagging on, heading our way. Laurence swayed his body towards them like a matador, inviting them to contest the space with us. The body language was almost tangible as we swayed around, dancing in the centre of the ring created by the girls. We danced down showboat street – as the saying goes - and straight into flirt city and it felt great.

It was the professional flirt master, Laurence, who signalled to me when he decided that it was time to take a break.

'Top quality, mate!' I shouted over the din of the music as we rested at the bar.

Laurence grinned. He was wetter with perspiration than I was, but somehow even that seemed to suit him as his skin glistened like an Adonis. We ordered a couple of drinks and stood against the bar watching the action. The place was jumping.

Suddenly, I thought I heard someone talking to me. I looked around and heard it again; a voice shouting, 'Hello!'

There were two girls standing on my left that I'd never seen before. This happens all the time, especially in places where pills are taken freely. The drugs make people more friendly than usual. Trying to be polite, I returned the smile and said, 'Hello to you, too.'

The girl didn't move. 'Do you remember me, Steve?

I looked, trying to make out who she was and then it hit me.

'Bloody hell, Andréa!' I blurted out.

She looked completely different from the last time I'd seen her at Tim's house. Perhaps the alcohol had distorted my vision a little, but there was no doubt she didn't look the same. She was taller somehow, with her beautiful black hair gleaming where the strobes hit it and she was wearing a black dress with matching boots. The only other colours that I could see were the silver of her jewellery glinting in the lights and the blue of her eyes shining into the night. She looked stunning.

'Sorry, you look different,' I said awkwardly, trying to hide my embarrassment at not recognising her at first.

Laurence, cottoning on to the situation, moved in closer looking inquisitive so I introduced him.

'This is Andréa and her friend...'

She interrupted me, helping me along with the stranger beside her. 'This is Diana. She is my Russian friend.'

The other girl was slightly smaller then Andréa, but no less pretty. She looked Eastern European with dyed blonde hair and piercing brown eyes.

'Pleased to meet you both. What a couple of beautiful woman,' he drooled, while at the same time giving me a look that seemed to say 'nice one!'

Andréa came closer so that I could hear her, leaving Laurence with Diana.

'Really nice to see you, Andréa,' I shouted, lost for words.

'Thank you, nice to see you too.' She seemed to ooze confidence through every pore in her body.

I tried to gather myself and make some kind of half sensible conversation.

'You look lovely, Andréa. Have you been anywhere exciting tonight?' I babbled inanely.

'To a wedding of Diana's friend, it was very good and now we come to dance.' Laurence heard her and grabbed my arm before I had a chance to say anything else.

'Come on, son, let's dance.'

Laurence knew how good he was at the dancing game and this was a chance to impress the girls with his class. I realised that and played along.

'Okay, Andréa, we go dance. You come too?' I found myself imitating her broken English.

'Maybe soon, Steve, you go enjoy yourself.'

She evidently wanted to play it cool.

I'd made my choice and I couldn't just stand there anymore so I looked at her before following Laurence back down to the floor where the girls welcomed us back with loud chants. I quickly slipped back into the action, finding new moves that seemed to have come from the adrenalin rush I'd felt at the bar. The music pumped my muscles into frenzied action while the DJ hit the beats.

Lifting my head between hip shaking, I suddenly noticed the girls separate a little to make a gap. Andréa and Diana slipped between them and came towards us and I saw that Sharon looked annoyed.

'You are popular!' Andréa said, as her body started to sway to the sounds. I just stared. She could really move and, by comparison, my dancing seemed awkward and clumsy. As I watched, I was seduced by her body movements. I'd never seen a woman's hips sway so sexily to a beat while her eyes sparkled with the confidence of a siren.

After a while we began to flirt with each other until Sharon and her group got bored and went back to the bar. As Laurence did his own thing, I became more and more involved. We drew closer, touching, letting our intentions show in the way we danced. Before we knew it the lights dipped and were replaced by bright, go-home beams. The club was closing. That was it. Jesus, it was two o'clock already!

People left the floor all around us until just the four of us were left standing awkwardly, waiting for each other to say something until the bouncers moved in and asked us to leave. It was then that I decided to jump in with both feet.

'Can we walk you home?' I didn't want to say goodbye again, at least not now.

'Diana, you want to go to my place or Steve's?' Laurence went straight for the jugular.

Diana shook her head. 'I have to go home.'

Andréa said nothing, then moved close to me and whispered, 'I go home with you for while. I feel safe with you.'

I nodded. 'One moment.'

Pulling Laurence to one side I whispered in his ear, 'I'm going to scoot with her back to my place. You're welcome back, mate, if you really want to join us.'

'Go ahead, Steve. Thanks - but no thanks.' He took the hint.

'You okay with that?' I said with mock surprise.

'No problem, good luck.'

The cold air hit our lungs when we left the club and went out into the night. While we had been dancing in the warm club, it had begun to snow. I guided Andréa through the crowd of people hanging about outside.

As I was wondering where we could get a cab at that time of night I found myself gazing at her.

'Are you okay, Steve?'

'Yes fine, just….' Before I had a chance to say anything else she tugged at my jumper and pulled me towards her. Our lips touched and I swam into her kiss. It was as good as her dancing - if not better.

Although the kiss couldn't have lasted long it seemed like an eternity as my mind swam into semi-consciousness. We drew apart and I saw something in her eyes that told me that this was not going to be just one night.

As we set off down the snowy street I realised the magic of the moment. At last, I had found a Christmas card like they sold in the shops. Except this time I was actually in it.

CHAPTER EIGHTEEN

Snow is wonderful.

With the blanket of snow that lay around, my world seemed a quieter, more magical place. Less traffic, less people and, to begin with, everything looking so tranquil and enchanting. Then humanity intervened as gritters took to the roads, followed by cars, followed by slush and dirt. Normal life returned as people went out and stood around grumbling about the disruption that snow caused.

Then snow is horrible.

For now the snow lay in its virgin state and it stayed that way, at least for me anyway. I walked in the Christmas card of my mind with Andréa by my side long after the slush turned to water. It felt like we were two lost souls who had found each other via an ancient computer. It sounds almost mythical, doesn't it? My belief in destiny was confirmed more then ever.

I had never met such a distant, different person as I had in Andréa. That in itself was more alien to me than I could have imagined. With Susie, I had felt only the language barrier and minor differences when we spoke about WW2 but fundamentally we seemed pretty much the same. Here I had met someone completely unique to me. A tall, dark-haired maiden who reminded me of some kind of elfin princess. It wasn't just her jaw dropping good looks but her language and her history. To hear Czech spoken is like hearing a mythical language. It has a dreamlike quality where even harsh words sound musical.

This perception was enhanced by Andréa's stories of home. As we saw more and more of each other I learned about her home city of Prague, "The City of a Hundred Spires". It was a place rich in history and Andréa told it so beautifully. She spoke of Charles Bridge, T?n Cathedral, St Nicklaus' Church and the Cathedral of St Vitus and many other places. As I listened, the land of which she spoke took on a new meaning as, intoxicated by her spellbinding voice, visions formed in my head. The Czech Republic now seemed to be the place where all fairy tales were made.

We dated regularly and became fonder of each other every day. Within a month, all my Clacton friends knew that she was the new woman in my life and most of them liked her. Sharon was a little bit wary while Laurence didn't seem to care too much and Harry simply said, 'I can't really understand what she says, mate, but she seems really nice.'

So, with the world spinning in the right direction, did I stop contact with Susie? Of course not! I asked myself if I should. *Of course I should* but it seemed irrelevant. I balanced the fact that we still emailed each other occasionally, by telling her about Andréa from the beginning. Susie's reaction suggested that she was a little jealous and I gained some satisfaction from reading words that carried a trace of sadness. At least I knew now that she *did* have feelings. Anyway, she was history and Andréa was the present.

****

The sun woke me with warmth likened to what I felt inside. I loved Saturdays! After a coffee and croissant I decided to give my bedroom a good spring clean, not only to utilise the sun-kissed energy I felt, but also to make the room look as fresh as the world felt to me that day. After whizzing around with a duster and Hoover on the main areas of the room, I pulled out the mass of boxes that fitted snugly under the bed to make way for the final assault on the dust and dirt. Spare computer parts, old football programmes and much more lay within the array of old shoe-boxes. As I did so, the lid of one of the boxes flipped over showing its contents of little pieces of memorabilia from trips and events in my life. Match tickets, bar mats, matches and some sprigs of plants I had long forgotten about.

I smiled as I held them in my hand. The warmth of the day reminded me of Spain and of the gypsy who gave them to me. I decided there and then that they should be on display to remind me of days like this.

A half hour later I had pressed the dried plants gently into a small wooden frame. They looked pretty and as I hung it up on the kitchen wall, I stood back to admire my handiwork, grinning happily. If they were meant for good luck, then it seemed to be working. Even my grandmother seemed perkier, although I was becoming increasingly worried by her forgetfulness.

The phone rang and I felt a bounce in my step as I reached to pick it up.

'Hello?'

'Hello, darling.'

'Good morning, Andréa!' I said cheerfully.

'Oh darling, I need you,' she blurted out the words, sounding as if she was about to burst into tears.

'Andréa, what's wrong?' I felt panic grip my stomach.

'Please come for me,' she said hoarsely.

'Of course. Where are you? At home?'

'Yes.' Her voice suddenly dropped a decibel.

'Okay, I'll be there as quickly as I can. Andréa…are you alright?' I sensed deep distress in her voice.

'I will be when you arrive.' The line went dead.

I jumped into the car and sped down the hill towards the edge of town pulling up quickly when I saw Andréa standing outside the front of the house.

'Hi,' I said, trying to sound cheerful while at the same time studying her face. There were obvious signs of dried tears that had made her make-up run a little and she stood next to a small pile of luggage.

'Oh, darling, thank you for coming for me. We must

leave now, this minute.'

'Leave, where?'

'Anywhere, I must go from here, things are terrible.' She ran towards me and into my arms.

'Hey, come on! Everything will be okay.' I hugged her reassuringly. 'Come on, come with me.'

I picked up her luggage and began to carry it to the car. She had three average-sized cases which just about squeezed into my tiny Mazda Roadster. I suddenly felt so sorry for this girl, not just because I was falling in love with her but because of the absolute sadness in her voice and face. She looked so vulnerable – like a little girl lost and miles from home. I realised at that moment that I was her only hope right now.

With Andréa crammed into my sports car and the luggage squashed on top of her, I headed back to my place. When we arrived I carried her world inside and dumped in it the hallway with her following behind me. I felt an awkwardness surface now, a responsibility I had no experience of dealing with. Instead of holding her or saying the right things I heard myself say, 'Would you like a drink, darling?'

'Yes please,' she whispered.

I pulled myself together, realising that it was she who was scared, not me. Taking her hand I looked at her and saw that her blue eyes were filled with fear.

'Andréa, sit down and talk to me.' I held her gently by her shoulders. 'Don't worry, darling, you're safe now. Everything will be fine.' I had no idea how everything *could* be okay, but it would have to be.

'Steve, it was terrible,' she said tearfully.

'It'll be alright,' I repeated, more calmly then I felt. 'Tell me what happened, baby.'

She seemed to relax a little; her face looked more composed as she began to speak.

'Last night Tim brings friends home, they drink and drink,' she sighed.

138

'You mean they had a party?'

'Not really, just drink and swearing and drink. Then one man, he talks to me. At first he was nice and friendly.'

'And then?' The way she said "at first" made me sense something was coming.

'Then he asks me for kiss.'

'Go on.' I saw her hesitate as if embarrassed.

'I say "no" - of course I say "no" - and I go to walk away to look for Tim but he stops me. I am left for that moment with just me and him.'

'So what happened next?' I asked, my imagination beginning to slip into gear. As it did so I visualised the story unfolding, not wanting to believe what I was thinking.

'He smiles and leans to kiss me, I push him away. "Please no!" I say to him, he says "Alright" and steps away looking angry.'

'Right, then what happened?' I felt anger flare up inside me, I wanted to know what the hell happened but in a strange way suddenly I didn't. I wished she could stop now and that nothing bad happened.

'I thought that was it, Steve, I did.' She paused to wipe the tears from her eyes.

I passed her a tissue and waited, a feeling of sickness creeping inside my stomach.

'So I try to act like nothing happened,' she continued, as her composure returned a little. 'I go to get glass of water and then I creep up to bed. I shut door and get undressed, then....'

'What?' I interrupted. 'Are you saying he followed you?' I paused because I could see that my anger was upsetting her. 'Sorry, Andréa, please carry on,' I said trying to sound as calm as possible.

She wiped her eyes again. 'He come in, this man, he come in room and he say with horrid smile, "Ah, you are ready for me now?" I say "Please go away"; I say "You are scaring me now" but he still smiles this horrible smile and comes near. I smell his drink on him and he pushes me back on bed. I am so scared and I start to cry. He grabs me and says things, rude horrible things that scare me more so I do only thing I can do.'

'What, Andréa, what did you do?' I held her hand tightly, the main event was unfolding and I was not looking forward to the finale.

'I kick him in place that hurt, I kick him so hard.' I saw a look of pure hatred in her eyes as she recalled the moment.

'You did *what*?' I was momentarily stunned.

'I kick him where it hurts,' she repeated. 'He fall back on floor and his face go red and he starts to look sick and breathe badly. I get up and he say, "You cheap bitch!" I say "You English scum!" Then I run downstairs and I tell Tim to come outside and I tell him what happened.'

I started to laugh.

'Why you laugh, Steve?' She looked confused while I felt my face relax with laughter.

'Andréa, that is brilliant!' Relief washed away my anger and I knew that I admired the girl more then ever.

'Steve, I do not understand. Do you want to know what happened or just laugh at me?' She looked irritated and rather hurt.

I stroked her hand gently. 'Please. I'm sorry, I just think that what you did was the right thing and, to be honest, I was scared you were going to tell me he…raped you.' I felt a surge of adrenalin as the word "raped" came out. I suddenly didn't feel like laughing at all.

'No, darling, no!' She clasped my hand reassuringly as if it were I who needed the counselling.

'So what happened then?' I asked.

'Then my trouble really begin, I tell Tim. First he laughs and tells me not to worry, that the man was just joking. But he was not there and this man was not joking, you know that don't you, Steve?' Her voice wavered.

I knew just by looking at Andréa. There were no lies written on her face - I felt sure of that.

'Yes, Andréa, of course I believe you,' I replied reassuringly.

'Good.' The moment's uncertainty was replaced by calm. 'So now I have to leave.'

'What…here?' I pretended to sound confused.

'No, silly man!' Andréa laughed. 'I have to leave Tim. I wake up this morning and he asks me not to tell anyone. I say I was scared and it was wrong and you know what he says?'

'I have absolutely no idea, Andréa.'

'He says, "It is best if you leave", so I call you.' She paused, looking at me for a reaction.

The situation grabbed me by the scruff of the neck. She had nowhere to live, not strictly true, she had one place to live, and she was in it right at that moment. *My* home would have to be *her* home. What other options did she have?

'Eh, Andréa, you could stay here if you want.' The words sounded insincere to my ears as if my wall of independence was suddenly crumbling around me. The deep love I felt for this girl should not have made me fear anything, yet a tinge of doubt remained somewhere. It was just so sudden.

'Oh, Steve, I knew you would understand! I love you! I love you!' she shouted, before grabbing me and squeezing me tightly.

I didn't say anything else. I wasn't sure what else there was to say.

And so Andréa moved in.

****

My life changed in the following weeks as I adjusted to Andréa's constant presence in my life. By a twist of fate I was fortunate enough to be shown what a wonderful creature a woman can be and, in so doing, discovered what it was to truly love another human being.

Andréa had such depth, such strength, such beauty. The

words alone could not do her justice. She had no fear of her love, no barriers, and the magic of the love in her eyes shone through into mine.

'She's just right,' my grandmother said approvingly on a rare visit to our shared home.

We watched as Andréa demonstrated how to plant herbs and vegetables in a handmade basket that she had crafted from bits of wood and straw.

'She does that kind of thing all the time,' I said proudly - and it was true. She constantly did things I loved to hear and see. I would watch her skilful fingers effortlessly arranging delicate flowers into a bursting chorus of prettiness. Or listen to her singing softly in her native tongue while she prepared food I had never even heard of, let alone seen, and then see her big eyes scanning my face for reaction while I ate it. I learnt so much from her.

In return I learnt to give. I learnt to think unselfishly of another as she taught me the unique undiscovered freedom of loving. She taught me how to shed fear and temptation; to listen as well as being heard. The barriers that society and I had erected vanished to be replaced by an openness I had never experienced before. She was my equal, my love, my friend. At last my soul felt free.

Andréa always had the ability to surprise me and one evening, just as we had finished a meal at a small local restaurant, she did just that.

'Steve, may I ask you something please?' she said, as she sipped her wine.

'Of course, you know you can.' I was surprised simply because she didn't need to ask first – she didn't usually.

'Will you promise me something?'

'I'll promise you *anything*, baby,' I smiled.

'If you find our love is not what it seems in the future, if you think you want another woman - will you do something for me?'

I hadn't considered the possibility but now I had, the

answer seemed easy. 'I can't imagine feeling like that, Andréa.'

She ran her finger around the rim of her glass so that it made a humming sound. 'Perhaps not, but if you ever do, will you please go to a prostitute, do that and then come home and try to continue with me as normal?' She spoke with a meaningfulness I had to take seriously.

I did not know whether to laugh or smile or say anything at all. I was completely thrown by this strangest of requests.

'Why would you ask me that, babe?' I couldn't imagine ever needing anyone but her.

She leaned towards me and looked straight at me as she spoke. 'I ask you because one day that temptation *will* or *may* come into your life. I ask you not because I would wish for this but because I would be able to live with this thought now, tomorrow and forever, but I could never live with the thought of you having an affair, of having feelings for another woman. Do you understand what I am saying?' Even as she spoke her face paled as if the words had drained her.

I held her hand and looked into her eyes and heard myself say, 'I promise, Andréa, I promise.'

Pushing back her hair, she ran her hand down into her pocket and produced a coin. Smiling, she said. 'In my homeland we have a saying. It is something like....'

'See a penny pick it up, all day long you'll have good luck!' I intervened, laughing.

'Yes... It is something like that.' She smiled, pushing the coin across the table. 'I was once told,' she continued, 'that I would know when the moment was right to give it away. I know now what that meant.'

I saw love in her eyes as I reached out for the coin. It looked old but had no date marked on it. It featured a dragon in battle on one side while on the reverse was a cross set against a faint outline of a crown.

'It's very lovely, Andréa,' I said looking at her again. 'Is it for me then?'

Her face shone and her eyes became watery.
'Yes, it is. It is meant just for you.'

****

It was in May when I received the email from Susie. I was
slightly surprised as we had lost contact as our separate
relationships had progressed, and she had become nothing
more than a distant memory of a different time. I ran my
mouse arrow over the email and clicked:

Hi schatz,

How are you? I have missed our emails and I have missed you. Something
told me to write to you and I had to, so I hope you will not mind. I know you
are with someone else and that your life has perhaps moved on. So what am
I saying?

I want to come to England. I feel it will be too late if I do not soon. Something
has happened to me and I just know I need to see you even it is one last time
before our lives continue on without each other.

I am coming to London in two weeks with two friends. Would it be possible
to see you and perhaps stay with you in Clacton? I understand if you say no
but I hope you will not. Please do not.

All my love

Susie xx

I reread the email over and over again before looking out of
the window to see Andréa in the garden working on her plants.
She looked so pretty and happy. She was the girl I would
never want to harm, the girl I had promised I would never
hurt.

I looked back at the message and thought of the

consequences of my next actions.

I looked outside again at Andréa. I could reply and say "no" and end it there or say "yes" and risk destroying her love for me. I could not even believe I was capable of such emotional brutality.

As I wrote my reply, I hated myself completely.

I said yes.

CHAPTER NINETEEN

'It's not a problem, son,' he said nonchalantly. 'They can stay at my place and I'll kip at my mum's. It's only three days - don't worry about it.'

Laurence sat opposite me in the pub garden as we sipped beer while plotting my plan of deceit. After much thought about how exactly this meeting would - or could - occur I had decided he was the best chance of a trouble free visit. I had told Susie it would be okay without actually thinking about *how* it would be okay.

Laurence was just doing his job as a pal. He cared little for girls' feelings, so he seemed the best option if I wanted to avoid getting into trouble. I'd decided, in my mind, to just spend a last weekend with Susie and then say goodbye. I balanced the scales of my conscience and the theory seemed good but I puzzled about why, if that was the case, would I even *want* to take the risk?

****

The two weeks leading up to the visit were hell on earth. I carried the twin burdens of my foolish vanity and the terrible power. The beach became my residence of repentance but it did no good. The position I had found myself in, or put myself in, was one of agony. I had it all, yet wanted to take a gamble that could have terrible consequences and I still couldn't figure out why I was doing it. I was happy. I felt I was in love. I had everything a man could want. So why? I was a weak-willed human being who had become the disciple of temptation.

At first Andréa didn't seem to notice anything. She had no

reason to see change because nothing had changed for her. For me it was a case of waiting for the impending storm to gather its pace and knowing the exact day it would begin to consume everything in its path. With Susie due to arrive on Friday, I could hide no more and on Monday I approached Andréa. My mind was filled with the words that I wanted to say but all that came out were prettily wrapped lies.

'Darling, I've something to ask of you.' I paused, trying to summon up the courage to continue.

'Yes, darling?' she smiled warmly.

I dived in head first. 'I had an email from some old friends who are visiting this week. Would you mind if I went out with them…you know… caught up on old times?'

'Why should I?' She gave me a bemused look. 'If they are old friends that would be lovely for you, I know that.'

I saw her smile with its unblemished innocence shining through as she added, 'Perhaps it would be nice for me to meet them, don't you think?'

I hadn't thought of that possibility. Of course I hadn't thought, and of course that's the kind of innocent, trusting response Andréa *would* give.

'Well, that sounds good,' I said slowly, trying to think of a way out, 'but I think at first I'd just like to see them alone. You know, to catch up.' I felt nothing but contempt for myself. The lies were flowing and I felt sure that any moment she would see through them.

I needn't have worried. Love has a way of both protecting the heart as well as tearing it apart. In this case, her love for me answered for her. 'Oh okay, darling, whatever you want.' She shrugged easily and went into the kitchen humming a cheerful tune as she went. It had all been much easier than I had expected although my conscience troubled me. My tainted heart spoke to me telling me that I could cross the bridge of their meeting later but for now I had deceived her.

I turned to walk into the garden and as I did so my mobile began to hum. It was Ray and as I answered him I heard

Andréa call out. 'Where are they visiting from, darling?'

The sentence sent a chill down my spine. I somehow knew my answer would be the beginning of the storm.

'They're just popping over from Germany, sweetheart.' I heard my pathetic words spill from my mouth and form the sound, weeping with weakness, which travelled to her ears.

'Hi, Ray, how you doing?' Standing outside, the call seemed to offer a brief respite.

'Hi, Steve, things are good, how's England?'

As I held the mobile to my ear, I watched as Andréa stormed out of the kitchen and came to stand in front of me. Before she had so much as uttered a word, I knew that *she* knew. Her entire body language showed it and although she didn't speak for a few minutes, I remembered the one sentence that had ripped my insides apart.

"Not an affair, please do not do that to me."

'Yeah, good Ray, look, can I call you back in a mo?'

'Sure,' he said, sounding somewhat confused. 'Talk soon, Steve.'

'*Germany*!' She shouted with real venom in her voice. 'You never told me about anyone from Germany before!'

'What's wrong with Germany?' I attempted to argue but my legs felt weak. 'My friends are from Germany. So what?'

'It is not the country, you idiot!' she said angrily. 'Why did you not mention them before? We talk about everything.' I saw her hesitate. 'Who do you know in Germany? You have never mentioned anyone from there before.' I sensed that love had now awoken something else inside her. The most powerful force on earth had alerted something resembling a doubt she had not felt before. Her eyes portrayed a painful effort to hide her emotions as she said those words.

I said nothing. The destruction had begun.

****

I sat on the beach and dialled Ray's number. After making a

feeble excuse about needing to buy food for dinner, I had fled from the mess I'd created.

'Hi, Ray, sorry for the delay, little problem cropped up.' I tried to sound relaxed.

'No problem, anything you want to talk about?' His voice was tinged with concern.

'Nah, it'll be alright,' I lied to myself and him. 'Just girl stuff you know. Got Susie coming over and, well... Andréa isn't too happy about it. Enough said, buddy.'

'Right.' Ray's reply indicated that he didn't want to get involved. Either that or he knew it was going to create a problem.

'Anyway, Steve,' he continued, 'I've got some good news for you!'

'Fire away,' I replied. Any good news sounded exactly that. Good.

'Well,' he said, 'I'm over the first week in July and it just so happens that Knebworth is on!'

'Sounds good.' I guessed he was waiting for some kind of reaction. Knebworth Festival was where some of the top bands around played. I'd heard of it and seen it on television but never been.

'I also happen to have two tickets for it so I thought of you. Am I a good pal or what?' His voice oozed generosity.

'The best,' I answered, smiling to myself. It was too good a chance to miss. 'Count me in, Ray, and thanks for the thought. You're a top man.'

'I'll be in touch to sort out the arrangements. And oh...good luck with the girls, Steve. Rather you than me!'

I felt better – albeit briefly - after the call and lit up a cigarette and sat looking at the view. I had made a decision which did not include thinking of any girl at all.

****

The week leading up to Susie's arrival saw an inevitable

change in atmosphere. Andréa began to withdraw from me. My behaviour must have told her that something was happening; our body language said it all. My vagueness about the visit seemed to infect our lives and our moments of love became moments of pain. In the days leading up to that Friday it seemed that we were falling out of love. The division widened hourly. I saw her suffering and I suffered with her because of my own betrayal of our love, although I had not yet betrayed and I still hoped that, somehow, I would not; that there was still a chance for redemption. I wanted there to be.

Friday arrived, warm and sunny with the sea smelling especially fresh. I awoke early feeling a surge of excitement that I found hard to contain. Tonight I would see Susie again! I attempted to hide my feelings from Andréa but as I slipped from between the sheets that we shared she awoke and watched me dress. She didn't say anything. Just a look etched with pain. I had to escape the house.

As it was such a wonderful day I decided to take my bike out. I'd planned an easy day at work; just a couple of routine maintenance jobs so there wasn't much to carry. As I walked the bike around the side of the bungalow I saw Roz standing, clippers in her hand, near the fence.

'Good morning.'

'Good morning, Roz, how are you?' I grinned, feeling better now that I was out of the house with a few minutes to spare to talk to her.

'Where're you going on your bike?'

'I've some work to do and as it's a lovely day I thought I'd make the most of it.'

'Mmm.' She looked at me and then at the sky.

'How's Andréa?'

'She's fine,' I lied. 'She'll probably be out in the garden before long. Did you know she has a job now?' I added, trying to ease the subject along.

Roz picked out a yellow rose and gently clipped it from the

bush. 'Yes, I heard. At a restaurant in town. She'll be popular there.'

I thought for a moment knowing that she never missed a trick.

'I'm sure she will be.'

'She's a special girl, isn't she?' Roz looked at me kindly.

'Yes.' I felt a pain surface inside me. 'She is.'

I suddenly wanted to wriggle free from our conversation.

'Well, I have to go, Roz. Enjoy the sunshine.'

I mounted my bike and turned to go but she just nodded and carried on with what she was doing.

****

Nine o'clock. My heart balanced on a tightrope. Thirty minutes to go until the train arrived. I'd taken Andréa to work an hour before and tried to sound as normal with her as was possible. She said little except to wish me a good time and to tell me she'd be home by midnight.

Laurence and I had swapped cars as part of the deal. I needed more room and he was happy with the swap. The battered Vauxhall Astra was not my idea of luxury but it was more suited to the job in hand.

Standing near the railings at the train station, it had a feeling of timelessness about it. I watched the narrow platform which ran alongside the railings. The main station building, unchanged since Victorian times, was behind me. It was probably busier in those days too, what with all the holidaymakers and nobody having cars. Now I was surrounded by an almost ghostly silence.

I walked over to the dingy café bar in the main building and ordered a coffee just to pass the time. As I paid for the pale liquid disguised as coffee, I noticed a small flower stall at the far end of the station. An idea came into my head. I'd get the girl some flowers. It would be a nice touch.

I wandered over to the stall and saw that there were a few

flowers dotted around the edges for display but nothing special. I waited for a moment as the stall holder continued to sweep the floor surrounding the area, apparently oblivious to my presence.

'Hello?'

Turning her attention away from the broom towards me she said, 'How can I help?'

I felt a momentary chill creep up my spine. She was of medium build, slightly bent, her dark clothes lightened by the striped apron she wore over them. I was sure that her tangled, grey hair made her face look older than it was. At first I had thought that she was an old lady but somehow her face confused my judgment. She seemed both old and young all at once.

'Can I help you?' she said again.

That was it! The voice, I'd heard the voice and it didn't belong to the person in front of me. It was from a different woman - a different time.

I tried to compose myself – to stick to the job in hand. 'Yes, eh, I'd like some flowers please. Something small - pretty. Maybe roses?'

She chuckled. 'For someone special, eh? I've got just the job.' She set about picking a selection. 'Who's the lucky girl?'

I didn't really want to talk about the details so I simply replied, 'Oh, it's just a friend visiting from overseas. I thought it would be a nice touch.' I tried to sound nonchalant.

Her fingers worked quickly and I watched her create a posy of red roses entwined with delicate green foliage. Occasionally she looked up as she worked. 'Do you think she'll like it?'

'Yes,' I said, 'it looks good, thanks - very nice...' I hesitated. 'I'm sure I know you from somewhere, don't I?'

'I don't know,' she replied, twisting the paper into a decorative horn around the roses. 'Do you? Where would that be from then?'

I studied her face. I couldn't be sure but I had an

overwhelming feeling of familiarity. 'I'm not sure,' I said slowly. 'I just feel I do.'

She laid the roses on the makeshift counter in front of me. 'There, all done!' She must have noticed my confusion because she added, 'Oh don't worry. It can happen. It could be from anywhere - could even just be from a dream.'

I noticed her expression change as she spoke, making me feel even more confused. It was as if she *knew* that I knew her.

'I haven't seen you in a dream. It's somewhere else, I'm sure of it.' I said firmly. 'Now - how much do I owe you?' I was eager to escape.

'Oh, just five pounds. I'm closing up now anyway, my work's done for today.' She took my money and dropped it into a small box beside her.

'Thank you,' I said picking up the bouquet from the table.

'My pleasure - thank *you*. I hope you make sense of your thoughts.'

'Sorry? I don't quite get you.'

'You know, finding out who I am and all that,' she chuckled. 'Some things are a little harder to understand, I think.'

I felt déjà vu without the vu, somehow I knew this woman. As she smiled it just made the point seem more eerie.

'Well thank you and goodnight,' I said, walking hurriedly away towards the train platform.

CHAPTER TWENTY

The train rumbled in and came slowly to a halt. I watched carefully as the first people marched through the gate. My eyes scanned them until I saw her. She was dressed in a white summer blouse with a cream-coloured silk shawl over her shoulders. Her trousers were a pale brown check design. As she came closer our eye contact sealed the moment, The two friends alongside her melted into the background. It was as if she was the only person walking towards me.

'*Schatz*!' she called, her lips forming a wide smile. We drew close to each other and embraced. Instantly the feelings that we had shared on that last day in Spain returned and I knew that somewhere, deep in my soul, I had craved this moment.

As we slipped from our embrace, I turned to see Danni beaming at me.

'Schatz, you remember Danni, of course... and this is Markus.' Susie introduced me.

'Hi, Danni.' I kissed her on the cheek before offering my hand to Markus. 'Good to meet you, Markus.'

'Hello, Steve, very good to meet you,' Markus replied. I liked him instantly. He had an air of cheerful confidence about him.

'How was your journey?' I said, taking Susie's bag as we walked towards Laurence's old Vauxhall.

'Very nice, we flew into the City airport which was good. One train across London and then this train and here we are. Easy!' Susie beamed.

'I did all the planning, may I say, Steve!' Markus grinned.

'You did not!' Susie retorted good-humouredly. 'He always thinks he is good at these things. He works for German airlines and gets around a bit but he did nothing, I assure you. Did he, Danni?'

Danni reached out for Markus's arm, gazing lovingly at him. 'He is wonderful,' she said, leaning towards him so that their lips met.

'God help us, she falls in love as easily as the wind moves the leaves,' Susie whispered in my ear. I smiled, guessing that to be the case.

It wasn't long before we were at Laurence's house. It was a nice enough maisonette set in a small estate about three miles east of the town. A small entrance hall led to a largish lounge where Markus and Danni would sleep for the next few days. Upstairs I had made the bed with clean sheets for Susie. Laurence was very generous but not so hygienic and I didn't fancy letting this pretty girl share in his unwashed linen filled with the history of his conquests.

After settling in we cracked open some beers I had brought round earlier when I'd come to make up the bed. The hours slipped by as we relaxed in each other's company. I glanced at my watch when Susie began to talk about Andréa. Perhaps she sensed that it was almost time for me to go.

'So, Steve,' she said, a smile touching her lips. 'Do you think you will marry this girl?'

I felt as if I had been caught off guard. 'Who you? I hardly know you!' I joked, not wanting to answer her question but Susie didn't laugh. She looked and waited for my answer.

I saw that she spoke with sincerity.

'No, I don't see that happening,' I said, before putting the same question to her. 'And you? Will you marry Raimund?'

I watched Susie take a slow sip from the bottle of beer and then looking straight into my eyes she said, 'My heart lies elsewhere so that could not happen or I would be betraying myself, don't you agree?'

I was caught off balance again but this time by her honesty. 'It would indeed,' I replied without losing eye contact, 'now that you put it like that.' I suddenly didn't want to leave.

Later – in the early hours of the morning - we said "goodnight" to the others and I followed Susie upstairs. We immediately moved close to each other – we didn't need words. Our lips met in the darkness and we kissed gently, our hands exploring each other's bodies. Apprehension was mixed with desire as the urge to push myself onto her rose. I wanted so much to make love to her at that moment.

She seemed to understand what I was feeling because, pulling back from my embrace, she whispered, 'It would not be right.'

'I know,' I said gently, feeling slightly relieved. Not because of the desire which burned bright, but because I could not bring myself to betray Andréa there at that moment while at the same time feeling disgusted with myself for even getting that close to doing so.

We didn't speak again but just held each other in the night shadows as I decided to stay for a while longer before going home. But the power of the moment and sleep took over. When I next opened my eyes, the morning light filled me with panic.

'Shit!' I shouted out loud. Susie was still asleep when I hurriedly scrambled out of bed and into my clothes. I had no idea of the time but guilt filled my mind. Leaning over I kissed her on the cheek. 'I'll be back later.' She murmured agreement as I ran down the stairs.

Markus was sitting watching the television, smoking. 'Practice is good,' he nodded towards the sports programme.

'What's the time?' I shouted.

'Half past nine and I have been up since six, Steve. The bloody phone kept ringing.'

I felt nervous. 'You didn't answer it?' I asked trying to sound calm.

'No, I was going to, but Danni said not to.' I looked at Danni lying on the sofa. She gave me a little smile but I was in no mood for more chat.

'I have to go,' I said, looking at Markus. 'Listen, tell Susie

I'll be back this afternoon. I'll text her and we can meet up and do something, okay?'

Guilt drove me as much as I drove the car. Pulling up outside the house, I felt scared of what this moment would be like and images of Andréa flashed in front of me.

I entered the house cautiously. 'Andréa?' I called her name tentatively.

No reply and it soon became apparent that she was not in. Instead of worrying about where she could be, a feeling of relief washed over me. My discoloured heart told me that it was good because it meant that I didn't have to face my pathetic self for a little while longer.

I didn't hang around long. I showered quickly and changed my clothes and left within twenty minutes, almost running to get out of there, heading for the beach. When I arrived I found that it was almost deserted except for the odd dog walker and a lone fisherman. Sitting on the stone steps, looking out to sea I concocted my game plan; attempting to hatch something believable. I wouldn't be returning to the house for the rest of the day but I *could* say I had gone there with them and waited for her. The only danger with that idea was if she had gone home and waited for me, then I would have to concoct something about just missing her. Many scenes played out in my mind, mostly fat lies to try and make *me* feel better instead of her. I knew in reality I was killing everything we ever had but I just could not stop.

To be aware of destruction is a sin indeed.

An hour or so and a few text messages later, I left my beach sanctuary and drove to meet up with the three Germans. As soon as I saw Susie, I felt better. The drug of her being injected me with new vitality. The day was fresh and warm so I suggested we walked into the town from Laurence's house. They agreed immediately and within an hour we were sitting down outside the pier with me acting as their tour guide. Telling them about the "good old days" and the English tradition of holidaying seemed to make my visitors happy –

and me too because it was with more than a degree of enthusiasm that I went with Markus to buy fish and chips for everyone.

'This is wonderful,' Susie said as she pulled a piece of cod apart and delicately ate a small morsel of the white fish.

It *felt* wonderful and as we ate and talked my guilt seemed to evaporate in the heat of the sun. After we'd finished eating we strolled around the town where the girls bought gifts and souvenirs to take home. Tea consisted of warm doughnuts and candyfloss - hardly healthy but very much in the theme of the day.

I'd arranged, via text messages, to meet Harry and Laurence to introduce them to my friends. I hadn't risked Sharon or anyone else because I was scared of being lectured about my loyalty to Andréa.

They arrived just after eight o'clock and we all sat outside The Moon watching the sun dipping low over the horizon. Everyone seemed to get on well and Harry was in good form, enlivening the night with his friendly ways and humour. Laurence, as usual, acted pretty cool but his contribution of his home made him instantly popular. The evening was easy and relaxed but somewhere in my subconscious I could not erase Andréa and wondered what had become of her.

'She's a lovely girl.' Harry commented, as we stood at the bar waiting to order.

'She is, Harry - and I'm mad about her - but I feel like shit,' I said, my head filled with confusion.

'I meant Andréa,' he replied.

'Oh, you don't like Susie?' I said defensively, trying to cover up my mistake.

'She's nice enough but don't worry what I think, Steve. It isn't *me* who has to make a choice, is it?' He flashed me a grin as he picked up a couple of drinks and walked outside.

I decided at that moment to stop thinking about it all. Just to enjoy the night and worry later, my heart told me.

Follow your heart, they say.
Not that easy.

****

At three o'clock in the morning I once again lay next to Susie in Laurence's bed. The night had turned out to be fantastic, ending with dancing at The Zone. My earlier meeting there with Andréa was now a distant memory; my senses were numbed to everything except Susie. We fell asleep in each other's arms. No questions. No thinking.

For the second time in two days I awoke with panic, only this time it was worse than before. I'd done it again. The drink hit me as I leapt from the bed like a groundhog. Too much of it the night before had dulled my senses but now it surrounded me. I felt a thumping pain in my head combined with guilt and panic. I felt sick. Rushing to get dressed, I kissed Susie quickly as I had done before except this time she was awake.

'Do you love her?' Her brown eyes looked appealingly at me as she spoke.

'I don't know,' I said, pausing for a moment, panic clouding my thoughts and opinions. 'Yes, but in a different way, Susie. Look I have to go - talk later.' I rushed out of the building.

As I pulled up at my own house I saw that the windows were wide open, telling me that Andréa was at home. My head hurt more than ever and my breathing felt erratic. Not only had I committed the ultimate sin but I'd done it totally. No explanation would suffice. I took a deep breath and turned the key.

There was no need to search or call her name this time. As the door swung open she was standing in the hall. Her naturally black hair was accentuated by heavy make-up that Marilyn Manson would have been proud of.

For a few minutes she didn't say anything - just stared. Not able to look her in the eyes, my own wandered around like a child in front of an angry parent, anything to avoid eye contact. It was then that I noticed the four bin liners by the front door.

I moved towards her but as I drew near, instead of stopping I walked straight past, my nerves in shreds. As I walked into the kitchen I looked at the floor and saw that it was covered in an array of smashed china: dinner plates, saucers and much more. I felt a crunch under my foot and looked down to see I was standing on the broken handle of my prized cappuccino cup.

As I stumbled over the debris my shoes crunched on the shattered pieces which seemed to represent Andréa's anger. I carried on into the garden not knowing what to do or say but wishing, like I'd never wished before, that a hole would appear and I could leap into it.

My feet took me a few more paces before they gave way and I felt them crumple as I slid down onto the warm grass. Andréa had followed me out into the garden and now stood towering over me. Although I could feel her presence, I couldn't raise my head to look at her. I just could not find the balls to do it.

I heard her say, 'I am leaving.' The words hit me deeply, cutting and twisting their way into my mind as I digested their meaning.

I wanted to curl up and die.

CHAPTER TWENTY-ONE

The next thing I remembered was a cup of tea being lowered in front of my face. I took the handle and looked up to see Andréa. She slid down and sat cross-legged next to me.

'Thank you.' I felt full of shame. 'I'm so sorry, Andréa. I know I've been selfish, but please...I don't want you to leave, not like this. Not *for* this.'

'I do not want to leave but you have hurt me. I have done nothing wrong to you, Steve. *Why* after all we spoke of? Why could you not share any of this with me?'

How could I explain? No words *could* clarify my feelings or my confusion. I wanted to open up and tell her everything but the thought of that made me feel even weaker. 'I don't know.' I sighed. 'I just thought it wouldn't be this hard...I don't know.'

The silence that followed was broken only by birdsong. It was a beautiful, sunny day yet the two of us were covered in a cloud of doubt - or in my case - deceit.

'Tell me about your friends,' I heard her say quietly. 'Who are they? How many are there? How do you know them?'

'Two girls and a boy. I met them on holiday and we stayed in touch.' I let the words stumble out, but even as I spoke I imagined how I would have felt if it was her in my place.

She looked at the ground. It seemed that it was *she* who was looking for the answers now.

'Look, they go home tomorrow.' I pleaded. 'I'll see them for a little while and then come home. I promise.'

Perhaps she didn't hear the desire in my voice or else she was simply troubled by just one thought.

'You said two girls and one boy. This girl, did you get close to her?' I heard the tremor in her voice as her mind created the scene. She faced me, tears welling up in her eyes. 'Did you sleep with this girl - this German girl?'

'*No!*' I moved my hand towards hers in desperation. 'No, Andréa, I didn't. I just fell asleep there and woke in a mess. I'm so sorry. I let you down, but not like that.' I prayed she would ask no more. Prayed she would not ask if I had feelings or love for Susie. I had no idea what to say if she asked that.

She did not. She sat in silence, her hand holding mine while she continued to stare at the ground for some time, lost in her own thoughts. After what seemed aeons she finally spoke again.

'Please come home as you promise.'

Relief flowed through me. 'Of course,' I said, knowing that I would not, and *could* not let her down again. Her forgiveness made me feel guiltier than ever.

****

'I can only stay for a while, Susie.' I stood in Laurence's kitchen.

'Was she mad at you, Steve?' Susie seemed to be enjoying it.

'It's unfair,' I said firmly. 'Unfair on you, on me, on her, on everyone. I want to be here with you, but this isn't right.'

Susie pushed gently against my chest before taking hold of my hands.

'You are right, it is not fair but I cannot help it and you know it to be true. Steve, we are in love.'

I felt my stained heart cleanse a little and its voice speak through my lips. 'I know.'

The remainder of the time that we spent together became meaningless. The clock ticked and the hours were numbered. It had all happened so quickly and now the cracks had begun to form around us, opening up the void.

At dusk I took them back to the train station. I couldn't kiss her "goodbye" when the time came. I wished that I would never have to let her go, so not touching her seemed the best course of action.

I hugged Danni and Markus and bid them a safe journey. To Susie I could only whisper the words, 'See you soon.'

I watched as the train's wheels began to turn, taking a piece of my heart with them.

****

Andréa was waiting up when I got home. It wasn't late and she greeted me with a warm hug. After what I had put her through I deserved a punch in the face. We sat for a while and I told her briefly about the weekend. Once again I found myself lying at certain points where I feared things could get messy.

Lying beside her in bed she soon fell asleep while I continued to look up at the ceiling in the darkness. Things were going to be different now. Susie was gone but in my mind I could see her clearly. A long selection of pictures flashed before my eyes, a slideshow of the last seventy-two hours paraded itself, each snapshot releasing a different emotion. I had no idea how long I lay like that before the dream began.

****

The narrow passage was a place I knew. I felt for the wall on my right. Yes, it was there. I felt somehow as if I was awake within my own dream.

I walked with newfound confidence, as if the faith that had been buried within me for years had surfaced. Ahead I saw the door and I saw the light clearly whereas before I had only seen darkness until I had reached it. I felt an urgency surface. Not of fear but a new sensation. Suddenly I was aware. The door pushed open easily. Inside I saw a warm light glowing from a lamp which was hanging about thirty metres away from me. I walked towards it, slowing my pace as I got closer. Things were not the same as before. Caution crawled over me.

As I approached I saw that there was a figure standing to the left of the lamp. The silhouette became clearer with each step I took. It was a woman, dressed in black and she seemed to be tending a stall, a flower stall.

As I neared she looked at me as if she had been expecting me. Her face looked familiar; bunched up dark hair surrounded her pretty, kind face. Although I guessed she was in her mid-fifties, her features didn't give much away; she seemed almost ageless. She didn't look like the lady from the train station but there was something about her demeanour that made me feel that she was somehow connected with that night and that woman.

She smiled and I returned her smile but mine was more automatic than meaningful. There were many different types of flowers spread around her stall and it looked as if I had interrupted her at work. I waited a few moments before speaking and then whispered, 'Now I know who you are.'

'Do you? Then you'll know why I'm here.' Her voice was familiar.

I thought for a moment, noting that I still I had the ability to think. 'No, I don't.' I replied.

Her look sent a shudder down my spine.

'Time and numbers, they guide us all.' She whispered the words softly, as if to herself.

'Can you tell me more?' I asked.

'The fabric of us all is counted by time, by numbers. Days, years, age, birthdays, history, all judged by numbers. We all live by this law, even choosing our own favourite numbers.'

My mind flashed back to Spain and the gypsy woman. She had asked me my favourite number but what could this woman know of that? It seemed that somehow she did.

'What does my number mean? What does it tell you?'

'You have seen things that have passed or will come to pass;

three moments, you will know them when you see or feel them.'

I stood motionless, watching her arranging flowers, just as the lady at the station had done. I scanned my mind for answers trying to link the pieces together.

'Dreams... I have dreams,' I said cautiously.

She laughed. 'Of course you do – you're in one now, aren't you?'

I felt frightened, as if I had lost my grasp on reality. I searched for reason.

'If my dreams - or visions - or whatever the hell they are - have substance, tell me this,' I said impatiently. 'You say numbers have meaning and you know I chose three so tell me this...why do I have *four* in my dream then?'

She stopped moving her fingers and glanced away. 'You have three. If you think you have four, then the fourth will be through choice.'

'I don't get it, what do you mean three?' I said in a puzzled voice. 'How can you know that? I had four, I know what I had. There was no choice, it was what happened!'

She didn't answer immediately, instead she moved to the table and took two bunches of flowers and held them out to me. 'I know because you chose the number three, Steve. Remember?'

I held the flowers in my hands as her words sank in. I felt frozen in time; she knew my favourite number but not only that...I had also seen those flowers before.

They were on my parents' graves on the day of their funeral.

The realisation hit me. That was where I had seen her before. She was the lady that I had met on that day all those years ago. I wanted to speak but the words wouldn't come out.

And then I woke up.

****

If peace had come in my dreams it certainly hadn't in my life.

167

For a few days things appeared to return to normal, but Andréa and I were not as close as we had been before Susie's visit.

Then she made an announcement: 'Darling, we need to talk.'

My first thought was that it would be about the "German people" as she had referred to them in recent conversations. I prepared myself for her.

'Sure, Andréa.'

She took my hand. 'My visa runs out in December, Steve. We have to make a choice about things … about us.'

I was shocked. I hadn't even thought about that at all. It had never crossed my mind nor had we even talked about it.

'What does that mean?'

'It means exactly what I say,' she said coldly in answer to my question. 'We have to decide our future. If I am to remain here in England, it would mean we would need to discuss a way.'

'Fine,' I said. 'Tell me a way and we can look at it.'

'We would need to be married.' It was obvious from her expression that she was irritated by my lack of awareness.

Her words created a vacuum of silence. Danger signs flashed in front of my eyes as I suddenly saw Andréa in a different light. Married? I weighed up the girl who stood before me. She had put on weight recently - maybe a stone or so - it was hard to tell. I couldn't see the beauty that I had observed just a few months before. I suddenly saw someone who wanted to live in the UK and me being the best answer to her problems. My cynical mind took over. No wonder she was so relaxed about the Germans! Everything we had shared had been replaced with suspicion.

Just then we were interrupted by the front doorbell and I almost ran past Andréa to get to the door in an attempt to gain some breathing space.

'Oh, hi, Roz,' I greeted my neighbour with a distinct lack of interest.

'Hello, Steve, is Andréa in?' Roz smiled, obviously in

control of her hearing aid for a change.

'Sure, come in.' She followed me, humming, into the kitchen where Andréa smiled awkwardly at her.

'Hello, Roz. How are you?'

'Ooh, I'm good, my dear,' Roz beamed. 'Just checking that it's still alright for our little lunch tomorrow, that's all.'

'Of course,' Andréa smiled. 'I am looking forward to it.'

I watched silently as Roz studied my framed picture of the flowers I had brought back from Spain.

'That's nice, Andréa,' she commented.

'That was not me,' she said, glancing at me coldly. 'It is Steve's, from before he met me.'

'Oh,' Roz looked at me. 'Very nice… oleander, osmunda and palm… beware spiritual dreams.'

'Excuse me?' I said, remembering the gypsy. Roz knew the plants alright but I didn't understand the rest.

The old lady chuckled quietly. 'The plants, Steve, what they represent. Oleander means "beware", osmunda "to dream" - or "dreams" while palm is for spirituality. You didn't know that?'

'No.' My pulse raced. Beware! The meaning grew as her words sank in.

'Oh well,' Roz laughed. 'Now you do. See you tomorrow, dear.' I was sure she winked and then she was gone, leaving just me and Andréa standing in awkward silence.

'I need to think about it, Andréa.' The hesitancy in my voice was apparent. The word *beware* invaded my thinking and my mind whirred.

'Then think!' Her face was filled with anger and hurt and as if reading my mind she said, 'You don't have to worry. I would not marry you just to stay here.'

Guilt overtook suspicion so I said nothing.

****

I needed advice. A new lesson was about to be taught to me.

To seek advice on matters of the heart is to seek further confusion. Each answer made it harder to see what I should really do. Follow my own feelings.

'Definite trouble, dude. She's after one thing only - a passport,' Laurence advised.

'I'm not sure, bruv.' Sharon was doubtful. Her uncertainty could have been caused by the drugs so I ignored her opinion for the time being.

'I like her, Steve,' said Harry, 'but, like I said before, only you can decide and the visa is really the least of your problems. It's whether you want to be with her or Susie.'

His advice seemed to hold the most truth.

'How the hell do I know? I don't know her, mate, but it does seem a bit dodgy,' Ray spoke over the phone and threw Harry's words back into the wind.

'You can't ask me, Steve, I never even met the girl.' Pat was more matter of fact about it.

More advice was needed so I decided to seek that of the older, wiser generation. My grandmother would surely be able to help.

'Granny, may I ask some advice, please?'

'Of course, Michael,' was her reply as I sat down beside her with the usual cup of tea, while she prepared to listen.

'It's Steve, Granny, not Michael,' I said, softly but firmly. This kind of thing was happening more and more frequently and was beginning to annoy me. She was forgetting names and places and everything around her seemed to be more hazy.

'Sorry, Boy.' She focused her attention on me and seemed to have lost the earlier image of my father.

'What would you like to ask?'

I took a deep breath. 'Andréa can't live in England after December. She's got a visa, Granny and you know what that means. It means we have to marry or separate.'

'I know what a visa is, Boy. My Cyril needed one in the war,' she said curtly.

I failed to see how that could be compared with the world

we live in today and she must have seen the doubt.

'Well, it's simple,' she continued. 'Do you love her? Do you want to spend the rest of your life with her or do you still care for that damned German girl?'

Dear Granny! Straight questions laced with answers. She knew I still cared for Susie, of course she did, and she probably knew I did not love Andréa enough to give her my love forever.

'Thank you, Granny. I need to think about that.'

My grandmother leant forward. 'No you don't, Boy. If you need to think then you've already answered. You just need to realise it yourself.'

The last person I asked was Roz. I knew she liked Andréa; she might be able to put things into perspective.

'My advice is to ask yourself and not others,' was her simple opinion.

Terrific, I thought. 'Thanks, Roz.'

'I've one piece of advice, though, that may serve you better,' she added.

'Thanks and what's that?' Perhaps it would actually help me a little.

'Watch out for your grandmother.'

'I will. Thanks.' I wondered about that woman sometimes. She seemed so worldly, yet sometimes her behaviour was quite bizarre. She either knew a lot or was leaning on the side of insanity. As I looked at her I sided with the first view.

I would watch out for Granny. She hadn't been herself lately.

****

I once heard that the worst vice is advice. For me that cliché seemed truer then ever. Confusion still reigned within after seeking the damned stuff. Andréa tried hard to act normally around me but of course the subject of the visa and our future was on the surface of both our minds. Meanwhile, like a snake I slithered around, when she wasn't at home, emailing Susie.

I didn't discuss my dilemma about the visa with her because it felt like a breach of my loyalty to Andréa and would probably influence me further.

As July approached I found myself looking forward to Ray's return and a welcome respite from it all.

I had decisions to make, dreams to unravel and destiny to follow.

It seemed time was running out.

CHAPTER TWENTY-TWO

If I'd had problems with myself before all this happened, then they just seemed to grow as each day went by. I found myself being more critical of Andréa. Little things would make me impatient with her. I could feel myself rejecting her, trying to force her to leave, without actually saying it. If I was the man who had been trying to find his inner self, then the man I had found was one I was beginning to detest. I had searched everywhere for answers, but I was still a mess.

The following Saturday was the Knebworth Festival and I tried to put thoughts of Andréa and visas to the back of my mind and look forward to meeting up with Ray. As he was in London in the days leading up to the concert, I'd arranged to get the train up to the flat that he rented in Poplar. From there I would ride pillion on his bike down to Knebworth. Ray was taking his small two-man tent for us to sleep in so that we could party the weekend away without moving from the venue.

I returned home on Thursday evening to find Andréa slouched on the sofa. My growing frustration made me feel irritated that she seemed to have it all so easy.

'Hi, looks like another busy day then, Andréa.' My voice was laced with sarcasm. 'Anything actually *happened* while I've been at work?'

She twisted her head towards me seemingly oblivious to my tone.

'Not really, darling.' Her head turned back towards the television.

Great! I turned to leave the room.

'Oh, darling, there is one thing,' she turned to look at me again. 'A lady called and booked an appointment for computers, I took down the details for you - they are on the breakfast bar.'

'Thanks,' I said, still feeling annoyed with her for having such a relaxed way about her; didn't she realise the pressure we were under?

I picked up the note and read Andréa's writing, noting the details. The lady lived in Great Holland. Eight computers - Saturday morning. With a surge of anger I stormed into the lounge.

'Andréa, this job, do you know what day you booked it for?' I didn't give her time to respond. 'Bloody *Saturday*! That's the day I'm going to Knebworth!'

I half expected an apology or some sign of regret but she responded calmly.

'I know what day, Steve. The lady said that was the only day she would be there and she would pay you well. I thought you would be pleased.'

I was beginning to feel really angry now.

'How can I do the bloody job on Saturday if I'm going to Knebworth, Andréa?' I shouted. Now it was her turn to be sarcastic.

'That is why I wrote *morning* on the note.'

'Well, it can't happen.' I said furiously. 'Where's her number? I'll call and let her know my girlfriend's a little slow.'

At last I saw some kind of remorse in her eyes, whether it was because of my insult or regret, I couldn't be sure.

'I did not take the number,' she said slowly.

'What a crock of shit, Andréa.' I glared at her, stopping myself from screaming because it would be pointless.

I went out into the garden for a cigarette and some breathing space and after a while I calmed down a little. The thing was it did *sound* like a good job but it could take some time. Time I didn't want to lose.

I decided that I would have a word with Ray and tell him what had happened. Then, if he was alright with it, I would go to the job early and then drive to Knebworth. At least that way I wouldn't miss out and if the woman wasn't up that early then I would bloody wake her up.

Ray was good as gold when I explained what had happened. I didn't tell him how angry I had been with Andréa. She didn't deserve that. After all, she had only been trying to help. I felt better after I had spoken to him and went back into the lounge.

'It's all sorted out,' I said, kissing her on the cheek as she lay on the sofa. 'I'll go to the job and then drive to see Ray.'

'Good,' she said quietly but I noticed that there were tears in her eyes.

****

I woke up early on Saturday and prepared myself for the weekend ahead. After packing my case of computer tools and software I went about the business of selecting some clothes. Although it was a warm, sunny morning I added a couple of jumpers and a waterproof just in case it rained.

I left at half past seven, leaving Andréa still asleep and headed slowly over to Great Holland. The village, a pleasant suburb of Holland On Sea with a rural feeling about it, was not large - perhaps four thousand or so inhabitants. The houses were notoriously expensive and, in the main, huge. I was pretty sure that this lady's house would be no exception, especially as she had eight computers that she wanted me to look at. It could be a good earner.

The address I had been given was in a small lane off the main road which approached the village. As my car bumped along the unmade track, I noticed a big farmhouse on the left surrounded by fields stretching as far as the eye could see. There was only one other house, right at the end of the lane so I guessed that it must be the one.

As I pulled up outside I saw that it was the number that Andréa had given me but the windows were boarded and the house didn't look lived in. In fact it looked totally deserted and derelict. I walked to the door and banged loudly. No one answered. I fumbled in my pocket for the note to check the address again.

'Can I help you?' I heard a voice behind me.

Turning around I saw a tall, well built man. He was wearing Wellington boots and jeans and a jumper that seemed heavy for the time of year.

'Hello,' I said, 'I'm trying to find the owner of this place. I was given this address for a job.'

'Nobody lives here and hasn't done for a few years.' He looked surprised and added, 'I live in the farmhouse and as far as I know, this place is going to be condemned.'

'Sorry, it must be a mistake with the address. I'll call the lady,' I said, feeling a bit foolish.

I drove back home cursing all the way. The job had sounded too good to be true and now I had nothing. I would give that Andréa a mouthful when I got back.

She was awake when I arrived home.

'Nice one,' I snarled. 'Turns out the job you gave me was at a derelict house. Nice one.'

'It was the right address. I did not make a mistake. That was the address she gave me.' She glared at me.

I was in no mood for an argument. 'Okay, Andréa,' I said, taking a deep breath, 'I'm going to try and catch Ray and forget about the whole mess.'

I called Ray on his mobile but it was switched off which meant he must be on his way. There was nothing for it, I would have to drive there and call him when I arrived. I gave her a peck on the cheek as I left the house but the atmosphere was stone cold.

The journey would normally have taken me about two and a half hours but today, with the build-up of traffic around the concert, it took over four. As I waited in the massive parking queues I tried to call Ray again but there was still no answer. With the speed he drove he should have been there by now. Once I was parked I'd try to find him in the crowd. I'd heard that the year before there had been something like a hundred and fifty thousand people every day at Knebworth and, judging by the gridlock of people around me, it looked like it could be even bigger this year.

It took nearly an hour to park the car and with the sun beating down on my head I wandered towards the main entrance. There were stalls set up around the perimeter, offering everything from beers and soft drinks to food and souvenirs. The concert was already in full flow and I checked down the list of bands that would be playing. It looked like it was going to be a good day.

With still no sign of Ray, I had to buy a ticket which proved more difficult than I had imagined. The only option was to buy from a tout who did me the favour of selling me a ticket at three times the face value while at the same time, telling me I'd got a good deal. When I finally caught up with Ray perhaps I would suggest that we could become touts for a while to claw back some of that money.

Once inside, I went about the task of getting a beer which, because of the number of people, took a long time. With the drink in my hand, I found myself a good spot about three hundred metres back from the main stage. It was impossible to get much nearer but because the organisers had put up massive screens all around, you could see the action from pretty much anywhere. I called Ray again but his phone was still switched off.

I tried his number again between each band. I was getting a bit worried, time was moving on and it would soon be early evening. I decided to have one last beer and then if I still couldn't contact him, I'd think about driving home. I didn't fancy a night hunched up in my little car.

The music was excellent and I found myself swaying to the beats of some great bands. As dusk became dark, I still kept trying to call Ray but to no avail until finally I gave up until as the last band played out to a massive standing ovation, it finally occurred to me to call home. Andréa would be at work, but if the answering machine was on I could check to see if he had left me a message. It just wasn't like Ray to blow somebody out without a good reason. It wasn't his style at all.

Feeling uneasy, I dialled my number and waited for the machine to cut in. Only one message, it had to be Ray.

'Steve. Are you there? Steve?' It wasn't Ray's voice. It was his mum's.

'Please pray for him. We must all pray for him.' The voice was choked with emotion. My heart froze as I listened.

'Steve, Ray has had an accident on his bike. He's in Stevenage hospital. Please tell the others you know and pray for him.' As the message ended all I heard was her sobbing.

'Oh, God,' I said the words out loud.

Pushing my way through the crowd, I ran to my car and set off for the hospital immediately. Stevenage could only be a few miles from Knebworth but it took me nearly an hour to get out of the car park.

My mind was filled with thoughts of Ray. He must have almost been at the festival when it happened.

I kept repeating to myself, *please Ray. Be alright.*

****

'No, I'm not family but if you want to call this number they will verify that I'm a close family friend – his *best* friend, in fact.' I stood in the hospital reception trying to explain to the receptionist who I was. Trying my utmost to remain calm with the girl who was just trying to do her job. Knowing his parents would be on the way now, I persuaded her to call Ray's mother on her mobile. She confirmed what I had said and the receptionist then pointed me in the direction of the intensive care unit.

When I reached the ward a short man approached me who introduced himself as Doctor Zamir. 'I understand you are a close family friend, Mr. Bidante,' he paused. 'I am afraid the news is grave.'

'How bad, doctor?' I heard myself say, feeling like I was in a television drama.

The doctor paused. 'Ray is in a critical condition - but he's alive. The motorcyclist he collided with died instantly at the scene.'

'That's terrible.' My voice sounded strange to my own ears.

'From what we can gather,' he continued, 'the two motorcycles collided head-on. They were both riding on the white lines at around eighty miles an hour. You can imagine the impact and result.' His expression said everything.

'So.... how's Ray? What....' I wasn't sure what I was saying but no doubt the doctor was used to dealing with people in shock.

'I will give you an idea of what you are about to see. Up till now, Ray has had six litres of blood transfused into his body as a result of the repeated loss of blood. As you may know, the average amount for a man of your friend's size is approximately five and a half litres so the severity of his blood loss is of major concern. He has shattered the left side of his body but more importantly, despite the crash helmet, his head suffered a massive blow. We can't be sure of the long term damage at the moment.'

'Oh, God,' I repeated.

'I wish I could give you and his family better news but at the moment all we can do is wait and see and I can assure you we are doing all we can.'

'What are his chances, doctor?' I didn't want to ask, yet I *had* to. My voice quivered as I spoke.

He didn't speak for a few seconds as if weighing up what he was going to say. 'We're running tests - when we get the results we'll take it from there. We may have to operate.' His voice sounded vague, as if he didn't know the answers himself.

I wanted to swallow but it was as if the saliva had dried in my throat. I tried to remain calm but inside it felt as if a jelly-like substance had been released into my mind and body.

'Thank you, doctor,' I said, while sterilising my hands with pure alcohol from the dispenser above the washbasin in order to prepare myself for visiting Ray.

He nodded, swinging open the doors with me following behind him. There were only five beds in the ward and each one contained a person who seemed to be either clinging to life, or recovering from the worst of their own tragedy. I felt like a god myself with my fully functioning body as I trailed behind the saviour of lives who led the way.

As we took each step across the scrupulously clean and shiny floor I could feel Ray coming nearer, but when the doctor stopped next to one of the beds I wondered why he had. The person in the bed couldn't be my best friend.

He spoke quietly to the nurse who was attending the bed before nodding at me and walking away. I stared at the body in the bed until gradually I saw what I didn't want to believe, that it *could* be Ray.

A metal frame that looked as if it had been constructed from a vast Meccano set, covered a skull that looked far too big to be Ray's. His head was half that size, wasn't it? He lay limp and broken, covered by snowy white sheets and there were more pieces of metal surrounding the left side of his body. I still couldn't believe that it was him.

I moved closer, peering carefully, as if scared that the body would wake up and jump at me. When I looked more closely I saw that his head had been shaved and that it was definitely Ray. It was his features but where was his body? He looked so small.

'He's heavily sedated. I'm sure the doctor's briefed you.' The nurse spoke quietly.

I nodded. 'Is it okay to sit here?' I whispered.

'Of course – but please don't touch him.' Her voice was filled with compassion.

I pulled up a chair and sat as close to him as possible. Tubes attached to an array of bottles filled with blood and fluid and God knows what, were poking from him. The more I looked the more wires and metal I saw. Could this really be my friend Ray Skee? The powerful fireman who saved lives and lived without fear?

'Ray, talk to me.'

Of course he didn't respond. I felt sick inside. What could I say? I decided to just keep talking anyway.

'Ray, I can't believe this,' I said. 'I can't fucking believe this. You're my friend, my best friend. Please wake up. Wake up, Ray.' But he lay silent and motionless seemingly oblivious to my pleas.

I bowed my head over the bed, careful not to touch him, and felt the tears begin to come. They pattered onto the sheets as I was overcome by sadness. I hadn't known that I had that many tears to shed. I was consumed by my sorrow. Never in my adult life had I felt as completely shattered as I watched my friend clutching onto the last strands of life.

I stayed like this until the nurse came over and asked me to leave.

'They're going to operate,' she said, confirming what the doctor had told me earlier.

Leaning over Ray, I kissed him gently on his cheek, trying to stem my tears as I did so. The nurse took hold of my hand and led me out of the intensive care unit, whispering words of comfort as we walked. But I had no words to reply because I was shaking from the aftermath of my tears. All we could do now was to wait and pray.

CHAPTER TWENTY-THREE

When Ray's parents, June and Alfred, arrived, the doctor explained the situation to them and told them that their son was about to be taken down to the operating theatre. We hugged tightly, trying to draw comfort from each other. They were, naturally, both deeply shocked that their son was facing death. The waiting room couldn't have been more aptly named.

I felt as if I was being suffocated by grief and emotion and after a little while left the room and went in search of the hospital chapel. Alone, I prayed for Ray. I prayed he would live and I prayed forgiveness for him. I prayed for all the good he had done. For all the lives he had saved. I prayed for his family who should not have to see their son on the edge of life. I prayed for God to show mercy. But my prayers were in vain.

Ray's parents never saw their son alive again.

I was the last person to touch his skin, to kiss him while he was alive. At four thirty in the morning, a massive brain haemorrhage claimed the life of that wonderful human being who was Ray Skee.

****

I must have been dozing and when I awoke events seemed to be unfolding in slow motion. I heard the doctor talking to June and Alfred followed by sobbing and wailing. I felt numb, unable to comprehend, as if I was not yet awake, and then…I saw Pat Reilly. He walked into the room at a snail's pace and I lifted my head to look at him. His shirt was covered with sweat, his eyes carried a glazed sense of madness within them.

He was still ten steps from me but I saw, rather than heard, the words drop from his mouth in big, bold capitals. **'RAY IS DEAD.'**

I held out my arms to him and he came to me. I didn't hear what he was saying, I just hugged him and sobbed like I had never done before. The blow ripped my soul apart and left me feeling exposed and vulnerable to the tragedy that this world could bring.

'I couldn't save him. I couldn't save him,' I heard Pat say between my sobs. Desperate words that magnified the tragedy when I realised that it had been he who had been given the last chance to save Ray. The irony was absolute and obsolete. Emotions ran riot.

When I next became aware of my surroundings, it was to see Pat standing nearby, holding Ray's parents. Although I found myself crouched on the floor, I felt neither embarrassment nor the need to apologise. As I rose slowly to my feet I wiped my eyes on my sleeve which was already drenched with sweat and tears. I tried not to think for a minute or two, wanting to believe that it wasn't real but I knew, like I guessed they all did, that there were moments when you couldn't hide. One thought triggered the gun inside and fired bullets of emotion again.

Ray Skee's death hurt as much as anything I had ever experienced in my adult life and reawakened inside me the deathly ghosts of my parent's death. I knew that I would never forget him and while we all kept remembering, his memory would live on - and my memories of Ray were vast and beautiful. I had loved that man.

****

One week and many sad moments later, Ray's funeral took place at the chapel near my house. I hadn't walked through those arched doors for many years and now it was to witness the burial of a man who had died too soon.

Mourners – family and friends streamed into the chapel. Ray's coffin was carried in by six of his colleagues from the brigade whilst the remaining members formed a guard of honour. I was waiting outside with Andréa and my grandmother when Laurence, Harry and Sharon arrived. No words could help us to understand why it had happened. It seemed that we could make no sense of anything. Nothing seemed real.

I saw Pat walk towards me accompanied by his elderly parents. I tried to raise a smile but as he came nearer I saw that his eyes reflected the pain that was in my own. Mr. and Mrs. Reilly nodded before seeking out June and Alfred and embracing them wordlessly.

Pat came closer to me. 'I failed Steve. I failed,' he whispered, his voice filled with emotion. 'I should have done more.'

I felt his pain. 'No, Pat, you did your best, please believe that.'

As he took a step back I saw that he was a broken man; that he had been as much, if not more, affected by the tragedy than anybody.

I tried to find the words to console him but failed and, looking at him, endeavoured to send him a telepathic message:

'Everything is for a reason,' I wanted to say.

****

Ray hadn't left any special requests of course, because he couldn't have had any idea that his life would be cut short. His parents had given the priest details of Ray's life which he handled with dignity and respect. June and Alfred had given me the job of writing a few words on behalf of us all and as the priest signalled to me, I fought back my tears and walked tentatively to the front of the chapel and stood so that I was facing the crowd of mourners.

Clearing my throat, I began speaking the words that I had written:

I stand before you today to dedicate a few words.
It is with a heart full of strife that I speak of a lost son and a lost friend.
We will all need time to let our hearts heal and our faith grow once more
For Ray Skee was stolen from us in the most tragic of circumstances.
He was a giant of a man with a gentle smile who loved life and saved lives.
I loved him dearly as did all of you.
Today we feel the bitter loss of a loved one taken.
But today we must believe whilst remembering
Angels came and took him under their wings,
And now he belongs in a safer place.
We are all left here to bear the sad scars.
I say on behalf of us all, Ray,
You were the best. I - we - will treasure you in our memories.
We will never forget you.

The sound of throats clearing from some and gentle sobbing from others broke the silence that followed before a few hands offered gentle applause. As I walked back to my seat I felt nothing until, as I drew level with them, I saw the sadness and appreciation in Harry's and Sharon's eyes. Harry just nodded but Sharon whispered. 'That was lovely, bruv.'

Then we all walked across the road for the burial which was close to where my parents had been laid to rest. I felt numb as I watched the last part of Ray slowly drop into the earth.

I would never see Ray Skee's smiling face again.

****

Many hours and many drinks later, I lay next to Andréa who

was asleep in her own pain free place. The dreams returned that night; brought on by the uneasy drink-induced sleep and I dreamt, in vivid detail, that same recurring dream.

I knew which way to go and what to expect and I sat in the seat and waited for the images to appear. This time I would try to see more because I was aware that each time I felt more awake or as if I was more conscious of my surroundings.

I saw the funeral and the images of the two people and the girl all with the same clarity as before, offering me nothing new to cling to. Yet one image was missing.

When I awoke I was sweating profusely with a realisation that had not occurred to me before. The person I had seen leaning over the bed was me. It was me leaning over the body of Ray.

I sat bolt upright as another terrible realisation dawned on me. I looked at Andréa, her face gently lit by strips of moonlight blinking through the slatted blind.

The phone call about the computer job on that Saturday morning.

The house where no one had been. It had been the right house after all.

Oh God.

I would have - *should* have been on that bike.

CHAPTER TWENTY-FOUR

The month of July was filled with pain. While I tried to make sense of Ray's death, Andréa and I seemed to become more and more distant with each other. The division grew as we struggled to come to terms with the alien scenario we were in. As the month neared its end things came to a head. It was to become a day that would be etched on my mind forever.

The day began normally enough. A little bit of work followed by lunch with Sharon and more talk of what I should do regarding Andréa and the visa. I was becoming sick of the whole subject, snapping at anyone who tried to push me into doing "the right thing".

When I arrived home in the early evening Andréa was in the kitchen cooking. I went into the lounge and saw that she had put cushions around the large circular coffee table, presumably so we could sit and eat Japanese-style. There were candles dotted about the room giving it a warm glow.

'Darling, dinner will be soon,' she called. 'Can you get ready please?' She sounded happy.

As I walked into the kitchen I smelt something really good cooking. Andréa was standing over the stove, stirring something in the wok and humming happily to herself. She had her hair pulled up in a ponytail and had made the effort to put on some make-up. It was the prettiest I had seen her looking for a long time.

'You look lovely, Andréa.' I kissed her on her cheek and wrapped my arm around her waist, pulling her close. 'Really lovely.'

She rewarded me with a big smile and a kiss but all she said was, 'Hurry, sweetheart – dinner is almost ready.'

Soon we were sitting on the cushions around the table where

she served up a delicious combination of beef and pasta in a sauce that was indescribably good. The warm glow of candlelight made the moment feel special yet we said little as we ate. When we had finished she poured some more wine into my glass and motioned me to stay seated.

'I have something for you,' she whispered.

I lit a cigarette and waited. A moment later she returned with an envelope which she handed to me before dropping back down onto the cushion beside me.

'Thank you.' I opened it carefully noticing that she was watching me as I did so. A piece of paper fluttered face down onto the table. I turned the page over immediately recognising what it was.

I felt my heart race as I scanned the page, looking for the details. They leapt out at me:

July the twenty-ninth, Stansted to Prague. Return date - none.

A one-way ticket!

I looked up at Andréa. She continued to sip her wine, holding my gaze. The glow of the candles appeared to spread around her and sitting opposite me, she looked almost angelic.

'I don't understand, Andréa. We haven't spoken about this for….'

'Steve, we both know why,' she interrupted. 'I have just made the choice easier for you. Now, at least you will know I did not want to be in England for a visa.' Her face softened and became sad as she added softly, 'I was only ever going to be with you because I love you with all my heart.'

The sense of loss felt vast. I'd been so busy making my choice I'd been ignorant of Andréa's feelings. Of what she had had to face when making *her* decision. I'd searched for answers everywhere except from the one person who really counted. As she spoke of her love for me I realised I had made a major choice in my life that could not be undone.

'I'm so sorry, Andréa, so sorry.' The child with no fear of emotion, no barriers around his heart awoke. The realisation caused a sickening sensation in my stomach. I moved towards her and we held each other tightly.

'So am I, darling.' She wept now as did I. The frustration and pain we both felt was released in the agony of our tears. We held each other tight, cuddling together until we could cry no more. I sensed overwhelmingly, that this would be one of our last embraces. Perhaps I could have begged or offered to change but something deep inside shut out any possible avenue of reconciliation. My soul felt trapped and my heart surrendered love at that moment.

****

I've been told that when people are terminally ill, their loved ones often notice that they see a vast improvement during the final days, before the cruel arm of death reaches out and takes them from this world. To compare our situation to this would be wrong because no one was about to die, but even so it felt as if a part of each of us was dying. The last few weeks we spent together gave us more moments of pleasure and love than many people experience in a lifetime.

We were so happy during that last week and behaved like children, never leaving each other's sides. Day and night our time was dedicated to each other as if it was our last hours on earth and in a sense it was - as a couple at least.

When the day finally came I woke up with a heavy heart not wanting to get out of bed. Andréa was already awake and dressed and, as I went for a shower, I noticed that her luggage was standing by the front door. A sickening feeling in my stomach brought tears to the surface as I ran a shower and cried along with the water that fell on me.

Her flight was early afternoon so we left around midday. As we drove onto the dual carriageway I realised we had not spoken all morning.

'Are you okay, Andréa?' I glanced at her, sliding my hand onto her lap, but she pushed it away from her.

'Don't do that,' she replied. 'I am fine, just drive.'

We didn't speak again. The pain of her rejection stabbed at my insides but it was probably nothing compared to the rejection I had shown her. I turned the music up as if to put distance between us.

At the airport I pushed the trolley piled with her luggage to the check-in desk and waited while she completed the formalities before following her immediately to the departure gate.

'Andréa.'

She was standing in a long queue of people waiting to go through passport control. She turned to look at me and I saw emptiness in her eyes. No smile, no tears, nothing.

'Have a safe journey,' I mumbled feeling sick inside.

I went to hug her, but once again she pushed me away. People were watching us and I felt slightly embarrassed.

'Andréa. Please,' I begged.

'Goodbye, Steve,' she said abruptly.

'Goodbye.' As I turned to walk away I heard her say something and looked back in the hope that she had softened, that we could hug, kiss, even cry. Anything except parting like this. Her last look was filled with pain. All the love we had exchanged had been replaced with pain. A pain that was of my making, not hers. All she had wanted to do was to love me.

I watched as she turned away and walked out of my life forever without so much as a fight. I doubt she would have listened to me anyway. Why should she? The man she had trusted had not had the courage to do the same. In order to protect myself, I had made a sacrifice. Andréa.

The drive home was filled with reflection and emotion. As I walked into the house the shadows of her presence surrounded me. Silence echoed where there had been voices and as I wandered aimlessly from room to room, I remembered all the things we had done together. How could anyone, after the way I had behaved, understand the sadness I now felt. In fact most people would probably be thinking that I was glad to have escaped her visa clutching fingers.

It was a warm evening and I sat alone in the garden, holding the coin she had given me. The memories of that night raced around in my head and now all I had was a piece of metal. The coin that had become a symbol of *her*. She had given it to me because she had truly believed we were going to be together forever. I had accepted it and, by so doing, confirmed what she was saying. Yet I had failed. I had given in to temptation and doubt. My stomach turned somersaults as my soul was filled with that truth.

Eventually tiredness took over, I could no longer function properly and my feet carried me into the bedroom. As I got undressed and climbed into bed I realised that it had been only last night that she had slept by my side. She never would again. The reality of the situation made me feel wretched. I had never wanted to hurt her - to hurt anyone. Yet that is exactly what I had done.

In my quest for love, for happiness, for my angel, I had hurt the one person that I loved the most. If this was what it cost I wanted to give up right now. I should live alone without giving pain to anyone except myself. It was all I deserved. My wretched lonely heart.

'Andréa,' I sobbed into the pillow. 'I am so sorry.'

CHAPTER TWENTY-FIVE

I received one last text message from Andréa to say that she had arrived safely and not to contact her. I seemed to be living in a void.

I had emailed Susie to tell her about Ray's death. She was, of course, shocked and sad but I didn't want to speak to her - not yet. It all seemed too soon; the wounds inflicted by my parting from Andréa were still raw. Part of the reason I had lost Andréa was because of Susie's visit. In truth I could not pass blame on to Susie because it was not her, but *me* that had done the betraying. My bitterness towards her was simply a reflection of my own heart.

However, my main concern had nothing to do with my love life. It was for my grandmother's health. As I had time on my hands, I decided to spend more time with her. Perhaps I had taken Roz's advice on board.

In the past months, I'd continued to notice small changes in Granny. Her forgetfulness with names or the incorrect use of them was now added to by her inability to remember the time. Perfect timekeeping had always been one of her idiosyncrasies but I'd picked up on more worrying changes in her behaviour.

She referred to my grandfather more and more frequently. If she didn't call me by his name, or my father's, then she would mumble about chats she'd had with him and how close they were. It was as if he had never died and had now returned from the war.

I considered talking to her doctor about it, but decided against it for the time being. I would monitor the situation for a bit longer to try to get to the bottom of it. I had to accept that Granny wasn't young anymore and that she needed to lean on me now.

Soon the last warmth of summer departed and autumn returned and golden orange leaves fell on the streets as the days became colder. One morning, during the first week of September, I was awoken in the early hours of the morning by a phone call from my grandmother. She was in a terrible state.

'Boy! Boy! I need your help! He's gone! I'm sure he's gone for good!' Her voice was crazed, as if she had gone a little mad.

I looked at the clock by my bed. It was four o'clock.

Although I was alarmed by her panic, I tried to sound as if I was composed. 'Granny, calm down. I'll be round in ten minutes.'

'Hurry, we have to find him,' she said before the line went dead.

I stumbled out of bed and slipped on some clothes while all the time my mind was trying to make sense of what was going on. I drove quickly through the empty streets and as I pulled up outside her house I saw that the front door was wide open. Although it was still dark there were no lights on in the house. As I approached the door I saw a dark shape in the soft glow of the street light.

It was my grandmother. She sat huddled on the small patch of lawn that ran along the left-hand side of the house. I ran towards her and knelt by her side. 'Granny, it's Steve. Are you alright?'

She was shaking uncontrollably and her face was as white as snow. When she looked at me her eyes were expressionless.

'Cyril?' she muttered.

'No, Granny. It's Steve,' I repeated. 'Come on, let me help you up. It's cold out here.'

She didn't resist when I gently lifted her up. In fact she was quite limp and I could feel her trembling. I wanted to cry. I felt so scared for her.

I guided her back into the house, holding her hand and supporting her waist with my free arm and gently sat her down in her armchair in the lounge.

'Would you like a cup of tea, Granny?' It was her medicine for everything – perhaps it would help her.

'Oh yes, Steve. That's just what I need.' She seemed more aware.

I hoped that my theory that a cup of tea would help would still hold true. If there was one thing still normal about my grandmother it was that tea was the answer to all problems. After flicking the kettle on and getting everything ready, I put my head around the door to see if she was okay. She was sitting with her head in her hands, rocking back and forth mumbling to herself. I knew then that something was seriously wrong with her.

'Here you are, Granny.' I held the cup out to her

She stopped rocking briefly while she took the tea. 'Thank you, Boy, you are a good boy.'

I sat in my usual seat and waited for her to drink her tea and calm herself. I didn't know what else to do.

'I think he has gone for good, you know,' she suddenly said after a few minutes of silence.

'Who has, Granny?'

She looked at me as if I was the one who was confused. 'Who? Cyril, of course! Who do you think?'

I absorbed her reply and tried to think of an answer. I didn't want to upset her more than she was already.

'But Granddad is dead. You know that, don't you?' I spoke as gently as I could, scared of the effect the words would have on her.

'Of course I know he's dead!'

Her answer took me by surprise. What the hell was going on?

'I don't understand, Granny,' I said.

She reached down and put her tea on the table and suddenly she seemed completely normal once more.

'Remember I told you I sometimes get messages from Cyril?'

I nodded.

'Well, for a while now he's been closer than ever. I've even *seen* him. Before you think I'm mad I *know* he's dead but only in this world. I know he's somewhere else but he still speaks with me because I've heard and seen him. Do you understand?'

Again I nodded. I didn't understand but she looked so genuine and I had never heard her tell a lie.

'He told me more of his story,' she continued. 'He told me of his last days and also he helped me to understand why he left this world. I used to see him often and it was so lovely, Steve, but now he's gone. His voice grew quieter each day until I couldn't hear anything anymore.'

I watched as my grandmother reached for a tissue and wiped her eyes. The emotion was definitely real and whether or not I believed in her was irrelevant, because it was apparent that she believed herself in what she was saying.

'Perhaps he's only gone for a while, Granny. Why don't you tell me what he said to you while he was here?' I wanted to try to stop her from crying again.

My tactic worked and she seemed to calm down again.

'Would you like to know what I've found out about how he died?' she asked.

'Very much,' I said, intrigued.

'Well, as you know, when Cyril served in the war, he was sent to the Sudetenland under the command of Captain Doug Gardiner. Their instructions were to decrypt highly important documents. They found plenty of deserted places to work from where they could hide during the day and work through the night. Their task was made easier by the help they received from some of the women and children. One of these women would slip food and supplies and any information that she received to them whenever she could. She took risks every day to help them while putting her own life at risk.'

My grandmother paused and took a breath as if she was trying to compose herself again. 'The house was on the edge of the village and Cyril and Doug would sleep in the cellar during the day. Some of the other women and children lived, squashed together, upstairs. It seems that one lady – her name was Helena – helped the most. She had a small child and had no need to help but she, like all the women, knew who the enemy were, so they did their best. Sadly, somehow they were betrayed, and the Germans came.'

'What? To the house?' I asked.

'Yes, early one evening. My Cyril and Doug were woken to the sounds of screaming and panic upstairs. Doug crept up from the cellar and saw several women being dragged outside with their children until only Helena and her child remained. They interrogated her, beat her and threatened her. Doug whispered instructions to Cyril and they made their move. In an instant they leapt from the cellar and challenged the German soldiers. What followed was death.'

'Go on, Granny,' I urged her, although she was looking more and more frail by the minute.

'Doug engaged the first German in hand-to-hand combat, taking him by surprise but, before he finished him off, a bullet from another soldier hit him, ending his life. Cyril fired from the top of the stairs, killing that soldier before spinning to hit and kill the third soldier. He then went to Doug and tried to resuscitate him but it was too late. He hadn't noticed that the soldier Doug had fought with first still had air in his lungs and with his last breath, he pulled the trigger. The bullet with death written on it raced through the back of my Cyril and out through his chest. Although seriously wounded he turned and shot the soldier in the head. The blood spattered all over the poor woman and girl who lay there on the floor, horrified at what they had seen.'

My grandmother began to sob as she relived the scene. My mind was whirring with the story. It felt so real - so detailed. Could it be true? Could people communicate in that way or was it some form of hallucination?

Whatever the reason or answer was, I was totally hooked. 'Did he die there and then?'

'Not straight away. He fell onto the ground and Helena pushed her child aside so that she could attend to him. She sat by his side for hours but it was useless. No doctor could be called and the dressings she made could not stem the bleeding, only slow it. The light gradually left him and he must have known because he gave Helena all his worldly belongings, including the documents that he and Doug had given their lives for. He made her go through Doug's belongings and take all his possessions as well before closing his eyes and saying "goodbye" to this life.'

My grandmother bowed her head and began to rock back and forth and seemed to be in a trancelike state as if she needed it to protect her. I glanced up as I heard the clock above the fireplace chime and saw that it was seven o'clock.

'Granny,' I held her bony hand, '*why* do you think that he's gone away now?'

She didn't lift her head. 'I just know he has,' she muttered.

****

I sat with her for another two hours during which time she did nothing but rock and mumble to herself. I had to speak with a doctor. I somehow had to help her.

Eventually she sat upright. The trance state seemed to have run its course and she looked and seemed completely normal again.

'I'll be fine, Steve. Sorry to have troubled you.' She eased herself up from the chair and walked into the kitchen. The sound of the kettle being filled broke the silence.

'Are you sure you'll be okay, Granny?' I watched as she set about washing the cups we had used earlier.

'Of course. Now you run along, Boy.'

I didn't argue. Confused, I kissed her on the cheek and left.

She might seem to be fine again, but there was definitely something wrong. Or was there?

I, who believed in angels, I who believed I would one day find one. Why should I of all people find my grandmother's story so hard to believe? So she was old but her account of what happened was lucid and descriptive and there seemed to be no errors. It dawned on me that she had not made one mistake with the names or the places.

I would ask the doctor to take a look at her.

CHAPTER TWENTY-SIX

A few weeks later, as I debated my grandmother's dilemma, I received a surprise when, one morning, an email from Susie dropped into my inbox.

Dear Schatz, I read,

I have an idea! Markus and Danni are living in Cologne at the moment. I have spoken with them and I am going to go and meet them for a weekend at the end of September. Would you like to come and meet me?

Hugs

Susie xxx

I sat and thought for a while because I still felt bruised and raw about Andréa and the sadness was still very much on the surface. After spending so much time on my own I had decided that that was exactly what I wanted to be – alone.

However, a few days later, while I was having a beer or two with Laurence, and with him egging me on, I emailed her back.

Dear Susie,

That sounds a great idea! I would like to come and if it is okay with you all then I would like to bring Laurence. He and I spoke about it the other day and he asked me to ask you!

Let me know.

Steve xxx

'See what she says to that, buddy,' Laurence said, sitting back on the recliner behind me. 'I fancy a break from England,' he grinned sipping from his can of icy cold Stella. I pressed the send button and smiled. It sounded a good idea. I wouldn't be going alone and the fact that Laurence seemed eager, enhanced my desire to go.

By the end of that day Susie had replied.

Dear Schatz,

That is fine. Markus & Danni said that is the least they can do after he looked after us all in June. It will be the last weekend in September so book your flights and we will come and collect you from the airport.

See you then!

Ich liebe dich,

Susie xxx

The words *"ich liebe dich"* - I love you - registered a warmth inside I had not felt since June. It was a "no lose" situation. Whatever happened I would have a good time with my pal and see Susie in her own world.

We planned our trip and I booked two tickets for the last Friday in September. Having never set foot on German soil I had no idea what to expect and I drew confidence from the fact that Laurence and I could at least talk to each other in English. I also knew that Susie was making all the moves to see me. The fact that she hadn't invited me to visit her in Berlin, told me that she was still with Raimund. At least for now.

Another early flight meant another early wake up call and Harry, who was our chauffeur as usual, was as cheerful as ever. It felt great to have Laurence with me as we chatted happily on the way to the airport. It was the first time we had been away together and I knew he was looking forward to it just as much as I was.

I had taken the precaution of making one thing clear though. 'No drugs, Laurence,' I'd told him.

'No way, mate. I'm going to be clean for this weekend. Just alcohol and cigarettes!' I had to laugh. That was a "clean" weekend for him.

It was a smooth flight and we arrived at Cologne airport just after nine in the morning. It was a small but apparently well-organized airport and my first experience of the cleanliness and efficiency of Germany. A short while after we arrived we wandered through the arrivals gate to find the three of them standing waiting for us. We greeted each other enthusiastically with hugs and kisses and it felt wonderful to see Susie again. I immediately forgot all about my troubles and sadness. This was a different place. A different time.

Danni and Markus lived in a modern one-bedroom apartment a fifteen-minute train ride from the centre of Cologne. We settled in and had a beer and then Markus suggested that we take the train so that he could give us a guided tour of the city. He was in his element describing Cologne and its famous features to us. He took us to the beautiful cathedral, which he told us had taken over six hundred years to complete and was dedicated to the Three Kings who were said to have visited the infant Jesus. After a tour of the city we entered the *Ringstrasse*, a large circular cobblestoned boulevard. I hadn't envisaged that any part of Germany would be so pretty or historic.

The first day was filled with laughter and drink. After our tour of the city we went to an Irish bar and stayed there for the rest of the day getting more and more drunk. Laurence suddenly seemed like a different man. Whether or not it was to do with not taking drugs or the new environment, he seemed to have greater energy and humour about him. In the evening when the *karaoke* began, Markus told us about his great skill at singing which caused the girls to laugh.

'I will prove it,' he said, going across to put on a song.

We listened to him singing a Tom Jones number with a German accent.

'Not bad!' I told him when he returned.

'Pretty good,' smiled Laurence.

'*Wunderbar*!' exclaimed Danni, while Susie just gave him a look that simply said 'Rubbish.'

The big surprise of the evening followed when Laurence got up and, scanning the book of tunes, selected two. One by the Mamas and Papas and the other by the Beatles. When it was his turn he pulled his baseball cap down to hide his face a little and stepped confidently up onto stage. The next six minutes were incredible. I hadn't known that my friend could sing - let alone sing so well. The crowd were singing along with him and suddenly Laurence had changed from zero to hero. An unknown English guy finding legendary status in an Irish bar in Germany. Amazing.

Wandering back to the train station, our only conversation was of Laurence's singing abilities. We were all amazed at his talent yet he took it all gracefully and spoke of his gift with humility.

'I used to sing for my supper,' he grinned with embarrassment.

We staggered into the flat and after one nightcap got ready for bed. It was at this point I realised that the sleeping arrangements were not ideal - at least not for Susie and me because - and as you would expect - Markus and Danni had the bedroom which meant that we three would have to share the hard floor in the lounge. Markus searched around and found a blow-up bed which, even after twenty minutes of blowing up, still remained flat. It was barely the size of one person, let alone three, so Susie suggested that we let Laurence sleep on it and we would lie together on some cushions.

As we had all drunk a lot it wouldn't be difficult to sleep although I felt a tinge of disappointment that Susie and I wouldn't be alone, but if that was the way it was, then I just had to make the best of it. .

We lay with our arms wrapped around each other with Laurence just three or so metres away from us. As we waited for sleep to come he sang softly in the darkness and my last memory of the day was of Susie looking at me and kissing me softly.

'*Ich liebe dich*,' I whispered in her ear before beautiful dreams took over.

****

Like all lovers the feeling of completeness is most acute when they are together. There is nothing better than the feeling of love and warmth that it brings and for two days I floated on air. Everything seemed perfect. For the first time since my painful experience with Andréa, I felt love. A love so different but a love I craved for.

After a German breakfast of cold meat, sausages and bread washed down with coffee my head felt much clearer after the previous day's heavy alcohol consumption. While we were eating, Markus and Danni suggested that we spend the day visiting a theme park in Cologne. This appealed to all of us and I agreed, despite my long-standing fear of fairground rides which stemmed back to when I was a child growing up near Butlin's at Clacton. One day, when I was about eight, the mechanism had snapped on one of the rides making the machine rotate at an incredible speed until the emergency stop had come into action. But love and pride made me push that memory to the back of my mind.

It was a big theme park with many attractions as well as rides. Laurence was without doubt the most daring and he and Markus went on as many rides as they possibly could, while I hung back with the girls after a water raft ride left me feeling both sick and wet.

After a few hours of fun, Markus suggested that we head for the banks of the Rhine, where he said we would find good food and spectacular views. Before we ate we took a tour on one of the boats that were moored up offering sightseeing trips. The day was fresh and sitting sipping champagne – or more likely a substitute for the real thing - on the boat, made me feel grand - especially as there were so many people on board – including Susie.

It wasn't until the late afternoon that we sat in a lovely restaurant beside the river. The day drifted lazily into the evening as our conversation flowed effortlessly along with our banter culminating in a tribute to travel and all the opportunities it offered for freedom and fate. We toasted the wonder of travel and new opportunities that our generation were able to share. The evening took a strange twist when Markus started speaking about religion.

'Do any of you believe in anything? You know…God? Religion?' His comments seemed to be spontaneous but maybe it was the influence of the wine, or the atmosphere, because I suddenly felt very much alive and jumped in with my reply.

'Yes, I do,' I said with sincerity, and then, after hesitating for a minute, continued, 'I guess you could say I believe in angels.' The words came out before I could stop them.

Laurence laughed hilariously at my words. 'Angels! What the hell are you talking about?' His look told me that he believed in no such thing.

I felt my face redden. 'Nothing really,' I mumbled, wishing I had kept my mouth shut.

Susie however, seemed intrigued. 'Tell us more, Steve. You mean angels from heaven?'

A fear of embarrassment overcame me. I looked up to see Susie, Markus and Danni waiting for me to explain. Laurence just grinned at me as if I was some clown that was acting out his performance in front of them.

I took a gulp of wine and attempted to explain my reasons. 'Well, as a kid - as you all may know - I lost my parents. Tragedy is part of life, I know that, but I found myself in a situation that I shouldn't have been in. At least I did later on.'

'What?' Susie asked.

'I shouldn't have been there,' I replied. 'I should have been with my parents that day and I should be dead now. If everything had been normal, I would have gone with them but I stayed with my grandmother. Why that day? Granny told me then that things happened for a reason and I believed her. Of course I did. We've all heard about "guardian angels", so why not believe that they do actually exist? All I know is something or *someone* changed my life that day.'

'Bullshit,' Laurence said immediately. 'That is total bullshit, Steve. How the hell did you work that out? You got lucky; it was a choice you made, not a fucking angel or whatever the hell.' He grinned at me as if I was some sort of moron.

I felt a fire ignite inside me and anger flush through my body at his dismissal of my words. 'I'm even more certain now that it was true, you idiot, because my grandmother told me.'

'So your *Granny* is the angel, is she?' he said sarcastically.

'Please explain more, Steve,' Susie spoke.

Although I felt angry with Laurence, I wanted to clear all this up and get it off my chest at the same time.

'If you don't want to listen then don't, Laurence. I'm only trying to explain. My grandmother told me that she had heard a voice that day that said that I should stay with her. Nothing else. Nothing of what was about to happen. Just that I should stay and she listened to that voice. Well, if that was the case then it was the voice that saved my life. Since that day other things have happened around me that have supported it. I remember a woman at the funeral, for example, who spoke to me. I'm not mad, but I do believe in something, like you all do, and if I have to give it a name then it has to be an angel. Okay?'

'In search of an angel, how nice,' he smirked.

'I think it's a beautiful theory.' Susie looked at me. Her voice and eyes were filled with warmth and I felt better immediately.

Markus and Danni didn't laugh either.

'Steve, you have to believe in something,' said Markus 'We all do, and for me that is as good a reason as any.'

'I agree,' echoed Danni.

Laurence didn't comment further. In fact he became subdued, retreating into his shell as if defeated. Walking back to the flat I sensed the sadness within him. I needn't have cared after his earlier attempt to humiliate me, but I found myself worrying about him.

Dropping back from the others, I fell in beside him.

'So, Laurence, you alright, enjoy the evening? Enjoy your little dig earlier?' I couldn't resist mentioning his earlier snipe at me.

'I'm sorry, Steve,' he said quietly. 'I should have been more thoughtful.'

His reaction made me feel suddenly sorry for him. 'No problem, just forget it,' I said, trying to make him feel better.

'I want what you've got.' He looked at me and his face was bleak. 'That girl loves you.'

As he spoke I knew that what he said was true. I knew it because I had always known that our feelings were intense and that I had even lost Andréa because of them. Now what I needed was the proof that it had all been worth it; that my sacrifice hadn't been in vain. As we walked the rest of the way back, I felt my mind spinning with confusion. With Andréa I'd felt that our love was timeless. No rush, no pressure. Just peace and joy, but with Susie I felt afraid, as if I was fighting against the clock. I wanted to be married. To be living with her. I wanted it all now.

We were all tired and went to bed immediately. I was conscious of the fact that the next day we would spend our last hours together before we had to return home. Once again we made up the makeshift bed and I soon found myself close to Susie and her warmth flooded through me. The drug I craved was free and, with her by my side, I could take of it freely until the morning. The last sound I heard before dreams enveloped me was Laurence's sigh. Almost a sad sound of lost hope.

When I awoke on Sunday the realisation that it would soon be over swept through me. It was my first thought of the day and it made it difficult to smile. Just twenty-four hours before, the days had seemed endless, yet now, before I knew it, I would be back in Clacton minus my girl.

The day was forgettable. We ate a little but said hardly anything. I found myself wishing we could have just woken and left just to get it over and done with.

We hugged at the airport and as before, and as usual, I waited until all the formalities had been done before I held Susie for the last time. The moment was as painful as ever and again I could find only the one word. 'Goodbye.'

I saw tears in her eyes and turned away. I couldn't face it again. The intensity of the last months with Andréa, the love that I had for both of them, culminated in another farewell. I felt at that moment that any chance of finding love, of getting it right would end up in some airport. Saying goodbye...again.... Uncertainty entered me like a thunderbolt. I could not be sure if I had made the right choice at all. I just felt utter sadness and emptiness.

****

'Are you okay?' Laurence sounded as if he was trying to show interest.

'No,' I replied, gazing out of the window and seeing only emptiness in the clouds. The beauty had gone. As the plane glided through the sky, and Laurence turned back to the magazine he was reading, I tried to reason with myself. I should have felt elated after the time I had had with Susie, but I didn't. Although she hadn't spoken about Raimund at all, I guessed that she would now be on her way back home to him.

For all I knew it might be the last time we saw each other. I was stretching an unrealistic dream to its limits when what I really had to face was the truth and admit that this wasn't the right time for either of us. Would there ever be a right time? Was she the right person at all? Doubt reigned supreme at thirty thousand plus feet.

When we reached Stansted Harry was there to meet us and it was then that reality kicked in. On our way home Laurence suggested that we should go out for a drink when we got back to Clacton. We would drink to us, to them, to friendship, to Cologne and to anything else we could think of, he said. Harry dropped us off and declined our invitation to join saying that he had to work the following day. He probably had the sense to realise that it was a bad idea to try to drown our sorrows while we were both feeling so fragile. I didn't, however, and four hours later I was still sitting in the bar in a nearly paralytic state.

Laurence seemed to be in another world. He'd slipped off for a while and when he returned had seemed full of renewed energy. I watched his jaw move and saw him rub his nose from time to time. I had to face the inevitable downer which followed my bouts of heavy drinking while Laurence was in full swing on his chosen drug. A part of me wanted to try cocaine that night but I resisted and suffered as the beer and shots I swallowed gradually ate me away. The drink didn't provide me with any positive feelings and there was no fun being with Laurence that night. We might as well have been on different planets.

****

I slumped down by the toilet oblivious to the grime and dirt and piss on the floor. It mattered not. The only escape lay in that filthy toilet, in the dirty pub that was filled with people drinking and no doubt feeling better then I did. Desperation, fuelled by the booze, gripped me. I'd got it all wrong. This couldn't be love. How could love feel like this?

'Hurry up, I need a crap!' A voice yelled out, breaking through my self-pity.

Levering myself away from the pit of misery, I bowed my head as I passed the waiting man just in case he knew me. A glance in the grimy mirror revealed to me the state I was in. Splashing water from the cracked sink onto my face in an attempt to smarten myself up, I knew that I had to get out of this dump.

I went back to the bar which was now emptier than it had been when I had left. It must be near to closing time but Laurence was nowhere to be seen. I didn't bother to ask after him. He'd be somewhere else now, sniffing another line and feeling great. We were two different people with different feelings.

After an unmemorable taxi journey home I stumbled into bed. As the room swam I tried to reflect on the art of travelling love and all its implications.

'Just like the first day at school,' I slurred to myself aloud.

However, unlike the first day at school I couldn't imagine it getting any better.

CHAPTER TWENTY-SEVEN

Life leading up to Christmas was a mixed affair.

Susie called three days after I had returned home to say she had finished with Raimund. She, like me, had suffered during her lonely journey from Cologne to Berlin and it had made her realise that there was only one thing for it. We had to take the gamble and try to be together. The relief was extraordinary. The cloud of depression that had engulfed me lifted instantly and I became a happy man once more. This love thing was indeed incredible, if not pathetic at times. I was as vulnerable as a newborn baby.

The downside was being able to actually see each other. There could be no popping round for a cup of tea or other small moments of contact. Each arrangement had to be meticulously planned around our lives and, with Christmas just over two months away, we were both busy. We spoke every day but the next time we would be able to see each other, couldn't be till around Christmas time. At last we were able to make some concrete plans. I would fly to Berlin on Boxing Day and spend a week with her. That meant that there was time for the dust to settle after her break-up with Raimund and also for her to spend Christmas with her family and friends and I could spend mine with... well, anyone apart from her.

In an attempt to make the time pass more quickly during those weeks, I tried to keep busy with my own plans. I found myself missing Ray more then ever. With only Harry around to talk sense and behave normally with, my sanity was often tested. Laurence hardly ever put in an appearance although I heard stories about him being out all night at parties and raves and frequently being off his head. It seemed to me he was heading towards oblivion. Add to that the fact that getting in contact with Pat had become much harder lately, I found myself having to fall back on my own initiative. Since Ray's death, it seemed that Pat had retreated from me. I couldn't be sure whether or not this was the case and I had to accept his being under pressure at work at face value. Something inside told me that perhaps Pat was actually fighting a battle with his own faith.

****

A more immediate concern was still that of my grandmother. Such was her behaviour that I eventually decided to call in the doctor. She had been getting worse and worse and I had noticed a big difference in her when I returned from Cologne. The house was untidy and, each time I visited her, she seemed to be in a dither. Her use of names and places was hardly ever correct now. I had tried to ignore the inevitable but with her increasing vagueness with everyone around her, I realised that something had to be done.

The local doctor arrived on the morning of the eighteenth of October for a talk with Granny who greeted him as "Ted" despite the fact that she and I both knew that his name was Doctor Alan Fityin. He just smiled at her and continued with his work and after talking to her for some time he called me to one side for a chat.

'I'm going to arrange for some tests at the hospital,' he told me quietly.

I nodded, relieved that he was going to do something for her. 'That's fine, doctor. I'll take her myself just to make sure that she keeps the appointment on the right day. As you can see she can be a little forgetful with things like that.'

'I understand.' His eyes were filled with concern.

'Do you have any idea what could be wrong?' I asked hesitantly.

'Yes, I think so but perhaps we should wait until we get the results of the tests,' he said, nodding as if in agreement with his own decision.

I felt a little irritated by his words. 'Doctor, I'd like *some* idea. She's my grandmother, and the nearest thing I have to a mother, and I need to know.' I could almost hear myself pleading now.

He looked at me for a moment or two as if he was trying to decide whether or not to say anything. 'I think your grandmother has Alzheimer's disease, Steve. I can't be sure, or even how far it has progressed, but from my experience it appears to be the case. But let's wait for the results.'

As soon as I heard his diagnosis I knew that the tests were unnecessary. Everything fell into place with total clarity. Her behaviour had been erratic enough recently but the more I thought about it, the more I realised that she had been declining for some time. I remembered simple little things that I'd taken no notice of at the time and now realised that it was I who had tried to remain blind to it all. As I showed the doctor out, Granny sat motionless in her chair, apparently unaware of us.

A week later I held her hand while she underwent a series of tests. Each one seemed to confuse her more. She was unable to name simple, everyday objects and, even when they were explained to her, she then had no idea of what they were used for. The specialist spoke calmly and kindly but I sensed that he was making the same diagnosis as her own doctor had done.

Granny sat in the corner ignoring the tea I had got for her while the specialist and I faced each other across his desk. I saw the look of doom written on his face.

'Mr Bidante, what do you know about Alzheimer's disease?'

'I've seen bits on television about it but I think everyone has heard of the word.' I paused. 'I only know it takes your mind and destroys those around you while the person who has it has little idea about what is happening,' I said carefully, trying to remember the comments that the woman on the programme had made.

I heard him take a deep breath before he continued. 'Alzheimer's is a very difficult disease to diagnose. There are many tests we can do, including a Computerized Axial Tomography - or CAT scan as you may have heard it called. This can reveal evidence of small strokes that can be the cause of dementia, but the clues lie more in the patient's behaviour. A characteristic of the disease is the shrinkage of the medial temporal lobe of the brain. However, I must warn you, Mr Bidante, that it *is* a disease. It can be treated to some extent with drugs but if I'm honest, they don't have a huge success rate and the disease is usually irreversible. I'm sorry to have to tell you that we are facing a difficult situation.' He sat back waiting for my reaction.

I thought that I had been prepared for this day but, now it was here, I felt totally unprepared. I knew a little about the disease as I had already told the doctor, and the bits I'd seen on television had shown people suffering and the effect it had on their loved ones but I hadn't taken it in. I suppose it meant little to me at that time. I'd known that it was a terrible illness but I had no idea that it was so cut and dried – so *final*.

'What do you suggest?' I asked, feeling a sense of desperation.

I guessed that although he must have been in this situation many times in the past, it never got any easier for him.

'First of all, I suggest we arrange some form of home help for your grandmother and that you spend as much time as possible with her. It seems that she still knows and trusts you, and that's very important for her.' His reply seemed to be full of instruction rather than the remedy I sought for her illness.

I couldn't disagree or suggest anything else myself though; after all, he was the expert. I thanked him as I left but my words of gratitude seemed empty. How could I thank him for the news he had given me? After I had shaken his hand, I turned to my grandmother who just smiled at me vacantly. I knew then that the pain and confusion was just beginning.

'Come, Granny, let's go home.'

She stood and took my hand, her face portraying innocence and trust. I felt the bony structure of her palm in mine which seemed to convey the frailty and weakness of this once strong determined human being. I had to accept that things could only get worse. All I could do now was to support her to the end. Everything else in my life faded away to be replaced by the woman in front of me.

****

The hospital took care of the arrangements for the home help who turned out to be more like a visiting nurse than someone who did the cleaning. I was given a schedule of when she would be visiting, so that I could work my times around them, maximising the help we gave to my grandmother while at the same time minimising the risk of danger.

I knew that the outcome would - or should be - a hospice but knowing how, ever since the war, she had despised any kind of hospital, it would be almost impossible to persuade her to enter one. I tried to stay with her at least three nights a week but she always hustled me out of the house in the mornings. At times, her determination overrode her illness.

My calendar was full with thoughts and actions concerning Granny, with the exception of the trip to Germany on Boxing Day. I gave up on the idea of helping the other old people because I didn't have as much time as I'd had the previous year. I was grateful to the nurse who not only tended to my grandmother with great purpose and skill, but who also spared me the pain of watching her decline into full-blown Alzheimer's. The acceleration of her illness was scary but I could only put that down to the fact that, by her amazing will power, she had hidden the early stages from me.

****

My release came from thinking about Susie and of our wonderful and bright future together. I would find myself daydreaming about golden fields and sunshine - moments that helped to replace the grey decay around me. I'd decided not to tell Susie about Granny because she didn't know her and now, more than ever, I wanted to keep that part of my life private. To separate the dream from the truth. A part of me wanted to keep those emotions to myself so that when I visited Berlin, it would almost feel like I was exchanging one world for another. It would bring respite from the agony by sharing in someone else's festivities.

I felt at my lowest ebb when I paid my annual homage to my dear deceased parents. Even though I was not the one who was suffering from the illness the strain was taking its toll. Anyone who has been unfortunate enough to experience Alzheimer's disease will know what effect it can have on those who are close to the sufferer. There were no prayers that could help me and my belief in angels or any such thing began to be eroded with each visit and each depressing day that I watched my grandmother's sad end.

****

The big day came but I wasn't prepared. Just a year ago I'd sat having Christmas lunch with my grandmother and now the hospital had contacted me to inform me that they were making arrangements for her to be admitted into respite care for the period that I was away. I felt guilt run riot within me that I was being selfish for going off and enjoying myself while Granny was being taken care of by strangers. The lady on the phone reassured me that she would be well looked after in my absence and I thanked her for her kindness finding that her calm voice lessened my guilt a little. After all they *would* take good care of her, wouldn't they?

With little to look forward to on Christmas Day itself, I decided to link up with Sharon in the afternoon. I'd spent the morning occupying myself by wrapping the gifts I'd bought for Susie. With everyone busy celebrating, I decided to walk to Sharon's hoping that the few miles would clear my mind and give me time to reflect.

I noticed that Roz was out because she had drawn the curtains the way she did when she was away for any length of time. I thought that I could have done with her chatter today. Her words, however idle, usually carried meaning and today, of all days, I realised that.

I walked down the hill past the graveyard and seeing that it was deserted, it made me wonder whether many people visited their deceased relatives on Christmas Day. Making my way through the gravestones I knelt down in front of my parents' grave.

'Dear Mum, dear Dad. If only you could be here now,' I whispered and as I spoke the wind seemed to pick up around me and I was surrounded by the chill of the day. I looked up at the sky before continuing. 'If there is an angel, if there is a God - then show yourself and tell me why this is happening.' This time I shouted the words, but there was no answer, nothing but the sound of the wind.

'I feel so lonely.' I bowed my head in front of the gravestone and kissing the cold concrete, I wept for my parents and for my grandmother.

My journey to Sharon's took me past many windows. Inside each I saw that the day held different meaning for different people. Some panes showed glowing lights and silhouettes of happiness while others displayed lone figures illuminated only by a dim lamp or the flicker of a television. I realised then that Christmas Day could be the loneliest of the year for some people and I felt sympathy for those like myself.

As I walked up the stairs to Sharon's flat, I could hear music.

Not the usual festive type that you would expect but more like dance - or trance. I knocked loudly on the door and waited until I heard footsteps and then Sharon standing there looking very much the worse for wear.

'Bruv!' she exclaimed, rubbing her eyes as if trying to focus on me.

'Merry Christmas, sis,' I smiled and hugged her tightly before following her into the small lounge where the first thing I saw was a figure lying on the floor by the coffee table.

'Happy Christmas, Steve,' the voice slurred from the carpet.

'Hello, Laurence. Happy Christmas,' I said with disgust as I took in the debris around me. He was wasted. I looked at the coffee table, half of which was crammed with empty beer cans and bottles of spirits. I saw traces of powder around the edge of the table. It soon became clear what the other side had been used for.

I remained standing but, although I felt angry inside, I didn't say anything. I simply looked at Sharon and then at the table.

'It's not what you think, bruv,' she tried to explain.

I could see now that she too was out of the frame. She was drunk and high on cocaine and Laurence looked like he had been on the gear for a week. He was a complete mess.

I paused, trying to compose myself while Sharon stared at me, waiting for my reaction and the only thing I could think of to say was, 'What's that song? Oh yeah. "So this is Christmas".' I said the words and walked out of the flat.

An hour or so later I sat in my garden with a bottle of wine and the stars for company. The night sky glittered like glowing dots against the inky emptiness. I ignored the cold and drank the wine.

'Everything seems so screwed up,' I sighed out loud.

The stars helped to distract me from my worries taking me away from this place. One more night and I would be climbing up towards them in a plane, away from all this, for a little while and at least I had that to look forward to. Here, in my little town, the doors were closing around me. Soon there would be nothing left here for me anymore.

Another bottle of wine later and I was having a full-blown conversation with myself. It seemed the right thing to do. Ask myself something and then answer. Self-counselling under the guidance of my shrink, Miss Wine.

'So Steve, how do you see your life?'

'Well, Miss Wine, I think it's changing as we speak.'

'Really, Steve, and do you feel happy about that?'

'I have no choice, Miss Wine. It's happening in front of me. I sometimes get the feeling I'm at the cinema watching my own life story.'

'We all have a say in our own destiny, Steve.'

'Apparently, Miss Wine, I don't seem to have much say in mine. I try not to hurt anybody but I always seem to get hurt.'

'Oh, but you have hurt others, Steve. Haven't you?'

I looked at the bottle and stopped talking. Too much counselling with this bloody wine and now I was starting to feel like it was *actually* talking to me. The guilt of past sins crept up on me as I tried to redeem myself with the now empty bottle.

'I've hurt people - but never intentionally,' I said, gazing at the bottle.

'Fear not, Steve. There is always tomorrow. There is always hope.'

I picked the bottle up and kissed it. 'Thank you, Miss Wine.'

Staggering indoors I carefully put the bottle on the table. I couldn't bring myself to throw her away after her counselling. Perhaps when I awoke tomorrow, having forgotten the ridiculous conversation, I would simply toss her in the bin, but now, as I stumbled around the kitchen, she was all I had.

The cold had crept all around the house and as I lay numbly in my bed, enveloped by the covers, my last thoughts were of the next day. The day I would be in Germany. The day I would be happy.

'There is always hope,' I mumbled, as sleep took over.

'There is always hope.'

CHAPTER TWENTY-EIGHT

'Steve! Wake up!' Harry's voice yelled into my sleepy eardrum.

'Eh, what time is it?' My voice sounded like I'd been eating sandpaper.

'Four o'clock – I'm on my way. See you in twenty.'

My head was killing me. Staggering up and heading into the bathroom I ran a shower and clambered in, eyes still half-closed and feeling sick. The water helped to wash away the sleep but the drums in my head kept on beating. My attempts at speed failed as I stumbled from room to room, my mind rejecting all thought of order. Eventually, after about fifteen minutes, I was in some kind of shape. Once I was showered and dressed all that was needed to chemically enhance Steve Bidante was a cup of coffee.

Flicking the machine on, I noticed Miss Wine sitting prettily on the breakfast bar. Last night's counselling came at a price and right now I couldn't remember much of our discussion. Having said that, I doubted she did either. All I knew was that she was sitting there looking the same as she had done the night before, while I, who was stupid enough to talk to a wine bottle, was suffering badly for my sins.

The coffee tasted good and washed down the Ibuprofen tablets which I was swallowing when Harry arrived. Grabbing my case, I walked shakily to the car. 'Morning, mate!' he greeted cheerfully, much too cheerfully.

'Morning, Harry,' I tried to raise something resembling a smile. 'Merry Christmas.'

Even in the darkness the small light inside the car must have highlighted my bloodshot eyes.

'Bloody hell, Steve. You look rough.'

'Like I said, "Merry Christmas",' I repeated, slumping like a rag doll onto the passenger seat.

Harry was apparently trying to do his utmost to cheer me up during the fifty-minute drive by relaying stories of Christmas. The lovely moments he had had with his children while at the same time making humorous comments about the arguments with his wife and the snipes at his in-laws.

'All in all a typical English Christmas,' he summarised with a grin.

'It wasn't all bad, Harry,' I remarked, starting to feel better as the pills kicked in.

'It was good and I loved it,' he replied. 'But Christmas here just isn't what it used to be.'

I leant my head back and over the course of the next few miles thought about what he had said. Sadly, he was probably right. The festive season in England seemed to have lost something. The days of family and warmth had given way to commercial greed fed by the long lists of children's demands. If the cards that were on sale these days depicted modern Christmas scenes I think card companies would go out of business and as for poor Santa. Well he would be overworked and definitely underpaid.

As the morning sky welcomed us up into its heights I gazed out through the small window at the pink marshmallow sunrise. The wonder of flight awakened my senses and I began to think of the times ahead. Soon I would be setting foot in Berlin, the capital of Germany, famous for so much and where history was etched on every paving stone. The thought filled me with awe.

Apart from my brief visit to Cologne, the last member of my family to set foot on German territory was my grandfather and he never came back to tell of the place and people. War. A hideous beast of carnage dressed up in a uniform of pride and propaganda. So many people had given their lives for their country yet here I was, able to hop on a plane and visit the enemy of years gone by. I doubt he would have understood what all the sacrifice was for. A part of me wished that the world could all be the same. No borders and everyone having the same beliefs. Would there still be wars? Would people like my grandfather have to die to become just a distant memory in a few people's minds?

I didn't drink any alcohol on the flight. Drink couldn't make me feel better - only worse. I was too anxious about what the future had in store for me while at the same time I found myself reflecting on my whole life. The image of my grandmother floated in front of me. She was telling me her views on my love of a German girl. It all seemed so long ago and now I was watching her falling apart. Life can be so many things.

Schonefeld airport was not very big but it was meticulously organised. It was this sense of order that I liked about Germany. As the frosted glass doors slid open, my eyes scanned the crowd for Susie and saw that some people were holding up signs as Ray had done for me back in Alicante. I walked slowly as if giving my eyes more time to pick her out but I needn't have worried. Despite her height – she was only just over one and a half metres – she stood out like the angel on the Christmas tree.

As I spotted her she called out, '*Schatz*!'

'Darling,' I called, my feet gathering pace as I ran towards her. We clung to each other, hugging and kissing like a couple of lovestruck kids.

Taking my hand she led me out of the airport chatting all the way about Christmas. I felt a little ashamed to think that my day had been so uninteresting and, in many ways, sad, but her energy gave me new vigour. When she asked me about how I'd spent it I exaggerated a little - leaving out the details of Sharon and Laurence's drug-filled day.

Schonefeld airport is set on the edge of the city and, as Susie drove towards Berlin, I saw that the approach to the city was marked by two large towers that belched out smoke and fumes. The roads were clear with a few traces of snow on the verges but, although the sky was grey and it was cold, I felt warm and happy beside Susie. We talked so much that we seemed to reach her place very quickly. I was interested in everything and asked lots of questions. The houses looked so different, more interesting than the ones back home - like something out of Hansel and Gretel. Susie disagreed saying she loved the style of English houses.

'I think I just love England,' she said, as she pulled up into her parking space.

My heart skipped a beat.

Her flat was set on the second floor and as we walked quietly up the stairs she whispered that Raimund lived on the floor above. It felt weird to know that her ex-boyfriend was on top of us, but I didn't comment, just nodded thinking that at least it wasn't *literal*.

Inside the flat was very large. It had two spacious bedrooms with a large hallway. There was a big bathroom on the right and a modern kitchen on the left. The lounge was the largest room of all, with a dining table at one end and big comfy sofas at the other. It was a beautiful flat filled with the style and flair that only a woman could achieve.

Susie wanted to take me straight out to meet her parents because she had planned that, later in the evening, we would go out and meet some of her friends. Her parents' house – just a short car ride away – was both big and beautiful. Set in a tree-lined lane, it was the stuff of millionaires.

As she jumped out of the car, the front door swung open and her mother came down the steps to meet us. She was taller than Susie, with glasses and a warm smile and seemed friendly. I stood behind Susie feeling a little nervous as they hugged and kissed until it was my turn.

'*Mutter*, this is Steve.' Susie spoke in English.

'Hello, Steve. It is good to meet you at last.' Frau Brocker - or Beate as I came to know her, spoke slowly. Her English wasn't as good as her daughter's but I appreciated her difficulties because my German was terrible.

I walked towards her and bent to kiss her on the cheek but she grabbed me and hugged me, then turned to speak to Susie in German.

Susie beamed at me. 'My mother says you are nice and also that you smell good!'

Beate reached out and took my hand and pulled me towards the door. I glanced at Susie who nodded and smiled reassuringly as her mother guided me up the small flight of steps and through the open doorway and into a large kitchen to the right.

There, sitting in front of a roaring fire, was Susie's father. My first impression was that he didn't look German at all. More like an American from one of those old films. His skin, like his wife's, was tanned and his rugged face was complemented by a chiselled chin. I liked him instantly.

Beate spoke rapidly in German as the man looked up at me. Susie had followed us into the house and now translated to her in German as well as continuing introductions to her father in English

'Steve, this is my father, Charlie,' she said, and the man stood up and held out his hand.

'It is good to meet you, Steve,' he boomed. 'I hope you will have a good time here in Berlin and of course look after my little girl.' I recognised the warning in his eyes.

Looking at him I hesitated a little before answering so that he would know that I was sincere. 'It's good to meet you too, Charlie, and of course I will look after Susie.'

Susie then told me that although he was called "Charlie" it was not his real name but he had been known by it ever since he was a small boy. This had come about just after the end of the war when Berlin had been split up into areas. His area had been run by the Americans who had, she said, treated them well and shared things like chocolate and sweets around.

'My father loved the Americans and has done ever since,' Susie said. 'And that's why ever since he has been known to family and friends as "Charlie McQueen". Personally I think it's crazy, but he's my father and it is the way it is.'

'Well, I think it really suits him, Susie,' I said, because I really did.

Then Charlie took me for a tour of the house that was filled with everything that money could buy and all of the highest quality. He talked to me like we had been friends forever. Perhaps it was because I spoke English and it reminded him of the Americans or maybe his first impression of me had been favourable too and he genuinely liked me. Either way it was lovely to be made to feel so welcome in their home and in their daughter's life.

The evening was a joyful experience all round and after a few happy hours with Susie's parents and a delicious meal, we returned to her flat to get changed for a night out with her friends. We met them at a bar with a Mexican theme and I was introduced to at least a dozen people – friends and acquaintances – who were part of Susie's life. At first I felt a bit nervous at the way Susie was showing me off but the good atmosphere and company soon dissolved my fears and I felt nothing but pleasure that I was finally in Berlin.

During the days leading up to New Year Susie gave me a tour of Berlin and we went to many different places. One of the highlights was when we walked under the Brandenburg gate and along Unter den Linden by the river Spree. There was so much to see and do that at times it all became a blur but I remembered particularly the bright lights of Potsdam Plaza and the huge offices of the major car manufacturers rising up around me. We passed the Berlin wall and Checkpoint Charlie on our way to drink fresh beer in East Germany while Susie told me about the history of her city.

Berlin, for all its notorious past, seemed a remarkably quiet city compared with London. In my ignorance I had assumed that every large city like Berlin, would be as crowded with people as London, but it was not the case at all. Susie told me that the Germans referred to England as "Monkey Island" because of the number of people who lived in so small a place.

Knowing what a busy place my country was I could understand what they meant but I explained with a grin that it was so busy because it was such a beautiful green land filled with opportunities.

New Year's Eve came round all too quickly and we spent the day in preparation for the night's celebrations. We were spending the evening at Susie's flat, with Charlie and Beate, and then, just after midnight, going to meet friends at a club in the centre of Berlin. Susie had prepared a meal of warm chicken and salad for her parents and we chatted as we sat sipping *Sekt* – Charlie and I had a couple of beers too. I was surprised when, at one point during the evening, we had to stop to watch a programme on the television. Susie explained that it was a traditional part of the German New Year celebrations, which would have been fine except that it was an English programme. It was an old black and white film called "Dinner for One" and lasted for just over twenty minutes.

The story was about an old lady named Lady Sophie who, having outlived her friends, now lived in her big house alone apart from her butler. Each year she'd arrive downstairs for dinner where the now almost blind old lady believed that she was sharing dinner with her long dead friends. The butler, played by a chap called Freddie Frinton, pretended that the guests were still alive and served them all drinks. Lady Sophie conversed with imaginary guests while Freddie had to drink all the toasts to Lady Sophie. As the meal progressed through all three courses he, of course, became more and more drunk.

I watched with some surprise as Susie and her family laughed their way through every minute of it. Apparently everyone in Germany watched the programme every year. It made me realise, watching Freddie fall about, that there wasn't as much difference between our two worlds as I had thought.

As midnight struck I celebrated with my new family. They sang some German songs and I sang Old Lang's Syne and when we had finished singing I moved closer to Susie and found myself whispering in her ear, 'I love you so much.'

Her eyes held mine and were full of love and suddenly it felt like there were only the two of us in the room. As if in a dream I heard her say, 'We should become married.' The words danced into my mind and it was as if I had been intoxicated by a love drug. I was helpless, lost in her gaze, nodding and then accepting wholeheartedly what she had said.

'You have to ask then,' she whispered, still holding my heart in her eyes. I saw my future deep inside those brown orbs of passion. The dreamlike state that I had felt when I was asleep, now seemed real.

'Will you marry me?' I said, as I released the words that would change my life.

'Yes, I will.' Her lips brushed against mine and I felt as if I had found my Utopia but the moment ended as suddenly as it had begun because my euphoria was interrupted when Susie pulled away from me and shouted across to her parents. '*Mutter*, *Papa*! We have something to tell you!'

I hung back suddenly overcome with embarrassment.

'Steve has just asked me to marry him!'

****

I don't know if it was my imagination but for a moment her parents seemed to freeze before regaining their composure while I just felt numb and slightly idiotic. I'd known the girl for such a short time and now I'd asked her to marry me in front of her family whom I had met precisely twice.

Charlie motioned us to sit down at the table and I followed in my somewhat dazed state. Beate seemed relaxed but I sensed something in him that I hadn't seen before. The usual smile was missing and he had taken on an air of serious authority. I sat and waited for him to speak and Susie held my hand. He swallowed a big mouthful of beer and then focused his gaze on me.

'Well, Steve,' he finally said. 'This is something of a

surprise. May I ask if you came to Berlin with this thought in your mind?'

'No, sir,' I answered awkwardly, suddenly feeling rather hot.

'So where do you propose to live?'

I hadn't thought of that one. The truth is, I hadn't thought about anything and I was beginning to wish that I had kept my mouth shut. At least thought it through.

'Well... I *was* going to talk to Susie about that,' I said defensively.

'So you haven't given it any thought?' He was relentless.

'Yes, of course I have,' I stammered.

I had a rude awakening from my brief moment of pleasure. My daydreams had been replaced by the reality of the situation. Of course Charlie had a right to be concerned. I sat waiting for the rest of the cross-examination.

'Tell me this then, Steve,' he continued. 'Do you propose to live in Germany with my daughter or to take her away from her job and family to live with you in England?'

I felt myself blush. I didn't have an answer to the question. My hands felt clammy as I felt the rush of uncertainty and I knew that Susie was looking at me, waiting for my answer. I took a deep breath and let the words flow.

'Well, Charlie, I've spoken to Susie a little and I know she loves England so I'm hoping that she will come and live in my home to begin with and take things one step at a time. I've asked for her hand in marriage because I want to spend my life with your daughter. Where we live isn't as important as that we love each other. All I know is that Susie speaks perfect English and would be able to get work in England, whereas my German is awful and it would be much more difficult for us to adapt to each other here in Germany.' I looked at Susie and saw that she was smiling her support.

Charlie looked at her. 'Is this true, Susie?'

Susie continued to smile. 'Yes, Papa,' she said casually. 'We have talked and this seems the best way forward to begin with. I would like the wedding here in Berlin and of course we will visit you often. The most important thing is for us to be happy.'

Beate nodded and reached out for Susie's other hand at the same time as Susie gave mine a reassuring squeeze. I could not believe she had again come to my rescue the way she had done in Spain - only this time in front of her *father*. Especially as I knew that we hadn't talked about anything and now here we were planning the rest of our lives as if it was done and dusted.

Charlie gulped more beer and when he put his glass back on the table he was smiling again. 'It seems you have given this much thought and for that I am happy. You must understand, Steve, that Susie is my only daughter and you are a man who I know little of. My interests therefore are for my beloved little girl and not you.'

'Of course,' I nodded. What else could I say?

Charlie seemed to relax. 'If my daughter decides that you are her choice of husband then you have my blessing.'

I felt a calm wash over me. 'I'll do my best to love her and be the right man.' I held her hand tightly as the words fell from my mouth. They did feel right and I did love her. I felt sure of that although I hadn't imagined this.

'Then let's celebrate. You have our blessing!' Charlie grinned and, standing up, raised his glass. Susie, her mother and I stood up beside him.

'A drink to our new family and to love,' Charlie boomed.

'To love!' followed Beate and then Susie.

'To love!' I was the last to speak.

Charlie held out his hand and I shook it and then he pulled me towards him and held me in a bear-like hug. Then Beate hugged me and kissed me on the lips and after she had let me go they watched as I kissed and cuddled Susie. It all felt a little unreal but I was happy. My life was indeed changing more then I could ever have dreamt.

Charlie was suddenly the man he had been before our announcement. He beamed and shook my hand again. 'We will talk before you go of plans for the wedding and all the details,' he said proudly.

'I'll look forward to that,' I grinned.

Susie signalled for me to get ready. 'Don't forget we are going to go to the nightclub now to celebrate more.'

'Come, Charlie,' Beate said. 'We must let the lovers enjoy their night and celebrate as young people do.'

'Yes, my love,' Charlie answered before raising his glass for one more toast. 'To your love, to your marriage and to our future grandchildren!'

I watched as the two women lifted their glasses with the word echoing in my ears.

'*Grandchildren*.'

I gulped my beer down in one as the noise of laughter ran around the room. With the unexpected acceleration of events, I had forgotten to tell my new family one vital detail.

We would be a barren family.

CHAPTER TWENTY-NINE

The remainder of New Year's Eve blurred into a ball of confusion and fear that span around my mind like the lights in the club.

Susie noticed little of course. She spent her time in deep conversation with her friends about my proposal and our future. Love at first sight? I found myself feeling uneasy and slipped away to wander about alone in an attempt to gather together my thoughts.

There were six different dance floors in the club, each playing a different style of music. Around me people were jumping around, celebrating the New Year and, I supposed, feeling happier than most, but I somehow felt as if I was a victim of my own impatience. I had wanted so much to have and to be with Susie.

I reflected on my proposal to Susie wondering whether it had been *me* who had actually spoken the words. I couldn't help thinking about the expression on Charlie's face when he had said the word "grandchildren".

I'd never spoken to Susie about my problem resulting from having mumps as a teenager. Like all children I'd had my share of childhood illnesses and all I really remember about it was being told I was well enough to try eating and eventually being back to normal.

I remembered my grandmother explaining to me after I was better that I might have difficulty in having children when I was older. Mumps, she said, could sometimes have this effect. I didn't think much about it at the time. Why would I? I was just a kid and kids don't think of the future in that way. It was only as I got older and my friends began to have children, that I began to think about it and wonder if there was any truth it.

I'd never had any tests to confirm it though now, as I wandered aimlessly around the packed club, I knew why I hadn't. It was because I had feared the moment when I would be with someone I loved who would assume that we would have a family. I had been trying to protect myself from the possibility. I'd heard the jibes about people like me and never wanted to be associated with that kind of scenario.

When Charlie uttered those words I felt surer than ever that I could not. It felt as if someone was twisting a knife inside me and all I could hear were Granny's words. It wasn't getting married that worried me at all, it was my inadequacy and the realisation that not only would I never be a father but also that the family bloodline ended with me. I searched for more drink to numb the pain.

Eventually after several more bottles of beer I went back to where I had left Susie and saw that she was still dancing happily amongst her friends. Leaning against a mock Roman pillar I looked at her, wondering whether or not I should tell her, and if so when. I would have to tell her - but not tonight.

When the song ended she glided off the dance floor and came towards me. 'Darling, where have you been?' Her face was glowing under the lights. She looked so happy and it made my stomach somersault.

'Oh, just admiring the place and thinking about children.' I forced a grin which felt as phoney as my words.

Susie moved to within kissing distance and our lips met briefly until she pulled away. 'Steve, you are so lovely. I love you so much,' she whispered.

'I love you, Susie. This really will be a happy new year,' I said, wishing that I could believe my own words.

****

A kaleidoscope of images flashed through my mind while I dreamt. A slideshow of flickering snapshots probed my subconscious. Too many to make sense of, just the overbearing weight of decisions past and present. I saw them all.

I shivered and then felt warmth envelop me.

'Steve, are you okay?' I heard the voice reach out, as if a hand was saving me from the abyss of my own mind. I grabbed at it, feeling myself wake as I did so. I was in the bedroom. It was flooded with a light that hurt my eyes and I realised that it was morning. Blinking, I tried to take in my surroundings. Flowers were the first things that came into my mind together with the words: *Beware, spiritual, dreams.* They all seemed to belong together.

'Steve, are you okay?' Susie repeated her words. 'You are scaring me.'

'Sorry.' I sat up and saw her concerned expression. 'A bad dream, that's all.'

She came closer, hugging me so that the heat from her body warmed me.

'You were so cold, darling, so cold.' She sounded worried.

I pushed the dream away so that I could get on with the day, but the thought that was still uppermost in my mind was that I was in all probability obsolete when it came to contributing a daughter or a son.

Susie and I spent the day with her parents where everyone was cheerful and lively. I heard and saw everything, but registered little. I answered Susie mechanically when it was expected of me. We talked about our wedding and of our future but I wasn't sure what I was really saying apart from agreeing with her. I could not rid myself of the sickness in my stomach which grew bigger as the day wore on.

****

I didn't dream that night and the following morning reality returned together with the sadness of leaving Susie. When she awoke we lay together letting the silence embrace our souls while we gazed at each other with the now familiar sense of emptiness that grew as the hour of departure approached.

'It won't be long now until we're together all the time,' I said, trying to sound more cheerful then I felt.

She smiled. 'I know. I cannot wait for that day when I no longer feel the sadness of parting.'

I would be back within a month to discuss our wedding plans and in the meantime Susie had promised to visit me in England. Things weren't that bad; we just had to be patient.

After one more emotional parting I stood alone in the airport waiting for the flight to take me the wrong way. Back to England, to an empty house filled with nothing but shadows. Away from Susie. I tried to concentrate on the joys of the past week, my mind switched off from my surroundings and the people around me. I sat alone on the flight surrounded by my own demons.

A smiling Harry was, as usual, there to meet me. We sat and had a beer together and everything seemed back to normal. Despite it all, I put on a brave face, telling him only the good things and leaving the best till last.

'Harry, can you do me a favour?'

'Anything pal, anything,' he answered cheerfully.

'Will you be my best man?'

He stared at me for a moment or two before replying. 'Are you serious?'

'Yes, I am. Completely.' I laughed at his reaction until his gaze made me feel uncomfortable.

'Harry?'

I saw the uncertainty in his eyes. 'I don't want to be rude, mate,' he said eventually, 'but I'm... well... just not sure.'

I felt my happiness being squashed under the weight of his words - as if I had sobered up from the effects of alcohol.

'I don't understand,' I said slowly.

'Look,' he said, 'if you like, I'll think about it.' He paused. 'You know how it is, Steve. Logic and all that.'

I pondered his words as they sank in. I felt rejected and wished Ray had been there so that I could have asked him. But he wasn't and Harry didn't want the job - I had no doubt about that. Indecision flared up in my mind as I tried to come to terms with his answer.

****

I didn't get home that night. After some gentle influence from Harry we ended up back at his place. He tried to explain how he felt that he was worried that I'd made the decision too quickly and how he felt gutted by his own logical views. I listened as each gulp of Scotch made me accept his advice while at the same time I kept thinking about my future. With or without him, I was going to get married.

I relaxed as the alcohol took over until everything became a blur. I felt Harry help me upstairs and flick on a light before guiding me towards a bed.

'Sleep well, mate,' I heard him say and I thought he sounded sad.

'I will. You're a top mate and I understand.' I heard myself slur the words before falling face down onto the bed. I heard him laugh as he said, 'Just make sure you aren't like that on your wedding night, son.'

The light went out and I was in blackness again but now it was a calm and numb darkness. I knew that soon my whole life would change. I seemed to have more control then ever before, yet no control at all.

'Got to see a doctor, got to find out,' I mumbled to myself before giving in to unconsciousness.

CHAPTER THIRTY

'Roz, can I ask you something, please?'

I watched as she leant her bike against the rail next to the cemetery gates near the chapel. It was Sunday morning and I'd spotted her across the graveyard where I had been visiting my parents. It was two weeks since I'd returned from Germany and I had serious issues to discuss and seeing Roz wheeling her bike through the gates had made me decide to ask her advice. She was the wisest person I knew and also my friend and I needed someone who was unbiased to talk to about what I should do next.

'What can I do for you on this fine day, Steve?' Roz beamed.

I hadn't even noticed what a beautiful day it was. She breathed small clouds of mist into the icy air. It was a day for living but with my latest news I felt half dead. At least my future did.

'Roz, I need some advice from you, please. It's personal but I think you may understand.'

She cocked her ear towards me. 'Did I hear you right? Advice?' she shouted.

I sighed because this wasn't something I wanted to shout from the rooftops.

As if reading my mind she moved closer to me, fiddling with her earpiece and smiling to show that she could hear me.

'Well… okay…,' I began, realising that I didn't really know *where* to begin. 'When I was a teenager, I was very ill. I had mumps very badly and apparently it was quite serious. I got through it of course, but my grandmother told me later that the doctor had said that I could have difficulty….'

'Difficulty?' Roz looked confused.

'Yes… eh… I have a problem downstairs so to speak.' I felt

my face flush as I emptied out my personal problem in the churchyard.

'And *is* it a problem?'

'Yes… I think it is,' I said.

'Have you seen someone about it?'

'Yes…recently… well last week actually…' I paused before continuing. 'They did some tests and apparently the chances are slim to none that I will ever have a child or children of my own.' I hadn't said those words aloud before and only now had I realised that I'd always known inside myself. It felt something like when you know a cold is coming or it might rain. That instinct that we all have if we open our eyes enough to see or feel it.

I felt a lump form in my throat as I waited for her to answer. I would never be able to have a real child of my own. Should I be worried? It was just that I now knew that I wanted to see my own child and to continue the bloodline of my family. I knew it was the last chance for the name of "Bidante" to live on or to disappear into obscurity. As I struggled to keep my emotions at bay, I looked at Roz who in turn seemed to be looking deep inside me. The way she did at times, as if she was some kind of body scanner or something. *I have nothing to hide now,* I thought. *Look all you want.*

'And who do you plan on having a child with?' she said after a minute or two.

I was momentarily thrown by her question and as I gathered myself I realised that she was probably assuming that it would be Andréa. I felt a flicker of sadness that seemed to come from nowhere and instead of answering directly, I dodged the question.

'That is not the point,' I said, feeling a little aggrieved by her remark. 'Do you know what it is like *not* to have a child?'

I instantly felt regret at my words. I was not sure if she had children but, in any case, my comment was out of place. Roz, however, didn't seem at all fazed by it.

'To have a child is one thing, but to have a child of your own making is beyond that. It is the continuation of your life on this earth…your legacy.'

'Well, thanks anyway,' I said sadly. 'I just hope that the tests show that I'm wrong.'

I heard Roz sigh before she said, '"Hope" is a strange word, but it's immortal in its meaning.'

As icy wind pushed against my face and I experienced a feeling I had never felt before. I didn't understand. 'Roz… are you saying that I have *hope*?' The words stumbled from my mouth and I watched as she considered them.

'There is *always* hope, Steve. In your case the odds seem stacked against you, and indeed medical evidence adds weight to your fears and medicine doesn't often make allowances for hope. I know enough about this world to tell you that, but hope can be all conquering. It can give us a reason to believe – to go on and to flourish. If you don't have hope you have nothing.'

I digested her words, her wisdom. This woman had seen much more than I – no doubt had experienced illness and even watched people die. I knew her as a caring person and I had always respected her views, but it hadn't seemed like an answer at all. How *could* she tell me what I wanted to hear?

Again it seemed as if she had read my mind. 'You won't find the answer you seek from *my* lips, Steve. But if it's hope that you want, then I can give you that.'

'How can you do that?'

'Because I've seen it prevail in my own life,' she said. 'And you must remember how old I am. I know you, Steve, and I know you are a good man. Perhaps better than you give yourself credit for. Your journey will teach you much and it will enlighten you - because you *care*. You think and you live not just for yourself but the most important part of you, the one that gives you hope, is that you know love and how to give it.'

Her words comforted me and despite the cold I felt an inner warmth. I had never imagined that she would think, let alone say, things like that. Although I'd helped her that Christmas, it had felt like it had been for my *own* benefit. Despite that, I knew that she wasn't one to waste words and that she meant what she said.

'Thank you,' I said quietly. 'No one has ever said anything like that to me before,'

She shook her head. 'Don't thank me. Just remember that love creates love. It's a gift you can give freely, yet still retain to give again.'

I thought I understood what she meant and I felt something that resembled hope flow through my body. I watched her pulling her scarf close around her face and remount her bicycle. There were no polite ends to conversations with Roz. They just ended when she thought it was time.

'Thanks again, Roz,' I said gratefully. 'You've made me feel better and helped, I think.'

She paused with one foot on the pedal and the other on the ground.

'It's the least I can do, Steve, because you've done something special for me already.'

'I have?' I couldn't think of anything I'd done.

'Yes, you have. You've given *me* hope.' With that she pushed her foot down on the pedal and rode back up the hill towards her house.

****

When I opened the door to find Pat on my doorstep I was more than a little surprised. It had been months since I'd seen him, but when I saw him standing there I could see that he was in need of a friend.

'How goes it, Steve?' He smiled wryly in response to my surprised look.

'Pat, bloody hell, Pat. How are you? Come in, come in!'

We sat in the garden drinking coffee while the cold morning air woke me up. I hadn't expected to see Pat, especially at nine o'clock in the morning. It wasn't his style.

'How have you been?' I asked cautiously.

'Well, Steve, it's been hard, you know,' he grimaced.

I felt the shadows in his voice and the pain of what he had been through.

'It wasn't your fault, you did your best. You know that.'

He put his hand up as if deflecting my words of sympathy. 'I *should* have done more Steve, but I couldn't. I *should* have done enough.'

We sat in silence while I watched him tormenting himself right there in front of me. I would never have thought that my tough Irish friend could be so affected by his work, but that wasn't the point. The point was that it had been Ray who had been destined to be there on that night to save his parents. It seemed that Pat was thinking about a balance of fate. That he should have been able to return the favour when destiny required it but he hadn't been able to. As I watched him struggle to control his emotions, I knew that his faith had punished him for thinking like this.

'Pat, I need some advice,' I said, in an effort to take his mind away from what seemed to me like self-inflicted pain.

He shot me a glance that was tinted with a smile. 'Fire away. I'm full of that ....and the black stuff.' He was referring to his favourite tipple, of course.

'I'm getting married,' I began.

'Jesus, Mary and Joseph, Steve! Who to?' He seemed surprised and I realised that he had missed out on most of what had been going on in my life recently. I told him about Susie and the speed with which our love had grown before finally telling him about her desire for a child and my possible inefficiency in such matters.

'It wouldn't hurt to get a second opinion - I can put you onto a friend who can run the tests. He's a top man in that department.'

I nodded slowly. 'Thanks, that would be great.'

'Who's your best man, mate?'

I'd been so obsessed with whether or not I could father a child that I had forgotten all about that issue. 'Um… I haven't got one yet. You fancy the job, Pat?' As soon as I said the words I felt like the job was up for auction to any bidder who fancied doing it.

'Heaven forbid!' he said with mock horror. 'I don't even know the girl!' But he was smiling his toothy grin and seemed more relaxed than he had been. 'Sure, I'll do it, if you want.'

I grinned and held out my hand and he took it and, as we were shaking hands, a thought entered my mind.

'Pat,' I said looking straight at him, seeking his support. 'Tell me I'm doing the right thing.'

He stood still for a few minutes as if deep in thought and then reached into his coat pocket and pulled out some photos and put them down on the table.

'I'm still a man of faith, Steve,' he said. 'Take a look at these and tell me what you can see.' He turned to look at me as if waiting for my reaction.

There were three and I separated them and laid them out in front of me. As I looked at the photos I felt a strange sensation.

'No!' Pat intervened, 'Put them in the correct order and *then* tell me what you see.'

I soon realised what he meant and put the photo of the baby to the left, a smiling couple in the middle and lastly, an old man sitting on a park bench on the right.

'Correct, yes?' I grinned. 'Okay, I see a baby, a couple and an old man, correct again?'

He nodded. 'Yes, but do you *really* see what's in front of you, Steve?'

I looked again and saw the same thing. 'Only the same as I saw before,' I replied, scratching my head.

Pat lit a cigarette and smoked for a few minutes before continuing. He seemed to be enjoying making his point. After a few more puffs he chuckled and said, 'It looks like another lesson from good old Pat.'

'Come on, mate!' I said laughing, 'Put me out of my misery!'

'It's easy, Steve, you just have to see things for what they are, not for what you're *supposed* to think they are.' He leant over so that he was close enough for me to smell the tobacco on his breath.

'The baby...' he said slowly, 'is you as a child. It knows nothing of its destiny. It has no knowledge of what lies ahead and it can make no choice. The couple in the middle - well let's say you're the man,' he grinned at the same time as he inhaled smoke. 'The man - you - makes some of the decisions while destiny makes the rest. The crucial thing is that there, in the middle so to speak, is the most important part of your life. What you do in those years shapes the future.'

He leant back and stubbed out his cigarette, as if the lesson was over.

'But, Pat,' I said feeling somewhat bemused, 'you haven't said about the last photo. What does that mean?'

He had obviously been waiting for me to ask because he immediately put his finger onto the last picture.

'Remember, Steve. Each of us lives our lives like an artist. So take care in the pictures that you paint, for in old age you will be left to view an exhibition of a lifetime's work.'

CHAPTER THIRTY-ONE

For once Granny recognised me. She opened the door and beamed at me. 'Hello, Boy!' Just hearing her say that made me feel brilliant.

'Oh, they're looking after me so well,' she said as she pottered around behind me. I was making the tea because she had forgotten where the cups were and I knew that that indicated that things weren't all good. My grandmother had been making tea for more than sixty years and she knew a cup when she saw one and to suddenly forget told me more than any doctor could have done.

All the same, it was lovely to see my dear Granny again. Her soft skin looked rosy, her eyes sparkled and she laughed at nearly everything I said. Perhaps it was a part of the illness but for me it was one of the best parts I had seen for some time.

As I took our tea into the lounge she scuttled alongside me chattering about things I didn't understand. She told me that Mr. Bush the window cleaner had sold his round and moved to Manchester. That Gladys Douglas at the church had found her husband lying dead on the piano. I didn't know whether or not these stories were true or part of her dementia. All I saw was that my grandmother seemed more vibrant and energetic than she had done for some time.

I played along with her though while we drank our tea together, realising that some of the things she was talking about had happened years before. What a strange illness it was that took away the present yet restored memories of days long gone. Sometimes even of childhood and Granny seemed like a child now. I felt her leaning on me more and more and was grateful for the care she was receiving.

'How are they looking after you?' I said, between listening

to the many unfamiliar stories that she told me.

'Ooh, Boy!' she exclaimed. 'I'm being looked after like a queen! They send two of those nurses around during the week and they clean with me and help me to do jobs and we chat. It's lovely!' She smiled happily.

'That's good, Granny, do you like them?'

She paused a moment and for a split second I saw my real granny again.

'One of them is very nice,' she replied. 'Her name is Rose and she's my friend. The other one, Mrs. Hammond, well, I don't really like her much.'

I smiled to myself remembering how she had always done that. If she liked someone she would use their first name but if she wasn't that keen she would remain formal by using their full name. Dear Granny! How I loved her.

'Well, I'll be around a lot, Granny, but I will be returning to Germany from time to time but soon Susie will be living here in England.'

'Who's Susie?' She looked at me blankly.

I felt exasperated. I couldn't go through all that again and now I had no idea how she would react. I'd just leave out the details for now and let events take their course.

'She's my girlfriend.' Sometimes less is better. It must have worked because she looked pleased.

'Ooh, Boy, a girlfriend at last! I look forward to meeting her. I told you it was about time you got yourself a good woman!'

I left her in good spirits a short time later. The next few months weren't going to be easy and I was finding more questions than answers. Now I had the added burden of my grandmother's illness and how to best take care of her. Would she remain well enough to realise that I was marrying the German girl who she had been so against in the beginning?

Would she want - or even be *able* - to come to the wedding?

My last living relative and she probably wouldn't even

understand what was actually happening.

****

In order to try and cheer myself up, or perhaps to fulfil a moral obligation, an hour later I found myself at Sharon's door. I knocked and after a few minutes she opened it carefully without undoing the chain and peeped at me through the gap.

'Hello, bruv.' She sounded nervous.

'Hi, sis, are you going to let me in?'

I watched her hands tremble as she undid the catch and as soon as I stepped inside she grabbed me and hugged me tightly.

'I'm in trouble,' she sobbed.

I held her for a while until she seemed to have gained the strength to explain. I didn't know what to say so I said nothing. I hadn't seen her since Christmas and hadn't really given her much thought since then. I listened in disbelief as she told me about her problems. I'd known for a long time that she had some sort of a drug issue but I hadn't known that it was serious. It seemed that as the amount of cocaine she needed to snort had increased, so had the debts. I listened as my self-adopted sister spoke honestly and openly for the first time in ages. I should have felt happy but it made me feel more scared than I had done all the time she had been hiding behind her veil of half-truths.

Now she had a debt to pay and a habit to keep.

'How much do you owe?' I knew that my voice sounded unsympathetic.

'Six hundred pounds...I think,' she replied nervously.

'What about Laurence? Where exactly does he fit in to all this? Has he offered to help?'

Sharon looked embarrassed.

'Sharon!' I pushed her to talk.

'I don't see him much now,' she said. 'He used to come round and he helped a bit at first but....'

'But what?'

Tears began to run down her face and she stepped towards me with her arms open and I let her fall into mine again.

'He said I was useless, bruv,' she whimpered.

'What do you mean "useless"?'

'In bed. He said I was useless in bed.'

I felt a surge of sympathy towards her combined with anger towards Laurence. Why would he do that? He knew Sharon and how vulnerable she was. It was almost as if she *was* my sister that was being abused by a friend. It felt wrong.

I didn't shout at her or anything like that because the girl I was looking at was not the girl I had known for so long. It was a desperate shadow of that girl, someone who needed my help.

'I'll get you the money, Sharon,' I promised.

****

When I spoke with Susie that night, I didn't tell her anything about my day and anyway she was too busy talking about out future plans in glowing terms to listen. I agreed with her that it would make sense for me to return to Germany early the next month. I told her that I would book a flight and we could get the wheels rolling towards our future life together.

I wondered after I came off the phone why I hadn't shared my problems with her. Why couldn't I? I told myself that there was no need.

Susie was my future. The present chapter of my life was drawing to an end and would soon be my past.

CHAPTER THIRTY-TWO

The dreams had left me these days.

With so much happening in the real world, the night became my sanctuary, my release. Before, when dreams had taken over from daylight, they had been my salvation. Ever since my grandmother's illness the roles had been reversed. I worried too about Sharon and about Laurence's behaviour. I suppose I had even forgotten just what an impact my dreams had had on me. They were a bit like an illness that, once it has passed, loses significance and is rarely thought of except when something comes up that triggers the memory.

In truth I was becoming disillusioned with England. Daily news bulletins reported nothing but crime, and drugs were rife as I saw for real in Sharon and Laurence. Now even my leisure time was threatened. Almost everywhere I went and everything I did was spoiled by the sound of credit card chopping and people sniffing. Only Harry and Pat remained constant in my world of friends, because of course my family of one was also declining in the saddest way possible. England was not doing me or my soul any favours. I began to think of a future in Germany in more optimistic terms. Perhaps I could learn the language and get work there; perhaps I could adapt.

To make matters worse, the whole of Europe was experiencing a bitterly cold winter and snow and ice ruled. Images of accidents and incidents brought about by the weather beamed across television screens and added even more doom to the already gloomy news.

As for Clacton, well it was like everywhere else: roads weren't gritted and life ground to a halt. One inch of snow and the English panicked! It always made me wonder why we were so useless as a nation when it came to snow and ice. You didn't see any of that in Iceland or Sweden. It was just the same when we got a few days of sun in the summer. A hosepipe ban came into force but you don't get that in Spain, do you?

As I contemplated my country's demise, it occurred to me that England had not changed so much as I had. It hadn't been that long ago that I had seen all the good in my town and country. Perhaps the events of my life had left more of a mark on me than I had thought.

****

The night was freezing and my heating was on full blast. It was only around nine o'clock but the artificial heat made me feel sleepy. I lay on the sofa gazing at the candles and felt my eye lids droop as gradually a warm, dreamy sleep embraced me.

I felt warmth all around me but everything looked fuzzy as if my vision was distorted. My legs wouldn't move and all I could see was what looked like fog but wasn't. The image was familiar, I had seen it before. I closed my eyes in an attempt to see more clearly and when I opened them, I noticed that there was a palm tree on my left. It towered over me and as I looked beyond it, all I saw was the same grainy image.

I become conscious of what I was seeing. It was the image from a previous dream, the couple embracing. It was Susie and me…. wasn't it?

I felt something brush against my knee and, looking down, I saw her. She was holding a plant in her hand. Oleander, just like the piece I had hanging in my kitchen. The girl was younger but she was the same little girl. There was absolutely no doubt and when she looked up at me I heard her mumble 'Da…ddy' as if it was the first time she had said it.

It must have been her voice that woke me and I sat up feeling cold but at the same time a line of sweat trickled down my face. I gathered myself together and waited for the panic and wonder to subside.

****

As the plane touched down in Berlin I saw that the landscape was white with snow and ice much the same as it was in England. Disembarking from the plane I looked around to see the other passengers all dressed in warm jumpers and coats. We really were caught in Eskimo Europe, I thought to myself, as I trudged inside the terminal building. Susie was harder to spot amongst the array of coats, scarves and jumpers but I eventually spotted her small frame, wrapped like a cute present, in a long brown woollen coat with a bright red scarf and matching bobble hat.

As we hugged I felt her warmth through the thick clothing. We were back together, everything felt right again. On the drive back to her apartment she talked of nothing but the wedding.

'*Schatz*, I have a date in my mind,' she said enthusiastically.

'Okay, darling, when?' I said, fiddling with my seatbelt adjuster.

'I think August would be perfect. You know, the weather, the *timing*.'

'August sounds lovely, Susie,' I said smiling. 'But why is it good timing?'

I saw that she was grinning happily. She had put emphasis on the word "timing" and seemed pleased that I had picked up on it.

'Well, I was thinking that we would have a wonderful wedding day and I was also thinking it would be the perfect time to begin thinking of starting a family. Steve, imagine! May would be a perfect month for our first child to be born!'

The words sank in as my stomach reacted. A twisting sensation inside translated into an answer only I could hear. *So soon*? was the initial reply of my subconscious followed by the haunting thought "A barren family".

I didn't speak aloud for a few minutes and then I heard Susie say, 'Steve?'

'Sorry darling, I was just taking it all in.' I tried to smile reassuringly at her as I spoke and I saw her take her eyes from the road briefly and then smile as she was convinced. I needed time to think and I needed to talk to her about the problem and it ought to be sooner rather then later. Jesus, things were moving too fast.

We dropped my bag off at the flat and then headed for a bar in the centre of Berlin. Susie had arranged to meet her parents there and I ordered a cold beer and a coffee for her while we waited for them. The foamy German beer tasted wonderful and when Susie excused herself to go to the lavatory I found myself gazing out of the window absorbed in my own little world.

This could be home, I thought to myself. The city was clean and pleasant, the people friendly and the girl I loved was here. And of course the beer was wonderful! I smiled and then became serious again. What could I offer her in Clacton?

The more I thought, the more I found myself doubting that we could be happy in my home town and I decided that when Susie returned I would discuss it with her. Now all I had to decide was whether to mention it before or after I'd told my future wife that I could not give her a child.

Charlie and Beate arrived in less than an hour and greeted me as if I was their own son. It was good to see them and I felt the affinity between Charlie and me more than ever. As we grinned at each other, Susie and Beate looked on wearing identical smiles of satisfaction.

We stayed for a bit longer drinking beer and chattering away in a mixture of English and German before making a move. I had little understanding of German and, because of this, misunderstood where we were going but it didn't seem to worry my new family. Susie held my hand reassuringly as we got into Charlie's brand new Mercedes.

There was little traffic in the snow-covered streets and, as we swished through them, I thought at first that we were travelling towards Susie's parents' house. I've never been very good at direction and as usual I was wrong. Our destination turned out to be a beautiful church near to their home. As we got closer I marvelled at its size. Wow! Was this the place we were to be wed?

Susie noticed me staring and squeezed my hand tightly. 'You like it?'

'It's lovely,' I said, craning my neck to stare at the gigantic building. It looked like a church that royalty would get married in. Not someone like me.

'Mum and Dad chose it.' She grinned at me as if to tell me that her use of English was for my benefit.

Charlie pulled the car up inside the church grounds where I guessed the gardens would look spectacular without their covering of snow. The icy gravel crunched crisply under our feet as we walked towards the huge wooden doors. Charlie opened the door and we filed in behind him into that vast monument to religion.

'Do we have to pay for this?' I whispered curiously to Susie.

'Of course,' she laughed.

I suppose it was a silly question because I knew that in England you had to pay for church weddings but somehow this was different. I'd never seen anything like it before, except in London, and that was St Paul's Cathedral.

I felt dwarfed by the size and the whole thing fascinated me. The detail on each window was amazing. Heraldic glass containing holy images stained carefully into the glass in wonderful detail. The ancient brickwork of the wall dwarfed me and the flagstone flooring seemed to go on forever – untouched by history.

'I sing in the choir here, Steve. I chose this place because I love it so much – it's like a friend to me, and the priest speaks a little English. You like it, don't you?'

I nodded because the splendour of my surroundings had

rendered me speechless. I began to picture guests from both our lives filing in just as we had done a few minutes before. I was sure they would feel the same sense of awe as I, and suddenly I felt like I was someone special. I looked at Susie as she stood talking to her parents and there in front of me I saw my wife and everything fell into place. There, in that church, our two hearts and minds would become one.

'I don't know how we'll fill the place!' I joked.

'We will do our best,' was Susie's laughing response.

It was then that the thought occurred to me. She must have a lot of family and friends if that was the case whereas I had little to bring to my wedding. A scattering of friends and perhaps one family member. My life was not exactly packed with masses of friends and family, let alone those who could be persuaded to make the journey. Looking around the magnificent building, I felt slightly embarrassed about my own sad life.

We continued to walk around the church for a while before the priest arrived. He seemed as if he was a man of character and wisdom. His white robes were complemented by his wispy grey hair and his black sash matched his thick dark eyebrows. He spoke in German, first to Charlie and Beate and then to Susie. I stood and listened trying to predict what they were saying and when the pastor with an unpronounceable name did eventually speak to me, he said just five words in German.

I looked at Susie. 'What did he say?'

'I will see you soon,' she replied.

'Thank you.' I smiled acknowledgement. '*Danka shun.*'

'So, August the fifth, my love,' Susie informed me as we were leaving.

'Excellent!' It seemed okay to me.

'Now we have to discuss the arrangements for the week before the wedding. You call them stag and hen nights, I believe, *schatz*?'

'Don't forget the rings,' Beate chipped in with a grin.

As we walked to the car behind Charlie and Beate, I put my arm around Susie's waist and squeezed her gently. 'I hope we'll be like them,' I said, nodding towards my future in-laws.

'Of course we will,' she replied without hesitation.

'How long have they been married, Susie?'

'Thirty-five years.'

As I climbed into the car it dawned on me that Susie *and* her parents, seemed to have it all mapped out.

The next two days of my short visit were filled with arrangements in which I had little say. It wasn't that I minded because I had no knowledge of their customs or ways. I had assumed that they wouldn't be a lot different but I soon found out that I was wrong. One of the big differences was that we would wear our wedding rings on our right hands instead of our left. The other was that we would share our "hen" and "stag" nights – same time – same place. That way, Susie told me, everyone would meet before the wedding and it would make it easier to socialise on the big day itself.

I decided to agree with everything and made an effort to really get into the swing of things. Susie was my world now – my beautiful future and once that ring was on my finger I swore that I would be hers forever. I'd always believed in marriage and for the time being I pushed aside my fears of a childless future and the practicalities of where we would live and replaced them with faith in, and love of, the girl beside me.

When it was time to return to England again, it was as usual with a heavy heart.

'I will be over in England within a month. I want to party with your friends and celebrate there too!' Susie told me happily.

I hugged her and agreed even though I couldn't think of many people who actually cared about us. How had my world seemed full before?

I slept restlessly in my own bed that night but thankfully

there were no dreams. The morning, however, brought a nightmare.

****

I was woken by the telephone. Looking at the digital clock I saw that it was still only six in the morning. I lifted the receiver feeling tired and angry at being called at that early hour.

'Are you up, Boy?' It was my grandmother's voice.

'I am now, Granny,' I said, with a degree of sarcasm, but my anger soon dissipated. Perhaps there had been trouble while I was away.

'Then I shall be round to see you soon, Boy.'

'But....' the line went dead.

I pulled the covers back over me. This wasn't the first time over the past few months - and I was sure it wouldn't be the last - that Granny had called me at odd hours then not remembered doing so. Forgive her, Steve. She's not a well woman, I thought as I snuggled down under the covers.

I soon fell asleep again comforted by the soft warmth of the quilt until I was woken again by a loud bang followed by the continuous ringing of the bell. I leapt out of bed bleary with sleep and angry at being disturbed again but I softened when I opened the door to see her standing on the step.

'Hi, Granny,' I welcomed her wearily.

'Don't you "Granny" me, Steve!' She barged past me into the house and I followed behind her, wondering exactly where she could be going at that time of the morning. I didn't even know whether or not she knew herself but I soon discovered that despite everything, it was one of her more lucid days.

'Cyril is back.' She pulled out a kitchen stool and sat down on it. 'Put the kettle on.'

I obeyed without even questioning her. It was too early in the morning for discussion and if it helped her to believe her husband was back, then let her.

As I made the tea I glanced at her and saw that anger was flaming in her eyes. I decided then that the best thing to do would be to go along with her story.

'That's great news, Granny. Will I get to see him too this time?'

'We are *not* happy,' was her reply.

.'What's the problem?' I stirred the teabag slowly into the water and as I did so she suddenly grabbed my wrist so that the cup tipped over and the tea spilled onto the worktop.

'Jesus, Granny! Be careful!' I exclaimed.

'Don't marry her, Steve.'

The shock made me drop the spoon and it clattered onto the table.

CHAPTER THIRTY-THREE

'How did you know, Granny?'

My brain was rotating faster than a spinning top. There was no way she could have known about my plans to marry Susie. I'd purposely kept them from her. Now with this and recent events, I felt completely certain that there was something, or someone, else involved in my life. There must be, and as I listened to what she was saying I had no choice but to believe. Whatever doubts I may have had about my grandmother's state of mind could not hide the fact that she believed totally in what she was saying.

'Cyril told me, Boy. He came back and told me that you were going to marry the German girl and that it would be the wrong thing to do.' Her words were as brittle as she was.

'Why does he think that way, Granny? I love Susie.' I tried to placate her.

She let go of my arm and at the same time dropped her head as if the moment of strength was past and she was again giving in to the weakness of old age and illness.

'I don't know, Steve.' I heard the tremor in her voice. 'I...can't remember.'

I sensed the frustration in her voice and pushed her gently back down onto the stool. Passing her the cup of tea I saw that her hand was shaking as she took it. I tried to reassure her. 'Don't worry, Granny. It'll be alright,' I spoke earnestly. 'Next time you meet him tell Granddad that you've told me and that I'm thinking about it carefully. Okay?'

She smiled at me but it was obvious that she no longer had

any idea what the hell I was talking about.

****

The narrow stairway leading to Sharon's flat was in darkness despite the time of day. It looked dingy as always and the carpet on the staircase was dark with grime.

Although I'd decided to help her with the debt, I had two main concerns about it. One was that she might not use the money to pay off the debt and the other was wondering where we would go from there. I couldn't afford to do it again and there was little chance that she would be able to pay back the money.

I banged on the door and waited while Sharon once again peered cautiously at me through the gap between the chain and the door. I moved closer so that she could see that it was me and said, 'It's only me, sis.'

She looked blank and then said, 'Oh, bruv,' and unhooked the chain to let me in.

Sharon looked so different now; not at all like the girl I had grown up with. As I went to give her our customary hug, I saw that her face was bloated and one of her eyes was bruised. She was wearing her glasses and the lens that covered her black eye was cracked. I felt nothing but despair as she began to cry.

'No, Sharon,' I said firmly. 'No tears today. We're going to get you sorted out.'

I took hold of her hand and walked the few steps into the kitchen at the rear of the flat. Once Sharon had been a woman who had taken pride in her home but the days when her kitchen was spotless were long gone. Now there were filthy cups stacked up alongside plates and bowls containing all manner of aged food. The smell was overpowering.

'Sit down, sis,' I said firmly.

She obeyed immediately, looking like a lost child. I felt so sad seeing the shadow of the girl I had known. I walked over to the window and wrestled to open it in an attempt to let in some fresher air.

'Can't you *smell* the stench in here?' I said harshly.

'Yes, bruv, sorry,' she whimpered.

Forcing the window open I felt a blast of cold air enter the room. I had difficulty keeping my feelings of resentment from her but she looked so pathetic that I had to relent. I knelt down in front of her and took her hands in mine.

'Look, honey,' I said softly. 'Go and get a shower and freshen yourself up. I'll make some tea and toast and then we'll talk. You can tell me all that's been happening. Alright?'

She nodded nervously.

'Sis, we'll get the money paid and then between us we'll make sure you get over this. Okay?' I hoped that my promise to wipe out her debt would calm her.

Her long brown hair was matted and greasy but I still saw how pretty she had been. I watched as the tears rolled unchecked down her face.

'Why are you so nice to me, Steve? I don't deserve you as my brother,' she sobbed.

'Of course you do, sis,' I said. 'We need each other. Now come on, go and get a shower and clean yourself up.' Despite my feelings I remained firm and my voice seemed to have the desired effect because without another word she got up and went out of the room.

While she was in the bathroom I set about tidying the place up a bit. Piling the dirty crockery into the bowl, I discovered that there was no hot water. The electricity had apparently been cut off so I filled a kettle and put it on the gas ring which, thankfully, was still working. I looked around and found some stale bread that was now inedible. It was no good. I would have to go over the road to the shop.

There was also no milk or tea. After putting the hot water in the bowl together with some of the encrusted crockery, I made a list in my mind. The place hadn't seen bleach or any cleaning agent for weeks - if not months.

'Sis, I'm going over the shop, back in a mo,' I called as I put the door on the latch.

'Okay, bruv.' I heard the renewed sense of security in her voice and smiled to myself as I leapt down the stairs.

I shopped quickly and when I went back into the flat with my purchases I saw that the bathroom door was ajar. That seemed like a good sign so I busied myself with getting some breakfast ready. I doubted whether Sharon had eaten anything much for a long time.

I unpacked the shopping and put the kettle back on the stove to boil. The thought occurred to me that she might like some dippy eggs and soldiers – the classic kids' meal that had always made me feel better. I went to find her to ask her.

The hall of her flat extended from the lounge to the kitchen and was about thirty feet long. Sharon's bedroom was next to the bathroom about mid way between the two and as I walked along it I was about to call her name when I heard a sound that stopped me in my tracks.

Chop, chop, chop, scrape. Chop, chop, chop scrape. Then a long snorting sound. Cocaine. I didn't need to listen to the other nostril repeating the dose. I just knew she was piling the stuff up her nose as soon as my back was turned. I felt a combination of hurt and anger but instead of barging in I walked quietly back to the kitchen. I would just make the eggs anyway.

I rested my elbows on the worktop and put my head in my hands in desperation. What could I do? I wasn't a doctor or a specialist who could help her to rid herself of the drug that ran through her veins. I decided that it was no longer time to be angry; what I had to do was to seek professional help for her.

Ten minutes later Sharon came into the kitchen and sat down.

'Feel better?' I said, putting the tea down in front of her.

She sat there in nothing but her once white dressing gown that looked as if it needed a good wash. She scratched her nose and sniffed as if she was trying to hide what I already knew. I didn't question her about it.

'Much better thanks, bruv. Just got to shake off this cold.' The lies slipped freely from her lips.

'I've made you eggs and soldiers, sis. Do you good to get some food into you.' I knew she wouldn't want to eat now with a fresh dose of coke up her nose, but it would make her think that I hadn't noticed.

'I'm not hungry but thanks, bruv. I had breakfast before you got here.'

'Oh well, two eggs for me then,' I said cheerfully.

She said nothing while I bustled around the kitchen accompanied by the sound of her sniffing. The wretched drug was consuming her the way it did everyone. If Sharon didn't get help soon, the future looked bleak indeed and as far as I could see, there was no one else around who gave a damn.

A faint smile touched her lips as she sat and watched me tuck into the eggs and I occasionally nodded my appreciation of the meal. She looked better now after the shower but the cocaine had made her eyes glazed. I wondered, not for the first time, how any drug taker could think that their habit could go unnoticed.

'So!' I said cheerfully when I had eaten the last mouthful. 'How did you get that black eye then?'

'It was a warning, bruv,' she replied hesitantly and I knew that she was speaking the truth. 'About the money I owe.'

'Well, don't worry about that, sis,' I said dismissively. 'I have the money and I'll go and pay it with you but I'm not going to just give you the money, okay? I want to see it given to the right person.'

I watched her face for reaction. I saw that she was tempted when I said that I had the money. I guessed that she was probably wondering how she could get to keep some of the money back so she could feed herself more of the crap.

'I can take it round, bruv,' she reasoned. 'You don't have to put yourself out anymore. Just by helping me with the money you've done enough.' She sat back looking slightly smug and I saw Gollum in front of me.

I gave Sharon a fierce look. 'No room for discussion, sis. I go with you or you get nothing. I'm not feeding your damned habit. I'm trying to help you. End of discussion.'

Sure enough the drug had been talking or thinking for her.

'Alright, bruv! No need to go on at me,' she said, obviously trying to make me feel sorry for her. The cocaine was still master, at least for another half hour or so.

I ignored her – didn't even look at her in case I said something that I would regret. I loved the girl as if she was my own flesh and blood. We'd shared great moments and her loyalty to me had never wavered. I owed it to her and to myself to try and get her through this. As I washed up my breakfast dishes she just sat there in some kind of daze. I figured she'd forgotten *how* to act in front of someone who wasn't a user. Her days and nights were filled with people looking and feeling like she usually did. I probably didn't *look* normal to her!

'Right then, sis, we're going to go and pay this debt and take the first step towards the new you!' I forced an enthusiastic smile for her benefit but she didn't seem happy about it so I tickled her in an effort to bring her round. As our eyes met I saw the pain in hers. 'Sis, please. I'm only trying to help. For Christ's sake, please let me help you.'

'I know you are, bruv,' she said. 'I'll get ready.'

I knew then as she got up and left the room that I had at last got through to her.

As I waited for her, I listened for the telltale sounds of chopping but there were none and ten minutes later she appeared looking much better. Her glasses needed replacing but maybe I would treat her if things went to plan and I could convince her to get help. She'd put her hair up in a ponytail and it went a long way to making her look half respectable. Taking her hand I bounced happily along with her attempting to make it seem that we were going somewhere nice.

Once in my car I asked her for directions to where the guy she owed the money to - or should I say to the home of the *dealer* who was feeding her the stuff. She didn't tell me the address outright but simply pointed out the directions as we went along. I felt a little like a rally driver being directed by his co-driver - all that was missing was "sharp left twenty metres ahead" because what I got was 'Left here, bruv.'

When we finally reached our destination, Sharon turned and looked at me as if she was waiting for my reaction but I said nothing - just got out of the car.

She knocked on the door and as I expected by the address it was opened by Laurence. Although he looked surprised to see me, he soon regained his composure.

'Steve! What are you doing here, mate?' A smiled touched his lips but he must have known damned well what I was doing there.

'Six hundred quid, is that right?' I said, coldly.

'Er... yeah... give or take a couple of quid.' His voice was emotionless.

Taking the money carefully from my pocket I shoved it into his hand. 'There. Debt paid. Come on, sis.'

I nodded at her and she turned and began to walk towards the car. Her head hung low as if she was cowering from Laurence. I waited until she had taken a few steps before I moved closer to him and putting my face right up against his, I said, 'Now do me a favour and leave her alone. Don't go fucking near her. You hear me?'

'Easy on, Steve. I'm not the one with a problem.'

At that moment I hated Laurence with all my heart. He was part of the reason why Sharon was in trouble and he should have known better.

Screw him, screw Clacton.

I guessed by the way that he returned my look that he knew what I was thinking. There was no need for either of us to say anything more.

We both knew that a friendship had died on that doorstep
.

****

I got back in the car and without speaking to Sharon, revved the motor and span off towards the seafront and didn't stop until we had reached the short stretch of gardens in the middle of the promenade.

'Come on.' I got out of the car and she followed me without argument as I walked down the slope which led onto the beach. When we reached the bottom I stopped and lit a cigarette and looked at her for the first time since we had arrived at Laurence's house.

'Are you angry with me?' she said nervously, but I ignored her question.

'I couldn't *not* tell you, bruv,' she persisted. 'I felt so embarrassed and I'm so sorry - I really am.'

My mind was in turmoil. How could I take out my disappointment on her? She was partly to blame, of course she was, but she was also the *victim*. Laurence should have helped her, should have stopped her, but he did nothing except make money out of her and rape her personality from her. No. I wasn't going to get angry with her.

'Sharon, I need you to promise me something.' I pulled her round to face me. 'I'm not angry, but please promise me just one thing.'

'Anything - just don't be mad at me anymore,' she pleaded.

Taking a deep drag on my cigarette, I breathed the smoke out into the air in an attempt to steady myself. 'Look, Sharon, I won't be here forever. I'm getting married to Susie and I'm not even sure if I'm going to still be living in England. I want you to know that the one thing I promise to do before any of this happens is to help you.' I paused, feeling overwhelmed by the sorrow inside me. 'My grandmother's dying, I don't have many true friends left but I have you, my adopted, pretend sister and friend whom I love dearly. Please don't let this happen to you. Please let me get you help - professional help.'

She didn't reply for a few minutes and then she said, 'Okay, Steve. I'll do it for you *and* for me.'

I knew she meant what she said and I sensed that she felt as relieved as I did. As we hugged it felt as if we had been reprieved. Maybe there *was* one thing that I could do in that town that would count for something.

I would do my best for her.

****

The weekend and Susie finally arrived and after a lovely night together we decided to meet with Harry in the town the following evening. The three of us sat in the Moon where Harry bought us a couple of celebratory bottles of champagne to drink to our future. Good old Harry! The drinks and chat flowed and it was a good night. That was until I heard a familiar voice.

'Well, well, a party I see!' A voice taunted us.

I looked up and saw that our table was surrounded by a group of men and at the head of the pack was Laurence.

CHAPTER THIRTY-FOUR

I glared at him at the same time as Susie leapt from her chair.

'Laurence!' She crooned as she approached him.

I was shocked to see him take her in his arms and squeeze her tightly. Susie, of course, had no idea about what had been happening and I couldn't blame her for being pleased to see him. Harry and I knew differently. The whole Sharon thing stank and the fact that good old Laurence was now a major cocaine dealer made me hate him even more. I felt sick inside as I looked on.

After he had stopped whispering in Susie's ear and she had stopped smiling and they had stopped holding, I saw him turn and speak to a couple of his cronies. I knew one by sight and he was bad news, but as they shuffled off Laurence sat down with us.

'How are we, fellers?' I saw the smirk on his face as he turned to speak to Susie. 'I haven't seen these guys for a while now.'

'Really?' She looked surprised. 'But you were all such good friends. What has happened, Steve?'

I had no wish to explain about "nice Mr. Laurence" now in front of the others. I would wait until later. For now I bluffed. 'I've just been so busy, darling, what with the wedding and everything. We'll have to catch up though, Laurence.' I shot him a glance that I hoped told him that I couldn't wait.

'You're right, Laurence. We should catch up more often,' Harry chipped in. 'I've just been real busy earning an honest living. What have you been up to?'

Good old Harry! Always ready to lend a hand. Not that it did anything to divert Laurence from whatever it was he intended doing.

'Same here, Harry. Enjoying my work as much as ever,' he mocked. 'So?' He looked at Susie again. 'I hear you're going to marry our Steve.'

Susie blushed. 'Yes, we are to be married in August. You will be coming, of course?'

'I would love to but only if my broken heart mends by then, pretty lady. I wanted you all for myself, you know,' he grinned.

I couldn't believe the cheek of the bloke. What made it even worse was that Susie was swimming in his bullshit compliments and actually responding as if she believed him.

'Now if I had known that, Laurence....' She smiled at him and it made me feel jealous in a way I hadn't felt before.

For another two hours I had to listen to him complimenting Susie while at the same time dropping in crafty little comments that I couldn't react to without causing a scene. By the time it was my turn to go for more drinks my blood was boiling and the final straw came just after I returned. Harry flashed me a look that told me that Laurence's behaviour was getting worse and worse the more he drank.

'I was just saying to your lovely lady, Steve. Do you all fancy coming to a party tonight? Beats going home and being boring, don't you say?' His efforts at being smooth almost made me gag.

'Sounds like a good idea,' Susie said enthusiastically.

I couldn't do it! I couldn't spend another minute in that man's company.

'Sorry, darling. I'm a bit tired tonight - maybe another time?' My efforts at wriggling out of the invitation sounded pathetic but it was all I could muster up in the way of an excuse.

'Okay. Sorry, Laurence, perhaps another time when Steve is more awake.' I saw her wink at him but I knew that she was disappointed.

Jealousy burned even brighter.

Laurence wore the smile of a torture chief who was enjoying

his work and it seemed that he still had one more stunt to pull.

'No problem, sweet Susie. Maybe next time we meet there'll be more of us anyway.' He turned to me. 'Where are the others by the way, Steve? I haven't seen Sharon and her pals for a while.'

'You know where she is, you idiot.' I scowled at him.

'No, last time I saw her she was out of her face,' he shrugged. 'Think it was my punch that did it?'

Susie grinned at his supposed joke but I couldn't hold on any longer.

Grabbing him by the throat, I shouted, 'Tell me if it was as tasty as my punch, you piece of shit!' before hitting him with the full force of my right fist.

I caught him flush on the nose and he sprayed claret as my knuckle ate into him. He reeled back, holding his face, thus avoiding my second punch, and fell to the floor. The last thing I heard him shout was, 'You prick!' before I found myself being gripped by two doormen who proceeded to walk me out of the building before pushing me down the stairs.

I heard one of them shout that I was barred.

Terrific!

The cold air helped both to sober me and to dissipate my anger and I sat on the wall outside waiting for Susie to follow me. After about five minutes I began to wonder where the hell she was. It was one helluva bullshit situation to be in. I couldn't go back inside and she hadn't come out. Just as I was deciding whether or not to make even more of a prat of myself, Harry appeared looking more than a little flustered.

'Hi, mate,' he said quickly. 'Look, I'll be back in a minute with Susie but Laurence is playing the victim and she's fallen for it. She's pretty mad with you right now, believe it or not. Give me five and I'll work on her.' With that he went back inside.

I continued to sit there. What the hell was going on? How could she fall for that rubbish? I'd held back and held back and now I wished I'd told her everything about Laurence earlier. If she'd known what he was like she'd probably have been the one to punch him on the nose.

Eventually both Susie and Harry joined me. I stood up to speak to her but before I could say anything she said, 'I am ashamed of you tonight, Steve.'

Her look told me that she was deadly serious and I suddenly felt like a kid who had been told off by his parents for something he hadn't done. I started to say something but Harry's look indicated that I should keep quiet.

He left us by the taxi rank and Susie and I went home together. After several failed attempts at explaining what had happened I gave up and spent the night on my own sofa while Laurence was probably still partying somewhere.

The next morning I found myself apologising to her for what had happened.

'Look, Susie. I know I shouldn't have hit him, but he was provoking me about Sharon.' I said, trying again to make things right between us.

'What, so *Sharon* is so important to you, is she?' She flared at me.

I was astounded by her reaction. 'What? Of course! But only as a friend, don't you get it? Laurence was selling her drugs, Susie. He's a drug dealer!'

Susie was having none of it. 'That is rubbish and you know it, Steve!' she said angrily. 'I heard she is the one who is the dealer! It upsets me to think you would defend her over your friend. Is she *that* special to you? Is it her you wish to marry?' She looked at me with contempt and I could hardly believe what I was hearing.

'Of course I don't,' I said unhappily. 'That's just ridiculous!'

It was a no-win situation for me and it seemed that she still hadn't finished.

'Then stop hanging about with her, and next time you see Laurence I think you should apologise to him. I felt so ashamed of you last night. Is that the man I am to marry? One who hits his friends over a girl or after a drink?'

'No,' I mumbled because I had no real answer for her. She had formed her own opinion of what had happened and whatever Laurence had said had added nothing to my cause.

Despite my resentment, I gave up arguing with her. We had only a few days left together and I wanted to make the most of them. After a while she forgave me and calmed down. Payback time for Laurence would have to wait because I didn't want it to spoil my time with Susie. Enough damage had already been done.

As usual, the time flew by and soon it was time for her to go home. We sat in the airport working out how many more times it would be before we would be together all the time so that there would be no more travelling. Susie said that she would miss her parents and friends and would at first want to travel home often. It was then that I mentioned my idea that perhaps it would be better to actually *live* in Germany.

'I think I could get work, Susie and I'd try and learn the language. It makes more sense because you have a good job. I think you have more to give up than me and I could adapt,' I reasoned.

She didn't answer for a moment or two and then she said, 'I would like to live in England, but...I will think about it.'

I nodded but remained silent. As I kissed her at the departure gate I was left feeling as if I was completely out of control of anything relating to Susie. She was in charge.

****

The next Thursday I went to a London clinic to see the doctor that Pat had put me in contact with. Despite the fact that I was understandably embarrassed about being there, I felt quite relaxed about the appointment. The procedure wasn't too damaging to my already shattered pride, the medical staff were helpful and the consulting rooms were bright, clean and well-equipped. After they had done the tests, the doctor told me that it would be a little while before they had the results but that they would be in touch as soon as possible.

'We must remain hopeful,' he said, as I was leaving.

Hopeful, always hopeful, remembering what Roz had said to me.

During the long drive home along the M25, I thought about Susie and me trying to analyse the doubts I was beginning to feel. Whichever way I looked at it, she seemed to be in control. Her way or no way! I reasoned that living in Germany seemed the better option for me but now that decision was in *her* hands. It was a sobering thought. I was an addict and Susie was my drug - my escape route.

Pulling into Clacton the big picture hit me and I was overcome by sadness. If Susie agreed then I would leave England and my history behind. The truth was, I had no life here any more. Everything seemed to have gone wrong. I sat alone in the car outside my house, thinking hard and wiping away the tears that trickled down my cheeks. Once my grandmother succumbed to the saddest of illnesses, there would be little or no reason for me to remain.

For the first time I actually felt all out of that thing called hope.

CHAPTER THIRTY-FIVE

The next week I went to Sharon's to collect her to take her to the hospital in Colchester where I had made an appointment for her to see a specialist. When I arrived at her flat I found someone who looked as if they had just done a few lines, rather than a person who wanted to stop the habit. I controlled my anger with difficulty and urged her to accompany me. After making some ridiculous attempts to lie to me about a job she had to get ready for, I grabbed her hand and practically pulled her out of the door.

As we walked in through the main entrance, the whole horrible hospital smell filled my nostrils and having an avid dislike for the whole medical scene, I had to put on a brave face. As we sat and waited our turn, I saw that Sharon was shivering and that her pale face showed the reality of where she was and why she was there. Before long the consultant called her name and smiled at me, but at the same time indicated that he wanted only Sharon to follow him. She gave me a scared look before following him into his room.

I just sat there waiting, trying to kill time by sipping coffee from the machine and once went outside for a cigarette. I felt as if a weight had been lifted from my shoulders. It was the doctor's turn to help her now; I'd done my bit and it had almost cost me dear. I still felt angry about what Laurence had tried to do with Susie by baiting me with Sharon. I comforted myself with the thought that soon it would all be over and I would be able to get on with my life.

After about half an hour the doctor came out of his room and came over to me and started asking questions about her. I gave him as much detail as I could about her drug-taking habit and where it had led her.

'You've done the right thing bringing her here,' he said, after listening to me. 'Sharon has agreed to be admitted for treatment which is the first step. She'll need some clothes and maybe a few home comforts. Will you be able to see to that? It's what she wants.'

I could see by his expression that he was worried so I nodded agreement both to his decision to keep her in and to fetch her things.

'Will she be alright, doctor?' It sounded like a cliché I knew, but despite this he answered me in a calm, professional voice.

'We're going to try and treat her for both problems because it seems that Sharon not only has a serious drug addiction, but also a potentially serious alcohol problem. It helps that she's been so open about everything, but frankly she needs to be here where we can look after her. I've recommended a three-month rehabilitation period which I hope will prove successful.'

I nodded again then spoke briefly to Sharon, who seemed relieved that she was at last receiving help. I took her keys from her so that I could get what she needed from the flat.

I didn't see her when I returned with her clothes and a bag of bits that she had asked for so I left them and her keys with the nurse.

Maybe it was for the best. I had done as much as I could.

****

It was I who now needed guidance.

It was a rain-soaked afternoon when I walked the short distance to my parents' grave. It had been too long since my last visit and although I thought about them often it was there that I felt their presence the most. Looking at their names engraved in the stone gave me a combined feeling of grief and strength.

'Mum, Dad,' I whispered like a child. 'I'll soon be leaving here. I'm destined to live somewhere else. I feel it and I just hope that I'm doing the right things by you both.'

I stood with the rain falling onto my face, immediately feeling cleaner. It was as if I had shed the pain and strain of all that had been going on around, like a snake shedding its skin. I heard no words in reply and I expected none, but I felt that something positive had happened within myself.

I didn't need voices in my head anymore. I'd started to believe in destiny and my faith would be my guide.

****

As April, the month of showers, neared its end, I went back to Berlin, the city that I hoped would soon be my home. It was for a three-day visit with nothing but wedding dresses and rings on the agenda and Susie had planned another visit to the church to make notes and take down all the information I would need to relay to Pat involving both his and my duties.

After hours spent looking at dresses and suits with Susie and her parents, I'd had enough and Charlie and Beate suggested that they treat us to dinner at a well-known fish restaurant on Potsdam Plaza. Charlie seemed to be enjoying himself and we were in agreement about wearing dark grey Italian-designed suits with lilac cravats and waistcoats. The girls had given their approval so all was going well. Now we just had to wait for Susie to decide between three different gowns, the outcome of which I apparently would not know until the day I saw her walk down the aisle.

I chatted with Charlie as we walked together to the restaurant.

'Are you happy, Steve?' he suddenly asked me.

'Of course. I'm looking forward to it all very much,' I replied.

The girls were as usual in front and Susie turned back towards us and said, 'Come, hurry! Papa! Steve!'

Charlie raised his eyebrows in acceptance. 'This is the life with a German wife! I am a poet also!'

I joined him in laughter. 'Is it always like this then, Charlie?'

He stopped and turned to me, becoming serious. 'Steve, when you have a family with Susie you will become the third person in the relationship. That is neither a good or bad thing but that is the way it will be. It is the way that she knows and you must be prepared for that.'

I hadn't asked the question but he had sensed what I meant. I would be the third person. I hadn't even mentioned a child!

We sat in the restaurant and I remained quiet while the others chatted away happily. The fish was superb - a selection of trout and sea bass, but I couldn't stop thinking about the talk I was going to have with Susie. For some reason I thought about the woman at the flower stall in my dream and wondered about the meaning of it all. If there was one. Suddenly everything in my sleeping world - the visions, the strange moments, seemed just as real as the world I was in.

I felt suddenly as if I was losing control as Charlie's words echoed in my mind. I felt distanced from those sitting around me. I didn't feel the same as them and it brought an overriding emotion to the fore, with or without a child I didn't want to be third in *any* relationship.... I felt a bead of sweat on my forehead and quickly wiped it away.

'Are you okay, *schatz*?' I heard Susie's voice from somewhere in the distance and snapped out of my daydream.

'Susie, we need to talk.'

CHAPTER THIRTY-SIX

I ran my lucky coin through each of my fingers as I waited. I *called* it lucky but I doubted if it really was. It was just that it was the only memory I had left of Andréa and our time together. It had become my talisman and I would hold it before getting on a flight or, like now, when I needed a friend.

I watched as Susie stood outside the window of the small bar talking to her friends on her mobile. I guessed that she was explaining why we wouldn't be meeting them after all, that we had things to discuss. It had been hard enough to get her to agree to a one to one with me after the meal, but eventually she had relented – with a smile – no doubt thinking that I had some big surprise for her. After meeting with the doctor before I left I did indeed have some news. Oh boy, did I!

A waitress came over and I ordered a bottle of red wine. The bar was like a small converted cellar. Small paned windows let in narrow rays of light but now as night was falling, candles glowed on the tables around us. Old wooden floors added to the atmosphere and I imagined that in days gone by, important men – perhaps future presidents and generals, or even poets and writers - would have met to discuss or write about their countries. Mine was not such a big issue - just one man and one woman.

Susie arrived soon after the wine and I watched as she unravelled her scarf and pushed back her hair before sliding out of her coat. As she sat down, the candlelight softly illuminated her face capturing the warmth in her brown eyes. We were face to face and she looked at me lovingly, slipping her hand into mine.

'So, *schatz*, what have you brought me here for then?' Her voice echoed with anticipation. I wished that I had a lovely gift for her or something wonderful that I wanted to tell her. As I poured the wine into the glasses I wished more than anything for this to be the case.

'Susie,' I began, 'you know I love you very much and I'm looking forward to being your husband, don't you?'

'I do, Steve, and I love you too, of course. Why do you talk of this now? Is something wrong?'

I figured there was no easy way to say what I wanted to say. 'Well no…I mean yes…I mean…maybe, Susie. I need to find the right words and talk to you about something. Something I should have told you about before, I guess.'

She looked confused and I wasn't surprised because I knew that I was procrastinating and it wasn't making it any easier. My mind felt as if it was a ball of fuzzy words.

'Well? What is it?' she said impatiently.

I took a deep breath. 'Okay. When I was young I got ill with what we call in English, mumps. Apparently it was a serious case but all I remember was being sick and having a fever. When I recovered, my grandmother told me that when I was grown up I might have problems with having children. She'd tell me that if I ate my vegetables up it would help.' I smiled, trying to make light of it with the last words and then realised that my timing was terrible so I tried to look serious again.

'What are you saying, Steve?' Susie's voice was filled with concern.

'Well, darling…I didn't think about any of it for years. I suppose I even forgot about it until I met you and it was only when we spoke about having children that it all came flooding back to me. That I might not be able to have children.' I knew what was coming next.

'And can you?' She pulled her hand away from mine. I saw the fear in her body language and began to feel weak.

'I went for tests, Susie, and the consultant's opinion is that the chances would be very slim.' I blurted the words out.

We looked at each other and I tried to work out what her reaction was going to be but I could saw nothing but hurt in her eyes. At that moment I felt like a man waiting to be told that he has a terminal illness. I waited for her to smile, to grab me and say it would be all right but I knew that would not be the case. Her eyes told me that it wouldn't.

At last she spoke. 'Why have you not told me this before, Steve?'

'I was waiting for the right time, darling. The tests aren't completely reliable...I mean...the chances are slim, not nil.' I knew I sounded feeble.

'And you think this is the right time, do you, Steve?' She leant towards me and although she was whispering I could hear the resentment in her voice. 'You think that just months before we are to be married would be a good time to tell me that you cannot father a child? You think that it is fair to leave it until now to tell me this?'

'Susie, I.....'

'You *nothing*!' Her voice was louder – angrier. 'You did not think because you knew if you told me it could ruin everything. So why tell me now? Why didn't you just wait until we were married and trying for babies before we discovered that you couldn't even have them?'

Her voice was now loud enough for everyone else in the bar to hear and I saw a few faces turn to look at Mr. Sterile and his angry woman. I wanted the earth to swallow me up.

'No, Susie,' I said desperately. 'That wasn't what I was thinking of doing. I wanted to talk to you about it but everything has moved so fast. One day we were just visiting, getting to know each other, the next we were discussing marriage! It all happened so fast and I hadn't found the right time to discuss it with you.'

The distance between the table and us now seemed to have expanded.

'So what do you expect me to do, Steve? Jump up and hug you? Sing a song of love for us? I wanted to marry you and have a family with you.' Her voice was icy cold.

The one word *wanted* registered above all others. It wasn't the word *want* as in I *do*. It was *wanted* as in I *did*. My heart sank and my stomach felt as if it had been punched.

'Please, Susie, we can still be happy. We can get treatment. There are other ways. We can discover them together and get through this. We can still have a family.' I heard myself pleading as I realised just how big a blow it was to her not to be able to have a child. I remembered her father's words about love fading and I began to feel that my sole purpose had been to support her and give her a child, before I too faded into the background. I hadn't wanted to believe it but the feeling was inescapable as I sat there facing her wrath.

'I don't know anymore, Steve.' Her face was blank, emotionless.

'Please, Susie. What do you think it feels like for me? Having to tell it to the woman I love?'

'I wish to leave now, Steve.' She stood up suddenly. 'I need time to think about everything. I do not know if I can marry you. I need time to think - alone.'

With that she walked out of the bar, throwing a fifty-mark note on the table as she left. I followed, scuttling after her like some faithful pet and feeling pathetic as I sat with her in the taxi. When we arrived at her flat she went into the bedroom and closed the door behind her and I heard the key turn in the lock. I made no attempt to say anything more to her because I knew that it wouldn't work and would only increase my feelings of worthlessness. All I did was lie on the settee and wait for the night and the nightmare that was my life to pass me by.

****

Early the next morning I was woken by the sound of the front door slamming. Leaping up and going to the window, I watched as Susie drove away. I had no idea if or when she would be coming back. Once again, as I waited for her to decide about our future, I realised that I had lost control over my own destiny. It seemed so unfair.

After an hour I knew that I couldn't stay in the flat any longer, but I had no keys to get back in. Damn it! I made a decision. I'd go for a long walk and then wait until she returned. Maybe she would have calmed down and be ready to talk. Surely she wouldn't throw everything we had - or could have - away? I felt completely alone. I had no way of getting about and, even if I had, knew no one that I could go and see. Berlin was suddenly a vast and lonely place to be in.

I walked for miles but I couldn't remember afterwards where I'd been. My mind was full of negative feelings and as much as I tried to argue that she loved me and we had so much between us I got the feeling that we had nothing between us. Not now. What could I take into her world? I felt more sorry for myself than ever before as if I'd been cheated by my own body. If only I was capable of fathering a child, I would have the girl, the wedding *and* the future. Why did it always have to be like this? Why was it that I always lost those closest to me? Each step I took was filled with contempt and bitterness.

I ended up walking to the outskirts of Berlin where I spent the afternoon in a bar, looking into one glass of beer followed by another and another. No one made any effort to talk to me nor I them. I was a foreigner in every sense.

As I got up to take one of my frequent beer-induced visits to the toilet, I saw that it was getting dark outside. I stood in front of the urinal hiccupping and feeling my legs doing strange things. It was then that I decided that I had to leave and try to find Susie. In my drunken state I, of course, knew that she wouldn't want to speak to me. The fine balance between logic and stupidity waged war in my mind as snapshots of memories raced through it. Moments of love fought with the jealousy I had felt the night when Laurence interfered and mingled with the exaggerated drink-induced sadness. Unable to focus I thrust a note into the barman's hand and stumbled out of the bar, almost falling over on the pavement.

I looked up at the night sky, swaying, trying to get my

bearings knowing that I could use the towers that stood out on the Berlin skyline as my compass. I decided not to go to Susie's flat but to head, instead, for Charlie and Beate's house, which I guessed must be nearer. Perhaps she would be there. If not, maybe they would give me a lift to her flat and help me resolve things. I tried to think positively.

After more than two hours of tentative, beer-infused steps that led me down unfamiliar street after unfamiliar street, I finally saw the house. Before I knocked on the door I attempted to make myself look less drunk, which, given my inebriated condition, was a ridiculous thing to attempt. I stood outside pulling faces and muttering to myself and noticing that passers-by gave me strange looks that said "drunk".

'Hi Charlie.' I heard the word slur from my mouth when I saw my future, or perhaps *ex* future, father-in-law in the doorway.

'She is not here, Steve,' he said abruptly. 'She has been and gone.'

We looked at each other for a moment in silence. I wanted to ask for his help but no words came out. I knew that she had told him about my problem. My defect. I even thought that I saw pity in his eyes.

'What shall I do, Charlie?' I felt tears begin to well up, helped along no doubt by the alcohol.

'I do not know, Steve.'

The answer was as straightforward as my situation and I watched as he went to go back inside. He was going to close the door, I could feel it. Just as the light in the doorway began to fade, he stopped and said, 'You should stay here tonight, Steve. I will get your things and take you to the airport tomorrow. It is the best I can do for you. I am sorry.'

I had little choice. I was in a mess and the invitation was as good as it was going to get. I followed him into the house feeling ashamed of myself. I must have reeked of beer and cigarettes, not ideal husband material at all. Beate was nowhere to be seen and I didn't ask any questions.

Charlie guided me into the spare room and motioned me to get some sleep.

'Thank you, Charlie. You're a good man,' I said gratefully.

'As are you, Steve. Tomorrow is a new day. Now get some sleep.'

I saw sorrow in his eyes. He probably already knew what tomorrow would bring but at that moment I appreciated his warmth.

He closed the door and I closed my eyes and let alcohol knock me out.

CHAPTER THIRTY-SEVEN

There was to be no meeting with Susie the next day. No chance to see or talk to the girl I should be marrying.

I was woken by Charlie who handed me a cup of strong black coffee. My head thumped with a combination of a hangover and the situation I found myself in. I was a desperate, washed up man with no answers to the problems facing me. Charlie gently controlled my day and I did as he said. I had no wish to offend him and hoped in some way that he might be able to help my cause. I couldn't expect too much, of course, because I was the outsider and his love for his daughter reigned supreme. I could only thank him for his kindness.

We parted at the airport with a handshake. I couldn't be sure whether or not it would be the last time I would ever see him and I doubt if he knew either, so we just shook hands and said goodbye.

****

I was in a state of limbo. The journey home had been fraught with destructive deliberation. Thinking of Charlie's behaviour, I reflected that the baby issue was even more important than I had thought. No doubt Susie had decided that she wanted a child before she even met me. How else could I explain her uncaring reaction? I felt like faulty goods, sent back to where I was made.

Now back in England, there seemed that there was no one around to help to repair me. The days passed and each time I attempted to contact Susie, I was rebuffed. I tried to think of something to do or someone to talk to, but there was no one. Harry was always working and Pat was booked up for a few more weeks. I avoided visiting my grandmother immediately after I returned because I knew that seeing her would only deepen my depression further. In the end, I put on a brave face and went to visit Sharon to find out how she was responding to the treatment. It had been a while since I'd seen her and at least it would take my mind off things.

When I arrived a nurse showed me into the day room where I saw Sharon sitting by one of the large bay windows. She looked so much younger already. As I drew closer I could see that her skin looked healthier - she'd lost that yellowness - whilst her hair looked clean and shone where the sunlight caught it. She beamed when she saw me and her smile made me feel better.

We talked for a good hour but I didn't mention Susie. I just listened to Sharon relaying the details of the treatment, the nightmares and the hope she had found since her admission. She would be in hospital for another two months and then undergo another consultation based on how she had responded to the therapy, before finally being released. Even after the short time that she had been there, I saw a girl who had rediscovered hope. As I hugged her when I was leaving, I consoled myself that at least one of us had some.

****

May came and went as I waited and I waited. I sent emails, made calls, sent texts but there was never any reply.

Apart from my preoccupation with trying to contact Susie, my life was a combination of work and looking after Granny who was now declining rapidly. Each time I visited her it became harder to bear and it wasn't just because of her illness. It hurt sitting there knowing that she didn't understand what I was saying anymore or that what I was saying was hardly worth listening to.

It seemed pointless going out on my own at night so instead I sat and consoled myself with my friendly counsellor, Miss Wine. We became closer than ever as she helped me to sleep and my mind became a dumping ground for dreams. My future, my past, and those damned visions.

****

After a month of self-imposed exile from my social calendar, I got a call from Harry who persuaded me to go out with him. After putting up a little resistance I finally agreed; after all, it was always good to see Harry. He would cheer me up. He always did and I would do my best not to let my depressed state bring him down. In fact I decided I would try and avoid the subject of Susie completely because I was sure everyone was bored of hearing about it by now.

We met in the familiar surroundings of The Moon having arrived by taxi so that we could have a good drink together. It felt good to be going out and I'd made the effort to dig out a decent shirt and trousers and had a real go at my appearance which had been neglected over the last few weeks.

We sat outside and from our table we could see the pier a short distance below with the glittering sea beyond. It was a warm and dreamy evening and as my lungs filled with fresh air I suddenly felt the happiness associated with being with a good friend. Something I'd forgotten about over the last weeks.

We chatted about work. I hadn't done much lately, just enough to pay the bills and my flights to Germany and of course for the little extras I enjoyed. Harry was as usual raking in the cash from his antique business. Judging by his luxurious lifestyle, money never seemed to be an issue, yet despite this, I sensed a hint of sadness in him.

'So how's life at home then, Mr Rich?' I said with a smile.

My intuition proved correct. 'Not so great, Steve. I've been thinking about it a lot recently, you know, and I can't go on like this any longer.'

'Come on, Harry! You always say stuff like that.' I tried to joke even though I knew that he rarely said anything of the sort unless in jest and he didn't even smile.

'It isn't just my marriage, pal. I know I joke about it being bad and all that but you aren't living in my world right now.'

It was uncharted territory for me. I hadn't heard Harry talk like that in all the years I'd known him. 'She's a good woman, Harry, and a brilliant mum,' I said, trying to sound positive. 'You loved her once so maybe you can find that again. You've got to think of the kids as well. You know where I'm coming from, don't you?'

He didn't speak for a moment or two and then said, 'Yeah, you could be right. I know all that. It's just that…Steve, I've been thinking about….' I watched as he struggled to find the words. 'I need to get things sorted…. I hate being in limbo like this.'

I sensed that something was troubling him that was beyond my reach, a deeper problem that he didn't want to discuss. It was unlike him. Harry was the clown, the guy who was always happy and cheerful.

'Come on, Harry, it could be a new start.' I tried again to sound confident and optimistic. 'You just have to believe it can work.'

'Yes, I know that too,' he said but I could tell that he wasn't interested. 'Like I said, it isn't all that. Logic, Steve, what the hell is that?'

His reaction surprised me as did his lack of eye contact. I skirted around a few familiar subjects but received nothing but a few nods interspersed with grunts in reply. The only thing we seemed to have in common was the speed at which we drank. The evening passed with words low on the agenda. Whether it helped Harry or not, I couldn't tell but as the bar closed I felt pleasantly intoxicated. I put my arm reassuringly around him as we walked to the taxi rank.

'Thanks for a good night, mate,' I said and it was only half a lie. It hadn't been the best and that seemed to be the case for both of us.

When we reached the rank, Harry paused before walking towards a waiting taxi. 'Steve, I think I saw Susie.' He blurted the words out.

'Really? Where?' I was thrown completely off balance.

'In Clacton.'

My first thought was one of joy. Good old Harry! He'd been keeping it back from me and now he would unwrap the present with his words. But why had he taken so long to tell me about it?

'Did you talk to her?'

'No.'

He didn't sound happy and I thought about what he had said. It didn't make any sense. If he hadn't spoken to her, then it wasn't her.

'You couldn't have seen her, mate, because if you had she would have spoken to you.'

He took a deep breath and said, 'She didn't see me.'

It was getting late and I was beginning to feel frustrated by it all and, besides, we had both had a lot to drink.

'Okay, Harry, I'm going now. I think you may have been mistaken so let's just leave it there for tonight.' I meant what I said because I didn't want to continue the conversation. I turned and as I walked towards the taxi he grabbed my arm and I tried to shake him off.

'Leave it out, Harry.'

'Steve.' He looked straight at me.

'What?' I felt angry with him.

'It was her. I'm certain it was.'

I pushed him gently away. 'I'll talk to you tomorrow. Good night.'

I got into the taxi before he could say another word.

****

I visited my grandmother during the first week in July to talk about her future. I wasn't sure how she would be so I decided to wait until I saw her, to judge her reaction. I would have loved to have been able to talk to her about my relationship problems, about Sharon. Anything, just to be able to talk like we used to.

I thought it was strange when I rang the doorbell and she didn't answer it. I guessed she must have been taken out somewhere by one of her carers. After a few minutes, I let myself in with my key. The house was clean and tidy and I walked through the kitchen and into the lounge calling her as I went just to make sure, but there was no answer.

I was about to give up, begin writing a note, when I heard a faint sound coming from upstairs. I put down my pen and walked towards the staircase.

'Granny?' I called up the stairs.

I heard the noise again, like a quiet mumble and climbed the stairs cautiously fearful of what I might find. My grandmother was lying in her bed covered in clean, crisp white sheets. By her side was a glass of water and some books and papers.

I walked around the bed. 'Granny, are you alright?' I spoke softly and she opened her eyes and stared vacantly, as if trying to focus on me.

'Rose?' She sounded confused.

'No, Granny, it's Steve. Where's Rose?'

I sat down on the bed next to her, studying her face. She looked older and weaker and I saw the confusion in her eyes as if she didn't know where she was.

Where the hell was the nurse?

'Don't worry, Rose will be back.' She pieced the words

together with difficulty as if she was drugged.

'Are you alright? Have they been looking after you?'

'Like a queen.' A smile touched her lips.

I tried to talk to her but her responses were slow and misshapen. I hadn't seen her looking this bad but at the same time I sensed a strange calmness or maybe it was a gentle realisation that she wouldn't be around for much longer. I didn't want to consider that possibility.

I sat beside her until she fell asleep and then went downstairs to find the telephone number of the hospital. I needed to call them to find out what exactly was going on.

'Hi,' I tried to sound friendly, 'I wonder if you can help. My name's Steve Bidante and my grandmother's receiving home visits from your staff. It's just that I've arrived at her house and there's no nurse here. Can you find out why?' I spoke in a firm but respectful manner. No time to be getting angry, there could be a reasonable explanation.

I heard the receptionist tap out something on a keyboard and then speak to someone else. After a few minutes she spoke to me again, 'Sorry to keep you.'

'That's fine, any news?'

She sounded vague – puzzled even. 'Mr. Bidante, we seem to have a problem with our records. Can I call you back when I have more information?'

'Of course. Is there something wrong?' I said, feeling unconvinced.

'No, sir. It's just our computer records seem to be out of date. According to them the home help was cancelled over a month ago.'

'Cancelled? That can't be right!'

'Please give me some time, Mr. Bidante.' She spoke calmly, yet firmly. 'I'll find out what's happening and call you back.'

I put the phone down feeling mystified. It couldn't be right! I'd been several times in the last month and my grandmother had seemed fine about it all. But still, I hadn't actually *seen* anyone for myself. But she must be getting help. The house was clean and tidy, everything in its place and, judging by her state of mind, I doubt that she would - or could - have cancelled her own home help and done it all herself.

Going back upstairs, I sat down next to her again. Looking at her lying there, I couldn't help but wish that she would wake and be the Granny I knew again. The person lying beside me in the bed looked like her, but in fact was nothing but a shell whose contents were slowly eroding away.

Fifty minutes and two cups of tea later the phone rang. I ran down the stairs and grabbed it anxiously. 'Hello.'

'Hello, Mr. Bidante, it's the hospital here.' It sounded like the same woman I'd spoken to earlier.

'Oh, hi,' I said, relieved. 'Any news?'

'Yes, our apologies for earlier. The nurse wasn't well this morning and we're sending another one who should be with your grandmother early this afternoon. The medication they've given her should make her sleep until then.'

'Thank you for that. I was a little concerned,' I said, feeling better. 'What happened with the records?'

'You know hospitals, Mr. Bidante. We get things wrong or mixed up from time to time. I can only apologise and hope it didn't cause you too much distress.' She sounded as if she was trying to make light of it.

'I guess that can happen. Thanks for getting back to me so soon. Goodbye.'

I took the pen and paper I was going to use earlier and wrote a note for the nurse, writing down my home number just in case they didn't have it and explaining what had happened. I thanked the nurse for all the help and support and requested that if she, or any of the other nurses, thought they were going to be late, that they would let me know so as to avoid any further worry.

After that I went to check on my grandmother again. She was in a deep sleep, snoring gently.

CHAPTER THIRTY-EIGHT

July brought a heat wave that made everything seem more of an effort. I picked up jobs where I could and tried to work during the cooler times of the day. I spent the balmy evenings, shirtless, in the garden or wandering down to the seafront and strolling along the beach, lost in my own dreams.

At the end of July Sharon was "released" - so to speak. She had completed nearly all her rehabilitation and the doctors were happy with her progress. It seemed that not only was she clean now, but that she wanted to remain that way. We spent the first couple of weeks of her freedom together and it was lovely. She hardly mentioned the rehabilitation process, wanting to talk more about the future and I was happy to go along with her. It was like having a new friend – or more like having my old friend back.

It was like the old days and I loved it.

When Sharon suggested we go for one of our walks along the promenade, I was more than happy. I loved strolling along the seafront, even more so with her. After parking my car on the left of the beach we headed down towards the pier. I of course spoke about Susie as we walked while Sharon listened and nodded without saying too much in response, just being the friend I had missed so much. Weaving our way through the crowds coming from the pier area, I took in the surroundings. I loved the feeling of peace it gave me, as well as hearing and feeling the mixture of people who were on holiday and those who, like me, lived there. The smell of candyfloss and hot doughnuts, combined with fresh fish and chips smelling of vinegar, made me feel nostalgic.

As we walked down the hill towards the pier, the sun beat down warming me both inside and out, and Sharon had a permanent smile on her face as if she hadn't felt so good for a long time. When we reached the bottom of the hill we turned right away from the entrance to the pier where the beach stretched out as far as the eye could see. We walked a little way along the promenade and then found a spot on the sea wall where we could sit and enjoy the view as well as the sun.

The beach was packed. I lit a cigarette and inhaled the nicotine, blowing smoke out into the warm air. I looked around me, taking in the scene. There were children playing in the sand, building sandcastles. Families eating together and some elderly people sitting in deck chairs doing as I was, just soaking up the atmosphere. When Sharon suggested that we walk a little further along the beach, I didn't argue. It was such a wonderful day.

We continued to stroll, hand in hand, along the promenade but before long she signalled for us to sit down again and as I did so I was suddenly attracted to a scene on my right. A couple were lying together on the sand and although they were too far away for me to see them clearly, I couldn't take my eyes away from them. I watched them for what must have been well over a minute, waiting for the scene to become clearer, wanting to get up and move closer but I couldn't because my legs felt as if they had been turned to stone.

Gradually, as the image became clear, I realised that I knew who they were. I looked at Sharon for confirmation but she just continued to hold my hand. I was almost certain that one of the shapes was Susie. As I watched them kissing and hugging each other my mind left the beach and scanned my dream world.

'Susie?'

My stomach felt as if it had turned to jelly as I tried to get closer to them without being seen. If I was wrong I would end up looking like some sort of voyeur ogling a couple of lovebirds.

I stood up carefully and walked in a straight line to where they were sitting, until I was close enough to see the scene and the people. What I saw was Susie sitting down there with a man when all the time I'd been trying to tell myself that it couldn't be her. I hadn't believed Harry when he'd said that he'd seen her. If she hadn't called me how could she possibly be in Clacton?

As I looked at them, I saw my future with Susie in front of me. There was none.

Clenching my fists, I turned away from the scene, bitterness and bewilderment, anger and pain burning inside me. How could she do it to me?

I hesitated, trying to decide whether or not to just run along the beach and launch myself at him and punch him with whatever I had until my knuckles bled or my anger was vented. I was tempted but what was the point? It was over. I had lost her. I had lost completely.

I walked back and past Sharon without uttering a word. She didn't attempt to follow me, which was probably a good thing because it was obvious that she had set me up. She must have known that Harry had been right all along.

I no longer felt the sun. Dark clouds of misery and humiliation encompassed me as I turned away from the ashes of my life. I wanted to scream *why?* I wanted to hit and punch the fury out of me but I did neither, instead I walked in the direction of my car and, as I did so, got out my mobile phone and called Harry.

As soon as I heard his voice at the other end of the line I let loose some of the anger I felt.

'Harry! You knew!'

For a few seconds he didn't say anything and then said, 'I tried to tell you, mate.'

'But with *him*,' I shouted.

'Like I said, I tried to tell you but you didn't want to hear.'

I knew he was right.

'I'm sorry, Steve, I tried to help, tried to tell you that night. It's been hellishly difficult for me, believe me.'

I knew that he was sincere and felt guilty that I had blamed him. I shouldn't have been doing it to Harry. He hadn't done anything wrong except try to warn me and I hadn't wanted to listen.

'I'm sorry, Harry. It's not your fault.'

'Me too.'

'Did you know it was with him? When you saw her, was it with him?' I had to ask.

'Yes,' he said and I could hear the sadness in his voice. 'It was the day that we went out. I saw her with him in the town and it was obvious that they were together. I went round to Laurence's house to confront him – told him that what he was doing was wrong, that he was destroying everything. He didn't care, Steve.'

Hearing the name "Laurence" irritated the wound further. Just *knowing* that he was with Susie and had been for some time while I waited around like a fool.

'I can't believe it.'

I heard his sigh down the line. 'Maybe it's for the best. Better to know now than later. I'm so sorry and you know where I am if you want to talk.'

'Yeah, I'll call you soon.' I heard the crackle of emotion in my voice and flipped the cover down on the phone. Getting into the car, I sat with my head back and my eyes closed feeling that my life was going into freefall. When Sharon arrived a few moments later I simply held her and cried.

****

Sitting alone in the garden, gulping down my umpteenth glass of wine, I couldn't escape the demons of my mind. The purpose of the drink had been to numb my emotions but it only seemed to heighten them.

It was a beautiful evening and from somewhere in the recesses of my mind, Pat's words surfaced. 'Follow your dreams.'

A cliché perhaps but what was I to believe in anymore?

When I was a child I'd held onto the belief that I would find an angel. My innocent, unblemished mind had believed without question what my grandmother had told me. As I grew up, the reality suggested that no such thing existed. So why did I still find myself believing?

I was no longer sure about *anything* except the fact that my dreams seemed more real than my life.

I finished the bottle of wine and went to lie down. Let the dreams come, let them clarify my destiny because I couldn't do it myself.

Soon, as I hoped, the gap between my two worlds was bridged. The dream re-occurred as I had known it would. The images were the same as before but now two were missing. I could only wake up and wait for the visions to fulfil themselves.

CHAPTER THIRTY-NINE

We sat alone. The nurse had called me to tell me that time was running out and that I should visit my grandmother and talk to her while I could. Today she was awake and looking almost youthful and it was hard to believe that her health was in such decline. But there I sat with Granny knowing it could possibly be the last time. It felt almost surreal and of course she wouldn't know herself, would she?

For the first time in what seemed like forever, my grandmother knew my name. She ran her bony fingers down my cheek and brushed away my tears and sadness just like she'd done when I'd fallen over or bumped into something when I was a child. She was my granny again and I was the small child she had raised so lovingly and unselfishly. We were back in those old days when she had run the house and I'd behaved like the boy I still was deep inside.

I talked about many things yet nothing of any importance because no subject had any real meaning and anyway Granny didn't seem to be concentrating on what I was saying and kept forgetting the point. It wasn't a day for talking but for holding hands and telling each other with our eyes how much we cared, how unconditional our love was. Knowing that she was still capable of doing this made me cry inside – I loved her so much.

I read to her for what would be the last time. Stories and articles from papers and magazines that were lying on the bedside table that I thought she would like. She smiled while my voice droned softly on, reading of matters that didn't matter. I felt as if I was trying to inject her with me – with my love. I heard my voice quiver at times but I battled on out of respect and affection for the dear lady beside me.

When I noticed that she was tiring, I picked up an old newspaper that lay on the table and flicked through it to the familiar piece entitled, *"Tragic End for Wife"* and read it to her again, wondering how many times over the years my grandmother had trailed through those words. As I finished I looked at her and realised that soon she would be with her Cyril again.

'Granny.' I spoke softly and she opened her eyes as if trying to fight off sleep. I knew that I had so little time.

'Yes, Boy,' she said feebly.

'Do you feel closer to Cyril today?' I stroked her cheek with my fingers.

'Yes, Boy, I do. Very close, very close. I'll see him soon… she told me I would.' Her voice trailed away as if she was tired of living.

'Who told you that, Granny? Who said that to you?'

'Why Rose, of course. She knows, you see,' she whispered, her eyes closing.

I kissed her as she drifted away not knowing whether or not it would be the last time. It felt somehow as if it was and as I sat there I felt cursed by my visions. I knew then that they weren't just passing dreams but a reflection of my fate.

I tucked my grandmother in just as she used to do with me so long ago. A wave of emotion gripped me as the tears came forth. 'Sleep tight, Granny.' My lips trembled as I whispered the words into her ear. I stroked her wispy grey hair and kissed her one last time on her cheek before leaving her. As I closed the front door it felt like the end, for the death of someone close to you is to realise your own mortality. You might *think* that you want to know how long you've got left, but I guess you don't really want to know the answer.

My beloved granny didn't last the night.

****

Wiping the tears from my eyes I looked at the headstones that bore my parents' names.

'*Who am I?*' I shouted the words out loud.

The next day I would attend the funeral of the last member of my family and then it would be me, Steve Bidante, alone in the world. My whole family would be reduced to memories represented by stone plaques. My sense of loss was complete.

'I tried to grow up believing that there was a reason for losing you both. A reason to go on and hold onto something, but now....' I whispered the words aloud.

Closing my eyes I knelt down feeling as if the weight of the world was leaning its full force against me, as if I'd always been destined to be there, at that moment.

I cast my mind back to the last conversation I'd had with Pat when he had told me about the photographs, and feared the image of me as an old man. That is, if destiny allowed me to live that long or if I had the will to go on living in so wretched a world.

'Steve.' I heard the familiar voice behind me. The reason I knew the voice was because I'd heard it twice before in my life. I didn't want to look - dared not lift my head for fear there would be no one there.

'Steve.' I heard it again. The voice was smooth as honey and although I dreaded it, I could no longer deny it. I turned and lifted my head and saw her. She was dressed all in black and was the woman I had seen at my parents' funeral. The same person from my dream who had told me of the three images. Yet now she was here. I wasn't a child any more with just a distant memory of her. She was here and she was as real as I was.

'Are you real?' I whispered, 'or are you a dream?'

'I am both and more,' she said gently.

Her face, that reflected both kindness and sympathy, hadn't changed at all except that she seemed even more beautiful than before.

'I don't understand. Why are you here? Why is this

happening to *me*?'

She held her hand out and I hesitated for a few seconds before taking it. Our flesh touched and I felt a lightness that lifted me effortlessly to my feet in one smooth movement.

'I'm here to give you hope, Steve.'

As I stood in front of her I noticed that she was slightly taller than me and that she seemed to give off energy. I struggled to find the courage to say what I wanted.

'Hope?' I said, trying to sound confident. 'I've seen you twice before and each time I've been surrounded by death and misery. You told me of three images and when I said that there were *four*, you told me that one was of my own choosing. I suppose I *chose* to let Susie betray me? Tell me, if that's true, what was the reason? Anger gave me strength. Tell me, what hope can I ever take from seeing you?'

Despite my apparent bitterness, her facial expression didn't change. She seemed to absorb my anger and deflect it, at the same time giving off warmth and making me feel as if she understood me.

'The first time you saw me you were a boy, Steve. I appeared before you then because I wanted to give you hope for the future. You never completely lost that belief even when it seemed you had. Despite the fact that you doubt me, you know that to be true.'

I couldn't deny it. All the doubts I had had over the years dissolved immediately and the madness suddenly made sense and the sense was now madness. She seemed to know that I believed her.

She continued, 'When you first saw me in your dream it was only because you *chose* to call on me through your subconscious. I did what I could within my boundaries to help guide you through your visions and dreams, but I didn't *show* them to you. Although you doubted their meaning at first, I knew that time and events would explain everything. As soon as you knew the answer to the first image, you began to believe that they were real.'

'*Why* did you come? *Why* did I call you? *Did* I call you?' I shouted.

'Steve,' she said quietly. 'You may not know me, but I've been watching you, I have a lot at stake. If I could explain more I would, but the laws of spirituality don't allow me to. There is a balance that needs to be adjusted and I've done all I can to help you realise your own destiny. You now know to recognise things for what they are.'

'I didn't know that she'd leave me though, did I?' Or *had* I known all along? The thought upset me.

'You knew it was so. If you want to be certain, look more closely into your heart.'

I thought back to when I first remembered feeling that there were signs and realised that I had seen them from the beginning. When I spoke about marriage, when I held back about discussing having children. I'd felt it when she spoke about her plans. *Her* plans, not *mine* and hers, but *hers*. My cowardice had clouded my judgement.

'*What about Ray, then, and Granny? Did I* know? *Could I help*?' The pain was so intense that I found myself shouting.

Again she answered calmly, 'I can't tell you everything, Steve, only what I'm allowed to tell you.' She paused and looked straight into my eyes. 'Other people will also have answers, just dare to seek them and ask.'

I battled to keep back the tears. 'And now what will become of me?'

She came closer and touched my face. 'All will become clear soon but for now you have hope again, Steve. Just close your eyes and feel it.'

I did as she said and with my eyes shut the feelings flickered behind my eyelids as if I had been looking directly at the sun. I felt the lights and colours filled with energy and certainty enter me. I stayed like it for a while until I could feel no more and when I opened my eyes she was gone.

****

My grandmother's funeral was to be a low-key affair. Unlike Ray, she had planned it all down to the last detail. I wondered how she had felt when she had sat down to plan her own death. I guessed that it must be a strange moment when you came face to face with the realisation of your own vulnerability and mortality. It must feel that time was against you as the clock gave you the first warning of life's shortness. So many of us ignore the signs and continue to live the mirror image life we have created without daring for change.

I followed the funeral arrangements to the letter and at ten o'clock on the morning of the service, I arrived at the funeral director's office wearing an immaculate suit, clean white shirt and tie. I sat alone as I would always be now. I would be the last Bidante after I had taken the penultimate to another place. I visualised that place where she would be reunited with her beloved Cyril and where she would see her son again. Would they still look young despite the fact that they had died at different times? Of course they would.

I waited outside the crematorium while one or two people arrived, offering me their condolences and I smiled, hugged and kissed them in no particular order. When I saw Roz appear I had to stop for a moment as a distant memory sprang to mind. 'Why, Rose of course. She knows, you see.' They were my grandmother's last words to me.

Rose and Rosaline and *Roz*. Could it be coincidence? As I looked at her I saw things that I'd only caught glimpses of before. If it hadn't been for the recent events in my life I would have been surprised that she had come at all. Now I felt that she was a big part of them. That there was a mystery I still had to solve - but that could wait. I was here now to say goodbye to my grandmother.

I sat alone in the front row and as the service began I recalled that the last funeral I'd been to with Granny had been my parents'. I remembered it in detail as I laid my surrogate mother and friend to rest and lost a huge part of my life.

As she had requested, we sang *Abide With Me* and although there were only a dozen or so people in the chapel, the volume and power of the hymn belied the numbers. I felt the hairs on the back of my neck stand up, so moved was I by the passion they conveyed in their voices. First the priest spoke about my grandmother's life with words of kindness and affection before signalling for me to speak. I wouldn't have wanted to speak at all except that she had requested it. I guessed that I was the only person left who knew her well enough to do so. As I walked to the pulpit I pulled my rough notes from the pocket of my jacket.

'My grandmother's name was Agnes Jane Bidante,' I began nervously. 'Some of you here knew her as Aggie but for me she was Granny. Like many of her generation, she lost her husband during the war and as if that wasn't enough, the hand of fate then deprived her of her beloved son and daughter-in-law in tragic circumstances. Before that happened I was her only grandson and after…well…I was *still* her only grandson. But for me she was much more than a grandmother.'

The words on the notes in my hand began to blur as I tried to summon the will power to continue, sniffing and gulping at the people in front of me.

'I'm sorry,' I whispered.

The faces in front of me blurred, I blinked and in their place saw my parents sitting there, smiling lovingly at me, just as they had done when they had watched me performing in a school play or when I opened a present at Christmas. Ray was sitting on their right wearing his best suit and looking as young as ever. Death had lent them to me.

Then I saw Roz except that she *wasn't* Roz. She was sitting three rows back next to two soldiers in full uniform. I recognised them both from the pictures as my grandfather and his commanding officer, Captain Doug Gardiner. Roz was younger – much younger - more than half a century younger and was wearing a nurse's uniform like the ones I'd seen in films about the Second World War.

And then I saw Andréa.

She was standing by the doorway, looking more beautiful than ever with her black hair touching her shoulders and her crystal blue eyes that seemed to penetrate me. I watched as she turned and left.

I bowed my head and closed my eyes trying to regain my composure from what must have been an illusion. Silence echoed around me as I tried to summon the strength to continue.

When I looked up again all I saw were the people who had come into the church at the beginning of the service and yet I was sure that I had seen those other people a few minutes earlier.

I began to speak again, carrying on as if there had been no break. 'My grandmother became so much more to me. She became everything I needed to survive in the world around me. She gave a part of her life to me to help me overcome my loss and treated me like her son. So far in my life I haven't connected with anyone else the way I did with her and I will miss her deeply and completely.' I paused again to wipe my tears away.

'I'd like to thank you all for being here today to pay your respects to a woman who shone in this life. May we all learn from people like my grandmother. I loved her with all my heart.'

With that I stumbled back to my seat avoiding eye contact with anyone and sat with my head bowed listening to the song she had chosen. It was "Moon River" and she had loved it. I tilted my face slightly to watch the coffin slide gently towards the waiting fire until I could look no more. I let the lyrics of the song consume me along with the tears of death.

CHAPTER FORTY

I saw Roz through the window and dashed out of the front door in order to catch her.

'Roz!' I shouted.

She half turned towards me.

'Did you enjoy the service?'

'Of course, it was lovely,' she said.

Suddenly I felt very uneasy and had to know.

'Roz... are *you* the angel?'

I wasn't sure if she had heard me. She looked at me, wax-like, her lips portraying a wizened smile.

'See you later then, Roz,' I bellowed on account of her more than poor hearing. She smiled but didn't answer. Our conversation was over for today.

I leant away from the crooked wooden fence that divided us as she gave that familiar little wave and turned away. I noticed she was not hunched in the way many eighty-three year-olds can be, especially considering the amount of gardening she has done over the years.

Roz had now wandered around the side of her small white bungalow and I stood alone. The sun felt lovely on my face as the delicate sea breeze flowed around me. I walked back towards my own front door. I didn't know how, but I knew I was close to knowing, to finding, at last...

****

I awoke early the next morning ready to face the questions I had to ask. I now knew that the lady who lived next door to me was someone - or something – that was crucial to my search. When I had seen the nurse in the church I'd known it was her and I was also certain that it was she who had looked after my grandmother during her final days. But why? If she was, then it was she who had sent the article to Granny. How long had they known each other?

I couldn't get my head around it, could only guess. I needed answers and she would be the one who would give them to me, whether I believed them or not.

'Roz, I need to talk to you.'

'Of course, Steve, it's nearly time,' she answered immediately, smiling knowingly.

'You *are* Rose Gardiner, aren't you?'

'Yes, I am,' she said quietly.

I swallowed hard. 'How did you know my grandmother then, because it *was* you who nursed her, wasn't it?'

She seemed to be lost in her own thoughts and didn't answer for a few moments and then said, 'You must understand that you are the last link to the past, the last chance for things to be as they should. . . .' She paused as if waiting for the cogs of my brain to adjust.

'I didn't know your grandmother, Steve, but she *believed* she knew me as Rose - not Rosaline. I'm more than you see, because in my brief life I was Rosaline Gardiner, wife of Doug Gardiner. . . and you know all about him, of course.'

'Yes I do.' I nodded agreement although I was puzzled by what she had said.

'When I took my own life I knew that suicide was a serious and sinful act but the truth is, Steve, I couldn't go on living without Doug, my husband. I know that what I did was weak but I had lost my will to live.' She paused as if to compose herself but I dared not interrupt.

'When I died I paid the ultimate price because instead of finding the beautiful place where my husband had gone, I lost my soul. You do believe in the soul, don't you?'

'Of course I do. . . but how do you fit in with my grandmother and Ray *and* with my visions?' I couldn't help myself.

'Patience, Steve,' she said, ignoring my outburst. 'First of all, you have to know about the laws of the soul in what you call the "afterlife". When my husband died alongside your grandfather, and *after* I had taken my own life, it came to me that to restore it, and to find peace and forgiveness with Doug, I would first have to salvage the soul of another person. In order to do this I've played many parts. I helped your grandmother to see the light in her final days on this earth. I also saved you from riding on the bike that killed Ray because it would have been the end of you too. Now my work is almost over and I will soon find eternal peace for myself.'

In trying to understand her words I found more questions. 'How did you help with me and Ray?'

'You're smarter than that, Steve,' she said, a smile touching her lips. 'I booked an appointment with Andréa for you to fix my computers. Remember?'

The pieces slipped into place but I needed to know. 'Roz, are *you* my angel?' The words stumbled from my mouth. I saw from her face that she had known that I would ask that question.

'I'm an angel of sorts, Steve. That is if you believe that angels are messengers sent by God.' She shrugged. 'Perhaps that's what I've become in my quest to save my own soul. By clearing the way I've cleansed myself in the process. In order to gain salvation I was destined to save you and to care for your grandmother and now my work is almost done because I have just one last debt to pay.'

'What is it, the last debt?' I needed to know.

She remained silent for a few minutes, looking slightly uncomfortable. Finally she spoke. 'The threads of time and destiny are much more complex than we can ever understand in the living world because there is such a thin line between fate and reality. I too am still aware of the boundaries and aware that my destiny isn't entirely in my own hands.' She seemed to relax a little. 'I told you once before that you gave me hope and that should be enough to tell you that you have a part to play in *my* destiny.'

'But…' I didn't understand what she meant and she seemed to pick up on it.

'I'm *not* your angel, Steve, although you could have seen one of your own if you'd looked carefully enough.'

I searched my mind trying to find the relevance of the lady in black. I hadn't thought of her as any angel of mine. Nothing seemed any clearer.

'So who are you, Roz? Who the hell are you?'

'Calm down, Steve. I've told you as much as I'm permitted to as an enlightened sentient.' She must have seen my puzzled look because she said, 'That means that I have knowledge of the other side and how to control it. I am, therefore, able to travel within the two worlds and have the ability to change them. But you must remember too that I am a damned soul. Don't you think some sort of an angel must have guided you in your search? After all, isn't that what you've been looking for all your life?'

'Yes, of course,' I sighed. 'I just don't understand what I'm supposed to do now.'

'You will in time, dear boy.' I heard the tenderness in Roz's voice. 'Steve, my work is nearly done. You may see me one more time if I'm to fulfil my part in your destiny and then I must go.'

As she stepped away from me she turned slowly around. 'Steve, the answer is in the palm of your hand.'

I watched her, knowing that it would probably be the last time I would see her. My mouth felt too dry for speech and all I could do was watch whoever's angel Roz was walk away. I knew she wasn't mine but I also knew that at last I had found one.

****

A month passed and I didn't see Rose Gardiner again.

The house lay empty.

No "For Sale" sign.

Nothing.

Just empty.

My time was spent sorting out my grandmother's finances and her few possessions. I took a few items that I knew had meant a lot to her and donated the rest to the charity shop. She'd left everything to me, of course, but I cared not for possessions during those first dark weeks when I mourned her.

****

I answered the door to find Harry standing on the step looking a little awkward. It was the first time I'd seen him since our telephone conversation and it still hurt when I thought about it.

He spoke first. 'Steve, I've come to say how sorry I am about your Granny and also...' he paused, 'to say that I'm sorry for everything.'

I forgave him instantly; after all it hadn't been his fault. It had been nothing to do with him except that he was part of it all, a piece of the jigsaw of my life. 'Don't be sorry, Harry,' I said, meaning it. 'Come on in, mate.'

'It was torment,' he said, as he sat opposite me at the breakfast bar. 'But I did learn something positive from it all.'

I laughed. 'That's you all over, Harry. Positive all the way! What "positive" could you get from all that?'

'You may well laugh,' he said solemnly. 'But I'm serious, Steve, because it made me realise that it isn't all about logic. I *do* have a soul and it was when I saw those two together that I realised how much it was going to hurt you. Logic disappeared right out of the window.'

'Harry,' I said with a reassuring grin. 'I knew that all along. I also know a few things more than I thought. You know all those dreams I've had? Well, it seems they all meant something. Now all I need is one more answer.'

If I'd spoken to him like that a year or so ago, he would have dismissed what I said as piffle or some such word without giving it a second thought. Now he seemed genuinely interested.

'What you got then, Steve?'

The corner of the breakfast bar was littered with strips of paper, each with something scrawled on them. I pulled them towards me and smiled at Harry.

'My dreams revealed four images, of which I've seen *three* come to pass. One was Ray, the next my grandmother, then Susie and the fourth was a little girl.'

I looked at Harry for some kind of response but he said nothing.

'Right,' I continued. 'So there were also three women – one in Spain who gave me flowers – all of which had their own meaning, then there was a lady in black who I saw both in my dreams *and* in real life... honestly, Harry,' I paused and looked at him and he nodded that he believed me. 'And...finally my neighbour Roz. They all played a part...I just don't yet know what it was.

Harry looked thoughtful. 'What about the girl? Where does she fit in?'

I shrugged. 'I have no bloody idea.'

'What about all this?' He pointed at the pieces of paper.

'I took this from my grandmother's house. It was all the memories she had of her Cyril.' I picked up the box and tipped the contents out onto the breakfast bar.

'Look at them. Just some letters and a newspaper.'

Harry looked at the letters for a few minutes and then, with a shrug, pushed them to one side. I guessed that he had been unable to understand them. Turning the paper to the obituary page, I pushed it across to him and watched as he read it. His reaction was predictable.

'Means nothing to me, pal,' he said.

****

I was in the middle of pouring us each a glass of wine when

Harry shouted, 'Steve, what's this?'

'I don't know.' I looked at the bright coin that he held out. 'Must have fallen out of the bottom of the box.'

He reached into his top pocket and pulled out a magnifying glass - he always carried one, it was the "must have" tool of any antique dealer - before holding the coin up to the light and examining it in detail. After a while he looked at me.

'Steve, I don't know if this means anything but....' He put the coin down on the table in front of him. 'If I'm correct, these coins are known to represent both good *and* bad luck. They were first introduced in France in the fourteenth century and are called "Angelot" or "Ange" coins. Later they were also made in England, but not until the late fifteenth century when they were reissued and first called "angel-noble" before they became known simply as "angel" coins. If I'm right, they were more touch pieces than coins,' he concluded.

I took the coin and studied it more closely.

'That's it!' I yelled leaping from my seat. 'Harry, you are *brilliant*!' He stared at me blankly looking slightly bemused by my excitement. Pushing my hand into my pocket I pulled out an identical coin.

'These aren't exactly common, are they, Harry?' I said, feeling the adrenalin rush through me.

'Not these days, Steve,' he replied, still looking confused by my behaviour. 'Why is that important?'

'*Because*,' I bellowed, 'I was given *this* coin! *That's* the key! Andréa gave it to me and when she did, she said that she would *know* the right moment to give it to me! Andréa has the answers!'

Harry looked gobsmacked to say the least. 'Bloody hell,' he said. 'What are you going to do now then?'

'It's simple. I have to find her. Don't you see? I have to go to Prague.'

CHAPTER FORTY-ONE

I logged onto the internet and looked for a flight. After searching around, the first one I could find left at six o'clock the next morning. It would have to do. I booked a one-way ticket before packing a small holdall. Now all I had to do was wait for the night to pass.

Again it was Harry who dropped me at the airport. I had no idea when I would be returning.

'Good luck, Steve. Let me know and I'll be here to pick you up' were his parting words.

I thanked him for the part he'd played and almost ran into the airport. I boarded the flight with just the holdall as hand baggage and the two coins safely in my pocket. Once we were airborne I gazed out of the window at a beautiful sunrise and wondered just where I should begin my search when, in less than four hours' time, I would be in the Czech Republic.

As the plane touched down I felt the adrenalin racing through my veins and, walking briskly out of the airport building, I looked for one of the white transporters that I had been told would take me into the centre of Prague. The city would have to be my starting place. As the outskirts of the city raced by I saw that the walls surrounding the beautiful city, had been vandalised with graffiti. The morning air was cool but the buildings looked beautiful where the sun's rays bathed them in yellow light. I would never have believed that I would be here of all places in search of my angel.

I got off the bus just outside the old town and headed off in the direction of the big square in order to find my bearings and to work out my next move. Joining the crowd of people who huddled beside the famous astronomical clock, waiting for it to strike the hour, I took out my map of the city, flicking to the back where the train routes were displayed. I studied all the different destinations, trying to guess where she might be and decided that the most likely place would be Lany, where she had lived before.

As I was standing there I suddenly heard a voice and realised that I had been half expecting it.

'You made it then?'

I looked up, smiling. 'Yes, I did.'

The woman I knew as Roz signalled for me to sit down beside her on a wooden bench that was close by. I nodded and followed her, and sat down beside her on the worn seat looking out over the main square. She remained silent and, while I waited for her to speak, my eyes idly surveyed the people who crossed the cobbled area. It was then that I saw her - less than ten metres away. Whenever I'd seen her before she'd been wearing black, but this time she wore a soft pale grey dress that complemented her warm beauty. She acknowledged Roz with a nod before sitting down slowly next to me on the opposite side from her. I just sat there wondering what the hell was going on but at the same time somehow *knowing*.

'I suppose you have more questions?' she said after a while. 'You probably want to know my name or who I am?'

'I can only guess that you're an angel of sorts,' I said politely.

She leant forward a little as if not wanting to be overheard. 'I'm Helena ...or should I say I *was* Helena. I was saved from death many years ago by two men who gave their lives to protect my daughter and me. One of those men was your grandfather, the other,' she paused and looked directly at Roz, 'you know about as well. After they died I found that they each possessed an identical coin. I sensed that they were important and sent one to your grandmother along with some letters. The other I kept for myself and my family, knowing that one day the connection might come through those coins.'

'Andréa is now the connection,' I said quietly.

'Yes,' she smiled. 'I died before Andréa was born, you see. She was - *is* - my granddaughter. She too suffered like you because she lost her mother, my daughter, from cancer when she was a little girl. Although Andréa never saw me alive, her mother had taught her well. She had followed my instructions, thus giving me an opening to guide her destiny. The coins you see.'

'Where exactly do I fit into this?' I wasn't sure what part I was supposed to play.

Helena looked straight in front of her. 'You have seen what you perceive as angels, Steve. Do you believe in destiny now? Do you believe in miracles or acts of God?'

I thought for a moment. 'Yes I do...but perhaps you know that better than I do.'

She glanced at Roz and I saw her nod.

'All things have balance in this world,' Helena continued, '*and* in what you call the afterlife. Both mine and Rose's destiny were intertwined many years ago. Our destiny - our *souls* if you like - are in the hands of you and Andréa now. You two are the future of the bloodlines for me and your actions will release Rose's soul from damnation. Do you understand now?'

I looked at Roz/Rose. 'Why me, Roz? I *don't* quite understand.'

'This may be hard to take in.' She looked relaxed. 'As you know we are led to believe that suicide is a sin. In a moment of suffering I made the decision to end my life. The only chance I had of being released from damnation lay in saving the life of another who was close. You were the only one who would do. I couldn't save your grandmother because she was suffering from a natural illness. I saved you because I *could,* yet for my task to be complete, I needed the one forgiving emotion which you still had to share. *Love.*'

'I understand,' I said eventually. 'But that was before it all went wrong. Andréa left - you must know that. I don't understand how *we* can be your destiny if we're finished.

I threw my love away.'

'You misread the flowers, Steve,' Rose continued. 'The symbol of oleander, meaning beware, didn't represent Andréa but *Susie*. Osmunda told you of dreams yet you *still* didn't realise that they were significant and the palm told you about spirituality. Eventually you saw that in a dream and by then you had started to accept everything.'

'You will understand love again when you see her,' Helena intervened with a smile, 'You have answers and so does she. You must find her only if you *choose* to. It must be of your own free will.'

'If *everyone* played a part, then what about Pat? Why did he become involved?'

Rose sighed. 'Destiny can be cruel. Ray was destined to die, you weren't. Thus the chance arrived for me to be the one to save you. I did that with the call to Andréa. You believed her and avoided being on that bike. That moment, sad as it was, did so much. You lived, I played my part in the salvation of a life and Andréa might still one day have your love. Do you understand fate now?'

'But Pat...I don't get it.'

'Pat played his part; he was - and is - your guide, the person who helps you the most in times of need. He tried to save Ray but he's only human and some things can't be changed. It's written that way. He's a good man and he'll save many other lives.'

I nodded slowly. Taking a big breath, I steadied myself to ask the one question I had thus avoided.

'I swore something to myself many years ago,' I began as I felt an inner shiver surface. 'I... promised if I ever met an angel then I would ask the one question.'

The words would not come out immediately. I looked at the two women in front of me and saw such compassion, such kindness in their eyes that I faltered, as tears welled up and my insides started to feel as if they were twisting, contorting with a long hidden pain. I already knew before the words finally tumbled out, that I was facing angels, and that they knew the answer to the one question that had driven me on. I knew the answer now.

'Why did you take my parents away?' The seven words poured from my lips with such meaning. I let them flow with the tears that the many years of heartache and confusion, of suffering and searching, had taken from my soul. As the words left me, I felt a long suppressed burden lift from my shoulders.

Roz and Helena both looked at me and I saw tears in their eyes too. They had known this question would be asked but, even now, it was not easy to answer. I knew the answer now and so did they but it made it no easier to say. I almost did not want them to speak. The words would only compound my truth.

It was Roz who spoke. 'You know why your parents died, Steve, don't you?'

I looked down at the ground and then slowly lifted my head, a glint of anger shone in my eyes. 'Say it! I asked you the question!'

Roz did not flinch but the pain was evident in her reply. 'Sacrifice…,' she whispered the word. 'The ultimate sacrifice was made. Your grandmother couldn't have known when she asked you to stay that day. She said that she felt a voice from your grandfather, and we can only assume it to be true. Something made that choice and that something was what caused you not to be in that car.' Roz paused for a moment to collect her energy. 'I am so sorry, Steve.' Her words were heartfelt. 'If that day hadn't happened, you would not have begun the hardest quest of your life and you wouldn't be standing here now following it through and believing and learning so much along the way. The balance would have been lost.'

I listened to the truth that I already knew. It seemed that the twists of fate held so much that was unknown. So much pain followed whatever choice was made. I had no choice, mine was made for me and now I had to follow it to the end.

'We must leave now, Steve,' Helena said, standing up. 'You won't see us again.' She kissed me gently on the cheek.

I looked at Roz knowing that it would be the last time that I would see her. My friend and neighbour and so much more. I could console myself that I had followed the right path – the one that she had foretold. She lifted her hand from the folds of her long, flowing coat and handed me a small piece of paper before smiling at me and turning to follow Helena.

I could feel the tension inside me as I held the paper in my hand.

I waited for a few moments until they were out of sight before carefully unfolding it. I read the words:

Take the train from Hlavnì Nádra i which is a five minute walk from the statue of Vaclav in Wenceslas Square. Buy a ticket for Boubin which is 200 kilometres from Prague. There you will find what you seek.

I followed the instructions and an hour later I was on board a train heading for Boubin and to whatever that would bring me.

****

I reflected on my life during the journey and for the first time ever it seemed to have some meaning. I looked out of the window at the changing landscape as the train rattled past villages and fields while at the same time saying a silent "thank you" to Helena for the decision she had helped me to make with Susie. And Roz for everything *she* had done. I mourned Ray but felt comforted by the fact that he was now amongst angels and smiled in memory of my grandmother who was now happily and peacefully reunited with her husband. For once I felt optimistic about everything. Even Sharon, who had found something new to believe in. It felt as if my quest was nearly over.

By the time the train finally stopped at Boubin, the afternoon sun was low in the sky and as I walked along the platform I tried to work out where to go next. I wandered around for several hours, lost in the fast approaching darkness. The temperature was dropping quickly and I needed either to find what I was looking for or book into a hotel.

As I was beginning to feel tired and was fast running out of ideas, I opted for the latter and found a small hotel in the town where I could spend the night. I had a couple of glasses of wine and a good meal in the restaurant before turning in. I lay there in the dark knowing that my only option would be to go in search of Andréa Sekhova, because she was the one who held the answer.

****

The following day was a trial in more ways than one. Firstly, it was raining and I was cold and wet because I hadn't thought to pack the right clothes. Secondly, it wasn't easy to locate a person by name in a country where I spoke little or none of the language. On the odd occasions when I thought I was getting somewhere, I became lost in a barrage of words that I couldn't understand.

As the day progressed the rain kept coming down and I was so wet that my clothes stuck to my skin. I knew that I had to do something drastic because I had little money, no return ticket and hardly any clothes. I began to feel a lack of faith again.

Walking towards a big forest I decided to go into it for a while to shelter from the rain and to ponder my situation. The vegetation rose above and around me as far as the eye could see, and many different types of trees and plants swayed in the cold breeze as if whispering my arrival to each other. I followed one of the many trails that led deep into the inner core like small veins leading to the heart of the forest.

Thankfully it had stopped raining and as I walked wearily

along the path, I breathed in the fresh autumnal air. After a while I stopped in a large clearing and lit a cigarette. Ahead of me I saw a group of people standing and talking next to what looked like a play and picnic area. I exhaled and their images became distorted by the cloud of smoke. As I neared them, smoking and deep in thought, I was attracted by one of the shapes and felt my heartbeat accelerate. I couldn't see her face but the shape was familiar and her hair was as black as the night. My heart thumped inside my chest. Could it be her?

Pausing for a moment to gather myself, I put the cigarette out on the ground with a swift turn of my foot, before heading towards the people who were now drifting away into the fading light. I couldn't make out which way she had gone because it seemed as if the paths went in all directions from the centre of the copse. I panicked and began to run, sensing that each footstep took me nearer to her. Reaching the place where the group had been there was nothing but a blanket of shadow hiding each path from me so that I couldn't be sure which one she had taken.

I ran down the nearest one, hearing the leaves crunch underfoot and in the distance seeing a shape. I increased my pace and within seconds I had caught her up. But it wasn't Andréa.

'*Prosím*! *Prosím*!' I grabbed the girl's arm and spun her towards me and she shrieked as I repeated the word *please* to her.

'No! Don't be scared!' I said without thinking that she might not understand any English. I gripped her arm tightly and although her face was pale with fright I couldn't risk letting her go. I needed to think of some Czech words to calm her.

'*Prosím,*' I said more calmly and slowly. '*Pomoc prosím*'. I asked for her help.

She seemed to calm down a bit and said something that I didn't understand. I searched my mind for more Czech words that I had learned from Andréa.

'*Prosím Vás, kde je Andrea Sekhová?*'

'Andréa?' she said, looking surprised.

I nodded and repeated the words, '*Prosím. Vás, kde je Andrea Sekhová*?' Where is Andréa Sekhova, please? I knew by her reaction that she understood me and that it had been her that I had seen.

The girl pointed into the forest. '*Andrea je má p ítelkyn?. Prosím.* She...is...my...friend...please...tell...me...where,' I said slowly.

She looked at me as if judging whether or not some foreigner *could* be Andréa's friend but my eyes must have convinced her because she began to walk in the same direction that she pointed.

I followed her into the now inky black forest and she held a small torch in front of her so that we could see the path. We followed it for what must have been more than two kilometres and although the coldness was now cutting into me I walked silently beside her. Finally, when I saw a line of lights shining faintly in the distance, the girl stopped.

'Where? Is she there? Which house?' I asked, straining my eyes to see.

The girl said something that I didn't understand and held up four fingers.

'Four?' I said, copying her by holding up four fingers of my own.

She nodded and turning, walked quickly back into the blanket of darkness.

****

I made my way towards the buildings and as I approached I saw that there were about ten big log houses separated from each other by small wooden fences. Looking inside them as I passed I saw soft lights and open fires that sent plumes of smoke upwards into the night air. As I walked past them I looked for number four and when I reached it, I hesitated before edging closer to the window. The silhouette told me that it was her and, as I peered through a small crack in the curtain, I saw Andréa. I was momentarily paralysed by her beauty and couldn't do anything until she had moved away from the light and into a room behind.

Taking a deep breath I walked to the door and grasping the small brass knocker in my hand, I paused one last time.

'Here we go,' I whispered to myself before letting the knocker drop onto the door. I felt the dull thud vibrating within me as the noise carried into the forest. I waited, hearing the sound of her footsteps approaching. She pulled the door open a little until the chain behind reached its length. I looked into her eyes for the first time in what seemed forever, the blueness of them shone out like two moons as I spoke her name.

'Andréa.'

Initially she seemed to react like a rabbit caught in headlights but after a few seconds she relaxed and without a word, undid the latch and opened the door. As the light glowed from behind her, I stared my destiny in the face. She held out her hand and guided me silently inside.

We stood in the centre of the warm room where a blazing fire flickered in the corner and lit up her face. We looked at each other. It was Andréa who broke the long silence.

'I was told you would come.'

'I was told you are the answer, that you have the answers.' I looked at her longingly.

'Maybe, maybe you do too,' she smiled. 'Now come and sit by the fire.' She took my hand and guided me to a chair. I watched the flames dancing while she went into what must be the kitchen and returned a few minutes later with two mugs of hot coffee.

'I saw you, Andréa,' I said as she handed me a cup. 'I saw your image at my grandmother's funeral and soon after I found another coin the same as the one you gave me. It was then that I knew for sure.'

She looked down at the floor. 'I knew a long time ago, I

think. When I met you, I knew. When we shared our time together, I knew.' She looked straight at me. 'I always knew.'

As I watched her beautiful lips speak those words, I knew that everything I had seen had been true.

I reached out and took her hand. 'It seems *you* are my destiny, Andréa.'

She squeezed my hand and I saw a tear falling down her face as she said, 'And you. You are my miracle.' She stood up and held out her hand, I took it and she pulled me to my feet.

'Come.'

Holding my hand she pulled me through the kitchen and into a long, narrow hallway. I sensed that I knew it, the shape and the smooth walls. Opening the door to a room at the back I saw that it was a big bedroom with a double bed against the far wall. The room was dimly lit and she pointed to the left where there was a child's wooden cot.

'There, go see,' she whispered.

I walked over to the cot and peered inside and there I saw a baby with blonde, almost white, hair and blue eyes that gazed up at me as she lay gurgling in the cot.

'Come, pick her up,' Andréa said softly.

I stood, unable to move. I *knew* this little girl. Of *course* I knew her. I'd seen her in my dream but not like she was now but as she would become. I picked her up gently and held her to me feeling her soft marshmallow skin and her warmth against my face.

'But...,' I mumbled, overcome with emotion, 'I thought I could not have a child.'

Andréa moved in front of me and I saw the tears running down her face, not sad ones, but filled with joy.

Printed in the United Kingdom
by Lightning Source UK Ltd.
125081UK00001B/1-42/A